To Catch a Fox

By Susan Calder

Print ISBNs
BWL 9780228606291

BWL Publishing Inc.

Books we love to write ...
Authors around the world.

http://bwlpublishing.ca

Cover art by Michelle Lee

Susan Calder

"—but the cruelty that condemned an unfortunate man to a living death. To catch a fox and put him in a box and never let him go." – Agatha Christie, *The ABC Murders*

Dedication

To Vivienne Mary Carty Arnold

Acknowledgments

BWL Publishing Inc. acknowledges the Province of Alberta for their Provincial Operating Grant for Publishers, for its financial support,

Alberta
Government

Thank you to Judith Pittman and BWL Publishing Inc. for bringing *To Catch a Fox* into the world. To editors Maya Berger, Susan Davis, and Rachel Small, for understanding my story and making it better. And to Catherine Bush and Lawrence Hill, my perceptive and encouraging mentors at the Sage Hill Writing Experience.

Thanks to my manuscript readers Will Arnold, Jean Humphreys, Stephen Humphreys, Shaun Hunter, Marilyn Letts, Pearl Luke, and Bernice Pyke, for helpful and appropriately challenging comments; Ruth Daly, Leslie Gavel, Lianne DesBrisay, and Pamela McDowell, friends on this writing journey.

And always, for your love and support, Will, Dan, Matt, Anne, and Vivi.

Chapter One

The code opened the gate, but Stuart hesitated before entering the yard. No matter how cool he played it, his father turned him into the kid. *What harm will it do to ask?* Her voice urged him onto the tile walkway. *You haven't spoken in three years. It can't make things worse.*

Fake gaslights illuminated the deck. The old man reclined on a lounge chair by the pool, alone, as Stuart had expected. They were creatures of ritual, his father with his evening swim followed by a glass of brandy, the trophy wife on her spa getaway the first weekend of the month. Except tonight, the old man holding the glass wore shorts and a shirt instead of a terry robe.

His father sat upright. "Stuart. This is a surprise. How did you get in?"

"You haven't changed the codes on me yet." Stuart stopped a few feet away. "No swim tonight?"

"I've come down with a cold." He sniffed, as though to make the point. "It's worn me out. What brings you here? Something other than money, I hope."

Stuart glanced at the pool shimmering in the faint light, and then at the dark windows in the house. The staff would be gone for the day. *He's sitting on all that money.* Her voice. *Why not put it to use while you're still healthy and young?*

"For your information, I bought the property you wouldn't pay for." Stuart straightened his stance. "Actually, with the delay we got it for a better price, thanks to the housing bubble crash."

"You're still with that woman?" His father sipped from the brandy glass. "How did you two come up with the down payment?"

"Work."

"What kind of work?"

Stuart looked at the pool. Fuck. Who cared? The old man would see through whatever he said. "Now we need to develop the property."

"With your foolish idea of a fantasy resort?"

"You might consider it an investment."

"Do you have a business plan?"

"Of course." A plan in their heads. But they could draft something on paper.

"Take it to a bank." His father coughed. "If it's viable, you'll get a loan."

They had tried. "Banks don't dole out money to people with no business experience."

"Exactly." His father set the glass on the side table and rose. He was almost Stuart's height. "Prove to me you can get this idea off the ground."

"How?"

"What work have you done the past few years?"

Surfing. Teaching people to surf. Hanging out on the beach. Scamming an even older man with too much money and inattentive relatives.

"I thought so," his father said. "Stuart, I'm glad you're here. I wanted to talk to you." He pulled a handkerchief from his pocket and blew his nose. "I've worked hard for my money, and I don't want you blowing it on some pipe dream—her dream, I suspect."

"Mine too."

"Or, for all I know, blowing it up the pipes."

"I've given up drugs."

"They all say that."

"You don't know fuck all."

His father stuffed the handkerchief into his pocket. "I've given this a lot of thought and have decided." He cleared his throat. "I'm changing my will so that everything I built when

I was with your mother will continue to the future, to our family. Your sister and her children—"

"They're getting my share?"

"Your sister will get her half after my death. Yours will go to any progeny you might have when I die, or on their twenty-fifth birthdays, whichever comes later."

Stuart rubbed his jaw, trying to absorb this. No money for him. Ever. Even when the old man expired. "You're disowning me."

"I see it as providing for your children."

"Fuck you. This is her idea."

His father coughed again and stroked his throat. "If you turn your life around—"

"You're doing this to manipulate me. That bitch talked you into it. She's always hated me."

"Don't talk about your stepmother like that."

"Or was it my bitch sister? So she and her snotty kids can rob me of my share?"

"If your line doesn't continue it will go to them, but that isn't the point. I don't want to contribute to a wasted life and schemes that are certain to fail."

Heat fanned out from Stuart's chest to his fingers. His father coughed once more, and his Adam's apple bobbed, exposed. *So weak.* Was that her voice? *So easy to get rid of him, make everything easy for us.*

Stuart raised his hands up to the grizzled neck.

No one will know.

He grabbed the bobble and pressed, pressed.

The old man coughed. Choked.

Teach him a lesson. Wasted life?

Surfing, fighting the waves, wasn't "wasting life." It made you strong—strong enough to kill a man withered by weakness.

The old man gasped, his eyes wide. Stuart's hands let go, released thc body. It collapsed to the tiles.

Stuart jerked backwards, blinked at the shape twisted on the deck, unmoving. He squatted and felt the wrist for a pulse. No beats. No sounds of breathing. He leapt up, stood astride the torso, formed his hands into position for chest compressions.

If the old man lived, he would cut him out of his will. If he died? His existing will would give Stuart more than he'd hoped for when he entered the gate, would give him the cash they needed now.

Stuart's gaze shot to the house windows, still barren and dark. When the wife or staff person found him, could the old man's death be taken as a heart attack or natural choking? Probably not. Fifty-eight wasn't technically old, and to Stuart's knowledge, his father had no heart or lung problems. There would probably be an autopsy, which might point to strangling. Trying to cover that up rarely worked on cop shows. Stuart scanned the deck. Fingerprints. What had he touched since he arrived? Had anyone seen their car in the lane, where she was waiting? She probably thought it was a good sign, his taking this long. It would be good if he could set it up right.

Stage a robbery.

His father would have left the house unlocked when he went out to the pool, and if he hadn't, Stuart knew the codes and where to find the valuables a thief would snatch. Jewellery, cash, expensive trinkets. With all the security, the cops might suspect an inside job. Stuart would be questioned, though only if they could find him—he had no phone, email, or fixed address. Service workers would be targets, someone his father might willingly let in. But cops always looked to the spouse first. The younger wife, who stood to inherit more than the children from his first marriage. They'd speculate she hired a hitman while away at the spa. Knowing his father, there were bound to be rifts in the marriage. Unlikely the old man had abandoned his habit of cheating.

Stuart looked down at the body crumpled on the deck, foam coating its lips. Strange the old man had held such power over him while alive. Dead, he was a mass of flesh and bones. Insects would be crawling all over the corpse by the time his wife found him. Stuart wouldn't mind if the bitch took the fall. Better her than him.

Chapter Two

Julie Fox formed the clay into a miniature barn roof. Smooth and perfect. Her psychiatrist called this self-directed art therapy. Creating the farm was supposed to keep her mind on concrete tasks and her goal of pleasing her daughter; away from self-indulgent thoughts. To Julie's amazement, it worked.

Someone knocked on the apartment door. A neighbour? Or had she been too absorbed to hear the downstairs buzzer? She hurried through the dining room and galley kitchen.

Through the peephole, a distorted face came into focus. Close-set eyes, thin nose, five o'clock shadow. The man turned to leave.

Julie opened the door. "Dad."

"A woman on her way out let me in," her father said. "What's the point of a locked entrance lobby if people do that?" He unwrapped the scarf from his neck and removed his boots. Under his parka he wore a flannel shirt and jeans.

"Why aren't you at work?" Julie asked.

"Doctor's appointment."

"Are you sick?"

"My cholesterol's still too high. He's talking about medication."

"You want a coffee or tea?"

"Anything warm," he said. "I only put an hour in the parking meter."

In the kitchen, he selected a packet of Irish breakfast tea. While the bag steeped in the teapot, they chatted about Calgary's arctic weather and the previous night's heavy snowfall.

Julie told him that she'd almost fallen on the slippery sidewalks during her morning jog that day.

Her shrink liked that she followed a regular routine. Jog, breakfast, art therapy, lunch, errands and cleaning, jog, dinner, and then reading or TV. Tuesday evenings she watched *NCIS* with her neighbour down the hall. Thursday was pub night with friends from university. She couldn't wait to return to work on Monday after two months away.

They carried their teacups to the living room. Her father took his usual chair by the patio doors so he could look out at the office towers downtown. She sat across from him on the sofa. Her grandmother had left her the Queen Anne–style furniture. It had suited the old house Julie had shared with Eric, her estranged husband, better than this high-rise. Her father blew on his tea. The cup and saucer shook in his hands.

He wouldn't normally drop by for an impromptu visit, especially knowing she'd be at his house tomorrow. "Is it more than cholesterol, Dad? The doctor—"

"He says I'm otherwise in A1 shape for a man over sixty."

She leaned forward. Was there a problem with her daughter? "Is it Peyton?"

"Peyton's fine. She's sleeping over tomorrow night. Eric has some kind of poetry event."

"So, is this about your work?" There had been talk of another round of downsizing at the oil company where her father worked.

"Looks like I'll hang on a few years more until retirement."

"So?" What else could have brought him here? A rift in his marriage? Was he cheating on Rosemary, or leaving her? Impossible. Although, this past year he had lost an inch off his waist and grown the shadow-beard to look cool, or perhaps to compensate for his thinning hair. Was he going through a midlife crisis? For sure, Rosemary wasn't leaving him. She'd never do that unless he provoked her.

Her father clunked his saucer and cup on the side table. "I wanted to talk to you, alone, without Peyton around." He cleared his throat. "Last month, I hired a private investigator to look for your mother. Your natural mother."

Julie carefully set her tea on the coffee table so she wouldn't spill it. She exhaled slowly. "Why?"

"First, I did my own search on the internet. Delilah tried too. She's good with the computer."

Julie stumbled to her feet and moved to the wall for support. Her father also stood. He didn't quite match the height she'd inherited from her mother. Julie had scoured the internet, too, years ago, and more recently while off work. Every link resulting from "Marion Fox" or "Marion Dejong," her mother's maiden name, had resulted in a dead end.

"The PI was Rosemary's idea."

"Rosemary."

"She thinks you need closure. And that I do, too."

Julie's ears roared. She hated buzzwords. "But last month? Why didn't you tell me?" He'd involved her stepsister, Delilah, before her.

"We didn't want you fussing before we got the result, one way or another."

"What did you find?" Julie's voice cracked.

"We knew Marion had been in LA, so Delilah found a Los Angeles PI online."

Through the fog in her ears, Julie heard her father explain that some twenty-five years ago—when she was about thirteen—a man had phoned their home and asked for Marion. Her father was at work, Julie at school. Rosemary took the call. The man said he was Marion's former surfing friend, but when Rosemary questioned him, he hung up. They didn't have call display, and the man didn't phone again.

"We got our number unlisted after that," her father said. "To avoid other cranks."

Julie felt dizzy. "What makes you think he was a crank?"

"Oh, he might have known Marion, I suppose."

Her back was sticky with sweat, the rest of her chilled. "So. You unlisted our number so her friends couldn't reach us. So she couldn't call us, if she wanted. And you kept this from me?"

"That PI was a mistake," her father continued, ignoring her question. "A sleazeball. Talks like some kind of Sam Spade. Do you know what private investigators charge these days?"

"What else did he learn?"

"Not much."

But something. She rubbed her freezing arms, afraid to hear what would come next.

"He located another man, who worked with Marion at a bicycle shop in the late eighties."

Her mother had left them in 1985. "She was into bikes?"

"She might have taken up biking after she split. I'm sure she took up a lot of things." He edged closer to Julie and stopped a few feet away.

Frost coated the balcony's sliding door frames and sealed them to the wall. Outside, the steel and glass towers acted as a fence that blocked any view of Nose Hill Park and the sky beyond.

"The man from the bike shop was high on drugs," her father said. "The PI couldn't get any more details out of him. Now, he wants another deposit to try the stoner again."

Julie turned to him. "He might not be stoned the next time."

"I suspect the PI is stringing me along."

But the man had found a lead. "It's worth a try."

Her father scratched his chin, as though irritated by the stubble. "He thinks I'm too far away in Canada to do anything except send money for his so-called sense that the stoner's holding back something."

"What makes him sense that?" Julie held his gaze, her stomach tight.

He kept scratching. "It's a scam, in my opinion. I have doubts this stoner exists. Delilah couldn't find him in any phone directories."

"You aren't listed in them either. Do you actually want to find my mother?"

"That's why I hired the guy."

She narrowed her eyes. "Her turning up would throw a wrench in your marriage."

"What are you talking about?" His hand left his face. Blood dotted his chin.

Julie rubbed her damp hands on her pants. "You have to give the PI the deposit. You can't just let it drop. If you don't want to spend the money, I'll pay."

"Rosemary came up with another plan." He stepped behind the sofa, so it stood between them. "We're sending Delilah to Santa Monica, where this stoner lives."

"Why her?"

He rested his hands on the sofa back. "Apparently, the stoner mumbled something about Marion's family not caring enough to look for her personally."

"Delilah isn't her family." Julie raised her arms, wanting to knock sense into him.

"She's your sister."

"Stepsister." She focused on the blood, which was crusting, not dripping from his chin. Sending Delilah was wrong. But why was it?

"She'll talk to the guy, find out what, if anything, he knows, and pursue any leads he gives. Same as the PI, without charging me by the hour."

"The PI has the skills. He's a professional."

"Delilah has time. She's not working."

Julie leaned forward, over the sofa cushions. "Neither am I.

"You start back next week." He gripped the sofa back, holding his ground.

"Otherwise you'd send me."

He gulped. "We—"

"You wouldn't send me because you think I'm not competent."

"Julie, of course you are."

"You think I'm fragile." Her voice trembled. Dammit.

"Like I said, it's probably a wasted effort."

She stepped back. Her calves hit the coffee table. Don't retreat, don't show weakness. "That's why you waited to tell me, because now I'm due to start work and can't go."

His hands eased up on the sofa. "Eric agrees."

"You told Eric about this?" Her damn voice was turning shrill. "Before me?"

"Delilah told him. I know you and he are separated, but—"

"All of you—Eric, Delilah, Rosemary—you're all in on this. It's my business." Her legs struck the table so hard, they would be forming bruises.

"Mine, too. Marion left me, not you. Julie, you need to understand it was never your fault."

Bullshit. She marched away from the sofa. "Stop talking like my shrink. He'd agree I'm the one who should make the trip."

"Not if he considers your best interest. Your recovery has gone so well. Why risk all you've accomplished?"

She glared from her spot by the window. "What have I accomplished except building a stupid barn?"

He squinted. "Huh?"

She paced to the sofa, the window, back to the sofa. Her father believed she would crack at the probable outcome. They'd discover her mother was dead. Why else wouldn't she have contacted them in thirty-four years? Even if Marion had flown to Africa, she'd have access to the internet, and Julie's name popped up on Google searches thanks to social media. Also, thanks to the local success of Eric's poetry book and Julie's personal website, which they had set up in case her mother was looking. Now Eric and the others thought she should be here when they got the news, so they could cushion the blow. She stopped to face her father across the sofa. "I can easily extend my leave of absence." She crossed her arms. "It's not like I have other responsibilities." She oozed sarcasm into her voice. "Child care, for instance."

He rubbed the congealed blood on his chin. Good. She'd made him feel guilty for that part of them putting her down.

"Work is what you need now," he said. "There's nothing like engineering to avoid the personal, as Rosemary always says about me." His forced chuckle twisted his face into a grimace. "And Peyton looks forward to seeing you every Saturday."

"One day a week. Big deal."

"At that age, they forget."

Julie had no mental image of her mother, aside from what she'd seen in photographs, most of them distant shots or fuzzy. She wasn't sure she had one genuine memory of her. They had no contact with her mother's relatives in Montreal and Boston. Her father said Marion had moved to Calgary to escape her family. He'd never met any of them.

"Weren't you curious?" Julie had asked once, when she was teenager. "Didn't you want to know where she came from?"

"She didn't make them sound too appealing."

Her father's relatives said Julie was the spitting image of his mother, as though the Marion side of Julie didn't exist. But Grandma Fox's hair had been spindly, not thick like Julie's and Marion's. And Grandma had been five foot five tops, nowhere near Julie's six feet and Marion's five foot eleven."

She hated that they were all treating her like a child. Couldn't they see it would drive her crazier to wait at home for the verdict? If, in the end, they told her the search had been a bust, how would she know they hadn't swept the gruesome news out the window to protect her?

Her father picked up his cup and saucer from the side table and skulked to the kitchen.

Julie followed him. "When is Delilah leaving?"

"We booked her flight for next Tuesday." He didn't look at her.

"Why tell me now instead of waiting until after she returned? You could have hidden the whole thing from me if her trip flopped."

He rinsed the cup under the tap, his face in profile, his gaze on the water. "Eric thought you'd be annoyed to learn we'd kept it from you."

"I am annoyed." She leaned into the counter for support.

"Perhaps we should have included you from the start."

"Well, it's too late for that."

"Delilah's eager to go." He set the cup on the counter. "It's the first oomph she's shown since she lost her job."

“So, the search for *my* mother becomes Delilah’s therapy.”

“Julie, that’s not fair. Or true.” He moved toward the far end of the galley kitchen.

She stared, daring him to escape from the narrow room. “Delilah’s trip will cost you more than a PI. She has no investigative skills.”

“She’s great on the computer.”

“So you keep saying. The stoner wants Marion’s relative to come. That isn’t Delilah.”

He shuffled from side to side. “The PI isn’t certain he heard him right. I’m not dealing with that scoundrel anymore.”

“There must be hundreds of private investigators in LA. We’ll hire another one.” She stepped closer.

“And put down another huge deposit?”

“It beats Delilah screwing this up.”

He was out of the kitchen, into the front hall. “Let’s sleep on it. We’ll talk more tomorrow during Peyton’s nap.” He yanked his parka and scarf from the closet. “Eric’s dropping her off around ten. If you come early, Rosemary can explain better than I did.”

Weasel. “Don’t you see, Delilah doesn’t care about my mother. She won’t push the guy like I would.”

He wrapped the scarf around his neck. “If Delilah fails, you can go later, maybe this summer or spring.” He reached for her arm. “You’d enjoy a holiday then.”

“Holiday? That’s all it means for her?” She shrugged his touch off. “What if she wrecks this so badly the stoner refuses to deal with us further?”

“I don’t hold out much hope that he’ll come through anyway.”

“It’s the one hope we’ve had in thirty-four years.”

“Why not discuss this with your psychiatrist?”

“I intend to.”

He gave her a stiff hug. “Why don’t you stay over at our place tomorrow night, to have more time with Peyton?”

She could ignore his questions too. Julie closed the door behind him, retrieved her cup and saucer from the coffee table, dumped the tepid tea into the sink, and strode to Peyton's bedroom. Julie used the space now for her art therapy. Peyton hadn't been to the apartment in over two months, since that horrible afternoon in November.

Julie sank into the desk chair and ran her palm over the barn roof. The clay collapsed inward. Her father had ruined her focus. She stalked down the hall toward her bedroom but paused at the closed bathroom door.

She nudged it open, visualizing what Eric would have seen when he'd barged into the apartment to collect Peyton that weekend. Thank God he'd had a key.

Julie blinked, her eyes watery.

She'd been kneeling at the bathtub. Her daughter's body—weightless in the water but too heavy to lift. She dragged her arms out from under the slippery skin. "Peyton, float."

Peyton's belly rose up and down. Her cheeks were blotchy with redness. The bath was too hot. Julie couldn't do any of it right, not the simplest thing. Almost four, Peyton was too big for the soaker tub, and too young to see Julie was no mother inside.

"Mommy, I'm swimming." Peyton fluttered her hands and feet. Her head struck the porcelain. Julie's baby, perfect the day she was born. Still unspoiled. Julie could save her.

"Mommy, look." Peyton's face sunk into the water. Her pink lips resurfaced. Her hands and feet fought to keep her buoyant as the water bore down on her.

"Swim, Peyton. Float free."

"Mommy, I'm tired."

So was Julie. Already her exhaustion seeped into her baby.

"I can't swim anymore, Mommy." Peyton's stomach and lips were submerged, her body suspended in a casket of glass.

Julie slammed the bathroom door shut. Never again. Never.

* * *

Delilah Trottier clicked the mouse. She scrolled through images of beaches, palm trees, and a glorious sunset behind the Santa Monica Pier. Who knew the prospect of a trip to a warm climate would boost her mood this much? She already felt eager to start a new round of job hunting after she returned.

The computer clock showed 2:07 p.m. She'd been lost in California for two hours. Without a snack. Weight loss might be an added bonus of the trip. She hoped she wouldn't let them all down and would get useful information from the man who had known Marion. With luck, not all his contacts would be druggies or creeps.

The doorbell rang. Delilah glanced at the frosted window. Who would be out in these subzero temperatures? She shuffled through the kitchen and dining room, cinching her bathrobe sash on her way to the front door. She opened it to see a tall figure in a white coat on the porch, the face half-hidden by a fur-trimmed hood. Narrow-set eyes stared down at her.

"Julie?" Delilah stepped back to escape the cold. She glanced at the street. "How did you get here?" Her stepsister had given up driving.

Julie closed the door behind her, lowered her hood, and pulled off her leather gloves. Her hands were red. "CTrain." She slipped the coat over her shoulders. "It took longer than I thought. I had the idea you lived close to the station." She shook her auburn hair over her sweater and removed her boots, which looked both stylish and comfortable. They must have cost hundreds of dollars.

Delilah crammed the coat into her closet, conscious of her pyjamas under the natty robe. She smoothed her curls as best she could.

"What a cute house." Julie surveyed the living room.

The house was small, old, and all Delilah could afford that wasn't way out in the sticks. Over the past two years, she'd invited Julie to birthday parties and other family gatherings, but her stepsister always claimed she had to work, or made a similar excuse. Delilah collected the empty chip bags and chocolate bar wrappers from the coffee table and studied her living room as if through Julie's eyes. Garage-sale paintings; their parents' castoff furniture; an old-fashioned afghan, knitted by her mother, draped over the sofa; a comforter bunched on the rocking chair. Rosemary raved about Julie's tasteful antiques.

"I was going to make coffee," Delilah said.

Julie opted for chamomile tea. The rosiness in her face had faded to her usual peach complexion. She wore no makeup and didn't need it with her dark eyelashes and clear skin. Delilah realized that only one thing would prompt Julie to trek across this frozen city. She wanted to grill her about the search for Marion. Julie had always been protective about her mother.

She set her coffee and the teapot on the dining room table.

"I'm going to California," Julie said.

Delilah tore open a box of cookies and put them on a plate. Misery swept through her like a wave. Without California, she'd be hurled back down to the pit of darkness she'd been in before Christmas.

"It's my business, not yours." Julie glared, as though defying Delilah to contradict her.

Delilah took two more plates from the wall unit. She passed one to Julie and grabbed a handful of chocolate chip cookies for herself. "You can't go," she said. "You're starting work."

Julie carried her tea to the living room and sat on the sofa. "I'll extend my leave of absence."

"Brad's already bought my plane ticket. It's nonrefundable. I can't transfer it to you, or cancel." Delilah dumped the comforter on the floor and dropped to the rocking chair.

"You can go on holiday in LA. I don't care about that. This means more to me than a free trip."

The crumbly cookie left Delilah's mouth parched. Her doctor insisted her dry mouth wasn't a side effect of her antidepressant and that it was probably stress. Stress from not working and having no life. She slurped her coffee. Julie rubbed her hands up and down her clingy jeans.

Julie had always pretended to be cool about her mother abandoning her. Delilah played the cool game, too. Her father lived in Vancouver, a cheap phone call or plane ride away, yet he limited his contact with her to sporadic calls and jokey electronic cards on her birthday and at Christmas. Delilah couldn't count the number of unreturned messages she'd left him as a kid. She'd finally given up letting it hurt her a few years ago and agreed with her mother—he was a charmer with no interest in parenting.

Julie's chin quivered, reminding Delilah of Peyton, caught in the muck of her parents' separation. In conversations with her mother, Delilah pretended to agree that Julie wasn't entirely at fault for the breakup, that Eric deserved some blame for being obtuse and unsympathetic. But it wasn't Eric's fault he'd been sucked in by Julie's on-top-of-it-all persona. They'd all thought she'd gotten over her postpartum depression.

"The apartment I rented on Airbnb's paid in full," Delilah said. "And it doesn't look too classy from the pictures. It's not a place you'd want to stay in."

"It's good enough for you."

"What I meant was it's cluttered with the owner's belongings. She rents it out now and then to make money. I think she moves in with her boyfriend. But it's cheaper than a hotel and will save me money on food."

Delilah's stomach churned in disappointment. Julie's determination always got her what she wanted. Top grades in school, a spot on their high school basketball team, job promotions. Brad believed Julie's engineering work was the ticket to get her back on track, but Julie was a grown-up. Brad couldn't forbid her to go. If he refused to pay, Julie had plenty of savings to travel to California at her own expense. She'd dig and dig and probably discover that Marion had died. Delilah suspected that Brad had gone along with the plan of sending Delilah so she could be the messenger with the dreaded truth. If Julie killed the messenger, figuratively, by cutting off their relationship, well, they weren't real sisters in any sense.

"What bugs me the most is how you all kept this from me. I'm not a little kid."

No chin quiver now. Julie had recaptured her cool. She would go to Los Angeles no matter what. The best Delilah could hope for was to salvage her own trip.

"The apartment has a sofa bed," she said, her mouth still dry. "I don't mind sleeping on that and helping you talk to the man the PI found."

Julie bolted to her feet. She lurched to the fireplace and then crossed to the dining room table to refill her tea. Delilah's coffee mug was empty, but if she went to the kitchen her tentative proposal might get lost in the air.

Julie stood by the table, teapot in her hand. "I'm sorry, I have to do this alone."

"Have you talked to your dad about it?" Delilah's voice was so weak, she could barely hear her own words.

"This isn't about him. He always got angry or changed the subject whenever my mother was mentioned."

"He's like that when Mom brings it up, too."

"He doesn't share his feelings with Rosemary?"

"Brad?" Delilah's mouth stayed open.

Julie's lip twitched. Almost a smile. Her first since arriving. Delilah and Julie had never directly discussed Julie's feelings about losing her mother. In that cramped apartment, engaged in the search, Julie might be glad for a confidant.

"You know, it took him ten years to take steps to divorce her," Julie said. "After tons of pressure from my grandmother."

And pressure from Delilah's mother, who had cried about it more than once with Delilah. "Do you think he's still in love with her?" her mother had asked.

"How would Rosemary feel if Marion turned up?" Julie said.

Dreadful. What was worse than second fiddle? Delilah should know, having played it since age eleven, when she and her mother moved in with the Foxes. Delilah had dropped to second, behind Brad, in her mother's life and slid into the role of younger child, even though she was a month older than Julie. After Julie's breakdown in November, Delilah's mother had pushed Brad to search for Marion—mostly for Julie's sake, but also for herself and Brad.

"It's hard living with a ghost," Delilah said, quoting her mother. Hard for all of them except Delilah, whose relative indifference might make her the best suited to tackling this head-on. But any argument Delilah presented regarding her suitability would only tick Julie off. "How's Eric doing?" Delilah asked, to change the subject. "Do you know if he's writing these days?"

Julie started at the non sequitur. "He has a poetry reading tomorrow night."

"Where?"

"Dad didn't say."

Delilah munched a cookie, while Julie poured her tea. Twelve years ago, after two dates with Eric, Delilah had invited Eric to a family dinner. How stupid and needy of her to rush their relationship after two dates. The sparks between Eric and Julie had been so instant that Delilah felt herself fading through the meal, and invisible by dessert. Three days later, Eric broke up with her. For years, Delilah had convinced herself she was over him—until Christmas Eve, when Eric had brought Peyton to her parents' home and the depression that had choked her through the fall lifted. How could she not love a man who would give up Christmas Day with his daughter so Peyton could spend bonding time with Julie? Eric and Julie weren't divorced, but they'd been living apart for ten months. By anyone's reckoning, he was free. A Google search might turn up a post about his poetry reading.

"I'm glad we settled this," Julie said.

Was it settled? Delilah looked at her crumb-speckled plate. Her trip to California was lost. She'd get fatter and fatter until she couldn't move from this chair. Julie would be the one sitting on the beach in the warm sun, cruising the freeway in a convertible, or rather, in the compact car Delilah had rented.

"How will you get around Los Angeles?" Delilah asked.

"There must be buses. Maybe trains."

"In LA?"

Julie's cheeks flushed pink.

Delilah's grew hot. She'd been surprised to learn through her Google searches that the sprawling, vehicle-obsessed city had a decent public transit system.

"I can take taxis," Julie said.

"They'll cost a fortune."

"Didn't you pick Santa Monica because that's where the stoner lives? I can walk to his place."

Delilah swirled a finger in the crumbs. "If he's too stoned to give you anything, you'll want to talk to the PI. His office is in another suburb. You'll have to drive there." Her voice croaked out the words that might or might not be true. "Or the druggie will direct you to someone who could have moved anywhere in the greater LA area during the past thirty years, or farther. Californians are particularly transient."

This wasn't lying, exactly. Julie could get around LA on transit, but she'd find it a hell of a lot easier by car. Even in her deepest depression, Delilah could drive. The one thing, perhaps the only thing, she could do better than Julie. And Julie wasn't protesting; she was thinking it through. What was Delilah getting herself into? Ten nights with Julie in an apartment with less space than this house.

Sunshine, sand, palm trees, the Santa Monica Pier.

So they'd spend the week quarrelling. It beat dreary home.

Julie left the dining table. Delilah met her in the middle of the living room and stared up at her, forcing her gaze steady.

"If you go, would you drive me to wherever I needed?" Julie asked.

"Absolutely."

In five days, Delilah would be in Santa Monica. But cooped up in three little rooms with Julie, who would likely turn nasty if the search for her mother ran dry. And if they discovered the worst, Julie might break down, go psychotic again. Delilah would have to deal with it. Could she? Her mother and Brad would have doubts. She'd leave it to Julie to tell them.

Chapter Three

Twenty-two faces in the amphitheatre gazed down at Aurora on the stage. In the predawn light, she saw them as silhouetted sunflowers drinking in her words.

"Every morning is an opportunity to renew yourself," she said. The natural acoustics carried her voice to Sebastiano, sitting high in the top corner. He was staring at Cassandra, who stood by the front row. From the corner of her eye, Aurora saw Cassandra's chin pointed toward her. That chin hadn't wavered in five minutes. The girl had focus—Aurora would grant her that. But she doubted she was capable of more. Sebastiano disagreed.

"An opportunity to break free of a past that cages you in," Aurora said.

Faces began to emerge in the sunflowers. Light glinted off eyeglasses in the theatre rows. The rising sun behind Aurora would make her silver hair shimmer. The pace of her speech was right on, even though her delivery was off today. Only she and Sebastiano would notice. She picked out the people she'd come to know this week. Lakie, with the swan neck, looked rapt. Mona glowed; Sebastiano called her moon-face "bovine," but Aurora felt Mona would make the best protégé of the ones they'd considered so far.

Aurora paused. What had she said? What came next? "Cast off the cage, let it tumble from the skies." She relaxed. She knew these words so well the emotion flowed through them even when her mind wandered.

People squinted at the rising sun; some shaded their eyes. A few put on dark glasses. From their perspectives, Aurora would be dissolving in the fiery ball, while her view of her followers grew clearer. After seven days, she understood what had brought each one here to California, to the New Dawn Retreat. They were all ages and shapes, female and male, but the largest chunk consisted of women in their thirties disappointed with their slices of life. Her role was to guide them to their individual paths. Usually, she succeeded on some level.

"Once you jettison the past, creativity flows." She was in the homestretch. One stumble, the hint of a stutter, would break the spell. She hadn't lost it once in ten years and was glad she wouldn't be here next week to watch Cassandra botch the daily morning ceremony and all the rest. Sebastiano would send her reports, and Aurora would wade through them to decipher the truth. Much as he'd tried to cover up his infatuation with Cassandra, Aurora had known him long enough to recognize the signs.

"Go forward." She raised her arms and voice. "Greet each dawn as a chance to dream. Live and love freely."

She soaked in each radiant face; the awed silence nourished her. Birds trilled from the cypress trees flanking the amphitheatre. Cassandra shifted her weight to one foot. The moment ended.

People edged to the aisles. Some trotted down the stairs, in a hurry for breakfast. Others lingered, hoping for a few words with Aurora, perhaps a touch of her robe. She adjusted the bodice, felt her clavicle and the evil lump. If the cancer had spread, Cassandra would have to fill in during the treatment. If it hadn't, Sebastiano's lady was out. Aurora would choose her own protégé.

She stepped away from the podium. Guests swarmed her. Where was Cassandra? Sebastiano?

Skeletal fingers squeezed Aurora's hand. "Thank you." Lakie's eyes were damp. "For teaching me to love myself."

"All I did was reflect what you already knew, Lakie." Would Cassandra learn everyone's name the first day, as Aurora did? Would she be able to subdue her bluntness? Most of Aurora's advice concerned delicate internal matters.

"You must be exhausted from all you've done for us," Lakie said.

Aurora extricated herself from the fingers. Did her tiredness show? She picked up her step on her way to the main building. Was this fatigue a sign the mass was infiltrating her body?

No. She would not permit that to happen. She was in charge of her future.

Mona caught up to her at the entrance. "In case we don't have a chance to talk later, I want you to know this was the best week of my life." The morning sun cast shadows on her pale, round cheeks.

Aurora smiled. Mona had told her this at the end of her three previous visits. She was too cloying to be a leader, and too short, although her strong voice with its hint of a British accent was appealing. Her father, who ignored her, was a diplomat. Mona, as Aurora's successor, might be able to propel the retreat's message beyond California, and the United States.

"I'm going to save every penny I earn so I can come back next year," Mona said. "If only it wasn't so expensive to fly from Australia. You know I'm moving there next month."

Aurora nodded.

"Have you ever thought of establishing, you know, branches?"

"The retreat needs one strong core of energy," Aurora said. "You could save money by taking advantage of our discount for the weeks I must be absent."

"It wouldn't be the same without you."

The muscle above Aurora's clavicle tensed. She had put her life into the retreat. All of it couldn't end with her.

Mona prattled on about her departure arrangements. In addition to her other flaws, she was too chatty. Not a good trait in a leader. Her trembling lips kissed Aurora goodbye. Aurora sniffed Mona's sweet scents, absorbed from the aromas of olive trees, flowering plants, and country air. The woman's chameleon qualities had helped her absorb the retreat philosophy. Yet, leaders had to be unchangeable, firm. The retreat needed someone who combined these contradictory features—a blend of Cassandra's strength and Mona's vulnerability.

Aurora entered the main building. In her office, she sank to the chair. Most days she enjoyed the paperwork, adding figures for income and expenses to arrive at a net profit that was gradually creeping up. It had slipped back into the red the year they purchased the farm across the hill at recession prices, but had recovered. This Christmas, they'd burned the mortgage. The profits would soar from now on. Sebastiano wanted to risk them on a large-scale development on the new property. He was still young enough to be careless and greedy, full of plans. To believe himself invincible.

She tried to concentrate on the spreadsheet. A sunbeam called her to the window. Through the round frame, she studied the expansive lawn, the swing underneath the valley oak, the olive trees rising up the hillsides, the stone guest residence. The sound of the door closing made her whirl. Sebastiano stood in the room, now quiet as a vault.

Aurora edged into the sunbeam so he could see her less clearly. "You disappeared after the sunrise service."

"I took Cassandra aside to brief her on some tips I picked up from your speech. For example, I told her to keep her eyes on the crowd in a way that makes each person feel she's speaking to her or him personally."

Sebastiano hopped onto her desk and dangled his legs, which were clad in pants most people took for tights. He considered robes unmanly and opted for a tunic vest and shirt, although the medieval garb didn't suit the retreat's Roman theme. He argued they'd already mixed the metaphor by building in the Tuscan style. His plan for the new development was an ancient villa that Aurora would lead; he and, presumably, Cassandra would run this retreat.

"I also told her to breathe from the diaphragm." His chest rose with his deep inhale. "She'll get the hang of it, eventually."

Sebastiano swung his legs back and forth as he elaborated on Cassandra's breathing difficulties. He was forty-two years old and as attractive as he'd been the day Aurora met him, nineteen years ago. His ebony hair still curled down the nape of his neck. Caps on his teeth had improved his ready smile. The hikes he led twice a day had sculpted his body into something resembling a Michelangelo statue. Eyes like the Mediterranean Sea. The scar on his cheek from a youthful surfing accident added character.

Thank the gods she was immune to him. Her attraction had lasted long enough for them to establish the New Dawn Retreat. Two weeks into the project, she'd decided sex and business didn't mix.

She interrupted his monologue. "By your own reckoning, Cassandra has a litany of faults."

"All of them easily fixed." He leapt to the floor. "Now, about the website."

"I know, a guest told you it needs to be 'more interactive and dynamic.'"

"What do you think of posting daily bytes of wisdom? Inspiring morsels that incorporate the retreat's values and ideals."

"You sound like a marketing representative."

"My old man would have been pleased."

"The message needs my breath, my voice. It will come off flat on a screen."

"A good ghostwriter will breathe life into your digital words."

"No outsider could interpret me." She sniffed his musky aftershave. He had, somehow, manoeuvred her out of the sun into the even light.

He leaned against the desk, his knee angled in a way that showed off the bulges in his crotch. "Pluck a scribe from the guests. God knows half of them spend hours scribbling in journals."

The website. A necessity, but the retreat's essence was to eschew the modern. "On the subject of Cassandra." Aurora wove through the slice of window light. "The minute I return, she's gone."

"You know we need an understudy. She's the best of the bunch. You agreed."

"I did not."

"You've objected to every woman I've suggested. 'This one's too chunky,'" he said, his pitch rising to imitate her voice. 'That one has a lisp barely detectable by the human ear. This other one's feet are too big.'"

"I never said that." She folded her arms.

He left the desk and eased toward her. "Darling, you have got to let go a little. Think of the future."

"I will, when the right person arrives."

"We need to send the message out to the world."

"Through cyberspace?"

His eyebrow rose, presumably in mock surprise at her knowledge of the term. "We'll need to figure out how to make money on the website."

"It's not about the money."

They stood so close her nose almost grazed his chin. He placed his hands on her hips, mussing her robe. Through his cologne, she smelled the peanut butter he must have nipped in the kitchen, unable to wait for breakfast. "Why are you against money?" he said. "It can't be all about power and adulation."

The bastard. She stared into the blinding sun. Her sole concern was the guests. Over the years, so many had sent her letters and emails gushing about how she'd changed their lives. Some included drawings they'd done of her. A few had composed songs and poems, some of which had been published in magazines. If she were an egoist, she would have posted them on the website.

"Give Cassandra a chance next week," he said.

"I will."

"She has the stuff we need."

She turned from the glare to his peanut-butter breath. "The stuff you need."

"You too," he said. "You could be out of commission for weeks, maybe months if you need radiation or chemotherapy."

"You'd like that."

He touched her sleeve. She drew back and bumped the filing cabinet.

"Supposing the worst happens and no one's been trained to step in for you," he said. "Do you want everything you've built dismantled and sold?"

"You would do that?"

"I can't run the retreat by myself."

He reached out to her shoulders. She let him caress her bones, too tired to shake him off. His strong fingers travelled to her clavicle and pressed the lump. Pain shuddered through her. She jerked away from him, back into the sunbeam.

"Must be time for breakfast," he said.

It would be her last meal here for a week. Or more. Not more. She would make it a week of opportunities. One: jettison the evil lump. Two: jettison that scheming Cassandra. Three: plan the retreat's future on her own terms. Sebastiano would come around. He always did.

* * *

"I thought she would never leave," Cassandra said.

Sebastiano glued his gaze to Aurora's Jetta. Dust spewed from its wheels as it rumbled down the road. The car disappeared around the curve.

Cassandra toyed with the ribbon on her robe's bodice. "She seemed odd today."

"What do you mean?" He looked at her.

"Oh, Aurora was riveting, as usual, at the sunrise service, but after that, I got the sense she was, I don't know, edgy."

Sebastiano clamped his mouth shut to avoid gaping. Even he hadn't noticed anything off about Aurora today, and he'd been watching for signs. Cassandra had sharp intuition, a vital trait in a leader.

"The retreat is Aurora's life," he said. With luck, Cassandra had missed his momentary lapse. "She gets tense when she has to leave it in the care of us lesser beings."

"Why is she leaving?" Cassandra scuffed her sandal in the parking lot's gravel. She unearthed a rock and kicked at it.

He'd have to train her to be less fidgety. Aurora was the master of otherworldly reserve. Who would have guessed from the way she efficiently and lovingly bid farewell to the guests that morning that she'd be under the knife in two days?

"Everyone needs a vacation," he said. "Even a goddess." He flashed a smile.

Cassandra's jaw tightened. "You shouldn't ridicule her."

"Isn't that my role around here? Levity? Even Aurora sees the need for balance with the sacred." This was true, although Aurora rarely admitted it. These past ten years they'd been a perfect team. Too bad change had to happen.

"You told me Aurora plans her breaks months ahead." Cassandra looked up from her kicking. "I heard talk of her vacation only yesterday. It wasn't advertised on the website."

"We're giving the incoming guests the discount."

"So they won't revolt when they learn they're stuck with me?"

Beneath Cassandra's self-deprecating smile, Sebastiano glimpsed determination. Another essential leadership trait. Her striking looks also wouldn't hurt. Taken individually, Cassandra's features were all wrong. Horse-shaped face, long nose curling into a bulbous tip, mouth too large for her pointed jaw. Together, they worked. At five foot ten, she was almost as tall as Aurora. Both had slim figures that looked splendid in robes. This ivory stola, in particular, enhanced Cassandra's dark skin. Aurora wanted an impressive successor, one who measured up to her standards, but she was jealous of those with the potential to become her equal and resented their youthfulness and glowing health. The paradox had made selecting a protégé impossible.

They moved into the sun. Sebastiano peered at the gardener riding the mower over the lawn, one of a hundred tasks happening during the few hours between retreats. Cooks were preparing the welcome dinner; trucks delivered fresh supplies of food. In the guest building, washers and dryers hummed, cleaning staff scrubbed and dusted rooms, all to make everything pristine and ready for Cassandra's trial week, which would start in two hours.

“I don’t think she likes me.” Cassandra paused on the stone walkway.

Since this discussion could take a few minutes, Sebastiano put on his sunglasses, which would also shield his eyes from her. “You mean Aurora?” He affected a mouth sputter to show the absurdity. “When has she ever indicated that?”

“On the surface, she’s all sweetness, but underneath…I can’t explain…”

Cassandra’s intuition was too sharp.

“We’ve been scouting potential protégés for years,” he said. “You don’t know how many Aurora’s dismissed. She lit on you instantly.”

“Really?” Cassandra’s face shone.

“Don’t worry about feeling insecure. Aurora’s a hard act to follow.”

“I’m not insecure.”

Yes she was, or she wouldn’t have forked out the big bucks for this retreat in the first place. “We all feel inadequate at times.”

“Including you?” Her lips broke into a teasing smile. She shifted her robed hip toward him flirtatiously.

Fortunately, no one was around, aside from the gardener riding toward them. Sebastiano kept his relationship with the leader ambiguous, a topic of curiosity that left him available for the attractive women and occasional man who attended the retreats. The lawn mower turned from them and manoeuvred around the oak tree.

“I should go practice my speech for tonight,” Cassandra said.

“Would you like more help with it?”

“That would make me nervous.”

“Don’t over rehearse, or the speech will go flat. You want it coming across polished, with some phrases apparently spontaneous.” Another Aurora art.

“I’ll check my email first.”

“Your mother’s still writing every day?”

“‘Cassandra,’” she said, mimicking a stern voice. “‘When are you coming home?’”

She'd been here a month. After he'd selected her that first week as a prospective successor, they'd kept her on to study Aurora and handle office details. Cassandra had opted to take a leave of absence from her job rather than quit before she knew if her role of Aurora's helpmate would work out. Sebastiano admired her common sense. So many others, inspired by the retreat, abandoned their former lives with no plans for the next step. Cassandra was smart, too. With only a high school degree, she had moved up from cashier to manager of a large supermarket.

Sebastiano opened the stone building's massive door. Cassandra loped past the lounge to the office. Her gait could use some work. Aurora glided. He closed the soundproof office door. Cassandra plunked down on Aurora's chair and rapped the mahogany desktop.

"Do you want me to leave while you e-chat with Mommy?" he said.

"If I phone her instead, I might set her mind at ease."

Whatever they talked about, she'd tell him later. He liked Cassandra's openness. Aurora thought she lacked mystery.

In the lounge, Sebastiano plumped cushions already plumped by household staff and adjusted chairs, all to keep moving. The retreat's future was in flux until Monday, when they would learn the results of Aurora's operation. She might be gone for months, undergoing chemo or radiation, or back in action next Saturday. No matter how well Cassandra performed, she wouldn't be able to get a foothold in one week. Aurora would whittle her down until she flew back to Mommy and her supermarket career. From subsequent crops of guests, Sebastiano could choose another trainee, but the result would be the same.

He grabbed a fireplace poker. They had built this place. Aurora's sickness was his chance to save it from dying with her. If her tests were clear, he'd need a plan B, one that would thwart her determination, intelligence, and intuition.

Chapter Four

"I booked a seat on Delilah's flight," Julie said.

Her father glanced at Rosemary. "I wished you'd waited to discuss this with us."

"So you could talk me out of it?" Julie inhaled the aroma of cookies in the oven. She didn't need her father and stepmother's approval for the trip, but she hated them thinking she would crumble at the first setback. "I need to be there because I'm more motivated than Delilah," she said. And because the answer, if she found one, would probably be bad. She didn't want to hear secondhand that her mother was dead. She had to know before Delilah, her father, her stepmother, Eric, and anyone else they had told. If that was being paranoid—

"Work would be better for you," her father said. "Delilah has time for this wild goose chase."

Rosemary opened the oven door to take out the tray of cookies. Had Marion baked? The phone rang from the family room.

"I'd go myself if I didn't have this project deadline," her father said.

The phone rang a few more times before dying. Her father and stepmother screened all their calls.

"That might be Eric to tell us he's running late," Rosemary said. "He finds Peyton a chore to hustle out in the mornings. Weekdays are the worst, he says."

That was Julie's fault. She'd walked out on them. When she and Eric were together, a nanny had come in on days they both worked. Now, Eric cut costs by taking Peyton to a babysitter.

Julie's father left to check the answering machine. Rosemary leaned over to put the mixing bowls in the dishwasher. Huge pockets on the seat of her jeans amplified her wide rump. She was pear-shaped, not slim like Julie's mother in the old photographs. Marion might have put on weight with age, although Julie was approaching forty and her stomach and hips showed no signs of spread.

Her father reported that Eric was stuck in traffic. Not a problem, since this wasn't his Saturday to work at the clinic.

"Thinking it over," Rosemary said, "I see Julie's point. California could do her good."

"Work and routine are what she needs." Her father sampled a soft cookie.

Julie crossed her arms. "I'm here in the room. You can talk to me."

"Routine will set her straight," he continued, ignoring her. "You can't beat the mental exercise of tangible, mechanical problems."

"The other day," Rosemary said, "I was watching Dr. Phil on TV—"

"Please," he said. "Don't bring that quack into this."

Rosemary closed the dishwasher, seeming oblivious to his insult. Would Marion have stood up for her hero?

"Phil talked about the mental benefits of choosing the uncomfortable path," Rosemary said. "It can lead to fresh solutions."

"Hmph."

Rosemary nodded conspiratorially at Julie. If her stepmother was climbing on board, Julie was almost there.

"It will be nice for you girls to spend time together," Rosemary said.

"Delilah doesn't have the private investigator's contact information," Julie said.

"That bloodsucker." Her father sniffed.

"He's the starting point."

"The drug addict's address and phone number are in one of the reports," he said. "Delilah will contact him directly."

The prospect of starting one step closer to any result was oddly exciting. "I'd like to read the PI's reports."

Rosemary plugged in the kettle. Julie's father loaded cookies on a small plate.

"That's enough, Brad." Rosemary tapped his hand.

Julie couldn't see Marion treating a husband that way, like a child. "We don't know he's an addict."

"Oh, he's addicted to butter and sugar." Rosemary dropped three teabags into the pot. "His cholesterol would plummet to normal if he gave them up."

"I mean the man who knew my mother," Julie said.

"Claims he knew her." Her father poured his tea. "I'm off to relax with the newspaper before Peyton arrives to keep us hopping." He retreated to the family room.

Rosemary looked at Julie. "He's nervous about all this."

"I can handle the trip."

Rosemary set a plate for Peyton's morning snack on the kitchen table. Watching her, Julie was struck, as she often was, by how much Rosemary and Delilah resembled each other. Same-shaped faces, wide eyes, and high-arched eyebrows. Their voices and laughs even sounded alike, although Rosemary's hair, dark like Delilah's when she married Julie's dad, was now tinted ash blond to soften her face. In the pictures, Marion's hair was light brown. Now it might be dyed or grey, assuming she was alive.

"Brad's worried about the effect on him too," Rosemary said. "Whenever we discuss it, he gets tense all over. That suggests he cares on some level."

Rosemary fiddled with a cookie, breaking it into pieces. Julie doubted Marion's reappearance would threaten their marriage, which seemed happy, or at least content.

"Marion's a part of your dad's life and history," Rosemary said. "But your grandma Fox didn't like her. I could never get specifics."

Neither could Julie. One time, when Marion's name came up, Grandma Fox spewed out that Marion was selfish and lazy. She stopped when she noticed little Julie staring at her. Thinking of her grandmother, who'd died two years ago, Julie felt a pang of loss. Her shrink attributed her breakdown, in part, to the death. When her father couldn't cope with raising Julie alone, he'd moved them in with his parents. His mother filled in for Marion until Rosemary came on the scene, when Julie was eleven.

"I think Grandma kept her views to herself to protect me," Julie said.

"That can't have been easy for her. She wasn't one to hold back her opinions."

Grandma had certainly ripped into Rosemary a few times, calling her lazy when she was depressed. Periodic bouts of depression were another thing Delilah had inherited from her mother, and possibly from her father. Rosemary had remarked that her first husband self-medicated with rum. Had Marion suffered postpartum depression, like Julie had? Was that why Marion left? Julie had to know.

Rosemary ate a broken cookie. "You'll be good company for Delilah in California. She'll be there for you, too, as family—a sister."

Sisters didn't always get along.

"I think you and Delilah could take and learn from the best in each other."

Julie pictured Delilah on Christmas Day, cuddled on the sofa with Peyton reading a silly children's story and enjoying it as much as Peyton. Her gaze glued to the pair, Julie had battled a paranoid feeling Delilah was trying to steal her daughter from her.

For sure, Delilah had more maternal instincts than she did. Julie could learn nothing from that except how to fake it.

* * *

Eric scrunched the sheet of paper into a ball and tossed it at the pyramid of paper wads on the kitchen table. The pyramid broke and spattered to the floor. Shit. Already 2:00 p.m. and he'd accomplished nothing, including lunch. Hadn't written a word.

He grabbed two pieces of bread and a slice of cheese to make a sandwich. The gum below his lower-right bicuspid throbbed. He didn't need a psychology degree to know this toothache was due to frustration with these poems about teeth along with worry about tonight's reading and Julie's trip to California. That was a rotten plan.

Eric downed two aspirins with milk and finished his sandwich while standing at the counter, looking out at his backyard, barely large enough for a strip of grass. Townhouse life focused on the front courtyard, with its playground in summer and snow hill in winter, great for Peyton. Selling the house and moving here had been Eric's one good decision since Julie left.

Back to work. Poetry had started as fun, not work. He ripped a fresh sheet of paper from the pad. *Root Canals*, he penned at the top. An evocative title for the new collection and its signature poem. Unlike the poems in his first book, *To Catch a Fox*, the new ones would be about him, not Julie. He, the dentist narrator, would ramble to patients in the chair. Mouths propped open, they'd be unable to respond, captive to the dentist's story, which would begin before his childhood with the three generations of dentists in his family, on both sides. Some poems might involve the dentist's imaginings about his patients, like the woman last summer who gushed about her engagement. The hygienists oohed over her diamond ring. Yesterday, she'd come in for a checkup, and Eric had asked about her wedding plans, pleased that he'd remembered. And then he glanced at her hands, which were resting on her abdomen as though she were laid out in a coffin. No ring on her finger. She didn't answer his question. His dentist narrator would speculate about what had happened, his musings circling back to himself.

Oh hell, that would make a boring poem. And once more, he'd be stealing from someone else's life. But what would make a good surface story to bring out the layers of personal meaning? *Root Canals*. Perhaps a burrowing into one's roots. Also, hair roots, if he were exploring further material about Julie, who dyed her hair those amazing shades of auburn. Copper, cinnamon, and nutmeg cascade to the small of her back, he'd written in *To Catch a Fox*. After Peyton's birth, Julie had cut her hair, but it still fell to her shoulder blades. He ended the book with a poem about Julie's postpartum depression and his assumption that she'd overcome it. But Julie had pushed it underground, where it abscessed and then erupted.

He stared at the paper covered with doodles, no words, balled the sheet up, ripped off another sheet, and wrote *Root Canals*.

Julie didn't understand that the Fox poems were only about her on the surface. Underneath they were about him, the fox pursued by ravenous hounds into a trap; the trap of a dental career that bored him, which might explain why he couldn't get into *Root Canals*. In hindsight, he should have shown Julie the Fox manuscript before sending it out to publishers, but she wasn't into poetry, and he couldn't bear the thought of her critical comments. *What does that mean? What's the point of this?* If she'd kyboshed the book, he'd have locked it in a drawer and wouldn't have readers, encouragement for more writing, and the poetry award. That had been a trap as well. People assumed because he'd published and won acclaim, he was a poet.

The doorbell returned him to the kitchen. He ran down the hall.

His neighbour, Nadine, stood on the step dressed in leggings, high-heeled boots and her purple jacket. No hat or gloves.

"I'm not sure if I can come to your poetry thingy tonight," she said. "Cody's dad stood us up again."

"I'm sorry." Eric exhaled in relief. He had regretted inviting Nadine on impulse.

"Cody asked if Peyton can come out and play."

Beyond Nadine's shoulder, in the courtyard, a kid who must be Cody jumped off the snow pile.

"She's at her grandparents." Eric shuffled in the cold air.

"I'd still like a copy of your book."

"I'll get one from upstairs. Come in a sec."

"I'll check on Cody first."

He closed the door, left it unlocked, and went up to the den. This would be Nadine's first time inside his house. So far, they'd run into each other only through their children, who went to the same babysitter in the townhouse complex. Whenever they dropped the kids off at the same time, he walked Nadine to the bus stop on his way to work. Since Christmas, this had happened enough that he wondered if she was timing her morning departures to meet him. Nadine had an accounting job with flexible hours. She'd raised her son alone from birth, although the father was peripherally involved.

"I'm not ready to date," Eric told everyone who asked. But if he were, he might go for Nadine. He liked her curly black hair and the way she let it blow all over on windy mornings, not attempting to tame it. She was slightly less slim than Julie and would be half a foot shorter if she ever wore flats. Both had similar athletic strides. Nadine dressed slinkier, in low-cut tops that he couldn't help notice since her jacket was always open, even in this frigid weather.

Downstairs, he found Nadine in his hallway, the front door ajar.

She looked at his handful of books. "That's more than I need." Her upper lateral incisors pointed outward like fangs. Otherwise, she had excellent teeth.

Eric felt his neck flush. "I have to bring some to sell tonight."

He set the box on the floor, took out a book, and passed her the thin volume. His fingers grazed her cool hand. Her cheeks remained ruddy from outdoors.

"Sharp cover," she said.

Both stared at the drawing of the red fox, huddled in terror.

"Cody loves animals as much as Peyton."

"The book's not for kids," he said. "Not at all."

She read the title aloud. "*To Catch a Fox*. How did you come up with that?"

"You sort of have to read it to see."

She tucked the book into her jacket's inside pouch. Since he'd offered to give her a copy, he didn't expect her to pay for it. But it would be nice if someone other than a poetry freak thought poetry worthy of payment.

"You must have a ton of things you want to do on your kid-free day." Nadine's glance at the kitchen couldn't have missed the wads of paper.

"I'm preparing my reading for tonight." He should start doing that rather than wrestle with *Root Canals*.

"I'll try to get a babysitter."

"Don't go to the trouble." Her presence would ratchet up his nervousness.

"No worries." She smiled and spun around to go check on Cody again.

Julie couldn't understand why he found reading his poems to a handful of people in bookstores, libraries, and bars scarier than speaking on a stage to hundreds at dental conventions. "They're personal," he'd told her. "About me, not anyone's teeth."

If he were a real poet, he'd be reading new material tonight, not the tired Fox poems. He had his excuse prepared. *I don't like sharing poems in the incubation stage*. The truth was, after four years, new work was nowhere near being birthed. *To Catch a Fox* had burst out of him in a frenzy that now seemed like magic. But it hadn't been magic. He had written those poems, worked on them, revised them, polished them to be the best they could be. His name was on a book that got rave reviews and won a major prize. He was a poet.

Was a poet. Was. Presenting himself as one tonight was fraudulent.

As Eric cleaned up the paper wads, his thoughts went to Julie once more. She'd answered the door when he dropped Peyton off with the Foxes that morning.

"Mommy!" Peyton lunged at Julie's knees.

Julie tottered and brushed her daughter's hair from her eyes.

"She needed a haircut last week," Eric said. "I never find the time."

"You could use one yourself."

Eric raked his bangs off his eyebrows, but they kept flopping down. In the old days, Julie's remark would have been teasing. He didn't know how to take it now. She was often surly with him, and he understood she hated his deal of allowing her to see her child only under supervision. A colleague thought Eric should have reported Julie. He'd considered this, but how would it help Julie or Peyton? Still, he couldn't trust Julie alone with Peyton until he was sure her medication and therapy had settled her back to normal, and even then, could he ever trust her alone with his child? His stomach still sank at the memory of seeing Julie in her bathroom, hunched over the tub. Intuitively, he'd known. He'd shoved past her, grabbed little Peyton and lifted her from the water, dripping, coughing, spewing a pale stream.

He shook the image away, but his thoughts of Peyton segued to this morning at the Fox house. She had dug out a miniature pony from her jacket pocket and handed it to Julie, who accepted it with pretend enthusiasm.

Peyton sniffed. "Is Grandma cooking something?"

"Chocolate chip cookies."

"Yay!" Peyton tore down the hall.

"I wish I had her energy," Eric said. "I'll pick her up tomorrow, late morning. Will you be here?"

"I'm staying overnight," Julie said. "By the way, I'm going away Tuesday, for ten days or so."

"On business? The day after you start back? For that long?"

"You can still bring Peyton here next Saturday. Dad and Rosemary love having her."

"Are they starting on a project already?"

"It's not for work." Julie tossed the pony from hand to hand. "I called my boss and he agreed I can delay my return."

"Where are you going then?"

"California." Julie looked over her shoulder at the sound of Peyton's squeals in the kitchen. "I better go rescue my parents."

They'd muttered goodbyes, and she'd closed the door behind him.

California. Damn. It had to be about her mother. The last Eric had heard from Rosemary and Brad, they were sending Delilah to Los Angeles to continue the search. When had that plan been changed? He didn't trust Julie not to crack up under the inevitable pressures. Yes, finding out what happened to her mother might resolve things for Julie, but only if done right. Damn those Foxes for screwing this up.

Chapter Five

Reclined on her deck chair, Aurora watched the sun slide into the Pacific Ocean. Reds, pinks, and oranges illuminated the clouds. On the sand, a group of thirty-year-olds batted a volleyball over the net. If Sebastiano were here, he'd leap off the deck to join the action. She wrapped her sweater around her arms. The sun's disappearance made the air brisk. Fortunately, since this was the low season, she and Sebastiano hadn't rented the beach house to tourists. If she had to be away from the retreat, she would rather be here than in a hotel, waiting for the operation.

The lump on her collarbone pulsed. Or she imagined it did. It wasn't a body part with nerves, but she sensed its presence, its cells. Cancer. She despised the word. The evil had attacked despite her efforts at self-care. No smoking, no drinking other than wine at dinner; healthy country air, purposeful work.

A cheer rose from the volleyball court. A group of teens on rollerblades whipped by on the boardwalk. Life was slamming her in the face, taunting. This minute, the cells could be spreading through her bones and flesh, killing her inside.

You can take control of your own life. How many times had she said this at retreat sessions, at the sunrise service, to guests in private conversations? *All it requires is will.* The teacher should listen to her own message.

The sickness had to be a remnant of her past. Dots of badness floating through her body had merged and bonded, coalesced into the lump. When she was the age of these volleyball players, she'd smoked, drank, snorted drugs, screwed around. Later, she and Sebastiano had founded the retreat with bad deeds, but they had redeemed them with the good the retreat was doing now. The worst was her childhood, her stepfather and her mother's boyfriends pawing her when they had the chance. Her mother slapped her and called her a liar and a slut when she complained. Her older sister got out, moved to Boston, and wasn't heard from again. Their mother would be over eighty, if she were still alive. Drinking and smoking had probably finished her off by now. The stepfather and boyfriends would be dead or shrivelled up in nursing homes. None of them could threaten her any more. And it wasn't her fault. That's what she told the guests who shared their stories of abuse. *Teacher, hear your own words*.

Aurora closed her eyes. She concentrated on the lump, let her mind travel its contours and depths. It felt mostly benign, only a few evil cells. Had more escaped, to invade the rest of her? *I will not let that happen. Make them return, like wasps to a hive at night. Spray the hive with poison and destroy them all.*

She focused on her fingertips. Was there cancer in them? She couldn't tell, but willed any sickness there up her arms, through the bones, veins, and flesh; rolled her shoulder to gather the evil into the lump. She sensed a weight on her collarbone. A burning. Success. A start.

Tonight, she would rest. She had all day tomorrow to cleanse her body, herself—to will all the cancer into the lump. Monday, the surgeons would cut out the putrid concentration. She would be free, freer than before with all the sin gone. So that was the purpose of the cancer. Jettison these remnants of her past. It would take a huge effort tomorrow, but she could do this.

* * *

"I totally blew it tonight."

"You did well for a first time," Sebastiano said. From his position in the dining hall observing Cassandra's welcome speech, he'd scanned uninspired faces and fidgeting bodies. He'd been almost bored enough himself to join the daydreams of a few young women who wished they were anywhere else.

"I noticed a man repeatedly checking an imaginary cell phone."

Sebastiano laughed. "More and more, we have to pry them out of their hands when they check in."

"It's not funny."

"I was trying for ironic." People came to the New Dawn Retreat to get away from the demands, the drudgeries, the limits of their everyday lives, and their first move was typically to resist letting go of the phones, tablets, and other gadgets the staff confiscated and locked up on their arrival.

Perched on the edge of the bed, Cassandra undid her barrette and shook her hair over her shoulders. Sebastiano stripped off his tunic vest and shirt.

Her lips quivered. "I'm glad Aurora missed my big flop. I doubt I prompted anyone there to 'slough off the past and free their creativity.'"

Sebastiano smiled. If Cassandra was as cynical about this as he was, she was even smarter than he'd thought and would be a refreshing change from Aurora's earnestness.

Cassandra unfastened her shoulder buttons. The robe slid to her lap, exposing her breasts. Sebastiano bent to his knees, cupped her firm breasts and kissed her nipples. He lowered her robe over her hips and nuzzled her belly until she moaned and pulled him down to the bed.

He fumbled in the bedside table drawer for a condom. "One day we'll do without this."

"You want children?"

Not a whit. "We'll need them so the retreat will continue."

"Or, like Aurora, I'll choose my own successor."

He raised her arms above her head and kissed her face all over, drinking in her sweet scent. "I'm glad she chose you."

"She hasn't. I'm terrible."

His lips slid to her neck. "You're beautiful."

"When she gets back, she'll turf me out."

He nipped her skin, wishing he'd turned off the lights in case her intuition got extra sharp. From the corner of his eye, he spotted the painting above his bed. Smudges meant to be a type of wild animal chased something through the forest. He bit harder.

She groaned. "I love you, Sebastiano."

He licked her breasts, peeled her panties down her strong legs, kissed her toes, moved his lips up her calves, her thighs.

"Sebastiano." Her body shuddered under his lips.

Later, in darkness, Cassandra lay in his arms while he drifted in the space between waking and sleep. Smudges chasing what? The painting didn't reveal. He loved that mystery.

"I've been meaning to ask," Cassandra said. "How did you and Aurora come up with the money for this place?"

His body and mind grew suddenly alert.

"This huge property in the orange growing belt," she continued. "The stone buildings, the amphitheatre, the gardens and groves. They don't come cheap."

"Inheritance." He had the answer down pat. "My old man croaked of a heart attack from working too hard in the rat race."

"That's sad," she said. "Did that prompt you to pursue the life you wanted?"

"Hmm." He was exhausted by a day in the fresh air, amazing sex, and figuring out how to handle Aurora. And Cassandra wanted to bond now?

"What about your mother?"

"The old bat's still alive, I presume. I haven't heard from her or my sister in ten years." Since he deposited the money.

"You have a sister?"

"She's a chip off the old rat race."

Cassandra stroked his chest. "I'm not crazy about my sister either. Who needs 'em?"

"Not when I have you." He squeezed her shoulder.

"I love you," she said again.

"I love you too." Why not?

Her body softened in his arms. She was perfect for him. Almost.

Chapter Six

Delilah entered Ospreys bookstore. The staff had dimmed the lights and moved the shelves to the side to create a reading nook with rows of chairs. Eric stood by the podium chatting with a young guy. The featured reader, Delilah guessed. According to the notice she'd found on the internet, the twenty-four-year-old was a dazzling new voice from Saskatoon. She gathered that Eric had been included to draw in the local crowd. His black T-shirt and jeans made her wish she'd dressed poetry rather than business—pressed pants, frilly top and a blazer to hide her stomach and hips. She edged to the refreshment table.

The store manager offered her a glass of wine. "How's the job hunt going?"

"No luck so far."

"Sorry we don't have anything for you."

A woman walked in, looked around, and fixed her gaze on Delilah, who hoped she wasn't an acquaintance from the old poetry-reading days. The woman was heading for her. Are you still writing? she was bound to ask. Not as much as I'd like, Delilah could answer, instead of the truth. Not at all, for years. Even at her peak, in her mid-twenties, she'd completed only a few poems, none good enough for an audience.

The woman zoomed in. "You look as lost as me. I've never been to this kind of thing before."

Close up, she looked to be early thirties. Curly black hair framed her face. Her open jacket revealed a low-cut top with a scalloped neckline.

"I'm Nadine." The woman extended her hand. "Eric's neighbour." Her firm palm was still cool from outdoors.

"At his townhouse?" Delilah said. "I'm his sister-in-law."

"From Saskatchewan?"

"On his wife's side."

"Julie?" Nadine's eyes lit up. "I think it's great that he's stayed close to her family, for his daughter's sake." She looked past Delilah's shoulder. "There's Eric."

Delilah turned toward the podium, where Eric and the store manager were adjusting the microphone.

"What's the setup here?" Nadine asked. "Do you think Eric will read early? I could only get a sitter until eight thirty."

"He'll probably go first, since it's the young guy's launch. Are you into poetry?"

"I'm trying to broaden my horizons." Nadine glanced at the table. "Is the wine and food free? I didn't have time for supper."

Delilah nodded. Nadine filled a plate with cheese, fruit and a brownie and picked up a glass of red wine. Her leggings and stiletto boots showed off shapely legs. If she needed a babysitter to go out on Saturday night, she was likely a single mother. Delilah's hand shook as she filled her wine glass. Eric must have asked Nadine to come, and he was shy about sharing his work. He'd also told her about Julie and his growing up in Saskatchewan. Crap. He was interested in Nadine.

The manager cleared his throat into the mic. Feedback ricocheted around the room. Static pounding each word, he invited people to take their seats. Delilah led Nadine to chairs at the rear corner. Sitting with her would feel less conspicuous than being alone.

Through more sputters of microphone feedback, the manager thanked the audience for braving the cold to launch the first of many books by the newcomer who had burst onto the poetry scene.

"I'm delighted to open the store tonight for my nephew's Calgary debut," he said. "First, we'll hear from celebrated poet Eric Lamond." He detailed Eric's bio, ending with his day job of dentist. "Ouch." The manager clutched his cheek and winced to ripples of laughter. "Now, all of you open your mouths, I mean your hearts, wide for Eric."

Nadine nudged Delilah, spilling drops of wine on her blazer, which at least was dark enough to hide the stain. Eric stepped up to the podium. He thanked his friend for the opportunity to help a rising poet from his hometown. The words reverberated through the mic, which Eric adjusted while thanking the audience. Nadine's gaze was glued on him. Delilah's stomach sank like a lump. Nadine was almost certainly here to broaden her horizons beyond poetry. If she and Eric were dating, even pre-dating, Delilah had missed the window with him after Julie.

"I'd hoped to share new work tonight," Eric said. "But decided not to inflict it on you."

People chuckled. Eric stared beyond the empty first row and apologized to those who would be hearing his ancient poems again. His face brightened at the sight of Delilah. Or Nadine.

He opened the book he held. "I'll begin with 'Foxtrot.'"

Nadine leaned into Delilah and stage-whispered, "That's the one I've got around to reading."

The opening poem in *To Catch a Fox* used the metaphor of the dance to portray Eric's first meeting with Julie.

"She pulls away from me and whirls," Eric read. "Skirt spins, heels clicking the ballroom floor / Falling into me / leading me."

Delilah knew the poem by heart. Was the fox pursuing the narrator or was he pursuing her? The poem's central question made no reference to Delilah, whom the poet had dumped for the elusive foxy lady. When she'd remarked to Eric, jokingly, that "Foxtrot" also played on her surname, Trottier, Eric looked blank, as though the thought hadn't crossed his mind.

Eric muttered into the mic, holding the book close to his face, his public-reading skills as pitiful as ever. How could he be nervous about this? He seemed confident about everything else. But Delilah loved his vulnerability.

"Reach for each other," he said.

Silence.

The poem's abrupt ending always startled her. The audience took a few seconds to clap. Nadine tentatively joined in. Eric brushed his bangs back from his forehead, his gaze shifting from Nadine to Delilah. His eyebrows shot up. So, it was Nadine he had noticed first.

A few poems later, the manager released Eric, who headed for Delilah and Nadine.

"That was fantastic," Nadine told him. "I didn't realize you were so talented."

"I'm just glad it's finished." He pulled back the chair next to her. "You got someone to look after Cody?"

"My sister," Nadine said. "She can't stay long. I should leave now so I don't interrupt the next reader." She gulped her wine.

Eric settled on the chair.

Nadine rose. "Now I can't wait to read the rest of the poems. See you Monday, Eric. Thanks for inviting me. I wouldn't have missed it." She glanced at Delilah. "Bye, too—I've forgotten your name."

Before Delilah could answer, Nadine squeezed by her and out of the store. Delilah considered moving onto the vacated chair beside Eric. The manager introduced his nephew, who could escape Saskatoon and his teaching job only on weekends.

Eric turned to the podium. Delilah studied his unkempt hair. That evocative 'unkempt' suggested he had better things to do than force his hair into place. Delilah guessed that he and Nadine hadn't evolved much beyond friendship.

Delilah might have a chance.

At the microphone, the young man droned in the monotone poetry style that Delilah found worse than Eric's mumbles. In case Eric asked her to comment, she tried to grasp some meaning but couldn't catch more than the swear words, which comprised about half of the poems. Eric used swear words selectively to much greater effect, in her view.

"Promising," Eric said, when the poet was finally done.

The people in front of them stood up.

"I didn't know you still came out to readings," he said, across the empty chair.

"I've been thinking of getting back into poetry."

"Me too."

She giggled, stupidly. "I'll bet you've got fabulous stuff in the can."

Eric's face looked tired. His dental practice and full-time parenting would be enough to keep him from writing.

"Julie tells me she's going to California this week," he said. "Last I heard, you were going to look for her mother."

"She decided to go with me."

"Is it a smart idea? For her, I mean." Creases deepened between his eyes.

"Eric." A woman behind them. She shoved *To Catch a Fox* at him. "Would you sign this? I was mesmerized by your reading. You totally captured your attraction to the troubled wife."

Delilah finished her wine and glanced at the lineup at the book-signing table. "Should you be over there?" she asked Eric when his fan left, giving him the opening to escape. Dumb. She felt like the lady in "Foxtrot." Pursue, withdraw. She had good reasons to withdraw from him. He was still legally married to her stepsister, he might be involved with Nadine and, most of all, he'd shown no interest in her.

A man with a shaved head leaned over the empty chair. "Eric, my man. Where've you been?"

"Around."

"Congratulations, you dirty pig. You were a dark horse for the Mustard prize, shooting past the rest of us. Everyone hates your guts." He grinned and bounded off.

"He's joking," Eric told Delilah. "Well, maybe not."

"Naturally, other poets would be jealous."

"It's all politics," Eric said. "I found out the final jury had gripes against the other two poets on the short list. I squeaked through the middle."

She laughed. "You still made the short list."

"Luck." He peered at the book-signing table. She would lose him in seconds.

"There's no point in my sticking around," he said. "It's the other guy's moment. Feel like going somewhere for a drink?"

Did she? This was more than she dared to hope.

"Don't you still live in the northwest?" he asked. "Did you drive here?"

Eric's townhouse was a good mile from the store. He'd told her he liked walking to his poetry readings to get in the zone and then walking home to clear his head so he could sleep.

"I could give you a ride home."

"I wasn't fishing for a lift."

"I'd love a drink," she rasped, her throat dry.

She was sure Eric wanted to pump her for details about her California trip with Julie and the part of it that interested him was Julie, not her. In exchange, Delilah would see his townhouse complex, find out more about him and Nadine, and slip a toe through the window that had opened a crack. Pursue. Withdraw. "Foxtrot," she said.

"Pardon?"

A chance. She'd kick herself later if she didn't grab it.

* * *

Julie leaned against the headboard. Peyton's small pyjama-clad body snuggled into her side. Rosemary had decorated the smallest bedroom in the house for Peyton. Pictures of cartoon animals stared from the opposite wall. A centipede, a giraffe, and a smirking hyena.

My Little Pony lay at the foot of the bed, abandoned. Tonight, it was Teddy. Other nights, Peyton chose her blankie. Unlike most kids, she hadn't settled on one special love object. If that signified a problem, it was probably Julie's fault. Julie opened *Goldilocks and the Three Bears*.

"I don't want that one," Peyton said. "It's a baby book."

Julie deepened her voice and did a growly Papa Bear. "You don't want to hear my ROOAARRR?"

Peyton twisted around to rifle through the collection on the headboard shelf. Some were Julie's childhood books, frayed from hundreds of bedtime readings with her grandmother. Not her mother. In her one possible memory of her mother, Julie was drawing on a sheet of paper; a woman was seated beside her, encouraging her. Was the young woman Marion?

Teddy dropped to the floor. Julie rescued him. On her way back, she and Peyton clunked heads.

"Ouch." Peyton rubbed her hair. Her other hand grasped a thin yellow book. On its cover, a fox huddled, shivering.

"What's Eric's—Daddy's book doing here?"

"I tried reading some." Peyton was recognizing simple words.

"Did you understand what they meant?"

Peyton shook her head.

"Join the club," Julie said. "You don't really want me to read these?"

"Daddy wrote them for you."

"About me."

Julie rolled to her back, her hair bunched behind. Since dinner, Peyton had been perversely energetic, as though she knew Julie wanted to get her to bed early so she could read the investigator's reports. A side benefit of the California trip was a break from this weekend parenting. One more shameful-mother thought.

"Do you feel motherhood is beneath you?" Julie's first shrink had asked her.

"No."

"Not all women are suited to it."

"Too bad you only find that out after you're stuck with the kid."

"Is that how you see it?" The woman stared. "Stuck."

Julie was glad she'd ditched that shrink for one who didn't look down on her.

"Mommy." Peyton batted Julie's arm.

"Sorry." Julie flipped through Eric's poems, looking for something non-sexy a four-year-old might possibly relate to.

"The fox tiptoes into the chicken coop," she read. "Hens shriek / flap wings / clutch their babies / shudder on roosts. Feathers fly." Julie paused for effect. She lowered her voice and spoke in an ominous tone. "The fox spies…" She enunciated each word. "One…little…chick…in…the…corner."

"Don't." Peyton wriggled against her. "It's scary."

"I agree," Julie said. "Daddy's poems are frightening." She closed the book. "Let's go back to *The Three Bears*?"

"Baby book."

"How about *Fox in Sox*? Grownups like Dr. Seuss."

"I want Daddy to read to me."

"Daddy's busy tonight."

Peyton's lower lip jutted out.

Julie couldn't blame her for the reaction. Eric almost always put her to bed. Plus, what kid wouldn't prefer to be in her own home? For Peyton, home was now her dad's townhouse, where her mom had never lived.

"Sweetie," Julie said. "I know it's hard."

Peyton jerked to her knees to search through the bookshelf. "Here." She held a large book inches from Julie's nose. *Fox in Sox*. Peyton squeezed Teddy under her arm. Yep, reading was easier than listening to the old story about her parents' breakup. Daddy and I have problems between us. They have nothing to do with you. We both love you. Wish I could live with you and Daddy, but I can't. Peyton always accepted it and didn't ask the obvious "Why can't you?" But Julie suspected her daughter didn't quite buy the explanation. Neither did Julie.

Julie stumbled through the tongue twisters to the end. She put *Fox in Sox* away with *Exploring the World of Foxes*, *Mr. Badger and Mrs. Fox* and the other books Rosemary had bought to play on her stepgranddaughter's name. Peyton Fox Lamond. Julie tucked Peyton in and kissed her forehead.

Downstairs, she found her father and Rosemary on the family room sofa, a blanket draped over their chests and legs. A man and woman argued on TV.

Rosemary put the movie on pause. "Brad, you make popcorn while Julie and I start from the beginning of the movie."

He groaned. "Do I have to? It's warm under here."

They kept the house cool to save heating costs. Both claimed they liked the bundling up.

"I'll make popcorn," Julie said. "But I'll skip the movie and go upstairs to read. Where did you say you put the PI's reports?"

"There's nothing much in them," her father said.

"Anything might help."

"On the desk in the den."

So, he'd taken them out for her. He truly was resigned to her making the trip.

The den had been Julie's bedroom until she moved out, after university. All that remained of hers was the single bed. Sprawled on the hard mattress, she opened the folder to the private investigator's first report.

People come to Los Angeles to either break into film or hang out on the beach, his opening line like a voice-over for a noir movie. She leafed through reports describing his interviews with connections in the film community or in suburbs along the coast. No one recalled Marion or recognized her from the pictures Julie's father had provided. One contact had put the PI in touch with the owner of a vegan restaurant who had lived in Santa Monica forever and knew the beach scene. After studying the photos of Marion, the restaurant owner thought, but wasn't sure, she'd seen her working at a beachfront bike-rental shop in the late 1980s. She knew a man who had worked in the shop around the same time, Terry Edwards, who still lived in Santa Monica. Julie's heart quickened. Investigators must find it exciting to slog through mud and hit solid ground. From his reports, the PI struck her as decent and thorough. Her father had probably been put off by his gumshoe writing style.

The PI had dug up Terry's address and gone to his house. People spill more guts if you take them unawares, he wrote. Terry was obviously stoned. The place reeked of marijuana. He couldn't focus on the photographs, staggered, giggled, admitted he'd worked with Marion at the bike shop but couldn't remember when, how long she'd been there, where she was living at the time or who her friends were. The PI asked if Terry had seen her or heard anything about her since. Terry possibly muttered that if the woman's relatives cared, they'd make the effort to come themselves. The PI tried other questions. Terry didn't grasp them or claimed he couldn't remember.

Julie closed the file. She could see why her father was skeptical about Terry as a source. Who knew if he'd offer anything of use, even if she and Delilah caught him sober. Still, he was their sole lead, and their trip was in motion. There were people in California who'd crossed paths with her mother. Whatever crumb Terry and the rest tossed her would be a feast. She hadn't realized before how much she wanted any connection to her mother.

Her father invariably shut down at the mention of Marion's name, yet he'd begun this search, hoping an answer would help Julie's problems. She shook her head. He had no idea how bad these problems were.

Her near drowning of Peyton was the worst, but there was more. She hadn't trusted it to her first shrink, and it had taken her a month to confess to her current psychiatrist.

On her way to the bathroom, Julie peeked into Peyton's room. Her daughter lay curled beneath the comforter, asleep, her small arms around Teddy, Blankie, and My Little Pony. No rosy face could be sweeter or more innocent. Eric used to say he never felt such pure love as when he watched their daughter sleeping. Where had it come from? he'd asked. The love that tore through your body, mind, and heart? Julie would nod in agreement, afraid to tell him the truth. She liked Peyton. Her fondness for her little girl ran deep. She felt responsible for her. But love? She'd never quite reached that feeling.

Chapter Seven

"Mrs. Jones."

Aurora struggled to open her eyes.

"Mrs. Jones."

Aurora recognized the voice of her surgeon, who sounded like Harrison Ford but looked like Will Smith. Only a hospital in Los Angeles would hire actors to be doctors. She should have gone to San Francisco, or farther away, like Japan. Less chance of being recognized.

"Mrs. Jones. Your surgery was successful."

Her eyes slit open. The surgeon hovered above her, dressed in mint-green scrubs. He held a clipboard.

She coughed to clear her dry throat.

"We were able to remove the whole tumour."

"That…that's good?" She shut her eyes. The ocean pounded in her ears, punctuated with the beep, beep, beep of the machine connected to her vitals.

"And more good news," he said. "There was no spread to the bone or chest. We removed a couple of wonky lymph nodes."

"Wonky?"

"As a precaution, we biopsy anything questionable."

"The results?"

"We should have them by the weekend," he said. "You rest. The orderly will be in to wheel you up to your room."

"When can I leave?"

"In a few days, if all goes well. We'll arrange for a home-care nurse to come in to change your dressing."

"Work."

"You'll need a few weeks' rest before you're ready for that."

"No."

"Your body's suffered a significant trauma. It needs time to recuperate."

She drifted away.

"Aurora."

The surgeon's skin had lightened to tan. He'd replaced his scrubs with a blue shirt.

"Sebastiano." Aurora tried to lift her head, but it was glued to the pillow. She raised her hand. The tube connecting it to the machine tugged it back to the bed.

Sebastiano leaned over and kissed her forehead.

She gagged on his aftershave. "Why aren't you at the retreat?"

"I can spare a few hours to see you."

"You're needed there." She hoisted her head an inch.

"I cut the afternoon hike short. No one will miss me at dinner."

"Ca…Cass…Cassandra?"

"She's getting the hang of things."

Good news and bad. Sebastiano dressed in something other than a tunic vest was strange. He had tied his hair back in a ponytail, which he sometimes did at the retreat. "Pig's tail" would be a more accurate description.

"I spoke to the doctor," he said.

"Wha…what did he tell you?"

"The operation went well."

"For him. I still might need chemo or radiation. 'Wonky'…"

"We'll face that if it happens." His smile pushed up his cheekbones. "I brought you flowers. Birds-of-paradise."

She craned her neck toward the bedside table. In the vase, a flock with yellow crowns peered from greenery. Their long beaks pointed in all directions, scoping the area for predators, or unsure of which way to go. If she could fly, she would soar to the retreat on Saturday to greet the incoming guests. *Screw the doctor's advice.* She supposed she had to keep Cassandra around until the final verdict came in. But if yesterday's meditation worked, if the nodes were clear, by next week, Cassandra would be out on her pretty ass.

Sebastiano stroked her hand not hooked to the machine. "I'll take off now and get back to the ranch."

And to Cassandra's bed. Next week, if the gods were with her, Sebastiano would be stuck combing the new flock for his next squeeze.

He kissed her forehead again.

"I must look like hell," Aurora said.

He smiled. "You mean your pallid skin, oxygen tubes up your nose, hollow eyes, oily rat's nest hair? You look beautiful."

* * *

She does look like hell, Sebastiano thought, as he left the room. But even though Aurora looked frail and about a hundred years old, no one could be more determined. If the doctor discovered her cancer had spread, Sebastiano wouldn't put it past her to forgo treatment in order to maintain control of the retreat, especially if the chemo or radiation wouldn't significantly improve her odds of survival. There was a good chance she'd lie and tell him they'd given her the all clear.

He stopped at the nurses' station. "I'm Mrs. Jones' nephew," he said. "When can we expect the biopsy results?"

"Hard to say." The nurse spoke in a nasal tone. "When she's released, the doctor will schedule a follow-up appointment."

In her condition, Aurora would need Sebastiano to drive her to the appointment. He'd be there to see through any lies when she emerged from the doctor's office.

"You know, you look familiar." The nurse stared up at him through lenses with diamond-studded frames. "Your aunt, too. Has either of you been in here before?"

"No."

Her gaze slid to his chest. "For some reason, I see you both in costumes. Last year I was at this carnival party…"

Permed hair, plump, late thirties, the nurse might have been among the thousands who'd passed through the retreat. He hoped he hadn't slept with her. Unlikely, with that grating voice.

He saluted the nurse goodbye and left the ward. Aurora should be grateful for the Mrs. Jones ID he'd kept from their days as petty cons. She would hate former guests seeing her in this weak condition, and feared that, one day, the police would connect her and Sebastiano to the long-ago scam of the old man. They'd carelessly used their real names for the bonanza that had bought the land for the New Dawn Retreat.

On the ground floor, he passed the gift shop. If hospitals could sell merchandise, why not New Dawn? Aurora had nixed selling anything other than the robes guests wore during the week, and the profits from those went to the local seamstresses.

"We need to keep the town's support," Aurora had said. "So they don't harass us and call us a cult."

"What's wrong with setting up a gift corner in the lounge the last morning of each retreat? We could sell mugs, pens, journals with a photo of the retreat on the cover."

Aurora had shuddered. "We will not become commercial."

Sure, they were swimming in money, but they could always use more to develop the farm property over the hill. Once that second retreat got rolling, they'd purchase land for a network of satellite retreats. And when they could afford a private plane, he and Aurora could fly from one satellite to another, supervising the leaders. That was assuming she survived. He shivered. Cancer.

He arrived at his car, glad he hadn't given in to Aurora's urgings to trade the sporty gas-eater for a hybrid. His role, and she knew this well, was to be the counterpart, a touch of the wild side. For that reason, he could never be a leader, even if he wanted to. Besides, the retreat as a matriarchy worked. He and Aurora were an ideal team. Ten years ago, when they founded New Dawn, they had drawn up wills leaving everything to each other. She was seventeen years older than him and expected to go first. He didn't want her to die, but her being sidelined would conveniently help him initiate his ideas and mould Cassandra into a leader.

He steered the vehicle onto the freeway. Two semi-autonomous retreats, the original and the newly developed property across the hill. Aurora leading the first, Cassandra the other. Any third retreat should be in a different location, say Northern California, or Oregon. Then a fourth, possibly in the mountains. He'd like Colorado for hiking.

But cancer.

What if Aurora's cancer hadn't spread? She would, essentially, be back to normal in a few weeks. Even if her health scare prompted her to seriously look for a successor, he doubted Cassandra would make the cut. His mistake had been championing the girl. Next time, he would lie low, let Aurora think the choice was hers. Things would be easier if Aurora's cancer had spread its tentacles, a little.

His exit was ahead. Traffic clogged four lanes to the right. Fuck. A car blocked him. Another. Another. Fuck LA. He spied an opening and scooted across the lanes. Environmentalism had its place, but this gas-sucking filly had pickup.

Chapter Eight

Eric wasn't sure how he and Delilah had wound up in his townhouse. They'd planned to stop at a bar. Now here she was peering at his furniture in the hall, the living room, the kitchen eating nook.

"I love the quirky, different-coloured chairs around the white table," she said. "It looks like most of what you've bought since Julie is modern."

"It's more practical for kids," Eric told her. "But I did claim the French Provincial–style Foosball table."

"Where is it?"

"The basement."

"I'll challenge you to a game later."

During the drive he longed to bring up her trip to California, but Delilah kept talking about the big change it must have been for him to move from a house to a condo. Had he offered to show her his place? Whatever, they were here.

"I've got a red opened," he said.

"Works for me." Delilah climbed onto a barstool.

He emptied the wine bottle into two glasses and joined her at the island.

"The title of your new book is cool," she said.

He regretted telling her about it in the car, but poetry was their common ground. And through Delilah he'd met Julie.

"I see lots of marketing potential." Delilah raised her glass in a toast. "Here's to *Root Canals* in dental waiting rooms across the country."

"Reading it will make patients grateful to get called to the dentist's chair." Eric grimaced.

She tittered, as though he were joking.

Time to steer their chitchat to his topic of concern. “I can understand Brad giving into Julie’s plan to go to California. There’s no arguing with her when she’s made up her mind.” He downed his wine, trying to appear dispassionate. “How long are you both staying there? Julie mentioned ten days.”

“That’s how long we’ve booked.” Delilah held up her empty glass. “Can we handle more?”

“I’ll do my bit.” He leapt from the barstool to get a Merlot from the rack.

“Maybe I’ll drop out of the trip,” Delilah said. “I should use my money and time to look for work, and Julie would rather be on her own anyway.”

The gum below his bicuspid pulsed. Julie alone, on a frustrating quest or discovering the worst news. He popped the wine cork. “What exactly was this lead that Brad’s PI found?”

Over their next round of wine, Delilah explained. Eric kept glancing at her feet. Her right sock had slipped off. She’d painted her toenails a burgundy shade and stuck on tiny pictures. Of what? He leaned over to look and felt his head spin.

“What does her psychiatrist think of her going?” he asked.

“You think Julie’s going to tell any of us what he says if it’s negative?”

“You should go with her.”

“She doesn’t need me.”

“You’re the driver.”

Delilah fiddled with her necklace. “I’ll show her the transit website and explain how their system works.”

“LA is huge for riding on buses.” He stretched his arms, bumping her shoulder.

“The search might be focused in a small area, Santa Monica. And do I want to spend a week cooped up with Julie getting all intense about her mother? You don’t know what she’s like.”

His brow raised. “I was married to her for five years.” And lived with her four years before that.

Delilah swayed to the side and straightened. "I don't think I should drink anymore."

"Are you okay to drive home?"

"I'm the driver."

They laughed. Delilah slid down the barstool. She bent to scoop up her sock, missed it and swiped at it again.

He couldn't send her home drunk. Had he been plying her with liquor to pick her brain about Julie and the trip? "You can stay over in Peyton's room."

Delilah stared at the floor, humming.

"What are you singing?"

"Was I?" She looked up at him, her cheeks dotted red. "I'm too used to living alone."

"Didn't your parents name you for that song 'Delilah'?"

Her flush deepened. "You remember my telling you that way back?"

He remembered Julie telling him that Delilah's parents had conceived her to the Tom Jones song. He'd asked why parents would tell a child something like that. His certainly wouldn't. Eric believed he and Julie had created Peyton on a hiking holiday in Utah. Julie insisted they couldn't know for sure.

"You're right." Delilah seized the sock. She grabbed the barstool seat and pulled herself up from the floor. "I'm not fit to drive. Can I use the washroom?"

He nodded at the hall and watched her totter to the powder room, her hips swaying. It probably wasn't smart to have his sister-in-law, whom he'd once dated, spend the night at his place. Did Delilah remember their dating? She'd never let on she did. There was no chemistry between them, but what if there had been? How different his life would be. Delilah suffered from recurring depression, but he knew that no matter how low she sank, she wouldn't dream of harming any child.

Eric collected their wine glasses and rinsed them in the sink. Who could have known that Julie would crack up? Had she inherited a predisposition to mental illness from her mother, who took off? Crazy family—crazy like a fox—although her mother was only a Fox by marriage. Delilah wasn't a Fox at all. She'd kept her father's surname out of stubbornness.

"Now I kind of regret it," she'd told him. "Fox is sexier than Trottier."

He pictured a horse trotting; Delilah's round behind retreating down the hall. Why was he thinking this? Julie would kill him if he got involved with her stepsister. It would be the end of any possible future between them, as well as taint their future dealings with Peyton.

Put a lid on it. Consider Nadine. She'd shown up at his reading. She had to be interested. Both single parents—they had that in common.

He looked down the hall at the closed powder-room door. Delilah was taking her time in there. Had she passed out? But to knock or call out might be intrusive. He plugged the opened wine bottle and adjusted the barstools so they lined up against the counter. These stools had come from their old place. He and Julie had sat on them numerous times, scarfing breakfasts before they dashed to work. She'd been fun in the days before Peyton. They'd whacked balls across the tennis court, each determined to clobber the other. The loser inevitably grumped, but oh it had led to amazing sex. About everything did back then, even the time Julie spilled the can of paint on the hardwood floor they'd just varnished. Stupid of them to varnish the floor before painting. They were crazy stupid. He missed the old Julie so much. But he would never, ever trade Peyton for her.

Still, he was the one who had pushed for them to have a baby. Julie had been dubious. He'd thought that her fear was natural. It was a big step. What if he hadn't pushed?

He wouldn't have Peyton.

Eric edged into the hall hoping Delilah hadn't hit her head on the sink or fallen asleep on the toilet.

"Delilah," he called through the door.

It opened. She stood inches away. He smelled the wine on her breath. She looked smoother. She'd touched up her makeup and combed her hair.

"You're right," she said.

"About what?"

"I'll go to California." Delilah touched her necklace. "I'll look out for Julie, drive her here, there, everywhere."

"Don't let her push you around," Eric said. "Only do what's reasonable."

"Mom will want me with her to send daily reports, so Brad doesn't go nuts with worry."

"I wouldn't mind hearing how it's going, too," he said. "Directly, not filtered through Julie's parents."

"Give me your email address. You'll get the scoop firsthand." Delilah twirled the necklace around her finger.

A step back into Julie's life, from a safe distance.

* * *

"Love doesn't always happen instantly."

Julie stared at her psychiatrist. "I've been Peyton's mother for four years. Before that, I carried her inside me for nine months."

Dr. Kumar jotted a note on the pad that balanced on his lap. He wrote frequently during their sessions but never looked down at the page.

"Love comes when it's ready."

"Other mothers…"

Julie knew his argument for this. She couldn't read other mothers' minds and hearts. How did she know some weren't struggling like she was?

She looked past him, at the avocado wall plastered with certificates for his numerous degrees. After the family meeting, her father had said he was impressed with Dr. Kumar's credentials. Rosemary praised his library of psychology books and classic novels like *Frankenstein* and *Sherlock Holmes*, books by Freud and Jung, and more by other classic shrinks. Dr. Kumar had requested and actually read *To Catch a Fox*.

"Interesting" was his only comment on Eric's poems about Julie.

"What if love is never ready?" Julie asked.

"Give it time."

At her initial session, Julie was astonished when Dr. Kumar remarked that there was hope. Her first psychiatrist had viewed her as a lost cause when it came to motherhood. Julie was sure this wasn't paranoia. Most likely that shrink had pegged her right, yet she trusted this man with the bald head and heavy-framed glasses. As always, today Dr. Kumar wore Dockers and a sweater flecked with cat hair.

"He can't be married," Rosemary had said, during the drive back from the family meeting. "No wife would let him out looking like that. I didn't notice any personal photos."

"I don't care how he looks," Julie's father had said. "All that matters is that he's qualified. Seems to know what he's talking about."

"And that Julie's happy with him," Rosemary had added.

Dr. Kumar crossed his leg. His pants rose up and exposed his beige socks. Why had Julie thought he'd support her trip to California? Instead, he agreed with her father that work and routine were the answer for her right now.

"This arrangement of seeing Peyton at my parents' house isn't working," Julie said.

"Why isn't it?"

"I can't be myself when they're around all the time. They think I'm incompetent at parenting, and I slip into their expectation."

Dr. Kumar swung his moccasined foot up and down. The nervous habit made him human. When she told him about trying to drown Peyton, she'd asked if he would report her to social services.

He'd paused, reflecting. "I see no reason for it."

She liked that he'd given it thought, rather than humour her.

"Don't you see?" she said. "I need to go to LA to find out why I'm this freak."

"You aren't."

"It's what Eric said when he walked into the bathroom. 'Julie, who are you? What are you?'" She shivered.

"Eric was reacting, in shock."

"You've had time to reflect these past weeks. What do you think?"

He jiggled his pen above the pad. "You said you felt you were saving her from future pain."

"At the time, in a weird way," Julie said. "And of becoming like me, a mother who kills her kid."

"You didn't."

Julie's lips tightened. "If Eric hadn't shown up, Peyton would be dead right now."

"How long did you hold her under?" Dr. Kumar's expression remained neutral, his body relaxed.

"Ten seconds. Ten hours." She stared at his glasses. "I have no idea of the time."

He tapped the pen, but didn't write. "It can't have been long. She suffered no physical damage."

"I thank God for that every day, and I don't believe in him."

"Your daughter was four years old."

"Almost." She rubbed her hands, which itched with dryness.

"Old enough to have fought you back."

"Not if she didn't know what was happening, if she trusted me. I told you, I pretended we were practicing swimming." She wanted to sink her hands, the whole of her, in water and never re-emerge. Would he call that suicidal?

"Can a four-year-old swim in a bathtub?"

"Floating. It's a soaking tub, big enough for two adults." Julie's nails dug into her palm. "Why didn't you report me?"

"Eric didn't."

"He can be a wimp sometimes." This digging was a waste; it drew no blood, but she felt it was less pointless than stopping.

"Your parents?"

"They wanted to handle it in-house. Parents protect their children. Good parents do."

Dr. Kumar wrote on the pad. "You said this occurred around the time Eric was due to pick Peyton up. Did you know he'd use his key to get in when you didn't answer?"

"He hadn't before."

"It was a reasonable assumption, given his concern for Peyton."

"Yes, Eric's the best dad." She crossed her arms.

"Perhaps you knew on some level he would stop you."

"I didn't. Even supposing I did, it was horrendous of me to cut it that close. Ten more seconds and she'd be gone."

One eyebrow raised above his glasses. "Are you sure you got so far as to literally push her under?"

"Eric saw me."

Dr. Kumar jotted another note. "How good was his view of the tub?"

Julie imagined herself at the bathroom door. "He could see over my shoulder." She'd like to be a bird looking over the doctor's shoulder to see what prompted his particular notations.

"Were you blocking his sightline of Peyton?"

"Dammit." She squeezed her fist. "I saw her under the water. Eric saw it."

"People see what they think is there."

"We both can't be wrong."

Dr. Kumar flipped the top sheet over the pad. "If Eric hadn't interrupted, your instincts might have kicked in. You might have raised Peyton up."

"Don't let me off the hook," she said. "The point is, you can't stop me from going to Los Angeles."

"That's correct."

"You believe I should stay home."

"Your mother has been gone for thirty-four years," Dr. Kumar said. "Do you have to find her this week? Leave the preliminary work to your sister."

"Stepsister."

"Does that make a difference?"

"In this instance, yes. Marion isn't her mother. Delilah's not as invested in the search. She won't push it to the limits." Julie dropped her hands to her lap. "Last week, you suggested I was blocked from loving Peyton. What if this trip unblocks me? Finding out, however bad it is, has to be better than this perpetual not knowing."

Dr. Kumar scribbled on the pad. "If you go to California—"

"When I go."

"Call or email the office if you run into problems." He held the pen above his notepad. His cheek twitched almost imperceptibly. Was he resigned like her father? Or, perhaps, supportive.

* * *

After supper that evening, Julie took the bus to Eric's condominium complex to say goodbye to Peyton. Silver lights strung on bare-limbed trees directed her along the pathway to his unit. She'd been here only once before, when she brought Peyton back on the bus as an excuse to find out what her daughter's new home looked like. It had been late summer. Now the lights reflected off snow blanketing the playground in the centre of the courtyard. Peyton raved about playing pirates on the jungle gym with the other kids. Someone had shovelled the ground below it to create the snow pile Peyton loved to climb. The families in the complex joined forces to enclose their children's world. Eric had chosen a good place to raise Peyton.

One of the units housed Peyton's babysitter, who looked after her and two boys, before and after nursery school, in addition to her own three sons. Julie had heard all about craft time, sing-along, reading nook, and the sitter tromping up the snow pile with the children. Peyton had given Julie a drawing she'd done at the sitter's, a typical kid-sketch of a house with a central door, peaked roof, and curlicue smoke coming from a chimney. Eric and Julie stood beside the house, Peyton between them. Peyton's and Eric's stick fingers touched. Julie was farther away, her scarlet hair framing her shoulders. Peyton had drawn Julie taller than Eric, even though they were about the same height. The absent parent always loomed larger.

Julie turned into Eric's walkway. Outside his door was the patio set he'd brought from their former house. His living room light was on, the upstairs windows dark. After 8:00

p.m., Peyton was probably in bed. A real mother would have anticipated this and made the trip during dinnertime. Julie had thought of coming over while clearing her dining table.

"Julie?" Eric stood in the door frame.

Had she rung the bell?

"I leave tomorrow morning for LA," she said. "I don't suppose Peyton is still up?"

Eric wore jeans and his T-shirt with the image of Shakespeare's face and the words "Will power" on it. "Do you want to come in?"

"For a minute."

She smelled curry. She left the door partially open behind her. The temperature had warmed during the day to barely below freezing. She'd packed light clothes for California due to a forecast warm front.

"I left Peyton upstairs with her books," Eric said. "She leafs through them until she falls asleep. She's picking out more and more words."

"I noticed."

"If she were awake, she'd hear us and come tearing downstairs."

"Ears like a moth."

"She gets that from you," Eric said. "I hate to disturb her. She'll take hours to settle down and be a bear to drag out of bed in the morning."

Julie nodded. She'd wasted an hour getting here, on nothing more than a whim to give Peyton a hug and kiss before taking off, in case her plane crashed, or she got struck by another disaster. Julie had flown dozens of times. *And now this anxiety?*

She glanced at the light coming from the living room. No sound of a TV. "Were you reading?"

"A book Delilah gave me for Christmas," he said. "Do you want to look in on Peyton?"

Julie's eyes watered. She shook her head.

In her teens, once, when she and her father were eating lunch without Rosemary, she'd asked him if her mother had said goodbye and hugged her when she left.

"She told me she did," her father had said. "I came home from work to find her dressed in a skirt. Her suitcase and backpack were by the door. She'd taken you to my parents' house."

"So I'd miss the blowout with you?"

"Thoughtful of her." His mouth narrowed to a slit. He carried his plate to the dishwasher.

Julie wouldn't let him avoid further talk. "Did she know it would be a permanent break? That she'd never return, even for a visit?"

"I doubt she'd thought that far ahead," he'd said.

Eric coughed. He dug his hands in his pockets, pulled them out again. "I've been thinking," he said. "This trip to California could be good, if it helps you resolve things."

Support.

Julie's eyes stung. She wouldn't cry in front of Eric; her sobs would wake Peyton. Julie had already ruined her daughter too much.

"I won't keep you any longer," she said. "Tell Peyton I love her." Julie bolted out, into the dark.

Chapter Nine

The condominium apartment in Santa Monica was even smaller than Delilah had expected. The oversized furnishings didn't help. Lidia, the owner renting her place to them, was waiting when they arrived. Dressed in a low-cut red tank top, zebra-print belt and tight capris, she led them to the narrow kitchen with zero counter space.

"We won't be cooking much." Delilah tried to sound upbeat.

Julie showed no response to the kitschy décor, which included leopard-skin-print throws and a shower curtain with stiletto-heel designs. In the bedroom, they squeezed single file between the queen-size bed and built-in closets.

Lidia opened a drawer. "I've cleared this out for you."

"One drawer for us both?" Julie said.

Until now, the trip had been going well, aside from their arriving at the apartment late on account of a botched exit from the freeway. Delilah hadn't been able to cross three lanes in time. The next exit had sent them winding through Santa Monica.

Julie rolled down the car window. "It's like summer. With palm trees."

"No snow and ice on the roads," Delilah had added.

A dozen pillows on Lidia's bed continued the apartment's faux animal-skin motif. Erotica was the second décor theme. The print above the bed was of a man and woman having standing-up sex.

Candles and a Virgin Mary figurine created a shrine on the bedroom dresser. Lidia looked no older than thirty-five, but she referred to a grown-up son. She said she wasn't ready to commit to her boyfriend full-time. Living with him for short periods worked for them and made her a little extra money.

"I wasn't thinking there'd be two of you." Lidia removed a small suitcase from a closet next to a print of nude females reclining on lounge chairs. From a second drawer, she pulled out scarves with animal designs.

"I sent an email saying I was bringing my sister," Delilah told her. "You said there'd be no extra charge."

Lidia grabbed hangers of animal-print skirts and leggings to clear room in a closet. "I'll show you how the sofa pulls out, unless you want to share the bed."

"We don't," Julie and Delilah said together.

In the living room, maps, brochures, and local guidebooks were piled between votive candles on the coffee table.

Lidia rifled through the brochures for a notepad and pen. "You'll want directions to the closest grocery stores." She wrote in a flourished script. "This deli's awe-delicious. And there's a French bakery to die for. The farmer's market's tomorrow. All organic. For a splurge, I love this cocktail lounge with a view of the ocean. Fabulous at sunset.

"We aren't on holiday," Julie said.

Delilah's gaze kept slipping to the painting above the sofa. A male and female, both naked, in a standing position, the man's buttocks to the viewer, his arm under the woman's breasts, either penetrating her or close to it. She asked Lidia for the internet password.

Lidia flipped over the notepad. Julie wandered away to the kitchen table, which was crammed into a nook. On the plane, they'd agreed the first step in their investigation would be to contact the PI and arrange a face-to-face on the off chance this would provide a new lead. Meanwhile, they'd visit the stoner, aka Terry Edwards, who knew Julie's mother. If both men turned out a bust, they'd rely on the internet.

Delilah handed Lidia cash for the balance of payment. Lidia wished them a fun week, hugged them both, wafting floral perfume, and then wove around their suitcases and out the door.

Julie returned to the coffee table. “It’s not so bad.”

“Aside from being crappy and cluttered.”

“I vote to stash away these forty candles,” Julie said, glancing down.

“Assuming there’s space in a cupboard or drawer.”

“I like her art.” Julie looked at the nudes above the sofa.

“You do?”

“Well, it’s interesting.”

Delilah bent over and tapped a sofa cushion. “The mattress is probably lumpy or thin.”

“Likely both.”

“I’ll sleep here. This place is my fault.”

“Tell me, again, why you chose it?”

“Anything decent in Santa Monica costs the moon.”

“I’ll take the sofa.” Julie went to get her suitcase. “You’re on holiday.”

Delilah tensed. “I’m here to help you, and really, Julie, I can sleep on a rock.”

Julie paused at the wall unit. “I didn’t notice these figures behind the glass. Women in bondage. Bookends of nudes. A nun in a strapless habit doing a cancan.”

“Combining two motifs, religion and sex.” Delilah came up to Julie’s side.

“I noticed her sex manuals on the bedroom shelves above the TV,” Julie said. “Do you think she has a hidden camera in there to film guests?”

Delilah smiled. “Another reason for you to take the bed. I insist.”

While Julie carried her suitcase to the bedroom, Delilah took out a few clothes to hang up and put in drawers. She stashed the suitcase under a side table displaying photos of Lidia and a young man who faintly resembled her. Voices speaking a foreign language mumbled through the kitchen wall. Delilah set up her laptop on the table. After several attempts, she connected to the internet. She opened her email and clicked on a message from her mother. ‘Did you and Julie make it to Los Angeles in one piece?’

Delilah typed a cheery reply. No email from Eric. On the plane, she told Julie she’d attended Eric’s poetry reading.

"He was good, the other guy boring." Only half a lie. Eric's poems were always special, even if his presentation sucked. "I drove him home afterwards."

"You did?"

Julie's cocked eyebrow prompted Delilah to say that she had dropped him off at the condo complex gate. The truth was she'd spent the night in Peyton's bed, but nothing happened except that Delilah hadn't slept as a result of thinking about Eric being across the hall.

A floorboard creaked, signalling Julie's return to the living room. On the laptop, Delilah opened her spreadsheet with the stoner's address and logged on to Google Maps. Julie peered over her shoulder at the Santa Monica street grid.

"Hard to tell which house is his." Delilah panned through images of modern homes and palm trees reaching to clear blue sky. A ranch house. A park. Spanish-style cottage.

"How far is it from here?"

"I'd guess a fifteen- to twenty-minute walk."

"Let's go see him."

"Now?" Delilah said. "What about dinner?"

"We'll eat after. First, we need to phone the PI."

While Delilah recited the investigator's number from the spreadsheet, Julie dialled. She left a message along with her and Delilah's cell-phone numbers. Above them, on the building's second floor, something thumped.

"Julie, I'm starved," Delilah said. "I can't approach this guy on an empty stomach."

"Okay, we'll stop somewhere quick." Julie put on her runners.

A half hour later, fortified by a free-range-chicken sandwich, Delilah trotted along the sidewalk to keep up with Julie's strides. How delightfully odd to feel warm wearing short sleeves when it was wintertime, dark at 6:00 p.m. She could get used to January in California.

"Maybe we should have called ahead," Delilah said.

"'People spill more guts if you take them unawares,' to quote our PI. Why give Terry a chance to plan his resistance?"

Five blocks from Lidia's apartment, they found Terry Edwards' street. They squinted at the numbers on the houses.

"Number 675," Julie said. "Something unreadable. 655." Her eyesight was sharper than Delilah's, at least at night. They passed the park. "635." Julie halted. "What happened to 45?"

"The park."

"Did you see a house in all those trees and shrubs?" Julie retraced her steps. "There's an opening between two giant ferns. How did we miss it?" She raced up the path.

Delilah caught up with her on the unlit porch. Two windows with drawn blinds flanked the front door. Tacked to a wooden mailbox was the number six. The next two digits were missing.

Julie rang the doorbell and pressed her ear to the door. "I heard a buzzing." She waited about twenty seconds, bounded down the stairs and disappeared into the trees. Delilah followed her rustlings through the branches to the side of the house.

"There's obviously no one home," Delilah said between breaths.

"Then he won't see us snooping around."

Delilah rounded a tree and rammed into Julie.

"Ow," Julie said. "You pushed me into his fence."

"Are you hurt?"

Julie reached over the gate. "Locked." She grabbed the fence posts, climbed to the top of the wooden boards and vanished down the other side, into Terry Edwards' backyard.

"I'm not doing that," Delilah said. "Even if I could."

"It's kind of a jungle back here," Julie said from behind the fence.

"There's a surprise." Delilah brushed leaves from her hair, reminded of summer camp. Their parents had moved in together that summer. They'd thought the girls would bond at camp. While Julie mastered swimming, kayaking, and the climbs and leaps of the obstacle course, Delilah floundered. They returned no closer than before. In the fall, their parents tried Girl Guides. It split them further. Delilah gravitated to the girly-girls, and Julie to the ones with the knack for survival skills. She won the prize for tying the strongest and most varied knots.

Something rubbed Delilah's ankles. She shrieked.

"What's wrong?" Julie's voice came from a distance.

"Mouse? Snake? Lizard? Are there poisonous ones here?"

"I haven't heard of poisonous lizards," Julie said. "His backyard is mostly wildflowers and trees. There's a gas lamp by a patio set."

Something tickled Delilah's leg. A snake. She seized the fence post, hopped up and perched on the lower crossbeam, high enough to see Julie's ponytail flap down a path lined with torch lights. Julie's silhouette reached a wrought-iron table and chairs illuminated by the gas lamp. Her silhouette slunk toward the house.

"Shit." Delilah couldn't crawl over. Stepping back down would be worse. She pictured the viper's tongue seeking her foot, its body coiling around her toes. Why had she worn sandals?

Julie reappeared on the path. "His back windows are dark. No curtains. There are boxes stacked in the kitchen, as if he's moving in or out. What if he's gone and left the boxes for the moving van?"

Delilah stepped down gingerly. Julie mounted and hurdled the fence. She darted into the trees.

"Where are you going now?"

"The neighbours'." Julie's voice flowed through the dark. "Those boxes might belong to the new people moving in."

"He'd have left them a forwarding address."

"Maybe he moved to escape us."

That sounded paranoid. Delilah stretched her arms out to fight the branches. Trust the stoner not to plant palm trees like a normal Californian. A chain-link fence separated his yard from the neighbours' pristine lawn. Julie was already over the fence and running to the porch. Was she hyper from nervousness about the search? Restlessness could be a side effect of her medication. Julie jogged down the porch stairs and met Delilah on the sidewalk.

"No one home here either," Julie said. "Let's try the house on his other side."

Delilah hoped Julie wouldn't want to canvass the whole street. Luckily, a man at number 635 answered his door.

Julie pointed to the stoner's yard. "We're looking for Terry Edwards, an old friend of my mother's. My sister and I flew in today from Canada."

"Usually he's home from work by now," the man said. "Might have gone to Malibu."

"What for?"

"Girlfriend." The man scratched his belly. "They visit back and forth. Where in Canada are you from?"

"What time does he leave for work in the morning?" Julie said.

"Early. Drives a recycling truck."

"How early is early?"

The man looked at Delilah. "Cold up there in Canada?"

"Yes, compared to LA," Delilah said. "What time does Terry get home from work?"

"Around three."

They thanked him and returned to the sidewalk, where the night seemed brighter. Delilah leaned her head back and noticed the stars emerging. The moon was over three quarters full. She rubbed her arms, chilled from the night air.

Julie toyed with the elastic around her ponytail. "I was afraid the guy would get suspicious if I pestered him about how early Terry got up."

"I'm sure it's before I'd like to go over."

"Yeah, and people are rushed in the morning. He'll have more time to talk after work." Julie took out her cell phone. "No missed call from the PI. If we don't hear from him, we can drive over in the morning to take him by surprise." Julie moved down the street, in the direction of their apartment.

Delilah quickened her steps to match Julie's.

"Terry wouldn't hold down a responsible truck driving job if he's stoned all the time," Julie said. "He might really be willing to cooperate with Marion's relative."

"Is this our street?"

"Let's go to the pier."

"Aren't you tired? You're supposed to be a morning person."

"I feel a little keyed up."

"Okay, if we stop by the apartment for our sweaters?"

"You're cold?" Julie said. "I'm steaming hot."

The waterfront might cool Julie down. Her nervousness or the medication side effect wasn't serious enough for Delilah to alert her mother—or Eric. But later tonight, after Julie went to bed, she'd send Eric an email report. A casual, sisterly message to let him know that she and Julie had landed safely in California.

* * *

Aurora forced her body down the hospital corridor. The intravenous unit was like an uprooted tree she couldn't wait to disentangle from her body. The doctors had said this might be as soon as tomorrow. She made it to the nurse station and stopped for air. Could she drag her body through one more run before bed?

"Mrs. Jones? You're still up?" the nurse at the station said.

"I want to be—" Aurora gulped for breath. "In shape when I go home."

That would be in two days, if all went well. Last night she had developed a fever for undetermined reasons. Antibiotics had brought her temperature down to almost normal.

"You've made incredible progress," the nurse said. "I wouldn't recognize you from post-op."

Aurora didn't remember seeing this nurse before. Pushing forty and overweight, she wore glasses with rhinestone frames that called attention to themselves, a fashion trend Aurora disliked. Bold frames rarely made women more attractive and had become too commonplace to be cool.

'Elaine' appeared across the name tag on her lumpy chest. Nasal voice. Adenoidal Elaine. No ring to that mnemonic.

"I know I've seen you before," Elaine said. "Were you at your nephew's retreat?"

"My nephew?"

"Sebastiano. It hit me last night it was him, who visited."

Aurora's collarbone area thumped, even though the lump was gone.

Elaine's jaw dropped. "You're Aurora. Oh my God. Aurora." She looked around, as though wanting to share her discovery. "Aurora. I recognize you now. Mrs. Jones. Is that your surname?"

Aurora tightened her lips and gave a faint nod.

"Talking to Sebastiano yesterday made me want to go back to New Dawn," Elaine said. "I didn't realize you and he were related."

Aurora gripped the intravenous pole and took a step away.

"New Dawn beats the pants off the other self-help seminars I've attended. It's a total experience."

Aurora cringed at the term 'self-help' and tried to shove the pole forward.

"You should market it more. When I tell people I've been to New Dawn, they've never heard of it."

Aurora took a breath. "We're at full capacity year-round." Aside from a few slow weeks in winter, which were useful for Aurora's breaks. She might need more of them as she got older.

"My husband says you should ramp up your website."

Aurora's hand slipped from the pole. All these people with ideas for her vision.

"The best sites do more than impart information. Interactive features would keep people returning to the site and hook them like you won't believe. They'll want to make a pilgrimage to the retreat, like Mecca. There are tons of creative possibilities."

"Like what?"

"I don't know. I'm not the expert. Excuse me a minute." Elaine sidestepped to a doctor who looked about thirteen. They consulted a chart.

A revamped site that drew people to New Dawn, the spider in the centre of a virtual web that reinforced the message and maintained a connection for retreat alumni. Sebastiano and the others had a point. The Net was the new community, and an international one. Her web would spread beyond California. For ten years, she and Sebastiano had buried themselves at the retreat and let the world come to them. That had been right for building a solid core. Now the message was ready to spin out to the world. Her body must not let her down at this pivotal moment. It must fight the evil. She would know in two days if her surgeon had excised it all.

Elaine returned. "Sorry about that."

"Where would I find out about developing our website?"

"On the internet, of course."

They had Wi-Fi at the beach house. Renters demanded it these days. Research would be a project during her recuperation.

Aurora shuffled back down the hall. A risk of expansion was exposure. Dare they chance that now? Surely, their connection to an old man's death was long buried. Two old men, one already dying.

As Elaine had said, New Dawn was unique, a 'total experience' with more potential than those programs that failed to lift people out of their everyday lives. Just as Aurora had to strengthen herself, she had to strengthen the retreat as the core of a virtual web.

Perhaps, after she was gone, daughter retreats would spring up across the hill and then around the state, country, and world. Sebastiano's vision of satellites wasn't so much wrong as premature. His recent push for expansion showed his willingness to take the risk, and he had more to lose than she did, with his father's murder under his belt. Together they had hastened the death of another man who'd loved her. Impossible to prove and that man might now be looking down from the skies thanking her for diverting his money from greedy relatives. True, it would be unfortunate if the retreat's increased exposure inadvertently led the police to

Sebastiano's role in his father's unresolved murder. She'd hate to see him in jail, and he would rather die than be locked up. Without him, the retreat would limp along. But only for a while. She was New Dawn's spirit; he provided an earthly balance, but he could be replaced.

Aurora's left foot skidded. She clutched the pole tighter and steadied herself. Before crawling into bed tonight, she would propel her body through two more circuits, even if it killed her.

Chapter Ten

"Do you like Chinese?" Nadine held up a takeout bag.

Eric still felt stuffed from his spaghetti dinner.

"I worked late tonight," she said. "I figured, who likes eating alone? I bet Eric doesn't either."

Cool air flowed into the house. Canned laughter rippled from the living room. Nadine's company would beat the dumb sitcom. Fortunately, he'd gotten Peyton to bed.

"Where's…?" Eric blanked on Nadine's son's name. Work and concern about Julie had made his mind too wobbly to concentrate on anything this evening.

Nadine shoved the bag into his hands and slipped off her boots and jacket. Her top was the loose kind that would make her look pregnant if she had any abdominal fat. Its V-front was alarmingly low. A pendant rested in her cleavage.

"My sister's staying at my place tonight," Nadine said. "She's with Cody."

Eric navigated his living room full of LEGO. After turning off the TV, he squatted to gather the little bricks.

"Don't clean up for me," Nadine said. "Who can keep a house neat with kids?" She set the bag on the floor and knelt to help, giving him a close-up of her breasts and a view all the way down to—

He scooped bricks into the bin.

"The living room is about relationships, marriage, love," she said.

"Huh?"

"Feng shui. Declutter a room in your house and you clean up the corresponding area of your life."

"It's that easy?" He moved into the hall.

She joined him. "This space is about health. You keep it reasonably neat."

"I'm pretty healthy."

"See what I mean? Let's check out your kitchen."

The dirty spaghetti pot sat on the island. He took it to the sink to soak.

Nadine studied the cherrywood cupboards and stainless steel. "This represents your career, your life path, the journey. Do you feel in a rut, like everything's an uphill struggle and you don't even know what you want to do?"

"How did you guess?"

"I can hardly see your counter for the coffee maker, rice cooker, vegetable steamer, chopper and mixer."

Julie used to tease him about his weakness for gadgets he bought with the idea they'd get into serious cooking together. The idea had never materialized.

"When was the last time you used that food processor?" Nadine asked.

Not once since he and Julie split.

"See?"

He didn't, really. More likely Nadine had sensed his frustration during their conversations on the way to work. He removed the containers of Chinese food from the bag. The Styrofoam felt warm, but the contents might need heating up. The garlicky and sweet aromas tempted him. He'd nibble. He got plates from the cupboard.

"White wine goes well with Chinese," Nadine said.

A white was chilling in the fridge.

She opened the cutlery drawer. "Do you have chopsticks?"

"I can never manoeuvre them right."

Julie had also teased him about his klutziness with the sticks. "Shouldn't a dentist be good with his hands?"

"All I do is manipulate a man-size drill," he'd bantered back to her.

"Where's Peyton?" Nadine asked.

"Upstairs, asleep." He hoped the noise from the kitchen wouldn't wake her.

Nadine spooned rice and chow mein onto the plates while he popped the wine cork. Did he like this woman he barely knew taking charge of his place, his home, his feng shui?

"That's enough for me," Eric said. "Save the leftovers for you and Cody."

"He won't eat anything more exotic than peanut butter," Nadine said. "I mainly came over to say how much I enjoyed your book."

"You read it?"

"I admit, I didn't understand most of it, but I sensed your passion for Julie at the start and the downward spiral. That happens in every relationship."

"Does it?" Couldn't passion evolve into something equally compelling and meaningful? He'd assumed this had happened with his parents and the other long-time couples he knew.

She clinked her wine glass to his. "Cheers."

Nadine hoisted herself onto the barstool, reminding Eric of Saturday night with Delilah. Two women here in less than a week. But Nadine wouldn't sleep over tonight. No matter how drunk she got, she could wobble through the courtyard.

"I finished your book last night," Nadine said. "I noticed the poems stopped before your marriage breakup."

He chewed the ginger beef she'd added to his plate, wondering why she brought this up.

"Usually the downward spiral is caused by the guy cheating, in my experience. But you don't talk about hitting on other women in the poems, unless I missed something symbolic."

So, she was fishing. "I didn't cheat," he said. "Julie thought I did."

"Why?"

"A few women showed interest in me, or at least in my poems."

Nadine sipped some wine. "Julie sounds kind of paranoid in the last poem."

"Really?" He wasn't aware of her paranoia until later.

"I could see the signs."

Eric ran his fork through the chow mein. He'd have to reread that closing poem, which was about Julie's struggle with fatigue and a colicky child who wouldn't stop crying.

"Postpartum's a bummer," Nadine said. "I had it, some, after Cody."

"How did you snap out of it?"

"I had to, with no real guy on the scene."

Eric's solution had been to take over the parenting tasks, which hadn't helped Julie in the long run. She'd escaped into her work, sent her problems underground, and grew away from him and Peyton. That's how the book and their marriage ended. He reached for his wine glass.

"Do you still love her?" Nadine touched his hand.

His skin tingled. "That's over." Since he wasn't pulling his hand away, he should be open with her. If that blew it, they probably weren't meant to work. "Part of it was my fault for being too dumb to notice Julie was faking it. On the job she was great and at home we were managing. Even after the split, I thought we might get back together, until a few months ago."

"What happened?"

He studied her chin mole. *She tried to drown our child.* "Let's just say something finished us forever." He'd like to continue this confiding, but he was sure she'd blab it around the townhouse complex and within days everyone would be staring. A kid might overhear his parents talking and say something to Peyton.

A speck of pineapple-chicken sauce clung to the hairs above Nadine's lip. The orange was strangely appealing against her olive skin. Her shirt had slid to the side, revealing a tattoo above her right breast. A flower or bird. Maybe she had other, hidden, tattoos.

"You know," she said. "It's unusual for a guy to have custody of the kid."

He stared into her eyes, his answer prepared for this fishing. "Why does it always have to be the woman? This arrangement works best for Julie, me, and Peyton."

Nadine nodded. "Okay." She held out a Styrofoam container. "More?"

He patted his stomach. “I’m done.” Coloured sauces formed swirls on his plate.

They cleared the counter and loaded the dishwasher. Nadine leaned closer. He breathed in her flowery perfume. His gaze travelled down her neck to her cleavage. He shouldn’t be thinking of this. But why not? He had told Nadine one truth. Julie’s action had irreparably severed their ties, except their shared one to Peyton.

“A bird,” he said.

“What?”

“Flying over your breast.” His feet felt stuck to the floor.

“Exactly.”

* * *

In the darkness, Eric nudged Nadine. He caught a whiff of garlic, flowers, and sweat. She rolled over, away from him. Her snoring eased. He pushed her bare shoulder.

“Wha…? Wha…?” she said. “What the fuck are you doing?”

“You have to go.”

“Where?”

“It’s after midnight.”

She curled away from him and drew the covers half over her head.

“Nadine, you promised.”

“For fuck’s sake.”

He didn’t recall her swearing this much before they wound up in bed. Her words had startled him during the act. Fuck me. Fuck me. He’d pressed his hand over her mouth to muffle her screams, and sensed Nadine liked him dominating her. Odd, given her pushy behaviour in the kitchen. Evidently, Peyton had slept through it all like a LEGO brick.

Nadine wriggled her bum against his hip. His erection rose. What a shock it had been, to find his body going all out during sex. Blame his year of celibacy? Nadine’s face had lit up when he confessed she was the first since his separation. He hoped she hadn’t read too much into that.

Thank God he'd remembered the condoms. And that he'd had the foresight—or rather, hope—to buy a box for his bedside table drawer. Nadine told him it didn't matter; she was on the pill to make her periods easier and also hadn't been with anyone in a year. Was that true? While he came, her slim body morphed into Julie's. Maybe that was normal when you'd been with one person a long time.

He shook Nadine's shoulder. "Please."

"Oh fuck. All right." She bolted out of bed, hauling the duvet with her. "Where are my fucking clothes?"

"Can you keep your voice down? Peyton…"

Nadine turned on the lamp on the bedside table. Light blinded him. He opened his eyes a crack to find her stomping over the duvet toward the door.

He leapt to the floor. "Where are you going?"

"Can't I have a pee?"

"Use the en suite, for God's sake." Not the bathroom beside Peyton's bedroom.

"I forgot. Your place is a different layout from mine upstairs."

Nadine slunk into the connecting room, her ass flat below her knobbly spine. He put on his sleep pants and T-shirt. The toilet flushed.

She reappeared and bent to pick up her panties and bra. "Peyton needs to learn the facts of life."

So much for his resolve that, when ready to date, he wouldn't let a woman into his bed when Peyton was in the house until it was serious.

Nadine shimmied her jeans over the butterfly tattoo on her thigh. The tattoo he'd kissed a few hours before. Her top covered the orchid on her ribs, beneath her left breast. He wondered if her tattoos had meanings for her, but asking now would resurrect the personal.

Moving into the hallway, he saw Peyton's bedroom door closed and no sounds came from behind it. Nadine flicked on the hall light and padded down the stairs. At the entrance, she put on her sneakers and slouched into her jacket. He recalled what she'd said about the hall representing health, and he had to admit he felt healthier after their night together. The physical release aside, it was a healthy step away from Julie.

Nadine patted down her hair, which stayed wild, sticking up all over. He loved that. Scratch the word love. He wanted to thank her, but that would make it sound as if she'd done him a favour. This was supposed to be mutual, which the sex had been, judging from her responses. She couldn't have faked all that grunting. Could she?

"Are you busy this weekend?" Nadine asked, half her lipstick smeared onto her chin.

He scratched his rough jaw. Would a second…encounter move this too quickly for him? He'd think it through when his mind was less tired.

"The usual. Julie's out of town, so I'll have Peyton."

"Odds are Cody's father will poop out again," Nadine said. "I could bring Cody over. The four of us can watch a family flick."

"Let's touch base later in a couple of days."

"Better yet, we could slip in a kiddie movie. Leave Peyton and Cody in the basement and fuck like bananas upstairs."

He glanced up the stairs. Not a rustle from Peyton's room. Did bananas fuck? It would be horribly risky, on so many levels. "How about I'll call you Thursday."

"Promise?"

"Why wouldn't I?"

"You're a guy." She leaned over and touched his arm, sending shivers to his chest. "We've got hours until morning. Sure you don't want to go back to your bedroom? Or to the basement?"

"Nadine." He pulled away.

"I know, naughty, naughty Nadine," she said. "All right, I'm gone."

She opened the door. He bent forward to do the decent thing and kiss her goodbye. She sauntered away from him and the porch light, to his relief. Or disappointment. Dating had been easier when he was young. Sure, he'd gone through a few breakups, but he'd had less baggage.

"Daddy," Peyton called from upstairs.

Shit. At the top of the staircase, she clutched her blankie like Linus in the old Peanuts comic.

"Who was here?"

He gazed upward. "Nobody."

"Mommy?"

"I thought I heard something and came down to check," he said. "It was just the wind."

"I want Mommy."

Even from this distance, he could see Peyton's face pucker. Tears would be streaming soon.

"I miss her too, sweet." No lie.

"I want Mommy back." Peyton's voice wavered. She plodded down the stairs, right foot first, left catching up to it. Right, left.

"Mommy needs to be on her own." The rote words wouldn't sway her. They were empty for him. Julie had left them. That was the fact. It wasn't his doing, mostly, and it wasn't Peyton's at all.

Peyton stopped halfway down the stairs, her blankie trailing behind. "You can get Mommy back."

"I can't, sweet. She has to live her own life."

Peyton blinked away tears. "Please, Daddy."

He dashed up to her. Peyton sniffed. Her small, damp face reminded him of the day they brought her home from the hospital. He had looked at the helpless baby, dependent on them, and vowed he would always do his best for her, whatever the sacrifice.

"I'll try," he said.

Her lower lip trembled. Hope lit up her hazel eyes.

"I didn't say I'd succeed."

She stared, the brightness fading.

"Sweet, I can't promise something I can't control."

Her chin, so much like Julie's, quivered.

"Okay. Promise."

She beamed.

Stupid. Never promise a kid what you can't deliver. But if he took it back now, Peyton's face would sink to the bottom stair.

He grabbed her tiny hand. Maybe she'd forget his dumb vow in the morning. "Let's get you and Blankie to bed, after a stop at the bathroom."

He tucked them in with Teddy Bear, her little pony, and her doll-of-the-moment. On the way to his bedroom, he noticed the den light was on. He'd overlooked it on his heated way up with Nadine.

At his computer, he discovered he'd left his email open. Three new messages, two from the dental association mailing list. The third was from Delilah and read, 'Arrived safe and sound to summer. Julie and I walked around Santa Monica earlier tonight and saw the pier. The Ferris wheel is amazing. Julie called it a kaleidoscope. She insisted we ride the roller coaster. Did you hear us shrieking all the way up in Calgary?'

He smiled. Julie was a big kid about midway rides. She loved the excitement and fear. Kaleidoscope. On their holiday in Utah, he and Julie had bought matching baseball caps in colours they called kaleidoscope. Did Julie still have hers? Most likely his was in a box stashed in the basement.

He typed a reply to Delilah, 'Glad to hear you made it. Calgary white and brown, no kaleidoscope or shrieks.' He reread his note, decided it wasn't too flirty, and added, 'Keep me posted.'

Chapter Eleven

Julie jogged down the slope to the Santa Monica Pier and spotted the sign she and Delilah had seen the night before, 'Bike and Skate Rentals.' Was it the beach bike-rental place where her mother had worked in the 1980s? A shutter covered the building's rental counter. The shop opened at 10:00 a.m., over three hours from now. With its peeling paint and rotten wood siding, the building could easily be thirty or forty years old. Something to look into before or after visiting the private investigator.

She continued east, into the rising sun, before circling back to the apartment.

* * *

As Julie and Delilah finished breakfast, the PI phoned. He said in a hushed tone, "I'm on a stakeout in San Francisco."

"When will you get back to LA?" Julie asked.

"Depends."

"Will you call—?"

"Can't talk now." He hung up.

"My dad's right," Julie told Delilah. "The guy's a drama queen."

"We can't go up to San Francisco."

"If we have to, we have to," Julie said. "Meanwhile, let's tackle the bike-rental shop."

They arrived a few minutes after opening time. A man with sun-bleached hair and bronzed skin was setting up bicycles for the day. His older colleague, in the booth, dealt with a grey-haired couple, who left the counter to select their bikes with the help of the surfer-looking dude. The older clerk with the bald head could be almost sixty, Julie's mother's age.

Julie hesitated, feeling foolish to hope he could provide any news; yet how wonderful, how easy would it be if he did.

He looked up, his eyes bleary red, and asked what type of bike she wanted.

From her waist pouch, Julie pulled out the three pictures of her mother she'd brought. "I'm looking for this woman, who once worked in a bike shop in Santa Monica."

"This shop here?"

"I'm not sure. It was in the late 1980s. Was this place operating then?"

The man's grin revealed a gold front tooth. "Beats me. I only bought the joint two years back." He picked up the pictures.

"Could you put me in touch with the previous owner?"

"Not likely. He's dead."

The man's pate glowed in the sun. He studied the top photo showing Marion from the thighs up; the most characteristic image of her face, according to Julie's father. Age about twenty, Marion wore slacks and a tailored shirt. Her light brown hair, parted in the middle, stopped halfway down her ribs, like Julie's hair now.

"Her name is Marion," Julie said. "Marion Fox. She might have gone by Dejong, her maiden name."

In the photo, Marion was looking down, laughing. At what? Julie's father didn't remember. He'd snapped the shot on their honeymoon, or what had passed for one. He'd had two years to go on his engineering degree, so all they could afford was a weekend in a cabin near Fernie, BC, nine months before Julie's birth.

The man scanned the other two photos and handed them all back. "Sorry."

Julie slumped in disappointment. "Are there other bike shops along the boardwalk?"

"A couple. Excuse me, I have a customer." He nodded at Delilah, who stood beside the back racks.

If they rented bikes, they could check all the shops. It would also pass the time until they waylaid Terry, at 3:00 p.m.

"Eighteen-speed or touring?" the shop owner called to Delilah.

"How many speeds do we need on the boardwalk?" Julie asked him.

"One," he said. "They don't call it sea level for nothing."

At the first bike shop north on the trail, the tanned clerk took the most interest in the second picture. "Is she an actress or model?"

The full-body shot showed Marion standing in front of a Chevy with a long hood. Julie's father had bought the used car a month after he started working. Marion wore a sleeveless sundress. This was the summer Julie had turned two years old. Like Julie, Marion had quickly regained her pre-pregnancy figure. She'd cut her thick hair to shoulder length and touched it up with blonde highlights.

The clerk slid the photos back to Julie. "I'd remember that chick if I'd seen her."

Julie raced her bike ahead of Delilah's to the boardwalk's north end, in Pacific Palisades. They bought Cokes at the takeout stand. Seated at a picnic table, they savoured the cold drinks and warm sun.

"A few years of this and we'll go as pruney as those bike-shop guys," Julie said. Was her mother pruney?

"Wrinkles would be a fair exchange for this idyllic climate," Delilah said.

They rode south past the original bike shop, now bustling with more business. Past Venice, they stopped at a third shop. The couple behind the counter said they'd bought the store seven or eight years ago as a retirement project.

The woman took the pictures. She paused at the one of Marion holding Julie as a baby.

Julie caught her breath. "Do you recognize her?

"She reminds me of the Madonna. Don't you think so, Al?"

"I've never met the holy mother," he said.

Julie doubted anyone could identify Marion from this picture, which was obscured by shadows, but she'd chosen it for the look on the young mother's face. Contentment. Joy. Connection with her child.

Around now, Peyton would be having lunch with the other kids at her babysitter's house. Julie realized this was her first real thought about Peyton since leaving yesterday. Had Marion found it that easy to forget Julie?

"I'm starving," Delilah said. "Let's stop to eat and get a drink."

Julie was grateful her medication had produced no excess thirst or other side effects, so far. These new meds seemed to be doing the trick, judging by her current mood—balanced.

She slowed her pedalling to ride beside Delilah. "It's a weird coincidence we both have psychiatric problems when we aren't related."

"Not really. Our parents met in group support, after all."

"They did?"

"Watch out."

Julie sped up to let a rollerblader pass. She dropped back again.

"Brad didn't tell you?" Delilah asked. "How did you think they met?"

"I don't know. He implied it was through friends, I think." Grandma Fox had told her that after her mother left, her father could barely function. "That's why you and your father moved in with us," her grandma had said. For her stoic father to seek help, he must have been in terrible shape. "Was it support for depression?"

"I guess. Or loss like divorce," Delilah said. "A friend recommended the group to Brad. So, they met through a friend, indirectly."

"And we inherited our mental problems from our parents." Had Julie's come from her father or mother? If both, she didn't stand a chance.

Riding their bikes, questioning clerks in bike shops, and checking out Santa Monica's restaurants and stores consumed their time until 3:00 p.m. The trees and bushes concealed Terry Edwards' home as much in daylight as they had last night. Close up, the house looked even more decrepit. The paint on the siding and porch had faded to mottled brown. Crooked Venetian blinds blocked the windows.

Julie pressed the doorbell and heard it ring inside. "If he's not home again, we're flying up to San Francisco to get that PI to—"

The door shot open. A scrawny, stooped man stared up at her. "I don't support Jehovah's Witnesses or Mormons or whatever the crap you're selling."

"Terry?" Julie said.

A scar zigzagged from the man's forehead to his chin. Thin white hair scraggled to his shoulders. "What if I am?"

"I'm…I'm Julie Fox. You and my mother, Marion Fox—or Dejong, if she went by that—worked in a bike shop, in the 1980s."

He started to close the door. Julie leaned in to block him.

"You did turn up." Terry chortled. "No fuck." He scanned her from head to sandals. "Marion's daughter. You're just as tall and skinny."

Julie's heart quickened. "You knew her."

He looked at Delilah. "She had two girls? No fuck."

"You'll talk to us?" Julie could smell onions on Terry. No marijuana.

He yanked back the door. Delilah squeezed Julie's arm in warning. She understood Delilah's nervousness. Going in was a dubious move, but they were two against one.

"Do you mind sitting out back?" Terry said. "Indoors is a mess. I'm getting ready to paint."

Meeting him outdoors felt safer. As Terry led them down the hall, Julie glanced into the living room, which was lined floor to ceiling with books. She stepped around rollers and paint trays into a kitchen filled with the boxes she'd seen through the window last night. In black felt marker, the word 'Trash' was scrawled on several boxes. Terry offered them a drink.

"Yes, please," Delilah rasped.

"Beer? Sangria?"

"I love sangria."

Julie asked for water. She had to stay sober for this. Terry grabbed a can of beer from the fridge while he rambled about the paint job being an opportunity to clear his cupboards of forty years of accumulated junk.

"You've lived here that long?" she asked.

"Mine's about the only original house on the street."

He'd lived in this place when he and her mother worked together. "Did Marion ever visit you here?"

"I only knew her from the shop. She worked with us a year, maybe ten months."

His stoop and shoe-leather skin made him look close to eighty, but he might be late sixties—no more than ten years older than her mother.

Julie took a breath. "Do you know if she's alive?"

"Can't say." He ripped off the beer tab.

"How did the private investigator track you down?"

Terry grimaced. "That prick."

"My father didn't like him either."

"Your father has good taste." Terry led them out to the backyard.

Flowers of every colour formed a ring around the patio and burst from sections of the yard not occupied by trees. The limbs of the deciduous ones were bare for the winter.

"I like your garden," Julie said.

"Years ago, I tossed out seeds and let it grow natural. What comes up, comes up."

Delilah chose a patio chair in the shade of the house. Terry dropped to one in full sun. Julie took the rattan chair shadowed by a tree limb.

"I notice you staring at the gash on my face." Terry looked at Julie.

"Really, I'm not." She truly hadn't been.

Behind Terry, birds-of-paradise poked up from a grassy shrub.

"Comes from an old surfing misadventure. I gave up dope after that." He grinned. "Did the asshole say I was high when we talked?"

"Were you?"

"I'm a pretty good actor after all." He chuckled.

"Why would you want him to think you were stoned?"

"Seemed the most efficient way to get rid of him." He crossed one boney leg over the other.

"But what if I hadn't come down here?"

He twirled his foot, flapping his thong sandal. "What if you hadn't?"

"This was a test of some sort?"

"One way of putting it."

Julie gritted her teeth and told herself to be polite. Terry was all she had, her only link to Marion, and she had passed the first hurdle. "You haven't heard a word about her?"

"In twenty years, give or take."

"Nineteen ninety-nine," Julie said. "Was she living in Santa Monica?"

"After she left the shop, I'd run into her from time to time at stores, on the beach."

"What was she doing? Was she working?"

He continued flapping his sandal. "She moved around to different jobs. Once she told me she was at an ice-cream store, once a hotel. Another time, she was a sort of tour guide."

"Sort of? For what company?"

"She didn't say. Or I don't remember. To be honest, I wasn't that interested."

"Did you like her?"

"I didn't know her well. She was distant, or she was with me." He squinted at Delilah. "I take it you're the younger daughter?"

"It's just her." Delilah nodded toward Julie then coughed and held up her empty glass. "Could I have another sangria? This is good."

"Who were Marion's other friends?" Julie asked quickly. She willed Terry to stay in his chair, to not disrupt the flow. "Do you remember any of them?"

Terry furrowed his brow in apparent thought. "You might try Hank."

"Hank who?"

"He hung out at the beach, in those days. You wouldn't guess that now. He's a successful businessman."

"Do you have his phone number or email?" Julie picked up her purse.

"If anyone knows, it's Hank." He glanced from her to Delilah. "Have you read *The Tipping Point*?"

"I've heard of it," Julie said.

"It talks about people who are connectors. Heard of six degrees of separation?"

"You mean about everyone being connected to everyone in the world through six steps of people?" she said. "I don't know that I believe—"

"Hank's a connector. He is now, anyway. 'Spect it was the same back then. It's his gift. Hank'll eliminate three or four of those steps and put you in touch with Marion's inner circle."

Julie's heart skipped, much as this seemed a wild shot. She held up her pen. "Hank's number…"

"I'd have to go through a few people to get it." Terry bolted to his feet. "Your sister's waiting patiently for that sangria. You too?"

Julie shook her head. "I don't suppose you could call your first step right now?"

"He works killer hours. I usually catch him early in the morning."

"Tomorrow?"

Terry hovered over her. "When did you last see Marion?"

"Thirty-four years ago." Julie was sure he could hear her heart.

"What's your rush now?" He loped into the house, favouring one foot.

She hadn't noticed his limp before.

"It's promising," Delilah said to Julie.

The sunshine having shifted to her face, Julie took out her dark glasses. Terry had a point. What was her rush? She would find out whatever there was to know in thirty-four years plus x days, xx days, or xxx days. But with each delay, something could break the connection. Terry could trip on a paint tray and break his neck. Hank could die of a heart attack. And six steps to Marion was a pop theory, not fact. There might be hundreds of steps, some fragile, and ever more variables. Across the patio, Delilah licked the rim of her glass. Her peasant blouse curved prettily around her neck; her floral-print skirt draped over her ankles.

Julie rubbed her palm on her capris. "Can you help convince Terry to make the call tomorrow morning?"

"Me?"

"He likes you."

"I've hardly said anything."

And Julie had pummelled him with questions. An old hippie like him might prefer Delilah's sixties wear and laid-back manner.

"Two against one," Julie said. "We have a chance."

* * *

Sebastiano stepped into his pants. A floorboard creaked.

On the bed, Cassandra rolled his way and bunched the covers over her shoulders. She opened one eye. "What time is it?"

"I have an errand to run." He tucked his shirt in.

"So early?" she asked. "In your town clothes?" Eyes alert, she bolted to her knees. Her matted hair dropped to her naked breasts. "Are you going to see Aurora again?"

He grabbed his shoes from the closet. How had she guessed that he wasn't simply taking a trip to town? She couldn't know about the hospital. He bent over to lace his shoes.

"What's going on in LA?"

Whether she'd somehow deduced his destination or made a wild guess, she would likely see through a total denial. "Every so often I have to catch up on matters like the overall food service. That local town can't provide everything we need."

"Why do you have to lie?" She raised her arms to the ceiling. "It's not like I'm jealous or anything. I know you're not sleeping with her."

Her certainty about this was interesting. Generally, the savvier guests, like Cassandra, speculated about the possibility that he and Aurora were lovers. This further confirmed his view Cassandra was beyond savvy—she was unusually perceptive. A useful trait in a leader, one he admired, but he had to be careful.

He kissed her warm forehead. "I'll be back by noon."

"I was counting on you to help me prepare this morning's session."

"You're well on your way to handling it alone. You've come a long way this week." True. He gazed down at her pale face. "Aurora will be impressed."

"You think so?" Her cheekbones flushed.

"I know it." Impressed to the point of feeling threatened. He nibbled the tip of Cassandra's nose. "It's good experience for you to be in complete charge." Aurora would be royally pissed at him for permitting it.

In Los Angeles, Sebastiano found Aurora in her hospital room, her back to the door. As he entered the room, she whirled.

"You?" she said. "Why are you here?"

"To drive you to the beach house."

"I told you I was taking a cab. You're needed at the retreat."

"It's in good hands."

A scowl distorted Aurora's pallid face. Rare to see her in street clothes. Her peach suit and silver hair up in a French twist gave her an air of elegance.

"Cassandra's become quite competent," he said.

Aurora turned and continued packing her suitcase. "You're out of luck if you came all this way to be present for the biopsy results. They're delayed."

"Why?"

"The usual medical inefficiencies."

Was that true? Aurora folded her dressing gown, her movements so smooth that no one would guess surgeons had cut her open three days ago.

"You look amazingly improved," he said.

"It took all my energies." She placed her slippers on top of the gown.

"When does your doctor say you can return to work?"

"He advises Monday."

In four days. She'd accomplished the first step, recovering from the operation, but chemo or radiation would pound her back to square one and suck up her time.

She slammed the suitcase shut. "I've been thinking. The solution for the retreat isn't your satellites. It's the World Wide Web. We need to expand our presence."

"Haven't I been saying this?" So, Aurora was doing her usual trick of appropriating his suggestion as her own.

"First, we strengthen the core," she said. "New Dawn is poised to break out, but not in the way you think."

A nurse bustled in for a last check of Aurora's vitals. Sebastiano took the opportunity to slip into the hall. Fortunately, the nurse at the desk wasn't the one who'd recognized him last time. He asked this prettier one if he could speak to Aurora's doctor.

"He's in surgery," the nurse said.

Fuck. Well, if Aurora later told him the tumour was benign, he'd phone her surgeon and say he was her nephew concerned that his beloved aunt was in denial. Doctors might not be ethically opposed to sharing results in the case of a patient rejecting necessary treatment.

Down the hall, Aurora doddered toward him, rolling her suitcase behind. This was a long way from her former confident stride, but what a show of independence. Would she follow her doctor's advice and take the weekend to rest? Not to save her life. He knew she'd be at the retreat on Saturday to greet the incoming flock of guests and implement her core-strengthening plan. He'd bet the beach house on it.

* * *

Seated at the apartment table, Delilah checked her email. No new messages. She reread Eric's remark about Calgary's white and brown, and then cringed at the stupid reply she'd fired off the night before, 'Don't knock muted shades. Kaleidoscopes and roller coasters aren't all they're cracked up to be.' She wasn't sure what that even meant. At least she'd had the brains not to mention they'd already met with Terry Edwards. Why get them all fired up about Hank, who might turn out to be a dead end? To her mother, she typed a chatty account of the day. She added that they hoped to meet Terry this afternoon, which wasn't a lie.

Julie burst into the apartment, her face flushed from her jog. She'd tiptoed out later this morning than she had yesterday. Over breakfast, she rehashed her worries about Terry. Yesterday, after he promised to call his friend first thing in the morning, he'd gone off on a rant about cell phones and email and today's pathological need to be constantly connected.

"What if a person doesn't want to be found?" He'd stared at Julie. "Doesn't she have that right to her own being?"

Later, at the pier, Julie had speculated that he knew what happened to her mother and was covering for Marion, or to protect Delilah from pain.

"He's sweet on you and thinks you're her daughter," Julie had said again. "No matter how many times we explain it."

They finished their cereal. While Delilah collected their used dishes, Julie called the PI and left a message, asking when he'd be back in LA.

"What do you want to do 'til one of them calls?" Delilah asked.

"Anything," Julie said. "I'll go nuts in this dump, waiting."

They began with Beverly Hills, since it was close to Santa Monica. Delilah steered the car through winding streets that offered glimpses of mansions behind hedges. They set the GPS for Rodeo Drive and wound up on a thoroughfare.

"I think we missed it," Delilah said.

"I'm not into shopping anyway." Julie took out her cell phone.

Delilah longed to see if Eric had answered her email in between seeing his patients.

Behind them, an ambulance shrilled. Delilah changed lanes to let it pass. The van ahead stopped. She jerked the car to a halt.

"How do you stand driving in this traffic?" Julie asked. "I'd have never got around this city on my own."

Delilah drove east, buoyed by Julie's implied thanks. "Look at that giant billboard of George Clooney's face. Imagine seeing your own head towering over everything like that."

"Imagine if we looked up and saw my mother's face."

"If she was that famous, we'd know. Let's go to the Walk of Fame."

Delilah circled the block and found a parking spot. On the walk, she squatted for a photograph beside the handprints and footprints of the Harry Potter cast.

Julie knelt by the prints of the Star Trek gang, original series. "Eric and I watched every episode at least twice."

Delilah flushed, thinking about how pissed Julie would be if she learned that Delilah was reporting to Eric behind her back.

While they had lunch in the Hollywood and Highland Center courtyard, Julie kept her phone on the table. Delilah guzzled her Coke, the sun beating on her head. Julie's baseball cap shaded her eyes.

"I should buy a hat like yours," Delilah said.

Julie tapped the multicolour swirls. "I got this on holiday with Eric. He thinks Peyton was conceived on that trip."

"Was she?"

"Eric's a romantic." Julie glanced at her phone. "Did you ever think of having kids?"

"You tend to need a guy for that," Delilah said. Should she open up more? Her mother had thought this trip was partly about her bonding with Julie. "Years ago, a doctor told me I had a small uterus. Or he might have said it was large. Either way, I felt he meant I'd have trouble getting pregnant."

"You don't know until you try."

"Did it take you a long time?"

"A few months after I went off the pill." Julie picked up her phone. "I thought it buzzed. Nothing. It's 1:15."

"We have time for the Griffith Observatory."

"If Terry hasn't called by the time we're finished there, we'll stop at his place on the way back."

"He warned us this could take a few days," Delilah said. "Hank or his connections to your mother could be out of town."

"No one's out of town these days what with cell phones and email—especially guys who are 'connectors.'"

Delilah drained her Coke. "I don't know if it's the heat or my meds making me so thirsty."

"Don't you hate being on them all the time?"

Delilah fished out some ice cubes. Her meds were less than ideal. They didn't stop her depression from recurring. In her deep drop last fall, the emptiness and pain got so bad that she spent days lying in bed imagining stabbing herself with a kitchen knife. All that stopped her was the effort of getting up, her cowardliness, and the hurt it would cause her mother. She hadn't told anyone, including her mother this. Should she share it with Julie?

"Taking them every day is a constant reminder I'm sick," Julie said, picking up her tray to carry it to the bin.

"Since we had lunch out," Delilah said, "let's buy groceries for supper on the way to Terry's. Give him more time to get home and reach his connector."

"You agree to us descending on Terry?"

"What harm can it do, aside from antagonize him?"

Chapter Twelve

Against the backdrop of the rubber dam, Eric drilled the cavity in Bill Brownley's upper left lateral incisor. The caries had been a challenge, given the way it had insinuated itself into the enamel. Through his protective glasses, Eric checked for any remaining specks of decay. At moments like this, he understood the satisfaction his parents and sister got from dental work. Clean out the rot and restore the tooth's function and integrity. But more often he shared his senior colleague's view of their profession, a job that paid better than most.

Bill's head stirred. He'd told Eric he welcomed his time in the dental chair to power nap. Eric was grateful he didn't need to entertain him with banter. Bill was able to sleep while keeping his mouth wide open. Eric envied his ability to relax.

"Someone to see you, Eric," the hygienist said from the door. "Says it's personal."

Eric left Bill with her and went to the waiting area. He froze as Nadine bounded toward him. The receptionists stared from behind the desk.

"Since you didn't phone," Nadine said, "I decided to stop by on my way home."

"I was going to call tonight."

"Cool to see where you work." She scanned the wood panelling, Western art, and chairs with waiting patients. Her open jacket showed off her cleavage. "Have you thought more about Saturday?"

He shuffled toward the far wall, hoping she'd get the hint. She planted her boots wide apart. Her short skirt clung to her thighs and shimmery stockings.

"My horoscope says this is my day to take action in relationships." Nadine raised her arms to the sides. "Here I am."

Eric glanced at the gaping receptionists. The new hygienist lingered at the desk to watch the show. His next patient looked up from her magazine.

"I'm real busy, Nadine," he said. "I'll phone tonight."

"What time?"

"Seven thirty?"

"I know you're disturbed by all your feelings, Eric. For you, in your situation, we're moving too fast."

With a glance at the reception desk, he took Nadine's arm. "I've got a patient in the chair and another waiting."

"I'm willing to go slower. As slow as you need."

He pulled her toward the exit.

"About Saturday?" she said. "If you pick up the movies, I'll bring dinner."

"Sure."

"Super. Saturday at six." She leaned forward as though to kiss his cheek, but halted and stepped back.

His face grew hot. The spectators were bound to notice the blush below his fresh haircut. Nadine clacked out the door. He was a coward to postpone the grisly conversation until Saturday, but he couldn't break up with Nadine on the phone or in front of the whole waiting room. He'd have to give her a reason for not continuing, something better than "I promised Peyton I'd get Julie back." Nadine would call him an idiot or punch him in the face, figuratively or literally. He deserved both.

* * *

"Here goes," Julie said.

She pressed the doorbell. Beside her, Delilah was visibly tense. Terry answered, dressed in what looked like the same rumpled shirt and baggy pants he'd been wearing the previous day.

His face lit up in recognition. "Marion's daughters. What can I do for you?"

“Have you heard back from your friend about my mother?” Julie asked.

“I’ll go check.” He hobbled down the hall, lurching to the right with each step.

Julie whispered to Delilah, “He’s been home an hour and hasn’t looked at his machine. Shows how much he cares.” She stepped inside so he couldn’t get rid of them quickly.

Delilah wandered into the living room. “I feel like I’m in a bookstore.”

Aside from the walls of bookshelves, Julie could only see an easy chair, a footstool, and a lectern in the living room. She continued to the end of the hall, which was still cluttered with rollers and paint trays.

“*Jane Eyre*,” Delilah called from the living room. “*The Electric Kool-Aid Acid Test*. *Baseball Legends*.”

“Shhh.” Julie strained to pick out words coming through Terry’s answering machine in the kitchen. The stacks of boxes blocked her view of him.

“Stephen King. Romantic poetry. Eclectic and disorganized.” Delilah came up behind her. “Exactly what you’d expect.”

“I’m trying to listen.” Either Terry had a lot of messages or one long one.

“I don’t see *Six Degrees of Separation*, or—”

“Shut up.”

Terry appeared beside a box. He showed no surprise at finding them in his house. “I hadn’t played that contraption in a week. While I was at it, I took the chance to get caught up.”

Julie tightened her lips to keep from snapping at him. “Was there one from your friend with the connection to Hank?”

Terry held up a scrap of paper. “He got through to him right away. Didn’t I tell you? Hank’s your man.” The paper fluttered between Terry’s gnarled fingers. “Hank wants to talk to you personally.”

“About what?” Julie’s legs grew weak.

“Marion, I expect.”

"Did he say if she's…?"

"Didn't drop a clue."

Julie touched the box for support. "It has to be bad news, if he wants to see me—like a doctor calling you into the office."

"Could be how connectors build up their networks, meeting you in person."

The box shook. Julie's heart pounded in her ears. She'd thought she could handle the worst. She'd thought she wanted to know.

"He's invited you both for lunch at this deli." Terry handed the paper to Delilah. "Here's the address and Hank's number. He asked you to call him to confirm."

Delilah looked at the paper. "Glendale. Where's that?"

"In the Valley," Terry said. "I'd be curious to know what Hank comes up with. How long are you in LA?"

"Another week," Delilah said.

"Drop by and let me know how it goes with Hank."

Julie let go of the box.

Terry stared at Delilah. "You remind me of her," he said. "Marion had the same openness and warmth around the eyes."

Julie clenched her fists. If she corrected him, he might tell Hank to cancel the lunch.

Delilah thanked him for contacting Hank. "It will save us the trouble of talking to the private investigator."

"He's an asshole."

"Does that matter?" Julie said. "He was working for our best interests. It would have helped us if you'd cooperated with him."

"He's not worthy," Terry said. "Your sister is."

Who was he to judge?

Terry wished them good luck at the doorway. Julie was conscious of him watching them walk down the porch stairs. Her leg spasmed as her foot hit the sidewalk.

"Thank you," she said to Delilah.

"For what?"

Julie shook out the leg cramp, which might be a side effect of her new medication. She could never escape them, it seemed. "I couldn't have got past Terry without you."

Delilah smiled, her cheeks dimpling. Julie vowed to thank and compliment Delilah more when she deserved it. Terry was right—they were sisters, in a sense. She was glad Delilah would be with her when Hank delivered the verdict.

* * *

The glass elevator deposited them on the hotel's top floor. Delilah followed Julie into the cocktail lounge. Tables lined the picture window on the west wall. Every booth was occupied.

"They're all here for the sunset," Delilah said. "We should have come earlier."

The section between the booths and bar contained sofas and chairs arranged in conversation nooks. Julie grabbed a vacant sofa. Delilah settled on the soft armchair facing west. The sky glowed yellow through the glass. A server brought them padded leather folders.

Delilah opened one. "This is some fancy bar menu. Eighteen dollars for a cocktail. I'm not paying that."

"You sound like my father," Julie said. "Don't worry about the cost. My treat tonight."

"We can get sunsets and cocktails cheaper somewhere else." Although even Brad might think keeping Julie happy was worth the price of a rip-off cocktail. Well, maybe not Brad.

Julie called the server over and handed him her menu. "Blackberry Bombshell's calling my name."

"Great choice," he said. "BB's my favourite."

Since Julie was going all out, Delilah ordered the weirdest. "Cucumber and dill." As the waiter left, Delilah glanced out of the window. The sun had become an orange ball.

"Tomorrow, at this time, we'll know," Julie said.

Hank had returned Julie's message within seconds, confirmed the day, time and place, then cut her off when she started to ask what he knew about Marion.

"It has to be bad," Julie had said, after she hung up.

The server returned minutes later with their cocktails. Delilah's was a pale green. She raised her glass to Julie. "Cheers." She sipped. Bitter and most definitely cucumber and dill. What would get tomorrow's meeting out of Julie's mind? "Eric said he's working on a new book of poetry."

"When?"

"Now, I guess, when he finds the time, between work and looking after Peyton."

"I mean when did he tell you?"

"Oh," Delilah said. "At the poetry reading. I told you I went."

"Yeah, right. You mentioned meeting his neighbour there. I suppose they're dating."

"I don't know about that." Delilah's stomach coiled, from the cucumber and dill, or the thought of Eric seeing someone, or his not yet answering her last email.

Julie swirled her dark drink. "It's strange how jealous I got last year of Eric and those poetry women. The obsession took over me. I couldn't control it, even though Eric wouldn't have cheated."

"How do you know?"

Julie stared over her glass. "Do you think he would?"

"No. Not while you were married. I mean, you're still married, but it wouldn't be cheating now." Delilah swigged the foul liquid. Eric was free now. He could have gone for her, could have tiptoed across the hall the night she'd slept at his place. But he didn't care for her that way. Never had.

Julie finished her drink. She signalled the server. Outdoors, the sun would sink into the horizon minutes from now. Delilah felt too tired to get up and watch the sight.

"Let's ask for the bill and pick up dinner to eat at home," she said.

Julie ordered a second Bombshell and a plate of wings. She nodded at Delilah. "And bring another whatever-that-is she has."

"No." Delilah held up her half-full glass. "I'm still working on this." At eighteen dollars a crack, she would nurse her drink drop by drop, which wasn't hard given its nasty taste.

The server soon reappeared with Julie's BB. "Wings on the way."

"Tomorrow I go under the knife," Julie said, when the server left. "Who knows what Hank will tell us?"

"He might say your mother is living happily somewhere."

"She didn't call or write."

"Maybe she tried to call after our number was unlisted."

"You can always reach someone if you want. Look at Hank, the connector." Julie gulped down half her second drink. "There hasn't been one word from her in thirty-four years. How can the news possibly be good?"

"There could be a reason you'd never think of."

"That's what Eric said."

"You talked to him?" Delilah stared over her glass.

"I emailed while you were getting changed. I don't know why I did."

Eric had answered Julie's message right away while Delilah's email sat in his computer.

"Guess I needed to unload on someone," Julie said. "But don't tell our parents any of this yet. They'll worry and make a big deal."

Delilah was no longer Eric's sole contact in California. "He'll tell them on the weekend if he takes Peyton there."

"I asked him not to right now."

Eric loved Julie. He always had. Delilah was nothing to him, could never be more than Julie's sister. So obvious, it blasted her in the face, and she had refused to see it. Stupid, stupid, stupid girl. For years, she had clung to a dream. Not a remotely attainable dream—the shimmer of a dream. She had thrown away her prime years for meeting someone, becoming part of a couple, having children, her eyes closed to available men around her—assuming any man would love a fat, depressive loser. Delilah downed the disgusting drink.

"She was like that, you know," Julie said.

"Who? What?"

"When she moved to Calgary from Montreal, she never looked back to her family there."

"Marion?"

"She was seventeen and had been through I-don't-know-how-many stepfathers, her mother's boyfriends. One of them beat her once, or worse. She wouldn't say more."

"How do you know this?"

"Rosemary sat me down when I was a teenager and told me what she'd learned from my dad. She thought it would help me to know."

"Did it?"

The server delivered the plate of wings, two side plates, and some napkins. He asked if they wanted more cocktails.

What the hell, Delilah thought. "I'll have a Blackberry Bombshell this time."

"Make mine a club soda." Julie watched the server leave. "I don't want to be hungover for Hank." She looked at the wings. "I'm not hungry."

Julie got up and strode to a vacated window booth. Delilah too had lost interest in food, but she grabbed a wing and bit into the crisp skin. She ate another wing and another. Julie knelt in the booth, staring at the setting sun, which cast orange and pink hues into the lounge. Delilah nibbled the last piece of chicken. She dropped the bone to the disgusting pile on the plate, wiped her fingers, and rose, too fast. Her head felt light, the room blurred. Eighteen-dollar cocktails weren't stingy with alcohol. Julie came back into focus, her auburn hair curling down her back. Eric still loved Julie. Delilah knew this in her heart, and intuition wasn't her strong point. She had done a rotten job of intuiting that Eric wasn't for her.

Delilah's mushy legs carried her to the booth. She stopped at the table. Six stories down, lights flickered along endless streets. Delilah tottered, touched the table for support. She was on a precipice, set to fall into that horrible mood she'd endured before Christmas, the hollowness and agony. Her gaze settled on the strips of light that outlined the limits of Santa Monica. Beyond lay the ocean, sky, and hills. Black. No relief.

Chapter Thirteen

On the beach house deck, Aurora scanned the computer screen. The information about podcasts, keywords, and search engines made her eyes glaze over. Voices called her attention to the boardwalk. People converged to help a rollerblader who had evidently crashed into a pedestrian. Both men looked dazed but were able to walk. Aurora massaged her neck, stiff from her two hours of research. Every site either wanted to sell her a service to increase her website traffic or teach her how to do this herself. Both options were equally unappealing.

She got up and stretched. The crowd on the boardwalk dispersed. A pair of cyclists whizzed by. Did no one in Southern California work on Friday mornings? Friday. Aurora doubted she'd be able to drag herself to the retreat tomorrow to meet the new guests. She returned to the hellish task.

'Content is king,' the next site declared. 'Choose an eye-catching name for your blog and posts. Make them funny and entertaining.' Funny? Aurora shuddered. What she needed was an office assistant to take care of this. Unlike Cassandra, this geek wouldn't infringe on Aurora's sphere and challenge her for the top job. Aurora could handle that type of delegating.

She skimmed more sites. Videos. Cartoons. Run a Contest. *Ridiculous.* Create a Facebook page. Tweet. Design a collaborative Pinterest board. Turning New Dawn into a brand would destroy its essence. She clicked to another page. 'Are websites dead?' Hers was barely born. The writer said apps were taking over from websites but a strong enterprise needed both.

A wave of fatigue rolled through Aurora's body. She closed her eyes, listened to the real waves in the distance, and inhaled the salty air. Enough of 'expanding your website.' The more important task today was to rebuild her strength. She needed rest.

She shuffled inside to the phone and checked her messages. Nothing from her doctor about the biopsy results, but any second now a phone call could determine the course of her life. Before the operation, she was convinced she'd driven all the sickness into the tumour. She touched her clavicle and glanced at the den clock. 10:30 a.m. Why did she have to wait for him? She punched the phone number for her doctor's office.

"Nothing yet," his receptionist said. "Should get them this afternoon, evening at the latest."

The hours of uncertainty and worry wouldn't strengthen her, physically or mentally. "Is the doctor working tomorrow?"

"He'll be at the hospital in the morning doing rounds."

"Don't phone me," Aurora said. "I'll meet him at the hospital for the results. What time does he go in?"

"Usually around ten."

If she caught him before he started seeing patients, she'd be done in time to go directly to the retreat during the lull between the outgoing and incoming guests. Before the newcomers arrived, she'd scope out Sebastiano and send Cassandra packing. A month from now, Aurora's illness would be no more than a blip in retreat life. Assuming the tests showed her body was clear. She rolled her shoulder, which ached from the surgery and computer, not from any cancer. Aurora was certain of that. It had to be true.

* * *

Vehicles on the freeway whipped by on either side of their car.

"How will we recognize Hank?" Julie said. "I didn't think to ask Terry or him."

A horn blasted. The driver speeding past in the right lane glared at them, but Julie was glad Delilah was a cautious and competent driver.

Delilah checked over her shoulder. "I have to get into that lane or we'll miss the exit."

Hank might leave if they weren't on time. A hundred possibilities loomed. A missed exit. An accident blocking the road. Hank having a heart attack. Julie having one—her heart was racing so fast. Her head was numb from last night's Bombshells and poor sleep thanks to sirens outside and music blaring from the apartment next door.

Delilah made her move and cut across two lanes. They were onto the ramp. Julie grabbed her cell phone from her purse to tell Hank they were on their way.

There was a phone message from the private investigator. *How had she missed the ring?* 'Back in town. Give me a jingle. We'll set up an appointment.' He could wait until after lunch.

She called Hank and left a message on his voice mail. "I'm tall, have long auburn hair, and am wearing a lavender T-shirt. My friend is shorter, has dark hair, and is dressed in a flowery skirt." She hung up.

The car wheels screeched around a curve. Delilah apologized.

"You're doing way better than I would. Even before Peyton, I wasn't keen on driving." Julie chatted to avoid thinking of Hank. "After Peyton, my driving reflexes were shot. In hindsight, the postpartum, I guess. Everything on the road looked fuzzy, like looking through cellophane. I went to an eye doctor. He said my eyesight was perfect, better than 20/20."

"That's the depression," Delilah said. "I'm sort of feeling it now."

"You better not be, or we'll crash."

"I can drive no matter what."

"Why are you depressed? I'm the one who'll be crushed by this."

"I'm coming to some understandings about me," Delilah said. "Shit. That bozo cut in. And why isn't the GPS telling us where to turn?"

The mechanical voice ordered the turn onto Glendale's main street. They found an angled parking spot and asked an elderly man on a bench for directions to the deli. Julie jogged the few blocks. Inside, she scanned the lineup that streamed to the counter. People milled around tables. A man broke from a group and strode to her.

"Julie Fox." He took her hand with both of his thick ones. "Thanks for sending your description."

Hank wore a suit and tie, well dressed, and was a bit heavy around the waist. He looked about sixty. His grey and black hair receded at the temples.

"Where's your sister?" he asked.

No Delilah among the crowd by the door.

"Hank," a man called from the lineup. "Haven't seen you in a dog's year."

"Excuse me a sec," Hank told Julie. He bounded toward the man, patted his back and spoke to him with animation.

Delilah entered, and they joined Hank at the end of the line. Julie thanked him for taking the time to see them.

"No problem," he said. "I love this joint. My wife always insists I bring home a loaf of ciabatta from the bakery side."

"Small world." A woman tapped Hank's arm. "Fancy running into you here, of all places."

Hank brightened, as though seeing this woman was the highlight of his day. "What's that son of yours up to now? He must have finished college."

"He found work at NBC."

Hank grinned. "Exactly what he wanted. Your daughter?"

"She's another story."

Hank's brow knit in sympathy. Julie edged forward with the line, feeling like Hank and these strangers were staging a show for her benefit, starring Hank, the great connector, to prove the story he was about to tell her was true. She scanned the menu board posted behind the counter, listing all kinds of sandwiches. Too many kinds.

"Hank." The counter clerk's face lit up. "What can I do for you, dude?"

"The usual."

"I'll have his usual, too," Julie said. "I'm paying for the three of us."

"Absolutely not," Hank said. "Allow me to treat."

Marion is dead. He's paying to cushion the blow. Delilah also ordered Hank's usual. The clerk handed them paper cups and said a server would deliver their food to the table. Hank led them to the soda fountain to fill their drinks and suggested they sit on the sidewalk patio.

"It's full," Delilah said.

"A table will magically appear." Hank winked at them.

On the shaded patio, a woman with a toddler and a baby in a stroller was gathering her used containers and napkins. Hank leaned over and cooed at the baby, who giggled in delight. While Hank carried the woman's garbage to the bin, Delilah sank into a chair facing the deli window.

Julie took the chair looking down the street. "Is optimism a connector trait? He sends out that vibe and everyone flocks to him?"

Hank grabbed the seat across from Julie. He rested his hands on the table, fingers linked. "So, you two are from Canada. What's happening up there these days?"

Julie latched on to the small talk to delay his revelation. A few minutes later, a clerk delivered their sandwiches. Hank's "usual" turned out to be shredded pork on a Kaiser bun, coleslaw, and oven-baked chips. He bit into his bun. Julie nibbled a chip that would probably taste delicious if her stomach weren't a tight ball. Delilah slurped her soda.

"You flew all the way down here to find out what happened to Marion," Hank said. "She'd appreciate that."

"Did you know her well?"

"I met her a couple of times."

"Lately?"

"Late eighties."

"What was she like?"

"Friendly. She fit in well."

"With whom?"

"Our bag of misfits, as we thought of ourselves. People outside the grid."

Hank nodded at a passerby and returned to Julie. His face grew blurry. Run. She could get up and run down this street. *Don't hear what comes next.*

"The past few decades," Hank continued, "I'd catch up on her activities periodically through mutual friends. As I recall, she stayed around Santa Monica for the next ten or so years then moved down the coast."

"To where?"

"That's all I know." He sipped his 7 Up. "Four or five years ago I ran into one of the old misfits. He was with a younger dude, who was close to Marion in more recent years."

Julie coughed to clear her clogged throat. "Close in what way?"

"He and I started talking about Marion," Hank said. "It always happened when I met her friends. She had a presence people don't forget." Hank's elbows hit the table. He extended his forearms, palms up. "I felt you should hear this in person. I hate to be the one to tell you."

Your mother is dead. Noise rushed through Julie's ears.

Hank's voice pierced the noise. "Marion died. Car accident. Driving down the coast in blinding rain. That highway can be treacherous. Stuart said her death was instant."

"Who's—?"

"The young dude."

"People always say 'instant' to make you feel better." Julie struggled to straighten her slouch. "It's not better. When did this happen?"

"Ten or so years back," he said. "Sorry I don't know any more."

Julie felt stuck to the plastic chair, her feet pressed into the cement. Delilah chewed in slow motion, her eyes damp with tears.

"Stuart told me she was married," Hank said. "Or, rather, living with a man."

"What was his name?"

"Wish I'd asked, to send flowers or a card. I couldn't remember Marion's surname."

"It was Fox."

"Funny, I'd forgotten that until Terry called. I'm usually good with names."

"She didn't go by Fox, that's why," Julie's body flushed with heat. "She rejected us." Dying got her mother off the hook for her recent non-contact, but it didn't absolve her of the first fourteen years' absence.

Hank picked up a chip. "You might learn more from Stuart. During the conversation, he mentioned that he and a business partner had started a type of holiday resort not far from the city. I Googled it last night. It's still kicking around. New Dawn Retreat. Have you heard of it?"

"Why would I?"

He drummed the table. "I knew of the place but didn't realize it was Stuart's. New Dawn has come up a few times with other people these last years. It's surprising to hear who's been there, or whose kids have been. From the website, it sounds like an all-inclusive deal with a New Age approach. Not my cup of tea, but it appeals to a lot of people here in LA."

"You say Stuart—"

"It seems he Italianized it to Stefano. A friend's daughter who spent a week at the retreat described Stefano to me. He's definitely Stuart."

"What's he like?"

"In the words of my friend's daughter, 'He's gorgeous.'"

"He and Marion were close?"

"He was considerably younger than her, nearer your age."

Julie looked at Delilah "We have to go see him. He might know the name of the man she lived with. I can find him."

Delilah rattled the ice remnants in her soda.

"They have free refills," Hank said. "I'll get you one."

Julie stared at him, silently commanding him to stay where he was. "Tell me more about my mother."

"I honestly can't remember more." Hank glanced at Delilah's cup.

"I don't mind going." Delilah got up and left.

Hank looked at Julie. "I know this is a blow, a shock." His tight brow oozed sympathy. "Tell me about yourself. Are you married? Children? Career? My guess is professional. A lawyer? Systems analyst?"

"Engineer."

"Good for you." He paused and frowned slightly. "Come to think of it, Stuart doesn't go by Stefano. It's Sebastiano."

Julie knew where she and Delilah had to go next.

* * *

Sebastiano entered Aurora's office and found Cassandra hunched over the computer desk.

She glanced at him over her shoulder. "I started checking the email. You can take over."

"I'd much rather watch you work." He dropped to Aurora's chair and raised his feet to her desktop. The chair rolled, toppling him backwards. He steadied the wheels. How did men do this so smoothly in movies?

Cassandra clicked the mouse. "It's way backlogged. Aurora can't be answering it more than twice a week."

"She's occupied with higher matters." Feet up and securely leaned back, he clasped his hands behind his head.

"You guys are sitting on a gold mine, and you're working it with spades and picks."

"She speaks in metaphor," Sebastiano said. "She types. What else does the girl do?"

He was conscious of Aurora's presence. The office was all her with elegant, cool lines and not one speck of the personal. That would change if he ever took over. He'd add life. Plants. A fish tank or birdcage in the corner. As a kid, he'd wanted a parrot. Dirty, messy creatures, his mother had told him. The old bat.

"Here's one addressed to you," Cassandra said.

"Read it. I have no secrets."

Probably from a former guest harbouring a fantasy involvement with him, one with whom he'd experienced a quick fling. Cassandra was cool about his past.

"It's from someone named Hank."

He couldn't recall a guest with that name. It made him think of an old man who fixed toilets.

"Who's Marion?" Cassandra said.

A misty image of a woman took shape. Sebastiano leapt out of the chair and across the room to the computer. He read over Cassandra's shoulder, 'Julie Fox, Marion's daughter, looked me up in LA. All I could tell her was that Marion died. Julie seems like a nice girl. If you want to talk to her, I'll put you in touch. Don't be surprised if she shows up.'

"Marion had a daughter?" he said aloud.

"Who's Marion?" Cassandra asked again, craning her neck to look up at him. "A former lover?"

"She never breathed a word about a child."

"Were you two involved?"

"Enough for her to have revealed that."

"Lovers keep secrets."

"She wasn't a lover."

Why was he lying? Marion was deep in the past. He paced to the bookcase. Hank had to be someone from Marion's old crowd. Whenever Sebastiano met one of them in LA, he'd tell the story she'd wanted spread.

"Marion died in a car crash," he said.

"When?"

"Ten years ago."

"Were you still lovers at that point?"

"Not me. She and my friend had been lovers."

A daughter. Should he contact this Fox woman? He certainly wouldn't alert Aurora. She wasn't good with surprises. Although, if this daughter appeared, Aurora's face would be priceless.

"Can you print out Hank's message? I'll never find it again if we leave it on the computer."

"Even you aren't that technically dense."

He pressed Delete once the print copy was made.

"Julie," he said. "Marion must have had her before I—my friend—came on the scene. She must be in her twenties. More like thirties."

"You better not fall for her." Cassandra sashayed toward him. She held the print copy of Hank's message in her long fingers.

"No chance of that." He massaged her robe over her hips.

"I want to hear all about Marion."

"She's dead, and I swear we weren't lovers."

"Then why has your face been sheet white since I mentioned her name?"

"I'm just floored by the thought of Marion as a mother." If this Julie burst into the retreat, or if he contacted her, nothing would change. Aurora would dismiss her, and she'd disappear. He and Aurora would never speak of her again.

Or…

There might be a way he could use this.

"I'm waiting," Cassandra said.

"For what?"

"To hear about Marion."

His subconscious must have spun those lies to Cassandra for a reason. What story was she most likely to believe? Could he steal one from Aurora, that Cassandra had heard before? He'd say the story was really about Marion, but Aurora appropriated it for herself for instruction and effect.

"Not here, in Aurora's space." He drew Cassandra to him. "Let's go to my cottage."

"Sex won't get you out of telling me the truth."

He ushered her out of the office and closed the door behind them. Their walk through the building and herb garden would give him time to work out a plausible tale.

Chapter Fourteen

Julie opened the laptop on the kitchen table and Googled New Dawn Retreat. The website described it as nestled between hills. Two hours from the bustle of Los Angeles.

"Find anything?" Delilah called from the sofa.

Built in the style of a Tuscan villa. Olive groves. Explore the inner you under the guidance of Aurora. Julie peered at the shadowy photo of Aurora, who seemed to be a sort of spiritual leader. Dressed in a blue toga, her blonde hair swept up on her head, she looked about forty. Another photo showed smiling people on lounge chairs around a kidney-shaped pool. Guided hikes. Three buffet meals a day. Julie clicked on the rates.

"It's not cheap," she said. "The site doesn't mention Sebastiano. I hope he's still there. Aurora could be the business partner Hank mentioned."

"Wouldn't hurt to email them." Delilah shuffled into the kitchen.

"We'll learn more going in person," Julie said. "Take them by surprise, our PI's motto. It worked with Terry."

"Are you going to phone the PI?"

"Why bother, unless we get nothing from Sebastiano?"

Delilah opened a bag of chips.

"You're hungry after those huge sandwiches?"

Footsteps pounded overhead—likely their neighbours returning home from work.

"Are you up for a day trip tomorrow?" Julie asked.

"Not another long drive." Delilah munched a chip.

"Only two hours."

"People always underestimate the time."

Julie returned her attention to the computer. She was tense, but not as depressed as she would have expected.

Maybe it was denial or the relief of knowing one fact after thirty-four years of uncertainty and of finally being able to do something. Sebastiano might lead to…she didn't know what, but he was one step closer.

Delilah carried the chips to the living room and collapsed on the sofa again. On the drive back from Glendale, she'd barely responded to Julie's musings about her mother, Hank, and the retreat. Sure, Delilah wasn't as invested in the search, but she'd shown a genuine interest before last night. Julie hoped her stepsister wasn't coming down with something that would prevent her from driving tomorrow. The retreat sounded too isolated to be reached by bus.

Julie clicked on her email. A message from Eric, 'What happened?' Sent from his mobile phone, presumably from work. One from Rosemary, 'How are you girls making out?'

"Your mother wrote me," Julie called out.

"She must be wondering why I didn't email today."

"Did you tell her about Hank?"

"You asked me not to."

"Let's keep it that way," Julie said. "All it will do is worry them." She typed a reply to Rosemary, 'We finally talked to "the stoner," as Dad calls him. He was pretty sharp, and not even stoned. A friend of a friend of his may have information about my mother.' She deleted 'my mother' and typed 'Marion' to make the quest seem less significant for her. 'The PI's been in San Francisco. He's back in LA and can see us on Monday. I doubt he'll offer much, but we'll leave no stone unturned and all that. Tomorrow Delilah and I are planning a drive in the country. We'll enjoy the break from LA.' She reread the message. It had the right balance of seriousness and lightness. After pressing Send, she checked the weather forecast. Sunny and warm tomorrow.

Her mother had died in a rainstorm. Was she the driver or a passenger in the car? Did it skid off the road into a post, the sea, or another vehicle? Maybe Sebastiano would know.

Julie stared at Eric's message, debating how much to tell him. He was obviously interested, perhaps concerned, but wouldn't brood on it like her dad and Rosemary. Julie typed,

‘We talked to Hank, the guy who knew my mother. Marion was in a car accident five or more years ago. She died. I’m surprisingly okay with it.’ Julie’s eyes stung. ‘Hank gave us a lead. Best not to tell my parents yet.’ Her throat constricted. She blinked away tears. Her fingers slipped off the keyboard. She wanted to tell Eric everything, but her fingers stiffened on the keys. ‘More later. J.’

* * *

“I think we’ve finally left LA,” Julie said. “The houses are farther and farther apart.”

“There’s a farm,” Delilah noted. “Or horses, anyway.” The GPS announced the upcoming turnoff. “And there’s a sign for Palm Springs. I wouldn’t mind going there sometime.”

Delilah acted, if not perky, less zombie-ish than yesterday. Last night’s solid sleep had made her feel better, she’d said, and settled some things in her mind. What things? Julie had gone to bed thinking about today, but exhaustion had knocked her out too. Somehow, she’d slept through the usual noises and her tension.

“We could stay overnight out here,” Julie said. “Might be a peaceful escape from sirens and the neighbours’ racket.”

They turned right at the major intersection and passed through farmland punctuated with scrub.

“I wouldn’t mind a coffee and a bite to eat,” Delilah said.

“Good idea,” Julie said. “It doesn’t sound like this retreat has a restaurant.” Food would fuel her for facing the man who had known her mother, perhaps intimately. “I wonder what Sebastiano is like.”

“Aside from ‘gorgeous’?”

At last they entered a town. Ahead was a motel, a gas station and Rita’s Café, which turned out to be a 1950s diner. Laminate counter. Red vinyl booths and chairs. Posters of Elvis and James Dean. Julie suggested they sit in a booth.

She flipped through the jukebox listings. Country...The Sixties...Queen.

"Do you think this place is retro or just missed the last half century?" Julie said.

A waitress brought them menus.

"We're on our way to the New Dawn Retreat," Julie told her.

The woman's middle-aged face broke into a smile. "That's right. It's turnover day."

"Pardon?"

"Saturday. The old crop leaves, new one arrives. Like you, they sometimes stop before going in, but they always zip past on the way out. It would be interesting to see if the week there changed them."

"Is it supposed to?"

"That's the theory, according to Sebastiano."

Julie sat up straight. "Do you know him?"

"He comes in for burgers and fries when he needs a break from healthy grub."

"What's he like?"

The woman's pencilled eyebrows rose. "You'll see for yourself," she said, and left.

"There's a motel next door with only one car out front," Julie said to Delilah. "If we decide on that break from LA noise, they'd probably have a room for us."

"What about toothbrushes, pyjamas, fresh clothes for the morning?"

The waitress returned with two glasses of water. Julie noticed her name tag, 'Trish.'

"Do retreat visitors ever come here midweek?" Julie asked her.

"Not much," Trish said. "When they do, it's to use the Wi-Fi. A few grumble about going stir-crazy out there, away from everything."

"There's no internet?" Delilah said.

"The management has it, I think. Don't get me wrong," Trish said. "There's only a handful who don't mesh with the retreat. Sebastiano says most love it and hate to leave. He wouldn't lie about that. There's no bull about him."

"Is there bull about anyone else there?" Julie asked. She glanced at Delilah, who was absorbed in her menu.

"It's just the two of them, Sebastiano and Aurora," Trish said. "The gardener also lives on-site. He's a quiet one. Never comes to town. For the most part, the town goes to New Dawn. They're the major employer in these parts. Cleaning staff, cooks, seamstresses, handymen, grocery suppliers. Before them, we were mainly retirees and orange groves."

"Your café must appreciate the economic spinoffs."

Trish nodded. "Without the retreat, I'd have had to leave for a job in the city. Have you decided on your orders?"

Delilah closed her menu. "I'll have the bacon burger and fries."

"Sebastiano's favourite."

"Make mine the same, without bacon," Julie said.

Delilah asked for a milkshake too. "Chocolate."

"Ditto, but strawberry," Julie said. "So, why would a holiday retreat need seamstresses?"

Trish chuckled. "They all dress up in these Roman-like robes. The seamstresses go out Saturday to fit the new arrivals. It sounds peculiar but feels normal there, so everyone tells me. Sebastiano and some of the men prefer tunics and shirts, with leggings."

"The owners are Sebastiano and Aurora?"

"Aurora's the main honcho. I'll be back with your shakes in a jiff."

Julie watched Trish leave and turned to Delilah. "I get the sense she doesn't like Aurora."

"She didn't say anything about her."

"It was her tone." Julie raised a brow. "Trish likes to gossip. She'd be good for information." Julie pictured a buff man in a Robin Hood costume. "I wonder if she's sweet on Sebastiano."

Minutes later, Trish approached again. She set the milkshakes on their paper placemats.

"What's Aurora like?" Julie asked.

Trish smoothed her apron. "I've only seen her a few times. Those who work for her say she's firm, pleasant, and fair. None of them feels they know her, really, but they seem loyal." Trish excused herself to serve the next table.

"That sounded positive," Delilah said.

"We'll find out for ourselves in an hour or so."

The milkshakes were thick, the burgers juicy. Despite her nerves, Julie found it all remarkably tasty. As Trish cleared their plates, Julie asked her for directions to the New Dawn Retreat, which didn't show up on their GPS.

"Take the road south out of town," Trish said. "When the orchards give out, you'll pass a few shacks in the brush and come to the end of the line. You can't miss it."

* * *

Shortly before 1:00 p.m., they drove up to the sign, 'New Dawn Retreat.' The gate was open. Delilah pulled into the parking lot. Another sign directed them to the office around the side of a stone building.

To the west, orange trees terraced up a slope. The sky overhead couldn't be clearer. Past the office building, an expansive lawn stretched to a similar building in the distance. A tree with spreading, bare limbs stood in the centre of the lawn. In summer, the leaves would provide welcome shade over the swing beneath it.

The door in the office building opened just ahead of them. Julie froze on the stone path. A woman draped in a pale-pink robe stood on the doorstep. She looked to be in her late thirties.

"Aurora?"

"She's away. I'm replacing her until Monday."

In the picture, Aurora did look a little older than this woman with long dark hair. Julie had been curious to meet New Dawn's spiritual leader, but that wasn't her purpose. Standing on the step, this other woman matched Julie's height.

"I'm Cassandra," the woman continued. "All of our guests this past week told me they didn't miss a thing with Aurora away. I'm sure you'll be completely satisfied with your week here."

"We aren't staying," Julie said. "I'm looking for Sebastiano."

"Can I help you?"

"It's personal. I have a few questions for him. My name is Julie Fox."

Cassandra's mouth fell open, like a hole in a tree trunk.

"A man named Hank—"

"We've been expecting you."

"You have?" Julie's gaze shot to Delilah, who looked equally surprised.

"Hank emailed a heads-up," Cassandra said. "Sebastiano told me about your mother. I am sorry."

"I was hoping Sebastiano could tell me more."

"He's in town now but should be back any minute." Cassandra scanned them both from head to toe. Her long face was beautiful in an odd way. Julie revised Cassandra's age—perhaps early thirties.

"Do you want to come in?" Cassandra said. "I can get you some tea."

Outside, in this glorious sunshine, Julie could deal with whatever horrors Cassandra dropped, and if she couldn't, she could run to the car. Inside, she'd be trapped.

A mechanical noise whirred on the lawn. Someone riding a lawn tractor.

"Is that the gardener?" Julie asked.

Cassandra stepped onto the path. "He does the mowing during this period between guests."

"I'll wait out here," Julie said. "We don't get winter like this in Canada."

"You came all this way to find your mother?"

Julie faced her. "I want the whole truth. Don't spare me anything."

The whirring got louder as the mower drove toward them. A man in coveralls rode on top. At the path, he steered the tractor away from them.

"Your mother was involved with Sebastiano's best friend," Cassandra said. "Romantically."

Julie steeled her legs for the rest.

"The friend was kind of an innocent," Cassandra continued. "This was some fifteen years ago. She was his older woman. You get the drift? He was infatuated with her. It was mutual until Marion lost interest."

Cassandra shifted so that her back was to the sun. Julie wished she hadn't left her sunglasses in the car. She moved sideways so Cassandra's body blocked the sunlight.

"The friend followed her everywhere, moping," Cassandra said. "Marion lost patience, and who wouldn't? When she finally brushed him off, the boy committed suicide."

Julie felt Delilah's fingers grip her arm.

Cassandra raised her hand. Was the gesture for sympathy or drama? Pink material flowed down from her wrist. "He walked into the ocean. A smart swimmer, he knew the tide was going out and he wouldn't have the strength to get back. This friend was closer to Sebastiano than a brother. His death broke Sebastiano but also turned him around from drifting, hanging out on the beach, scrounging a living as a surfing coach. Aurora was one of Sebastiano's students. She wanted to learn to ride the waves because 'that's what life is about,' she said, 'opening yourself to new experiences.' She'd saved money from her job at a bank and had a vision for a retreat."

Had Marion also been drifting, hanging out, scrounging? Did she feel responsible for the young man's death? Did it change her too? Lead her to the right man for her, or a wrong one; the one who died with her in the crash?

Cassandra motioned toward the path, the building, and the citrus trees. Sunlight sparkled through the sheer cape connected to her arm with a wristband. "Aurora and Sebastiano founded New Dawn, largely with money from Sebastiano's inheritance. He and Aurora are equal partners, although in the overall scheme he defers to her. Oh." Frown lines flared up from the bridge of Cassandra's nose. "I realize Sebastiano told me all about himself and almost nothing about your mother." She looked around Julie and squinted, as though blinded by the sun.

"There may be more he can tell me," Julie said.

“That’s Aurora.”

Julie spun around. A woman dressed in pants and a sweater rolled a suitcase down the path. She stopped to adjust her purse over her shoulder.

“I should have known she wouldn’t stay away,” Cassandra said. “Excuse me a minute.”

Cassandra approached Aurora, who let go of her suitcase. Julie edged closer. Aurora wore her thick grey hair loosely tied back from her forehead. Wavy tendrils shone silver in the sun.

Julie heard only bits of their conversation.

“…Sebastiano?”

Cassandra muttered something in reply.

“…if I returned Monday. It wouldn’t be fair to the guests…”

Then Aurora brushed past Cassandra. “Welcome to the New Dawn Retreat.” Her illuminated face gazed at Delilah and Julie. “Sorry to be late. You’ve arrived earlier than I expected.”

“They’re here to see Sebastiano on a private matter,” Cassandra said. “That sounds like his car.”

A vehicle clouded with dust entered the parking lot and disappeared behind the building.

“I’ll leave my bag for him to carry,” Aurora said.

Cassandra repeated her invitation to come inside for tea. Julie grabbed Delilah’s arm as a message for them to stay put. Aurora set her purse down and leaned on the suitcase’s extended handle, as though she needed a rest before moving. Her wrinkled neck suggested she was older than she appeared on the website picture. She could be close to sixty.

A tall man appeared from behind the building. He held a box to his chest. Sebastiano swerved around Aurora and set the red-and-green box down on the path. He brushed dust from his T-shirt and jeans. Tanned, curly black hair, lean torso, toned forearms. ‘Gorgeous’ covered it. Aurora’s hand left the suitcase.

He hugged Aurora, who remained stiff. “The cook discovered today we were short of olive oil. I picked up a case in town." His gaze shifted beyond her, to Julie and Delilah. "I see we have our first guests."

"This is Julie Fox," Cassandra said.

Sebastiano's eyebrows shot up. Aurora took a sharp breath. Her blue-grey eyes grew wide.

"Cassandra." Sebastiano pointed at the suitcase and Aurora's purse. "Can you take these to her room?"

Cassandra glared, clearly wanting to stay. She grabbed the handle, lifted the case and purse and stomped into the building.

"Julie Fox." Sebastiano stepped back to study her.

Aurora touched Julie's arm, her hand soft and warm. She pivoted to face Julie directly. "Do you know who I am?"

She was almost Julie's height. Blue-grey eyes. Like Marion's in the pictures. Julie shivered all over. Her knees wobbled, her vision blurred. Hands clutched her forearms, preventing her fall. Aurora's hands.

"Julie, what's the matter?" Delilah's voice was faint.

Aurora, Sebastiano, the stone building, the orange trees re-emerged in sharp focus. Aurora's kindly eyes shimmered with tears.

"Marion?" Julie said.

Chapter Fifteen

Eric stopped a few feet from his yard. Nadine sat on his picnic table. She waved hello, looking pretty in her purple jacket, yoga pants, and high-heeled boots. He moved toward her, his bulging shopping bags swinging at his sides.

"Your in-laws told me you were at the clinic," she said. "About tonight. Can we make it six thirty?"

Damn. Stupid of him to accept Rosemary and Brad's offer to visit Peyton at his place this Saturday.

"Cody's father showed up with this last-minute idea of taking him to the zoo. What could I say? I told him to be back by six, but he'll bring Cody late, full of junk food that makes him hyper. Make that closer to seven."

"I'm fine with us postponing it to another time."

"You and Peyton can eat earlier," Nadine said. "After all that sugary crap, Cody won't be hungry for anything except popcorn during the movie." She kicked her feet forward to leap off the table and came up so close that he could see the tip of the cormorant's wing on her breast.

"Your in-laws were shocked to learn we're seeing each other."

He stepped back. "Nadine—"

"You're shocked, too."

He glanced at his house. Front door closed. No Rosemary, Brad, or Peyton looking out of the living room window. "Nadine, it was wrong of me to sleep with you so soon."

"Eric, you've been separated from Julie for a year."

"Ten months. I'm still on the rebound. It's not fair to you to bring you into it."

"Where's Julie this weekend?"

"Away on business." And she had succeeded in tracking down a man who said her mother had died. 'I'm surprisingly okay with it,' Julie had claimed in her email.

"It's always hard, but we all have to move on." Nadine tapped her boot while studying his face. "But if that's how you want it, forget our date tonight. Forget all about us."

"I'm sorry, Nadine." He looked at the house. Still safe.

Nadine clacked backwards to the courtyard. "Give me a call if you ever get your shit together."

She turned and jogged away, toward her side of the complex. Her purple jacket disappeared around the corner. His body relaxed.

Inside, Peyton rushed toward him. "Daddy."

He grabbed her and bundled her up in his arms. Savoury aromas flowed from the kitchen. Brad sat on the living room floor surrounded by LEGO bricks stacked in towers and into rows of roads.

"We're building a city." Brad got up from the floor. "Peyton's a real engineer."

Like Julie and her dad. Engineers on the Fox side; dentists on his. Of Peyton's four biological grandparents, Julie's mother was the only wild card. The odds of mental balance were in Peyton's favour, but what if craziness trumped everything else, as it had in Julie? Plus, Peyton's nurturing environment wasn't so hot these days. And if his poetry bent expressed a hidden nutty side, poor Peyton didn't have a chance.

Rosemary stood in the kitchen doorway. "I've cleaned out your fridge and put all the leftovers into a pot to make a stew for your supper."

"You shouldn't have done all that with your bad back," Eric said.

She rolled her shoulders. "It's feeling good enough for me to take Peyton out to play. Brad hasn't had time for any of the work he brought home from the office."

"This engineering marvel was more fun." Brad beamed at Peyton, who was sliding a car down a ramp.

"I'll take her out," Eric said.

"It's fine, I'd enjoy some fresh air," Rosemary said. "That reminds me—a woman from the complex was here looking for you."

Eric tensed. He tried to read Rosemary's neutral expression. "I met her outside," he said, and quickly changed the subject. "Since you made the stew, you'll have to stay and eat some." Safer having them here, in case Nadine showed up to rehash their breakup.

He and Rosemary dressed Peyton in her snowsuit, hat, mitts, and boots. Then Rosemary got her overcoat from the closet and followed Peyton to the courtyard.

Brad motioned Eric to the stairs. "Do you mind checking your email? I've had no more word from Julie. Rosemary hasn't heard from Delilah."

They went up to the den, where Eric logged on. Only one message, from his sister in Saskatoon, saying she was going to a movie tonight with a friend who was new to town, a pediatrician who wrote poetry on the side. She was giving her a copy of *To Catch a Fox*. 'If you acquire a new fan, I'll introduce you the next time you visit.' A chatty email, and innocent on the surface, but part of him wondered if his sister was thinking of setting him up. At least her friend wasn't a dentist. Eric got up to give Brad the chair.

Brad slumped into it. "Why would Julie want to postpone telling Rosemary and me about Marion's death?"

Eric agreed they would find out eventually, and he hadn't wanted to spend the afternoon hiding that critical information. Julie would probably be mad at him for telling, but there wasn't much chance she'd find out. Her parents had promised not to let on they knew until Julie or Delilah came out with it. Would Julie have a reason to keep the news from Brad? "To spare you," Eric suggested.

"From what? Whether she's dead or simply gone makes no difference to me."

"Hadn't you always wondered?" Eric asked. "Wasn't that the point of this search?"

"For Julie." Brad rocked the chair. "Julie's like me, won't admit to weakness. Convinces herself she's coping when she's not. It can lead to trouble." He rocked harder.

Eric's thoughts flashed back to that afternoon in the bathroom. Julie crouched over the tub, Peyton under the water. "Delilah's there with her now."

"She's not much help. In some ways, she's a worse case than Julie."

Eric rubbed his jaw. "She and Julie wouldn't both go off the rails at the same time."

"Let's hope."

"Julie might get an emotional boost from their drive in the country."

"If that's all it was."

They had speculated that Hank's lead might be directions to Marion's grave. Eric's nose twitched at the aroma of the stew wafting up from downstairs. "Did you try their cell phones?"

"No answers. You try."

"If I push Julie, she'll think I don't believe she can handle this on her own. It's tentative between us." She'd reached out to him in her email. He'd betrayed her by spilling her findings to Brad, an act that could bite him later.

Brad gripped the chair arms and forced himself up, like a feeble old man. "I've got to get cracking on my work. It's due Monday."

Eric sat down and opened his email again, in case. Nothing. He clicked onto his last message from Delilah, which he hadn't thought necessary to answer. Julie might have told Delilah to ignore Rosemary's calls until they were ready to reveal the whole truth about Marion. But Julie had been open with Eric. Delilah might be, as well. It was worth a shot. He pressed Reply.

* * *

Julie let go of the woman. Aurora. Marion. Her mother. Her hands lingered on Julie's arms.

"We'll leave these two alone," Sebastiano said to Delilah. "You're Julie's friend?"

"Stepsister," Delilah said. "I don't understand."

Aurora looked beyond Julie to Delilah. "I'll want to get to know you as well, but first..." Her gaze settled on Julie again.

In the building doorway, Cassandra crossed her arms over her pink robe. Julie had thought she'd gone inside.

"I think I should stay with Julie," Delilah said.

Aurora smiled at her. "Would you like a beverage after your long trip?" Her blue-grey eyes glowed in the sunshine. "Cassandra," she called, although her voice kept its soft tone. "Can you take care of our guest?"

Delilah glanced at Julie, her face seeking permission to go inside. Julie scanned Cassandra, Sebastiano, and Aurora. All stared as though their lives depended on Julie's response. Julie nodded at Delilah. Sebastiano grinned. Julie handed her purse to Delilah to take care of for her. With a backwards glance at Julie, Delilah followed Cassandra into the stone building. Sebastiano brought up the rear and closed the massive door.

"Let's find a place to sit," Aurora said. "Inside or out?"

Aurora let her arms dangle, not reaching out, keeping her distance. Julie appreciated her understanding and reserve. They were effectively strangers. Julie looked at the stone building's large picture window, covered with curtains.

"Out."

Aurora's eyes crinkled. "I like natural air too. Shade or sun?"

Julie shrugged, afraid her voice would crack. Aurora led her into the yard and pointed to their right at an amphitheatre, which had been concealed by cypress trees. Hills rose up both sides of this valley. On the farther side, olive groves terraced up a high hill and merged into forest. Behind, in the distance, snow capped a mountain top. The stone building across the lawn was the guest residence, Aurora explained, and the same size as the main building used for administration, communal activities, and Aurora's bedroom upstairs. They stepped from the stone path onto rubbery California grass and angled toward the tree in the yard's centre. Julie became conscious of the silence. The lawn mower had stopped. Behind the administration building was a garden and the edge of a cottage.

"We grow our own vegetables behind the guest building," Aurora said, and motioned toward the trees to the rear of that building. "Behind the lemon grove is a pool." Her arm movement was so fluid Julie could almost see it draped in a robe. "We closed the pool for cleaning last week," she said. "If matters were handled properly in my absence, it will open this afternoon. Did you bring a swimsuit?"

"Why would I?" Julie stopped at the bench swing under the tree. "A friend of yours told me you were dead."

"Who?"

"Does it matter?"

Aurora stared straight at Julie. "I can't believe how tall you've grown."

"You last saw me when I was four years old."

"I know." A shadow of pain rippled Aurora's face. She fingered the collar of her turtleneck. "I'm sorry about that."

Julie coughed. Sorry didn't cut it. "Why did Sebastiano tell people you died? He even lied to Cassandra."

"Did he? Why would he say that? Unless…" Aurora sat down on the swing. "Could he have meant the death of the former me?"

"He said dead."

"A metaphor." Aurora stared at the grass. Threads of her silvery, swept-up hair fluttered in the breeze. "Death of the selfish Marion, who left you, Julie."

Julie's throat tightened. That was maudlin crap. Yet, Aurora's voice exuded sincerity and warmth. Julie felt awkward standing over this woman, her mother. She dropped to the swing's far end, three feet of varnished wood between them. The tree's bare limbs cast hatches of shade across Aurora's forehead, still youthfully smooth, although her age showed in the lines around her mouth and the wrinkles in her neck. Marion had been so young when Julie was born—only twenty-one.

Aurora's hands rested on her lap. Julie looked from the spotted skin to her own long, conical fingers. Their hands were startlingly similar in shape. In what other ways were they alike, aside from their height, slimness, and thick hair? Julie had the odd streak of grey under her dyed roots. If she were to let her hair go naturally, would it become splendidly silver, like Aurora's? Except, Marion's hair had been light brown, not Julie's darker shade. Julie's skin tones were darker, too. Aurora wasn't tanned. Evidently, she spent less time in the sun than Sebastiano.

"There's so much. Where to begin?" Aurora said. "How is your father?"

"Remarried."

"I know."

"How? Because I have a stepsister?"

Aurora smiled. "I haven't totally stayed away."

"What do you mean?"

"I want to hear all about your life. What were you like in school?"

"Normal."

"I bet you were a top student, like your father."

"How did you find out about his marriage?"

"He was bound to find someone suitable." Aurora pressed her hands on her pants. "His parents disliked me."

"Because you left us."

"Your grandmother hated me on sight. I don't blame her. That is, at the time, I felt it was my fault, that she saw through to my bad core." Lines etched themselves on Aurora's forehead. "It was my own self-loathing." Her voice wavered. "Are your grandparents still alive?"

"Dead. Why didn't you contact us?"

"I tried."

"When?"

"A number of times."

The gardener emerged from the lemon grove behind the guest residence, his hands full of tools. He loped to the flowers along the building and knelt down, his back to them.

"A year or so after I left," Aurora said. "When I felt settled in California, I called your father. The line had been disconnected."

The gardener's head bobbed up and down as he worked the strip of land.

"We moved in with Grandma and Grandpa Fox," Julie said.

"I thought your father might have been transferred. At his office, there was talk of a move to Houston."

"Did you look for us there?"

Aurora turned away, as though embarrassed. She could easily have lied and said she'd pursued them.

"A few years later, it occurred to me to try your father's parents. Your grandmother answered. I recognized her bark right away."

Julie smiled for what felt like the first time in hours. Grandma Fox had usually answered the phone sharply.

"She berated me for deserting you," Aurora said. "I deserved that. She told me how well you and your father were both doing without me, insisted you were both better off and that if I gave a fiddlestick for you, I would stay out of your life and not interfere and mess you up."

Give a fiddlestick had been one of Grandma Fox's pet phrases.

"I never heard about this call," Julie said.

"Even she would be sensitive enough not to share this with a child. Today, I would tell her to go..." Aurora paused. "F herself."

Julie smiled at the coyness. Her mother's coyness. She couldn't get used to the word, not in relation to this stranger.

"I was young and insecure. Your grandmother had always intimidated me. I slunk away, tail between my...I didn't try again for another five years."

"What happened then?"

"A friend had access to the Calgary phone directory. He found a number for a Fox, B. For Brad. My heart stopped." Aurora squinted at the sun.

Julie liked that the woman hadn't put on sunglasses, which would shield her expressions.

"I wasn't sure how your father would receive me," Aurora said. "I had the friend phone the number and say that he was looking for me."

This jibed with her father's story. Julie leaned toward Aurora.

"A woman answered, said she was Mrs. Fox. That's when I learned he'd remarried. I suppose he found a legal channel to divorce me."

"Abandonment is legal enough."

Aurora's brow creased with her frown. Good if that jab hurt her.

"Did you try to reach him again?" Julie asked

"I couldn't."

"Why not?"

Aurora rolled her shoulder. "It threw my confidence to hear he'd moved on. You had a new mother."

"Stepmother."

"In my odd way, I felt you had a stable family. My reappearance would shake that up."

"I wish you had." Julie realized she'd moved a foot closer to Aurora.

"You must understand," Aurora said. "I was still screwed up. My upbringing. How much do you know about that?"

"Dad told me some basics." The entire time he was with her, Marion didn't once phone or visit any of her family in Montreal and Boston. All Julie's father knew was that Marion had two older sisters and a mother, but no natural father on the scene. Marion had hinted at abusive stepfathers and mother's boyfriends. There was lots of alcohol in the mix. All of her damaged, sad past might explain Marion's behaviour, but it didn't excuse it, or change anything for Julie.

"The Fox family was so normal," Aurora said. "I wanted you to have that, untainted by me."

Despite the diffused shade, Julie felt flushed.

"Were they good to you?"

Julie nodded.

"What I said earlier wasn't quite true," Aurora said. "I did call again, in the evening. Your number was disconnected, the new number unlisted."

"Because of that call from your friend." Julie's father had made it impossible for Marion to reach them by phone. And Grandma Fox had cut Marion off when she told her to stay away. It wasn't completely Marion's fault.

"Let's get back to you," Aurora said. "I want to know everything. Did you go to university?"

Julie looked over her shoulder at the stone building. What was Delilah doing in there?

"She's your stepsister," Aurora said, as if reading her thoughts. "Is she the second wife's child? How much older is she than you?"

"A couple of months."

"You're thirty-eight now. So hard for me to believe, even though, in my heart and mind, I haven't missed a single birthday." She touched Julie's arm, now inches away. "Tell me about you and school."

"Starting when?"

"Grade One. Kindergarten. Your first day."

Julie didn't move. "That's a lot of story."

Chapter Sixteen

Seated on a plush sofa, Delilah nursed her fruit punch. Sebastiano had told her that the New Dawn Retreat was dry aside from wine at meals, but this punch had a kick thanks to herbs from the garden out back. He'd left to consult with Cassandra on a business matter. From him, Delilah had learned that within the hour, the week's twenty-two guests would begin pouring into this lounge. His job would be to entertain them while they waited for Aurora to register them in her office behind the massive mahogany door.

"You people are pretty hands on," Delilah had commented.

"Probably too much," Sebastiano answered with a grin.

He scared the shit out of her. Too handsome and tanned; confident, tall and muscled; his eyes an incredible blue, his cologne thick, his T-shirt and jeans tight. Was he sleeping with Cassandra? And what was it with everyone's elaborate names? It still floored Delilah that she and Julie had actually found Marion. Sebastiano had laughed when Delilah asked him why he'd told Hank that Marion had died in a car accident.

"Yes, why?" Cassandra repeated the question, hands on her hips.

Sebastiano had shrugged. "It came out the first time without my thinking. After that, it felt right to keep Marion's story consistent."

"Hmph," Cassandra said.

Delilah agreed. He'd evaded answering.

Behind her, the fireplace crackled. The fire seemed real, but it might be as fake as Marion's and Stuart's names and this Romanesque environment. Sebastiano had told her that after check-in, guests were fitted for robes. But this lounge décor was cozy, suburban modern, with overstuffed sofas and chairs angled in conversation nooks. Beige tones and plants added earthiness and lightness.

"Aurora holds her sessions here during downpours and cold spells," he'd said.

"Sessions?"

"You'll find out if you stick around."

Her punch finished, Delilah got up to scan the bookshelves that flanked the fireplace. She'd been told that guests occasionally hung out in this room on cool evenings, although most preferred the similar lounge in their building across the yard.

"Aurora prefers they stay over there," Sebastiano had added.

Many of the books were self-help with an exotic flair. Angels, tarot, and Pranic Healing, but there were enough novels, classic and modern, to keep Delilah reading for a year. If Sebastiano didn't show up in the next few minutes, she might tackle the Jonathan Franzen. She wouldn't mind spending a few days here, if Julie wanted. How was Julie managing with her mother? What do you say to someone you hardly remember, yet who played a crucial role in your life?

Delilah thought of her own mom, waiting for word in Calgary. She ached to phone her with the news, but she couldn't without Julie's permission. This quest was Julie's ride. She'd achieved the goal, with Delilah's help. Was it this success that was lifting Delilah's grey mood of yesterday to near buoyant in this oasis of green hills and trees? The first step up had been her acceptance of the reality of Eric. He would never be hers, and she was okay with it. She could live, even thrive, without him. Delilah cringed at the prospect of returning to LA smog and the cramped apartment. She sensed Sebastiano wanted them to stay the night.

Footsteps thudded down the hall to the lounge. Sebastiano apologized for abandoning her and offered to refill her drink.

"I'm good." She ran her tongue around her mouth, which felt deliciously moist. "Would you give me the recipe for this?"

"No problem. That's not one of our secrets." Sebastiano winked.

He led her to the hall and motioned to the stairs on their right. "Aurora's bedroom is up there. It's off-limits, except to staff and special invitees. Here's the dining room."

They entered a room on the right. A woman was setting places at three round tables. The white tablecloths and fern centrepieces would suit a wedding reception. At the far end, Cassandra adjusted a lectern beside a rectangular table. Another woman carried a stack of plates to a table along the opposite wall.

"Buffet style saves on service," Sebastiano said.

A third woman carted a chair to the head table. She wore regular clothes and an apron, like all the workers here except Cassandra. Sebastiano motioned Delilah across the hall to the kitchen. Workers chopped vegetables on a butcher-block island and bustled between stainless-steel industrial-sized appliances.

A short, fat man stopped beside them. His apron was spattered with tomato sauce as red as his face. "Is this our first guest for the week?"

"We're hoping," Sebastiano said. He loped to a woman stirring a soup cauldron. She offered up a spoonful to taste. His face radiated delight as he swallowed, and the stout woman blushed.

A soft material grazed Delilah's arm. Cassandra stood beside her. "I'd never in a million years have guessed Aurora had a daughter."

"How come?" Delilah asked.

"She's never talked about her, not once. Even Sebastiano had no idea."

That did seem odd. If Delilah had a child, she would tell the world. But what about a child she'd left behind? That might be too painful to bring up. "How long have they been business partners?"

"Ten years," Cassandra said. "For some reason, I thought Aurora was her real name."

"Are you really Cassandra?"

"Carrie." She grimaced.

"What's wrong with that? It's pretty."

"Lacks presence. What kind of ambition does a parent have for a kid if they write Carrie on the birth certificate?"

Was Julie any improvement? Delilah ambitious? The biblical Delilah had chopped off a man's hair to destroy his strength, but the sound of the name struck her as feminine and old-fashioned. Like Cassandra.

"Next stop, the herb garden." Sebastiano's voice startled her. "We decided the soup could use a touch of basil."

Delilah realized she'd left their purses in the lounge, but they should be safe in this place. Cassandra joined them on their walk out to the garden. She squatted to pluck herbs. Two stone paths crossed through the tufts of green sprigs and stunted trees. Each path led to a cottage.

"Are they six-sided?" Delilah asked.

"Eight," Sebastiano said. "I bunk here." He nodded at the larger octagon.

The path leading from the smaller cottage ended at the open lawn, where Julie might be with her mother. Cassandra started to walk in that direction.

"You can take the basil to the kitchen while it's fresh," Sebastiano said to Cassandra.

She turned and scowled, and then marched back into the building.

Delilah studied the cottage roofs. "Are those thatched?"

"A substance that looks like thatch."

"Why octagon-shaped?"

"I wanted interesting architecture."

"Who lives in the smaller one?"

"The gardener. Garth."

Forest arced around the backs of the cottages. A row of cypress trees between Garth's cottage and the main building blocked the parking lot from view.

Sebastiano guided her toward the lawn. "This is a big day for Aurora."

"Why did you all change your names?"

"To reflect our new lives." He smiled down at her. "You can keep Delilah. It works."

She felt herself flush from his approval. "Did you really not know about Marion's child?"

His lower lip dropped. He paused beside an olive tree. Had she actually caught him off guard?

"Cassandra told me you didn't," she said.

The backs of Julie's and Aurora's heads jutted above a double swing under the tree. Sun shining on Aurora's hair made it look like a silver halo.

"Knowing Aurora as I do," Sebastiano said, "my feeling is she kept Julie's existence to herself because it was deeply important. Aurora and I aren't that close, emotionally. Don't you find that people often hide things that affect them to the core?"

Delilah hadn't told anyone about her love for Eric, even her mother. It felt so peculiar now to only care for him as a friend. How could that sick, hopeless obsession have left her in less than two days? Was it a case of her mind subconsciously churning it through until the process enabled her to let him go? *But how wonderful to be rid of it.*

"They look deep in conversation," Sebastiano said.

On the swing, Julie and Aurora leaned toward one another. Given Julie's hand gestures, it looked as if she was doing most of the talking.

"My mom always says Julie looks like her father and even more like his mother, who helped raised her," Delilah said. "She does, close up, but I can see her resemblance to Aurora in the macro sense—you know, body type, height, movements."

"Julie's father married your mom?"

Delilah nodded. "They met in a single-parent support group. I can't picture him going to something like that, but he was devastated after Marion left him and found it hard to cope with Julie alone."

Sebastiano's lower lip quivered.

"I mean..." She hadn't intended it as a criticism of Marion.

"How old were you and Julie when your parents met?" he asked.

"Ten. They moved in together a year later."

"Julie was lucky to gain a sister. You too."

Delilah quick-stepped to match his stride past olive trees. "We aren't as close as sisters."

"From my years of experience with retreat guests, there are all kinds of sisters."

The hills on the far side, to the west, looked gentler. Semicircular rows of concrete rose up them.

"Is that an amphitheatre?"

"Bang on," Sebastiano said. "Aurora holds her sessions there."

"About these sessions—"

"Also, the sunrise service, which takes place daily at dawn. The theatre's designed so the sun rises behind Aurora."

At the moment, the sun was in front of them, and so blinding that Delilah only now noticed the person kneeling in the flower bed that lined the guest building. A straw hat covered the back of the gardener's head.

"How old was Julie when Marion left?" Sebastiano asked.

"Four. Same age as Julie's daughter now."

"Aurora's a grandmother, too?" He chuckled. "Is Julie married?"

"Separated. Do your guests like getting up so early every day?"

"Sunrise is late this time of year," he said. "And there's not much to stay up for at night. No TV or movie theatres or artificial outdoor lighting. My dream is to buy a high-powered telescope for star viewing. We're in a dark-sky zone."

"What about computers?'

"Most guests bring a tablet or laptops, but we're only wired in the office. They try to get the signal from the lounge or yard. The office walls are too solid."

No computer access; the retreat might not be for her after all.

"The point is to get away from the everyday world," he said. "I'll introduce you to Garth."

As they approached, the gardener jumped up. He's skittish, Delilah thought. She extended her hand. Garth shook his head, raising his dirty palms.

"I hope you enjoy your week here," he said.

"I'm not a guest, only visiting from LA," Delilah explained.

Garth looked about her age. He appeared slight standing next to Sebastiano, but was of average height and weight. With neither of them filling the conversation gap, Delilah struggled for something to say.

"Those are bright flowers, for winter. They must be shaded here most of the time."

"We do our best," Garth said. "In a couple of months, this patch will be a burst of colour." His cheekbones and the shape of his eyes reminded her of Eric.

"I like those orange trumpet-shapes."

Garth twisted around. "Lilies?"

"The yellow daisy-like ones, too."

"Gerbera?"

Her gardening knowledge was limited to turning on the sprinkler in her weedy yard. She spotted a plant she recognized. "Birds-of-paradise. Before California, I didn't know they grew on bushes."

"They're Aurora's favourite," Garth said. "Where are you from?"

"Canada. Short growing season. Snow."

"Delilah is a relative of Aurora's," Sebastiano said.

Garth's eyes widened. Their hazel tones had more yellow than Eric's.

"We'll leave you to your work," Sebastiano told Garth. "Delilah wants a look at the guest rooms."

"Is there space for her to stay?" Garth asked.

"We're fully booked," Sebastiano said. "But she and Julie can sleep in the main building."

"I hope we'll see more of you." Garth stared at Delilah.

"That's not up to me," she said.

Sebastiano nodded. "Depends on Aurora."

Delilah had meant that it depended on Julie. She glanced at her and Aurora on the swing. The dappled sun made their long, lean bodies look like mirror images. Delilah hoped they were building a bond, for Julie's sake. Aurora's too. Sebastiano ushered Delilah into the stone building.

"Do you think Aurora will want Julie to stay?" she asked.

"Knowing Aurora as I do," he said, "I have no idea."

* * *

Julie noticed she'd moved so close to Marion on the swing that their knees almost touched. Across the lawn, Delilah and Sebastiano looked like they were wrapping up their conversation with the gardener.

"So, you're an engineer," Marion said. "Like your father. And with published articles."

"Only in industry magazines."

"Do you like the work?"

"I did." Julie dreaded discussing her leave of absence, even with this woman she had come to accept as Marion, if not yet her mother. To avoid elaborating, she motioned toward the gardener. "He lives on the premises?"

"Garth? He came to us some years ago as a guest and found his place."

Delilah and Sebastiano padded to the end of the guest building and disappeared around the corner. Garth watched them the whole way and returned to his flowers. Facing the sun was hard on Julie's eyes, but she'd left her sunglasses in her purse that was with Delilah. Marion's shades were probably in her purse, too, although her eyes might be accustomed to the California brightness. Julie's mother had built this retreat, re-created herself, in part to shut off a past that included a husband and a daughter, but would she still want to know her child had grown up well? Except, Julie hadn't grown up entirely well, largely due to Marion's abandonment. Marion should know this. Finding each other wasn't enough.

If they were to forge a connection, on some level, it was time to end the rosy slant of the Julie life story. Loved by a devoted grandma to fill the maternal void, an ace high school student, point guard on the school basketball team, plenty of friends, boyfriends—decent ones but not so serious that they distracted her from her studies—graduated from university with distinction, worked in petroleum engineering, a male-dominated field, and married—happily for a while. She might as well blurt it out. "I'm on disability."

Marion blinked and her hand shot to her chest, above her heart. "Are you ill? You look perfectly healthy."

"I'm fine physically. Mentally, after my daughter's birth—"

"You have a daughter?"

"Peyton. She's four." Was that wince Marion's stab of recognition that the child was the same age Julie had been when Marion left her? If so, Julie was glad she'd made the link.

"I have a grandchild," Marion said. "I'd love to meet her. Peyton is a strong name. I like it. And your husband…?"

"Eric. We're separated. I had postpartum depression."

"Oh, Julie." The swing jolted with Marion's sudden movement toward her.

Julie stayed put. No advance or retreat. "I'd heard of it before I had Peyton, but I didn't think that I—"

"It was less known in 1981, when you were born," Marion said. "Or not as much talked about." Her voice sounded distant.

Julie looked up. "You had it?"

"In hindsight, I think I did. I was crying all the time and exhausted. I couldn't cope." Her mouth tightened. Her eyes filled.

Julie's eyes stung in response. For her mother or herself?

"Your father was impatient," Marion said. "He'd come home from work and there'd be no dinner, the house a mess, your soiled clothes in heaps, you wailing. 'What's your problem,' he'd say, or imply. 'Why can't you snap out of it?'

He'd take you, and you'd calm down right away. I felt hopeless."

Julie nodded, throat swollen. "Eric was a natural, too."

"Being more modern, he probably understood."

"Not really." He'd been good about it at the beginning, and he'd supported her choice to shorten her maternity leave and escape to work. The narrator of the last poems in *To Catch a Fox* was a sympathetic husband, reviewers of the book had noted. Julie had faked it at home, had concealed her continuing problems with mothering Peyton. Eric hadn't been sensitive enough to see.

"Without treatment, my depression dragged on for four years," Marion said. "The last straw—this will sound stupid—was when I read a newspaper article that said mothers should sing to their children to increase their brainpower and contentment. It implied—or I interpreted it this way—that if they didn't, the kid would be an imbecile. I felt like a complete failure. I can't sing for beans."

"Me neither."

Marion smiled through her tears. "I wasn't rational."

"No one's rational in that state." Julie had thought drowning Peyton would save her.

"That's why I left," Marion said. "I believed, in that horrible mind frame, you were better off without me."

"I wasn't."

"Julie, I'm so sorry." Marion's hands reached for Julie's. Gentle, loving mother's hands.

Julie drew away. She had to think about all this, before letting her mother off so fast. "Should we go inside? You'll need to get ready for your guests."

"They can wait."

"There's Delilah," Julie said. Delilah and Sebastiano had emerged from the guest building and were walking to the amphitheatre. "Do you have shows there?"

"It's not uncommon for guests from Los Angeles to have an interest in theatre or film. Sometimes they want to organize little plays or skits. We encourage it for self-expression and evening entertainment, although the theatre is mainly used for my sessions."

Julie could ask about them later. "How did you end up buying this retreat?"

"We built it from scratch," Marion said. "Largely from money I saved from my jobs over the years."

"You worked in a bike-rental shop."

Marion's forehead wrinkled. "Briefly, when I first moved to Santa Monica. I'd almost forgotten. From there, I got into hotel reception and, eventually, management. Not high wages, but I was frugal."

"Like Dad." He and Marion had at least that in common.

"Sebastiano also came into a small inheritance."

"How did you meet?"

"He was my surfing instructor."

That matched Sebastiano's story. Had his young friend really committed suicide when Marion rejected him?

"Surfing helped to change how I felt about my own worth—it pushed me beyond my physical limits. In addition, I read a lot and meditated with a wise guru. All of this led to epiphanies and a desire to help others achieve what I had. To my surprise, I find helping them nourishes me. I learn from every guest at the New Dawn Retreat. It's a beautiful circle that has made me a new person."

So, Marion had turned her life around. But meditation. Gurus. Surfing. Becoming a new person. Julie's father would scoff at all this, and he was likely even less hip in the early 1980s. His scorn would have shut down his insecure and depressed wife. How could Julie blame Marion for abandoning her child when she had done worse?

"I know what you're thinking," Marion said. "If I transformed myself ten years ago, why didn't I try to get in touch with you? But the longer I delayed the more awkward it felt. Another part, I think, is that I wanted to wait for you to find me when you were ready."

"What if I hadn't?"

"You did."

"Dad started the search."

"You pursued it."

"It was only luck that I found this retreat. So many variables could have gotten in the way."

"I don't believe in chance. You came to me when the time was right." Marion's eyes shone. "If your first approach hadn't worked out, you'd have tried another and another until a path led you here."

"Possibly." She'd said as much to Delilah, when she worried that their first lead, Terry, would brush them off.

Marion patted Julie's hand. "It's warm out. Shall we go in for some fruit punch? I'd like to show you my rooms. You'll be spending the night? You can't leave now."

"We didn't bring our things. Delilah might want to go back." Although now, she realized, they had no other business in LA. They'd found what they were looking for.

"No one needs things here. I have a collection of robes that would look lovely on you."

"Does everyone wear a robe, except the gardener?"

"Male guests wear togas, although some prefer the shorter tunic vest, with leggings."

"Sebastiano?"

"Definitely tunic."

Julie rose from the swing feeling as if a small weight had lifted. Dressing up would be strange, but she wanted to learn about her mother's new life. She hoped Delilah would agree to stay.

Chapter Seventeen

Delilah marvelled at the robes hanging in Aurora's closet, organized by colour. Each shade blended into the next like a rainbow. Aurora pulled several out, held them up to Delilah's and Julie's faces, returned some to the closet and handed others to the seamstress. A half-dozen robes now weighed down the tiny woman's arm.

Aurora took out a mint-green robe. "The ancient Romans called them stolas," she said. "I tried to use that name, but it wouldn't stick. This one isn't quite perfect for me but might bring out the red tones in Julie's hair and suit her darker skin."

"How do you not tan or burn if you're outside twice a day at sessions?" Julie asked.

"Herbal sunscreen." Aurora added the mint-green to the seamstress' pile.

The woman's arm sagged. Delilah offered to hold some robes, but the seamstress draped her other arm protectively over the pile as Aurora returned to the walk-in closet. Julie paced to the chaise lounge by the window that overlooked the path into the retreat.

"Aurora's robes will be too tight and long for me," Delilah told the seamstress.

"No trouble to hem and let out a few tucks," she said. "It's my job every Saturday afternoon."

"Looks like plenty here for your guests to choose from."

"These are Aurora's." The seamstress sandwiched the robes tighter. "Guests have their own wardrobe in the other building."

So that's what Sebastiano had meant by wardrobe room. It had been locked when he toured Delilah through the guest building's two floors. The lounge was similar to the one downstairs but had less plush furnishings. Each guest room had just enough space for a bed, dresser, and a small bathroom with a shower. A storage locker housed the guests' suitcases, filled with street clothes, computers, cell phones, watches, cameras, and anything else they wouldn't use for the week. Photography wasn't permitted on-site.

"Not so much for privacy," Sebastiano had explained. "Taking pictures reduces the immediate experience by shifting it to the future."

Delilah was too overwhelmed to ponder the depths of this. "I don't know if I'd manage without the internet."

"There are always a few who drive into town for their fix," he said. "More than a few sneak pictures when they're leaving."

"How do they contact family and friends?"

"They don't," he'd said. "And valuables like jewellery can be locked in the main building, although, in ten years, we've never had a theft."

"That's enough choice for us," Julie said, from her spot beside the velvet upholstered chaise lounge. She turned to the window.

Julie had seemed distracted since her conversation with Aurora. When Aurora took Sebastiano aside to consult him on a retreat matter, Delilah had asked Julie how the talk had gone.

"Not bad," Julie had said, and looked away.

Her evasive answer had prompted Delilah to jump in with babble about her discoveries. "The guest rooms are monastic. Bare walls. Sebastiano says the nothingness inspires people to conjure their own images, although he admitted that repeat visitors often bring pictures. About a tenth are repeaters. Sebastiano says they come for booster shots."

Halfway through Delilah's details about meeting Garth, the gardener, Julie had said, "What do you think about staying tonight?"

"Of course, you can't leave." Aurora had appeared beside Julie. "We've barely begun." She'd whisked them upstairs, showed them their bedrooms and led them into her suite, which occupied half the upper floor.

While Aurora and the seamstress continued searching the closet and Julie gazed outside, Delilah studied the suite, which looked like something out of a French château. Aurora's canopy bed, draped with curtains, had a tapestry headboard. The mattress was so high Aurora needed a footstool to climb onto it. A floral bedspread, oriental carpet, and fabric wallpaper picked up the room's dominant mauve and blue colours. Julie edged away from the chaise lounge.

"Wouldn't you love to lie on that all day?" Delilah said. "Reading Jane Austen, dozing in the sun, and wearing an Empire dress."

Julie crossed to a door that was slightly ajar.

"That's my bathroom." Aurora emerged from the closet.

Julie looked in. "Marble counter. Is that Italian tile? Oh, and a soaker tub."

Aurora smiled. "I'm on display downstairs every waking hour. I need comfort to regenerate." She nodded at the seamstress. "We'll try these on in Julie's room." She motioned for them to follow.

The bedroom Aurora had assigned to Julie was about a third of the suite's size. Its Italian Renaissance–style furniture looked less elegant than Aurora's furnishings, but more solid.

"Are these antiques?" Delilah asked.

"Copies," Aurora said. "We aren't rich enough to import originals." She helped the seamstress lay the robes on the bed, which was normal height.

According to Sebastiano, the retreat had taken eight years to turn a profit. It would have happened faster if they hadn't bought the farm across the hill when the owner defaulted on his loan.

"Aurora wants to let the farm revert to its natural state," Sebastiano had said. "Or, at most, dot it with cottages for guests who desire a more isolated experience. I say we have the money now to build a satellite retreat. Let's go for it."

Delilah had dared a joke. "You sound more like a businessman than a spiritual leader."

He'd grinned. "I'm the practical half of this team."

"We'll leave you two alone to change," Aurora said, and bustled the seamstress out of the room.

Delilah stared at the palette of robes on the bed. The room's only chair had walnut legs, with lion heads carved into them. It felt like days, rather than hours, since they'd set out from the tacky apartment with its fake-animal-skin cushions and erotic paintings. On this room's dresser, the cupids firing arrows at one another around a clock were classy erotic. Julie lingered by the dresser.

Delilah didn't like undressing in front of Julie—or anyone—but she pulled off her T-shirt and pants. "Our folks will be wondering what's happened." Feeling cool in her underwear, she quickly slipped a blue robe over her head. The neckband caught on her watch. "Sebastiano says they don't need watches here. A staff person rings a bell to signal the day's activities."

"Let's wait and see how it goes before emailing Rosemary and my dad," Julie said.

"Won't they be excited about us finding your mother?" Although, not necessarily in a positive way. They'd certainly be shocked to learn that Marion wasn't dead or destitute. She was alive and a blooming success. This property, now extending beyond the lower hill, must be worth...Delilah had no idea. And Marion—should she say Aurora?—exuded such confidence, holding her tall body so straight. It made Delilah conscious of slouching. She fiddled with the robe bodice that gripped her chest. It would need more than a few tucks let out. "You must have gotten along okay with your mother, since you want to stay."

"She had postpartum depression." Julie looked at the mannequin between the dresser and chair. "I'd wondered about that. It explains a lot."

"You mean, why she would leave you?"

If Marion had been as depressed as Delilah was last fall, it was easy to understand her doing anything to get away. In that flat mood, Delilah couldn't have felt the sensuousness of this cotton on her skin. Thank heavens for medication. She swished the skirt of her robe back and forth. It dragged on the floor.

"Oh, I forgot," Delilah said.

"What?"

"We left our meds in the apartment."

"One day without them won't kill us." Julie's elbow nudged the mannequin. The slim female torso on a pole wobbled and regained its footing. Julie stepped to the four-poster bed. "Might as well give the stola a try. As they say, when in Rome…"

Someone knocked on the door. Aurora asked if they were dressed.

"Come in," Julie said.

Aurora entered, trailed by the seamstress.

Delilah smoothed the robe over her hips. "With your tucking and hemming, will this look okay?"

"Okay isn't good enough." Aurora picked up the amber robe.

"That's not really my colour," Delilah said.

"How will you know until you've tried it?"

Julie took off her shirt and capris in front of her mother and the seamstress with no sign of shyness. And why would she be modest, with her slim body? And no stretch marks. Delilah squeezed out of the blue robe and put on the amber one.

"Is this silk?" she asked.

"Cotton so fine it mimics silk." Aurora stepped back to study the effect. "It's you, Delilah. Truly, it is. The hue heightens the gold tints in your skin."

"Mom always says yellow makes me look pasty." Delilah leaned into the dresser mirror. Her skin glowed. Amazing.

"You look great," Julie said.

Delilah smiled, her face looking radiant. "From now on, I'll shop for my clothes with you," she said jokingly to Aurora.

The seamstress fussed with the folds in Delilah's robe. Then, standing on tiptoe, she swept Delilah's hair up into a top knot.

"Wow," Delilah said, looking at her reflection. "Is it the lighting?"

"This robe brings out the inner you," Aurora said. "You're beautiful."

Delilah's gold-toned skin flushed. Her own mother had called her, at best, pretty.

The mint-green robe fit Julie as though it were custom-made. A clasp secured the fabric on one shoulder.

Aurora touched the mole on Julie's bare shoulder. "Notice the beauty of imperfections when you highlight them." She attached a sheer cape, the same mint green as the robe, to Julie's shoulder clasp and circled Julie's waist with a rope belt of darker mint. Aurora paused, her hands on the rope, which dangled to Julie's calves. "For a second, I felt I was dressing you for your graduation. I'm sorry I missed that."

"I'm sorry too." Julie's tone had a bite.

Aurora struggled to make a knot.

"Let me." Julie pushed her mother's hands away and secured the knot.

"Impressive skill."

"Dad signed me up for Girl Guides, so I'd have a female role model."

Aurora's lips tightened. Delilah wondered if this overnighter would be less fun than she'd thought. Julie was right again. Best to see how it played out before contacting their parents.

Aurora pinned Julie's auburn hair back from her forehead with a barrette, leaving it loose by her ears. When Julie wore this hairstyle, she usually tied it more severely. Aurora wove green silk leaves through the barrette. The seamstress gushed that Julie looked splendid. Delilah agreed.

"Now I must hurry to dress for my guests," Aurora said. "Some are already waiting." Suddenly, her knees sank. She grabbed the chair.

Julie, with a look of concern, gripped Aurora's arm. Perhaps a bond was forming.

"I'm fine." Aurora regained her balance and pulled herself straight. "I felt light-headed, for a second." She smiled shakily at Julie. "Must be the excitement of this astonishing day. I'll meet you downstairs." She shuffled from the room.

"Is there something the matter with her?" Julie asked the seamstress.

"I've not known Aurora to be sick for one day," the seamstress said. "Could be a blood-pressure drop. At her age and mine, it can do somersaults."

"I'll check if she's all right."

"She'd prefer you leave her alone. Aurora likes to dress herself."

"Then I'll go out for some air," Julie said. "It's stuffy in here."

The seamstress licked her lips, as though tasting the stale air. "That might have caused her dizziness. I'll open the window. This room doesn't get used a lot."

"Do guests ever stay up here?" Delilah asked.

"Only Cassandra," the seamstress said. "In the far bedroom."

"She's a guest, not staff?"

The seamstress extended her arms. "Give me your robe, so I can adjust it before the stampede starts."

"Sorry to put you to such trouble on arrival day."

"Aurora says you two are my priority." She glanced down. "Your sandals are slinky enough to wear with the robe. Julie can borrow a pair of Aurora's."

"What's wrong with these?" Julie raised her foot, clad in an athletic sandal.

The seamstress scrunched her nose.

Despite her clunky shoes, Julie glided from the room, looking like a Roman goddess. Delilah slipped off her robe. The seamstress opened her sewing chest and scrutinized the hundred or so spools of thread. She held several against the amber fabric before choosing the best match. Delilah put on her T-shirt for warmth and settled on the hard chair with its rigid back. There was a definite hierarchy at the retreat. Aurora, number one; Sebastiano, a close second; Garth, the gardener, far behind; and Cassandra, status unclear. Delilah wiggled her butt. This chair wasn't designed for sitting.

The seamstress sat on the bed, the lovely amber material flowing over her lap. Her fingers moved swiftly around the robe hem.

"Do you ever sew by machine?" Delilah asked. So far, she'd mainly heard Sebastiano's take on the retreat. It would be interesting to get the perspectives of others involved.

"At home. This works best for quick alterations on-site."

Twenty-two guests a week created a lot of sewing. "Do you do all the alterations?"

"I have assistants in town. I'm the only one who comes here."

Sebastiano had told her Aurora was so attentive to her guests that she'd remember all of their names by tonight. She also made every effort to get to know her staff on a personal level.

"What was your name, again?"

"Francisca."

"Do you make new robes in town?"

"Every week. To replace the ones people buy to take home at the end of their stay."

"For souvenirs?"

"And many prefer a change of robe for the last half of their stay. I come Wednesdays to fit them. Saturday morning, I go through the guest wardrobe to remove Aurora's colours for the week. None of the guests can wear the same shades as her."

"Like the Queen," Delilah said.

The seamstress kept sewing, her gaze on the material. Delilah hoped that hadn't come across as her mocking Aurora.

"How does Aurora pick her colours each week?"

"Instinct. Since we were occupied with you, I'll have to stop by Aurora's room to see which shades she's decided on."

"I've delayed the whole process."

"Finished." Francisca bit off the thread.

The bronze cupid clock said 3:55 p.m. Most days, Sebastiano had told her, dinner was at six, but Saturdays it was delayed to eight, to allow everyone time to arrive and get fitted and dressed.

"Can I help in some way this afternoon?" Delilah asked.

"We've got our routine and tasks in place."

There wasn't enough time to drive to LA for their meds and return for dinner. If Julie prolonged their stay, she'd go tomorrow alone to give Julie more time with her mother.

Delilah put on the amber robe again. It now hugged her curves firmly, no pinching. The colour truly enhanced tones in her skin she'd never dreamed she possessed. Her former jealousy of Julie's perfect skin and everything else about her seemed petty now, a waste of energy and time. The biggest waste was her twelve-year crush on Eric. He didn't want her. *Grow up, that's life.* Instead of letting go, she'd nurtured an obsession that might have been less about him and more about Delilah wanting to be Julie—wanting Julie's confidence and brains, her role as wife, super career woman, and mother.

"Go ahead and nap," Francisca said, as they left the room. "Read, explore the premises, anything you like. You're free."

Delilah would be free, in so many ways, if this mood continued.

Chapter Eighteen

Aurora entered the lounge, her body erect. The pain radiating from her collarbone area was bearable with her torso straight. She couldn't see anyone in the room, but went over to check a secluded conversation nook.

"Cassandra processed the first batch," Sebastiano said, from behind her.

Aurora jerked around. Agony shot up her neck, stabbed her arm and chest. She gritted her lips to keep from wincing.

"The lull before the onslaught arrives," he said. "She's registering the last of them now."

Aurora rotated carefully toward her office. The door was closed, but no sound would get through, even if Cassandra were screaming in there. She looked at him pointedly. "After which, she'll march upstairs to pack her bags. I want Cassandra off the property before dinner."

"That's small thanks when she's doing all your work so you can reconnect with your daughter." Sebastiano moved directly in front of her. "Who knew you had such maternal instincts? Who even knew that you had a child, and one as appealing as Julie?"

Her core inside tensed. How he was enjoying these upsets to her life. He'd better not make this situation worse. "Will you be chasing her like the others?"

He smoothed his tunic vest and the white shirt that set off his tan. The open collar provided a teasing glimpse of his muscular chest. "What was the biopsy result?"

"I saw the doctor this morning," she said. "No spread to the lymph nodes. They scraped everything out. My body is completely clear."

He squinted at her. "Is that the truth?"

"Why would I lie?"

"So you could be back here, in control."

She shifted her gaze between the hall and office door in case someone appeared. The building's front door behind her would chime for a new arrival. Julie was outside. From her bedroom, Aurora had watched her daughter disappear into the lemon grove between the pool and guest building.

"Any chemo or radiation would start this week," Aurora said. "You'd know soon enough if I needed it."

"Unless you opted out of further treatment."

"And let the cancer eat me up? I'm not suicidal."

He maintained his skeptical squint. Good to keep him guessing.

"Seriously," he said. "While you're recovering, why not let Cassandra relieve you of the drudge work? You hate computer crap."

They turned toward the door chime. A woman in her thirties entered. Thin. Dark bob. Red rectangular glasses. Her face lit up at the sight of Sebastiano. The woman's gaze remained on him as Aurora led her to a love seat by the window.

In a twangy voice, the woman described her flight from Little Rock. "Ah almost missed the connection in Houston. Ah had to run…"

Aurora was glad to sit down. Delilah soon appeared at the hallway entrance, and Sebastiano spoke to her briefly before greeting a couple walking in the door. Cassandra emerged from the office with a guest. She left her to shake hands with the new couple. On her way, she caught Aurora's glare and turned aside. Cassandra motioned the pair into the office, even though the Arkansan had arrived first.

"Ah can't stomach airplane food. Ah just can't…"

When the door chimed Julie in, Sebastiano flashed his largest smile. Above the Arkansan's chatter, Aurora strained to hear what Julie told him.

"Costume" was all Aurora made out.

"You too." Sebastiano made no effort to lower his voice. "You cut a fine impression."

Julie's body eased toward him. He said something that made her turn to Aurora. How beautiful Julie looked in the mint-green robe. Stately. She walked gracefully to the love seat, and Aurora introduced her to the guest from Arkansas. What was the woman's name? She'd neglected to ask. She was slipping. Too many distractions.

"Aurora's daughter? It's an honour." The Arkansan stood and grasped Julie's hand.

Julie could put herself to use by relieving her. "If you would excuse me." Aurora left them together.

As she edged toward Sebastiano, a trio of fortyish women breezed in and swarmed him, giggling. He guided them to Aurora and made a beeline to a pair of men, one handsome and compact, the other older and fat. Delilah sat on the love seat in the middle of the room, engaged in conversation with the guest that Cassandra had registered. Aurora took the three women to the sofa across from them. She sunk into the chair angling the sofa. How had she and Sebastiano managed this all on their own before? It made sense to let Cassandra do the grunt work.

Aurora struggled to follow the women's explanation of this girls' week away. Their laughs were spikes to her aching head. She glanced sideways and saw a man shuffling through the room. His tentative gaze suggested he was perfect for her to handle. She abandoned the gigglers and linked her arm through the man's just as Cassandra and the now-registered couple appeared from the office. Cassandra's smirk said *I beat you.*

Aurora lowered her eyelashes. *I'll let you think that.*

She eased the man toward a chair by the fireplace. He spoke haltingly and managed to stutter that he was an insurance clerk who wanted to improve his relationships.

Cassandra called the Arkansan in to register. Yelling across the lounge rather than going over to invite the guest in was crude, and typical of Cassandra. Sebastiano slid onto the love seat with Julie. From her chair, Aurora could only see them from their foreheads up. Julie had been born with brown hair, not red. Brilliant of her to have dyed it those splendid auburn tones, obviously done at a professional salon. The colour-riff on her Fox name was clever and attractive. Julie had learned, at a much younger age than

Aurora, that you didn't have to settle for what you were given. You could choose your own life.

The insurance man droned through his tales of failed girlfriends and relatives who were, naturally, fed up with his snivelling. Sebastiano's laugh rippled through the room. The gigglers stretched their necks for a better look at him and at Julie. She stood out as special, while Delilah blended in. That might also be useful. Delilah acted enthused about the retreat, less hesitant about it than Julie, and easier to influence.

Leaving Julie with Brad had been the right decision. Aurora's old ways, Marion's ways, would have tainted Julie, diminished her. Brad and his nasty mother, for all their flaws, had the strength of people who were sure of themselves and able to take what they wanted from the world. They had passed that strength along to Julie. Her postpartum depression was a glitch. With Aurora's help, Julie would work through that and secure the retreat's future. This was why her daughter had come to her at this particular time.

Sebastiano leaned into Julie. His flirting style came across as original to someone who hadn't watched him in action for ten years. Julie's head inched toward his dark hair. Sebastiano and Julie. Did Aurora want that for her daughter?

The insurance man stammered a thank you to Aurora for listening. She smiled warmly. Whatever he'd said she'd heard a hundred times before. Everyone who came here from the outside world felt disconnected and unfulfilled.

Sebastiano's hand grazed Julie's arm. She didn't shrink from his touch. He could be a key to inducing Julie to stay.

When the last arrival disappeared into the office with Cassandra, Aurora rose from her chair. The other guests had departed for their residence building to select their robes and have them adjusted. Delilah wandered to the bookshelves. Aurora approached Sebastiano and Julie and suggested they take the last guest to the residence so Julie could see the building.

Cassandra opened the office door. "All done, aside from a woman whose flight was delayed. She won't arrive before nine."

By then Cassandra would be gone.

Aurora mustered her strength to deal with her. "I'd like to talk to you for a few minutes."

Cassandra glanced at Sebastiano. He waved a hand in salute and guided Julie and the guest outside. If he thought Cassandra could stand up to Aurora on this matter, he was wrong.

Aurora motioned Cassandra into the office and closed the soundproofed door. "You've been a great help to me."

"Thank you."

"How did you and Sebastiano get along this week?"

"Fine."

Enough evasion. Aurora fixed her gaze, so she wouldn't miss a cue. "Are you sleeping together?"

Cassandra's eyebrows shot up. Aurora read the answer behind the slut's glare. If Julie stayed, Sebastiano would be forced to choose. Aurora suspected Julie wasn't the type to share a man with another woman, or even accept his ex-lover's presence.

"Unfortunately," Aurora continued, "we no longer need your services."

"By we, do you mean Sebastiano as well?"

"I'm certain he enjoyed your assistance. The situation has changed."

"If you mean your daughter turning up, do you really think she's interested in this?" Cassandra's arm swept the room of antique furnishings juxtaposed against the modern computer. "I'll make a deal with you."

"I don't deal."

"I'll take care of the office while you groom Julie."

The girl was too astute. She also wasn't fooling her. Cassandra wanted a foothold for her goal of replacing her.

"You used to be a store manager," Aurora said. "Will you be happy as a clerk?"

Cassandra edged to the bookcase. "All I want is to be part of the operation."

Bullshit. Aurora tilted her head.

"I really do. It's more meaningful than running a grocery store."

By her own account, Cassandra had been competent at her work but less successful in her personal life, with a habit of choosing men who lacked the capacity for commitment. Sebastiano was a continuation of that pattern.

"I realize your daughter will take precedence over me," Cassandra said.

Damn right. "My decision is final."

Cassandra bit her lower lip.

"Francisca, the seamstress, has a spare room in her house. I'll talk to her about putting you up tonight. You can take the next few hours to pack and say goodbye to the staff." Aurora extended her hand.

Cassandra brushed by her, out of the office.

Your anger is fine with me. Aurora dropped to her desk chair to regenerate, too tired to go over and shut the door. She closed her eyes and pictured the double swing moving back and forth under the valley oak tree. Forward and back, forward, back.

There was a tentative knock on the open door. "Aurora?"

She opened her eyes. Delilah.

"Would you mind if I used your computer to email my mother? I don't want to phone her yet, but she might worry something's wrong if she doesn't hear from me."

"Did you tell her you were coming here?"

"No, but we've been in touch almost every day."

Aurora massaged her neck. "You're fortunate to be close to your mother."

"I know." Delilah entered the office. "Sometimes I think it's too close, like I haven't grown away from her enough. I mean, how many thirty-eight-year-olds have a mother for a best friend?"

Aurora rotated her shoulder, inwardly cringing at the pain. "I blame myself daily for leaving Julie. It was the worst thing a mother could do."

"I didn't mean to make you feel guilty."

"Would you mind closing the door?"

Aurora stood and directed Delilah to the computer chair. By the time Aurora walked around her desk, Delilah had logged in to her email.

"You know your way around computers." Aurora hovered behind her.

"I waste hours a day on mine, since I lost my job. You know, social networking, games, surfing websites, email. It eats up your time."

"Do you know about blogging?"

"I thought of writing one, but what would I say?"

"I hear websites are dead. It's about apps."

Delilah cocked her head, as though considering. "Both have their uses."

"I'll leave you alone."

"It's not especially private." Delilah studied her inbox. "A whole bunch from Mom. One from Eric, Julie's husband."

Delilah's hand rested on the mouse, as though waiting for Aurora to move out of sight range. Aurora stepped back. Delilah clicked the message open.

"Julie told Eric that we learned you died," Delilah said.

"I thought she'd kept it from them."

"She did from her father."

But Julie had been open with her estranged husband. "Are she and Eric close, despite their separation?"

"I don't know." Delilah's gaze remained on the screen.

Julie had implied that Eric took to parenting more naturally than she had. "Julie told me about Peyton," Aurora said. "I'm thrilled to have a granddaughter. She sounds like a smart, strong little girl."

"Oh yes. Most kids who've gone through…"

"What?" Maternal abandonment?

Delilah's back tightened. But Julie was only away on a trip. She hadn't abandoned Peyton, had she?

Delilah appeared to be scanning Eric's message. She swivelled toward Aurora. "Do you think Julie would be okay if I tell him about the retreat?"

"I expect she'd like him to know I'm alive. Julie won't have time to do it herself today."

"I'll just say our information was wrong and reassure him that Julie and I are here with you and all is well. Julie can send more details later."

"I was wondering," Aurora said. "Do Julie and Eric share custody?"

"He has it. Julie sees her on weekends." Delilah returned to the computer.

The husband with sole custody. Unusual. "Is Julie happy with the arrangement?"

"She agreed to it." Delilah's fingers remained still on the keyboard. "I don't know if she's happy with it, exactly."

Much to probe. "Tell Eric I'm delighted that you and Julie found me." What else could she send through Delilah? She had to take care, since Eric might be less reticent with Julie's parents than Delilah thought. Being the bearer of news made people feel important. Quite likely, Eric would phone Brad to say that his first wife had been found. Aurora struggled to conjure up Brad's face. All she managed to picture were narrow eyes, a sharp nose, and brown hair in a business cut. In the beginning, she'd found his looks tolerable, but never attractive. What had drawn her to him? His steadiness, basic decency, and intelligence. And his obsession with her, which he lost when Julie was born and Marion wouldn't play the Mommy role.

Delilah's fingers flew over the keyboard. She would make an excellent clerk and website manager. At New Dawn she would find plenty to say in blogs, on apps, through social media. She would also be company for Julie, if Julie stayed. But what about Peyton and those unhappy weekend visits? Why not replace them with happy visits to the retreat? Peyton could visit here every few months to splash in the pool, run around the yard, and climb trees. Might it help convince Julie to stay if she saw how much fun her daughter would have at the retreat?

"Add that I'd love to meet my beautiful granddaughter," Aurora said. "She's welcome, any time."

Delilah turned around. "You mean, to come here with Julie on a future trip?"

"Or if Julie were already here, we'd pick up Peyton at the airport."

"I doubt Eric would let her fly alone. She's only four."

So, he was protective, like Brad. Predictable that Julie would choose a husband like her father. "Eric could bring her," Aurora said, unsure if this was wise. "I'd like to meet him, since he's a part of Julie's life."

"I can't see Eric here." Delilah stroked the robe over her lap.

As conventional as Brad. Aurora couldn't wait for Brad to find out that she'd turned her life into a success, and not fallen into ruin as he'd expected and undoubtedly hoped.

"You'll regret this, Marion," he'd shouted when she walked out of his house.

She wished she'd paused to spit back a clever answer. She had her answer for him now, but she'd let Delilah tell it her own way, naturally and honestly. Aurora leaned over Delilah, bracing her whole body against the pain. "Try to give Eric a positive impression of us."

Delilah smiled up at her. "That will be easy."

Chapter Nineteen

Delilah strode from the office, too pumped to return to reading in the lounge. Down the hall, staff shuttled trays and dishes between the kitchen and dining room, their movements orchestrated to avoid collisions. To not disturb their flow, Delilah avoided the back exit in favour of slipping out the front door.

Late-day sun glowed through the citrus trees on the gentle slope. If she weren't afraid of stumbling on her robe, she would run to the top of the amphitheatre and shout to the world, "I'm over Eric." Reading his message, writing her reply, she'd felt no more for him than sisterly affection. The fantasy obsession had vanished. She snapped her fingers.

She walked—floated?—toward the guest building. Was Julie in there? Delilah wished she could share her freedom from Eric with Julie. Or anyone. That was the problem with secrets.

Delilah continued on the path past the building and discovered a fruit and vegetable garden that extended south to a barbed-wire fence. Beyond the fence were hills and trees that had to be private land or a nature preserve. Strangely, while in the main building or yard, she didn't think of the outside world. That was the point of the New Dawn Retreat. She traipsed by rows of strawberries and ripening tomatoes, a few of them luscious enough to pluck. From the garden, she wove through lemon trees to the pool. A woman swam laps. A guest in a lounge chair waved at Delilah. She made a mental note to bring their bathing suits back with the meds tomorrow, assuming she and Julie stayed. In fact, she'd collect everything so they wouldn't have to return to the apartment at all. Their flight was six days from now, although this could be changed for a fee, if Julie wanted to remain longer. Delilah had nothing to run home to. At this moment, she would gladly live here forever.

She halted on her way back through the lemon trees. Was she replacing her obsession for Eric with one for the retreat? If so, this felt healthier, like progress. New Dawn was about finding yourself, being yourself, living your dreams, like Julie's mother did.

Two figures strolled by the olive grove terracing up the high hills. Julie and Sebastiano. He swirled his hands in wild gestures. Julie said something in reply. They disappeared into the trees.

Delilah continued to the middle of the lawn, where a man stood under the oak tree. The gardener, Garth, in his coveralls without his straw hat, bent over the glider chair. Delilah swished toward him, her robe brushing the grass. The seamstress could have hemmed it a notch shorter.

Garth looked up as she approached. "Delilah?"

Strands of sandy hair fell over his forehead, a colour and style similar to Eric's, yet longer, lighter.

Garth held up a can with a spout. "Aurora asked me to oil the squeak in the swing. To be honest, I can't hear a sound. Do you want to try?" He gave the large swing a push.

As it glided, Delilah leaned forward to listen. Silence. She shook her head.

Garth walked around the swing, pouring drops of oil on each nut and bolt. "Aurora can be sensitive."

"Is this part of your job?"

"I do odd repairs, like if they need someone right away to fix a toilet or faucet drip."

"Do you take care of that huge garden out back?"

"Occasionally guests help out, saying it's therapeutic," Garth said. "More help with picking and eating the fruit."

"You must have a ton of work." Delilah gestured around the yard. "All the flowers. The orchards, too? Mowing this huge lawn."

"That's only once a week, during the changeover between guests." Garth straightened from his oiling. "Let's see if that did the trick."

"How can we tell when we didn't hear anything before?"

He laughed. His plain features were suddenly handsome. "It might make a difference with someone on it. Do you want to try swinging?"

Delilah settled on the wood seat and pumped her legs forward and back. Garth circled the swing, listening. Without his hat, he looked younger than she'd thought. Around thirty-five, she estimated, a few years younger than her. The chair moved easily, noiselessly. Could she suggest he sit beside her?

She dropped her legs and dragged them to slow the motion. "What do you do when you aren't working?"

He held up the oil can. "I have to return this to the shed."

"Where's that?"

"Between the guest building and pool."

"I was just there. All I saw were trees." She hopped off the swing. The bare branches hovered a few feet above their heads. She pointed to the hill behind the amphitheatre, liking how her robe's sleeve expanded and fluttered downward. "Sebastiano said they bought a property over there that they use for hikes."

"The easier ones, due to the gentle lay of the land." He nodded the other way, at the olive-tree terrace. "The harder ones go up to the state park."

No sign of Julie and Sebastiano in the groves. "All these hills," Delilah said. "No wonder I can't get cell-phone reception."

"You'd think Aurora had planned it that way."

They scrunched over grass to the large shed that she'd inexplicably missed. "Buildings and people pop up from nowhere around here."

Garth chuckled. He unlocked the shed door.

"Was it intentional, keeping the mechanical operations of this place hidden from guests?" Delilah asked.

"As much as possible."

The lawn tractor, gardening tools, and pool equipment were neatly organized in the shed. Garth placed the can on a shelf and locked the door behind them. They passed the pool. The swimmer was gone, but a lone woman sat at the poolside, her legs dangling in the water.

"It's not fenced," Delilah said. "Do you ever get families with children?"

"Not since I've been here."

"How long is that?"

"Going on eight years."

They walked beside the olive trees. "What brought you here?" Delilah asked.

"Came as a guest," he said. "Chicago, my home city, made me a bundle of nerves. Few times I went back, it drove me crazy. I'm not going again."

"What about your relatives?"

"From now on, they'll have to come to see me."

"Have any done that?"

"Not yet."

"They could register as guests for a week."

His laugh was dry. "I don't think so."

In the herb garden, scents of oregano and rosemary mingled with cooking aromas flowing from the kitchen. Unlike Sebastiano, Garth didn't make Delilah feel inferior. Eric had done that, too, because she'd placed him on a pedestal. She and Garth stood on even ground, literally this instant, on the stone path.

"That's your house ahead?" she said. "The octagonal shape is interesting." She had an urge to see the inside.

"I read."

"Pardon?"

"When I'm not working. One of the kitchen staff brings me books from the town library."

"What kind of books do you like?"

He stepped off the path, bringing them to eye level. "History, philosophy. Gardening books, some fiction, especially modern classics. Right now, I'm reading *Catch-22*.

"I loved that novel," Delilah said. "It's hilarious."

"Makes me laugh out loud, but heavy meanings too."

"I'd like to see your cottage," she said, startled by her boldness.

Garth didn't appear surprised by her request. The octagon's door wasn't locked. Inside, a double bed butted against the west wall. He said the door behind it led to the bathroom. To their left, a jacket and sweater hung from hooks. A table and chair stood under the window, which angled toward Sebastiano's cottage and the woods. Garth opened the door on the east wall to show her the patio, where he liked to read on summer nights. Beyond, lay forest and his treehouse.

"Treehouse?" she asked.

Garth flushed. "Kid stuff, I know."

"I always thought they were neat."

"My parents wouldn't buy me one, said they were dangerous, so I built one here on my own."

"Do you go up to the treehouse to read?"

"When I want to be alone."

She glanced at the single chair. It didn't get more alone than this simple room. "Do you eat in here?"

"I have most meals with the kitchen staff. We clean up the food that's left after the guests. Saturday dinner's late, so one of them brings me a plate beforehand."

He rubbed his stained hands. His body smelled sweaty from his long day of work, and he was probably longing for a shower. She thanked him for showing her his place.

"Are you staying the week?" he asked.

"Not likely that long."

"I hope you do." His face went red.

Her heart raced. Garth's eyes, browner than hazel in the dim light, stared at her, his expression serious. Dirt smudged his cheekbone. She wanted to reach over and wipe it off his skin.

* * *

"No fair," Julie said. "You're wearing boots."

Sebastiano jogged ahead, up the steep, narrow trail. The show-off. She held up her robe hem, stepping daintily. Her sandal struck a root. She continued uphill, looking down at the path so she wouldn't trip, and banged into him.

"Why did you stop?" she asked, and then understood.

They had reached a ledge overlooking the retreat. From this height, the tiny buildings and trees reminded Julie of the farm she was making, her surprise gift for Peyton. Across the valley, the amphitheatre crept up a low hill.

"Is the farm you bought past there?" she asked.

"I'll show it to you later. First, I wanted to test you on this hike."

"Test?" she said. "You try hiking in sandals and a gown."

He laughed.

She folded her arms. "I don't like being tested."

"You passed with aces, considering your restraints. Guests who do the harder hikes wear tunics and boots."

Sebastiano raised a leg and crossed it over his other thigh to show her the deep grooves in the sole of his boot. He balanced perfectly. Hikes twice a day worked his leg muscles and core, he'd said. Julie sniffed his spicy aftershave. His upper chest, revealed by his open-collared shirt, was too smooth. She'd never met anyone with such navy-blue eyes.

"Do you wear contact lenses?" she asked.

"Only for looks, not vision correction."

"What's your natural eye colour?"

"Ordinary blue."

"Your hair?"

"Why? Is it vain for men to dye their hair?" he said. "I think it was a masterstroke for you to have chosen that gorgeous red to complement your name. Makes me wonder if 'silver fox' inspired Aurora."

"Her colour's not real?"

"My guess is she enhances a dull grey. That's Aurora all over, herself enhanced."

"Are you Stuart enhanced?" She detected a wince in him so slight she wasn't sure if she'd imagined it.

"In this fishbowl, we're all free to become our larger selves."

She followed his gaze down to the retreat, enclosed in hills. "That's deep."

He laughed. "Few people have accused me of that."

Below, a figure in yellow moved through the herb garden. Delilah. She disappeared into the main building.

"I'm curious about you and my mother," Julie said.

"Shoot."

"You two founded this retreat ten years ago, which would have made you…how old at the time?"

"Thirty-two."

"Young for acquiring an inheritance."

"My dad set up his will so the money he'd accumulated during his first marriage would go to his children from that marriage, my sister and me."

"He died relatively young?"

"The rat race killed his heart." Sebastiano's eyes narrowed. "I vowed that wouldn't happen to me, so I do my own thing, living healthily and simpler than he did. Ready to go higher?"

"More testing?"

"You nailed it already. The rest is for fun." He pointed to the trail. "Your turn to lead."

"Wait until I get a pair of boots. You'll be panting to catch up with me."

"I bet I will, Ms. Julie Fox."

Conscious of his footsteps behind her, Julie maintained a brisker pace than she found comfortable. Evidently, competitiveness didn't instantly vanish in this environment. Bird calls and breezes filtered through the trees. Sebastiano's aftershave closed in on her. If she stayed for any length of time, she'd convince him to reduce the dose. For a man so aware of his impression on people, he was obtuse on that point.

She hit a stretch of smooth ground and risked a glance back. "Do you keep in touch with your mother and sister?"

"What's the point?" he said. "They're in my past that doesn't matter anymore."

"Like Aurora's past family doesn't matter?"

Julie stumbled, managed to right herself. Sebastiano hadn't reached out to help. She liked that he trusted her to succeed on her own. Unlike her father, who was always worried she'd fall on her face.

"Aurora's situation is different from mine."

"How so?"

"You'll have to ask her about that."

"You two work closely together yet you share so little personally?"

"Is that impossible?"

Her father had shared a marriage and child with Marion, and he hadn't a clue why she left. The trail turned into gravel and shale. Walking down in sandals was going to be a horror. Sebastiano's breathing behind her was easy, while hers laboured.

"How much farther to the top?" she asked.

"The summit would take all day and involve a scramble over scree."

"I assume you've tried it?"

"On my own, in summer. I go in the evening, camp overnight, and return before dawn. Aurora nixed it for guests. Insurance reasons, and she's overprotective."

"I wish she'd protected me." Strange to say that aloud to a stranger, and not regret she did.

"Then you wouldn't be you," he said.

"Is that one of your bullshitty retreat messages?"

"Basically."

They reached another ledge. Julie caught her breath. Below, the retreat looked even more minuscule. A few gopher-sized people in assorted colours milled in the yard. She looked up at Sebastiano, who stared at her, his expression serious.

"The thing is, the bullshit works," he said. "I don't feel guilty preaching it."

"Do you believe in it?"

"I do and I don't."

"How does that work?"

"Yin and yang. Opposites make a whole."

She stamped her foot. "You can't escape the philosophy here. It permeates everything."

"I escape, more or less, on the hikes. For you, it could be something else."

"Such as?"

He pointed past the amphitheatre and hill. "We'll need an architect for the new development."

"What's that to do with me?"

"You're an engineer."

"Petroleum."

"Same difference."

"Hardly," she said. "Unless you want a pump jack on the new retreat lawn instead of an oak tree."

He smiled. "I'm thinking Roman villa."

"Haven't you done that?"

He looked at the hills glowing hazy in the late-afternoon sun. The dying light produced a sheen that obscured his face, but now the mask slid away. A scar marred his cheek. Childhood accident? Surfing mishap? Fight? Interesting that he'd perfected the rest of him and not the scar.

"When Aurora and I started this," he motioned toward the retreat and continued, "we winged the design. Threw in a mishmash of Italian fantasies without doing the research. A dab of Tuscan here, Roman there. She vetoed my idea of a Venetian canal."

Julie smiled at the over-the-top image.

"The new retreat will be pure Rome. We'll wear the togas and stolas. Guests in the old Tuscan buildings will sport Renaissance garb."

"You'll wear a toga?"

"No way."

"That leaves you in the old retreat."

"I get to switch back and forth between the two, in my tunic."

"You're special?"

He smirked. His mask returned. For a moment, she'd caught a glimmer of the person underneath, but she still didn't have a real understanding of him.

He edged to the trail. "We better get down before Aurora wonders what we're up to."

"Do you think she cares?"

"The question is, does she approve of us or not?"

"Us?"

He bolted ahead. "I dare you to keep up."

"You're on."

Chapter Twenty

Reclining on his bed, Sebastiano thought about Julie. She was like Aurora—Marion—around the age when he met her, except Julie was more genuine, and athletic. Marion was crap on a surfboard. He pictured Julie, in a bikini, cresting the waves.

Aurora hadn't looked angry when he and Julie had shown up in the herb garden, sweaty from the hike, Julie's robe nicked from her near fall on the way down. He'd grabbed her arm. She'd let his hand linger. He'd wanted to take her right there in the woods.

But if Aurora approved, did that mean involvement wasn't in his interests? He leapt to the floor. His gaze lit on the abstract painting above his bed. Part of Aurora's motive had to be getting him away from Cassandra, and he would hate to lose her.

He paced to the table, bare feet pounding the cool tile. Good chance that Aurora had lied and she was really near death. Her maternal instinct might be nil, but if forced to let go of the retreat, she'd want it to continue through part of herself: Julie, her flesh and blood. That reminded him—if Aurora didn't trot off for radiation or chemotherapy on Monday, he would phone her surgeon to get the scoop.

He looked outside. Since Julie's bedroom window faced the lawn, he couldn't tell if her light was on or off. During their hike down, she'd admitted that a lateral shift from petroleum to civil engineering wasn't out of the question, might even be a positive for her career. So, she was intrigued by his plan to develop the property over the hill. The real trick for him would be to juggle Julie and Cassandra without dropping either or both.

Outside, someone exited the main building. He peered to make out the person's stride in the dark. Cassandra. She moved purposely through the garden. He slunk back to his bed. She pushed open his door and slammed it behind her.

"While you cavorted with Julie, I spent the afternoon packing."

Sebastiano glanced at the dresser and closet. So that was why she'd removed her stuff. She wore a red jacket and capris, town clothes.

"Aurora turfed me out for good," she said. "I leave in an hour with Francisca. She'll put me up while I make flight arrangements."

Score one for Aurora, but he had to appease Cassandra. He reached for her arms.

"I don't suppose you could convince Aurora." Cassandra caught his expression and sloughed off his touch. "I didn't think so." She marched past him toward the back door. "Why do you let her push you around?"

"Open confrontation isn't how to play Aurora."

"What is?"

"I've been pondering that all afternoon."

"While you ponder, I'm headed up shit creek."

He drew up behind her, placed his arms under her jacket, around her waist, under her shirt. Cassandra at the retreat would ruin his plans for Julie. Cassandra nearby might work. He nuzzled her neck.

"Stay in town," he said. "Lie low. Not at Francisca's. She'll tell Aurora you're there. Get a room at the motel."

"With what money? I only have enough for a few nights."

She turned around, looking especially pretty with her wide mouth quivering. Like Julie, Cassandra had strength with hints of inner hurt, a combination he loved. He'd gladly help her stay by dipping into the bank account or petty cash, but Aurora kept her nose on every penny.

"Get a job," he said. "Temporarily, while we wait things out."

"This sounds like a long-term project."

"Talk to Trish, at the restaurant. She'll know about any openings."

Cassandra pulled her jacket zipper up and down. He closed all the window blinds, including the ones on the rear door leading to the forest, even though no one ever passed by.

"Things could happen quickly," he said. "I've been talking to Julie all afternoon."

"I noticed." Cassandra's breasts moved up and down beneath her tight T-shirt.

"Aurora sees Julie as her natural successor."

"I realize that."

He stifled his surprise. His theory had been a leap. "She'll open a path for Julie." He grabbed Cassandra's zipper toggle. "But Julie's not interested."

"I agree."

This was a negative for him. "Why do you think that?"

"Julie's got a life out there. Isn't there a husband and child?"

He nodded. Estranged husband with custody of the kid for reasons Julie avoided explaining. Had Julie given her child up willingly, like Aurora had? Maternal instinct or lack thereof could be hereditary.

"And a high-level career in engineering." Cassandra removed her jacket.

Julie was on disability, but she hadn't said why. Best to leave Cassandra believing Julie had too much to give up.

"So," he said. "Aurora steps aside to create space for her daughter. Julie flies home to Canada. You swoop in to fill the void."

"I can't see that working."

"I can. Trust me." He slid his hands around her hips. Cassandra tensed but didn't move. It was a long-shot, but what else did he have?

Cassandra's forehead wrinkled. "I still find Aurora a bit off."

"She seems normal to me." He smiled down at her. "Normal for Aurora."

"Since when does she nap before dinner? She's just returned from a week's rest."

"How about us taking a little nap right now?"

Her body stayed tense. "I won't sit forever in the motel."

It could be over in two days, if Aurora left for further treatment. He thought again how he didn't wish sickness on her, but it would make his life easier. Meanwhile, he had to string this along until he talked to the doctor.

"Tomorrow," he said. "Let's meet in town, after my hike. I'll find some excuse to go in. Make it four thirty, at the restaurant. By then, we'll have a greater sense of the situation."

"What about tonight?"

"You'll have to stay at Francisca's. Make Aurora think you're going home, tail between your legs."

He rubbed her lovely ass and pressed himself to her pelvis.

"Are you sleeping with Julie tonight?"

"No fucking way. Too skinny."

Cassandra chortled.

He kissed her. Their hands peeled off each other's pants. Keep your friends close, your enemies closer, people said. Which was Cassandra? At the moment, he didn't care.

After Cassandra was happily fucked, dressed, and gone to finish packing, Sebastiano tore across the herb garden and into the dining room. Faces around tables turned his way. From the podium, Aurora's subtle glare landed on him. Guests dug into their dessert as she continued her talk about the schedule for the week. Sebastiano stopped a server from yanking away the last main course dish from the buffet table. He scooped up the remnants of chicken cassoulet. Two women at the back table slid their chairs apart to make space between them. He grabbed a chair from the side wall, squeezed it between them and smiled greetings at his dinner mates. Aurora continued speaking, that glare her only sign of annoyance at his disruption, but inside she would be furious.

"This being winter," Aurora told her audience, "there is only a half hour between the sunrise service and breakfast.

For those interested, during that interval we'll offer tai chi on the lawn, led by Sebastiano."

He raised his hand to identify himself to the guests twisting toward him. Julie and Delilah sat at the head table beside the podium. They flanked Aurora's vacated seat. For years, Aurora had nagged him to join her up front. He insisted his role was to be one with the people. She no longer argued with him about it, a sign she saw he was right but wouldn't admit it.

Aurora began the next part of her spiel. "The morning session…"

Sebastiano forked up some chicken and legumes. When Aurora chewed him out for arriving late, he'd tell her he'd fallen asleep. And he had, after the hot, sweet sex with Cassandra. Julie looked beautiful in her pale-green robe, her shoulder bare. She tilted her head toward her mother, seemingly transfixed by the words, her crème caramel untouched on her plate. Incredible that Julie had turned up, the solution to both his and Aurora's dreams—if Cassandra didn't screw it up.

Aurora explained that the morning and afternoon sessions were held at the same time as Sebastiano's hikes. He flashed another wave at this new crop. Her sessions covered identical material, giving guests the option of doing the easier or harder hike scheduled. They included three rigorous hikes a week for those wanting an extra challenge. Sebastiano wondered which guests he would grow closest to this week. After ten years, this question continued to excite him each Saturday. Aurora added that their information packet provided details on hike length and elevation. After dinner, Sebastiano would answer anyone's specific questions in the lounge. He smiled and saluted.

Late afternoon was for relaxation, Aurora went on. She led yoga in the lounge. The pool had reopened this afternoon.

"Yay," said a woman at the table closest to the podium.

Aurora smiled down at her. "Expect the water to be cold. After refilling, it takes several days to warm up."

Aurora's ad-lib relaxed the room. Sebastiano constantly debated if her elevating herself from the guests was a positive or negative. She did manage to bridge the distance with a semblance of warmth. In the end, he always conceded Aurora was the expert on her own style, and it certainly worked. This didn't mean any successor couldn't shake up the mould. "A leader must create herself," to quote Aurora. He finished the cassoulet, which was lukewarm and bland. Female servers wove by the tables topping up guests' coffee and tea. One removed Sebastiano's empty plate. Another brought him dessert.

"For the remainder of the week," Aurora said, "dinner will be at six, as a courtesy to the staff, who need to get home to their families. Let's give them a hand for this wonderful meal tonight."

The room resounded with claps and a shrill whistle that suggested a fun week might lie ahead. The whistle came from a woman who had arrived with a pair of giggling friends.

"That takes care of business." Aurora paused. She spoke slowly. "The more important matter is this, why are we all here?" She scanned the faces fixed on her. "Some of you have come with clear ideas. Others, perhaps most, are searching." Another carefully timed sweep of the three tables. "I was once like you."

Silence. A cough.

"I was caught up in the ways of the world."

Sebastiano sipped his coffee and leaned back for what came next. The old story of the young man in love with Aurora fifteen years ago. Her insensitive treatment of him that led to his suicide; partially true, except Aurora's sin hadn't so much been indifference but callousness. What Aurora had really learned was how to hide her cruelty behind apparent caring. And she related the story in a way that made her and the retreat look good. Knock yourself down, repent, and show how much you've changed thanks to New Dawn's philosophy.

"This is a special night," Aurora said. "You may be curious about these two women." She turned from the podium and raised an arm to the head table. Her left arm, he realized, due to the surgery on the right shoulder. "At the far end is Delilah." Aurora smiled. "And this is my daughter, Julie."

Sebastiano clunked his cup to the table. An ad-lib and now a total departure from script?

"When I was young, so very young," Aurora said. "I did the worst thing a mother could do."

Even from this distance, he could see Julie's jaw quiver. She gazed down at her crème caramel, hiding her face from the crowd.

"When Julie was four years old, an innocent little girl, I left her with her father in Canada and split for California to do my own thing."

The audience tensed, not knowing how to respond. Delilah extended her hand to Julie, who didn't look up. Had Aurora told Julie she would talk about this? Was it the new repentance story?

Aurora described her narcissistic days in Santa Monica, making them sound like a real blast. And they had been. Sebastiano had been there for the later ones. He doubted that during that time Aurora had given her daughter more than a passing thought.

"I thought of her every day," Aurora said. "But I was too weak to do anything aside from call her home and hang up. I'd let her down as a mother. What turned me around was the tragic death of a friend. Suicide." She paused for the faint gasp in the crowd. "I saw the consequences of the careless life I lived. That revelation led to a host of fresh ideas. Ideas we'll explore this week." She glanced at Julie, who looked up, face flushed, eyes red. "When I was ready," Aurora said, "Julie found me. I thank the gods for bringing her here."

Aurora glided to Julie, leaned over and clutched her to her breast. Julie's arms hung by Aurora's sides then wrapped around her silver robe, shimmering under a spotlight. Aurora winced—from pain, he guessed. Viewers would think it was from emotion.

Delilah's hands drew together in a gesture of prayer. A woman across his table sniffed. The one next to him sobbed and blew her nose. Others in the room wept and clapped. The new narrative was a hit. Aurora made a show of extricating herself from Julie, returned to the podium and took out the box of tissues she stored underneath. She dabbed her eyes and handed the box to Julie. Even the servers were crying.

"I don't deserve such forgiveness," Aurora said.

Mutters from the audience suggested she did.

"But forgiveness benefits the giver more than the recipient." She smiled through her tears at Julie. "Already, I see my daughter, so capable of forgiveness, becoming whole." She looked at the guests. "This week, we will talk a lot about forgiveness."

Aurora paused, and then welcomed them all to a life-altering week, this one particularly special on account of Julie. She sat down to the room's applause.

Julie leaned in to say something to her. Mother and daughter talked and smiled. Sebastiano would kill to be a bird on Julie's shoulder listening. Guests murmured to each other. Typically, one or two went up to Aurora at this point, but this time everyone left her alone with her daughter. Delilah looked around the room, perhaps confused about her place at the head table. Aurora's speech hadn't included her stepdaughter.

"You're Sebastiano," the woman to his left said. "I wanted to ask about the tai chi. Do we need to have done it before?"

"I gear it to all levels."

"I've always been interested in trying it but wasn't sure I could concentrate."

Aurora led Julie and Delilah out of the room. Guests from the other tables followed.

"What brand of tai chi do you do?" a woman across his table asked.

"My own," he said. "A blend of the best of them all."

Aurora's story about abandoning her daughter had been a risk. Sebastiano admired that. It might have turned the audience against her. He guessed the response had topped Aurora's expectations. Her embrace with Julie at the end had sealed the moment. The story would certainly work best with Julie present. If Aurora had taken the risk to draw Julie in, she must really want her to stay. Again, he considered that Aurora's desire might be useful to him.

"I'll give the tai chi a try," the woman beside him said. "What do I have to lose?"

"No risk, no gain."

* * *

In the lounge, Sebastiano found Aurora and Julie surrounded by an admiring group. He joined Delilah and a gay couple, twenty years apart in age. According to his registration form, the younger man was thirty-three, lived in San Diego, and worked as a financial analyst. According to his tunic, he was handsome and fit.

"About those rigorous hikes," he said to Sebastiano. "What would be the rigours?"

He also had wit, not a common trait of New Dawn guests. His older partner's robe accentuated his paunch. Sebastiano described the hardest hike's rocky terrain, exaggerating its technical difficulties.

"I'd go for that," the young man said.

"You'd have to carry me up the hill." The older one rested a hand on his partner's shoulder. "I won't hold you back, Nelson. We'll do the different hikes."

"Then we'll be in different sessions." Nelson looked at his partner. "The point was to work together."

Work implied fissures in the relationship. Sebastiano hadn't had a man in a year. He pictured himself and Nelson hitting the peaks of adjacent waves.

"Do you surf?" Sebastiano asked.

"Every chance I get. Don't suppose you have waves in your pool?"

His companion laughed and fondled the hem of Nelson's tunic. The old guy was smitten. Poor dumpy clod.

"Working separately can have its benefits," Sebastiano said.

So much bounty this week in Julie, Cassandra, and Nelson. Tonight's focus was Julie, who planned to leave in the morning. Evidently, Aurora wanted Julie to stay.

Sebastiano would do everything he could to help. Right now, he couldn't wait to get into his cottage and unclasp the robe from her shoulder.

Chapter Twenty-One

While Eric gathered the cards from their game of canasta, Brad checked his cell phone.

"No email from either of them," Brad said.

"I'm sure we'll hear in the morning." Rosemary got up from her chair.

Brad scratched his thin hair into a peak, worry lines etched on his forehead. Eric took the pack of cards to the chest of drawers in the hall and glanced upstairs, where Peyton was sleeping with her stuffed toys. One day his daughter would grow up. If she took off to look for an absent Julie and failed to contact him for a day, he'd worry too.

"Can you check before we leave?" Brad asked Eric.

"I left my phone in the den."

"Brad won't sleep unless you have a look." Rosemary removed her coat. "I'll rest my back on your sofa while you're upstairs."

In the den, Eric bypassed his phone for the larger screen. He sat down at his computer desk and opened his email, aware of Brad hovering behind him.

"One from Delilah." Eric's heart rose and sank. Delilah might be writing because Julie had cracked up. "It says the email was sent 5:04 p.m. our time, but it wasn't here when I looked after tucking in Peyton."

"Aren't you going to open it?" Brad leaned over Eric's shoulder.

Eric took a deep breath, clicked the mouse and read aloud. "Julie and I are doing great, Delilah says. So is Julie's mother. Wow."

"What?" The chair shook as Brad gripped the backrest.

"Marion is alive." Eric's chair rocked back and forth.

Brad leaned closer. "That's a long message."

"Delilah goes on about how nice Marion is. Julie and Marion have had long talks. They've formed a bond, Delilah thinks."

"So much for their simple drive in the country."

"They're spending the night at Marion's place. Delilah hopes Julie will want to stay longer. Marion calls herself Aurora."

"Why?"

"She runs a kind of New Age resort, called New Dawn Retreat. She's the spiritual leader of it, according to Delilah."

"Marion?"

"Everyone dresses in robes, stolas, Delilah says. The atmosphere's like Ancient Rome, with olive trees growing on hills, lush gardens and amphitheatre."

The chair vibrated. Brad had let go of the backrest. "That's nonsense. It sounds like a cult."

Eric skimmed the next effusive paragraph. "Delilah insists that when you're there, it doesn't feel weird."

"I don't like it."

Neither did Eric. He swivelled toward Brad. "Isn't this good news, though? Julie found her mother. She's alive, doing well and receptive to Julie. It's all pretty amazing."

Brad dropped to the spare chair. "Marion running a cult."

"We don't know it's that." Eric returned to the computer. "Let's see what we find on the internet." He searched New Dawn Retreat and found the website. "Located two hours from Los Angeles. Buffet meals, sessions, and guided hikes included. Here's a picture of Aurora."

"Let me see." Brad brushed by Eric and peered at the screen. "Without my glasses, I can't tell if it's her or not."

"The picture's small and seems in soft focus."

"Marion would have changed with age."

"This Aurora looks in her forties to me, not late fifties."

"I can't believe it's Marion. This is a con."

"For what purpose?"

Brad clenched his fists. "They meet a stranger in Los Angeles, who sends them to this wacko place. Why?" His fists opened. "To get something from Julie. Money, most likely. Are they Scientologists?"

"The retreat people?"

"It wouldn't surprise me if that sleazy PI is in on it. I never did trust that man."

"Isn't that being—" Eric stopped himself from saying "paranoid." Like father, like daughter?

"If it isn't a con, it might be worse," Brad said. "This could really be Marion."

"How is that worse?"

"You don't know what she's like." Brad's voice was oddly high-pitched. "I've never told anyone this. Not even Rosemary." He went over and closed the door, settled on the spare chair a few feet from Eric and lowered his voice. "Those last few years with Marion, she constantly berated me. By then, she knew all my weaknesses and pecked and pecked and pecked."

Chills ran up Eric's arms.

"She left me a virtual basket case. I could barely take care of myself, never mind a four-year-old. If it weren't for my parents…"

Brad? A basket case? "I thought you were deeply in love with Marion."

"Not after I understood her." Brad leaned toward the computer and squinted. "If Aurora is Marion, we need to warn Julie."

"I'll reply to Delilah's email."

"Phoning would be better."

Eric returned to the New Dawn website. "There's a number for the retreat."

"No. Go through the girls' cells."

"Delilah says her cell phone doesn't work. We can try Julie's."

"Finish reading the email first."

Eric scrolled down Delilah's message. "There's no TV or radio."

"That's how cults operate. Cut you off from your family and real life."

"People only stay for one week. What harm can it do?" Eric clicked back to the search page and opened the first link, a blog entry. 'The New Dawn Retreat changed my life. I quit my unfulfilling job, left my oppressive relationship, moved to Vermont and took up pottery.' This wouldn't impress Brad.

"It's my fault for sending Julie and Delilah," Brad said. "I have to fly to LA and see what's up." He got up, shuffled to the window, and sighed. "No, I can't. Work commitments, and Julie would balk at my interference."

If Aurora was a con, Julie would figure it out. That is, unless the stress or her desire to reconnect with her mother clouded her judgment.

"I have work too," Eric said.

Something flickered in Brad's eyes. Hope that Eric would go in his place, if he was able? "This can't wait," Brad said. "Give Marion a week and…what does Delilah say next?"

"She raves about California. Palm trees, sunshine, summer weather every day. Sounds a heap of a lot better than Calgary in the dead of winter."

"I couldn't ask you to go, Eric," Brad said.

He just had. Eric's week was booked with patients, but they could be rescheduled or see one of his associate dentists if Eric claimed a family emergency. How urgent was this? Was Brad overreacting?

"Surely one of the girls will come to her senses," Brad continued, sounding unconvinced.

Eric finished reading the email. "Marion told Delilah that she would love to meet her granddaughter. Peyton's welcome there any time. Me too, apparently." Eric doubted Julie would want him butting in.

"Don't go for my sake," Brad said.

He'd be doing it for Julie. Whether he loved her or not, they shared a history, and she was the mother of his child. What was good for her was good for Peyton. And he'd foolishly promised Peyton to bring Julie back.

Eric swivelled in the chair. This crazy plan was actually possible. Rosemary and Brad would willingly stay here to look after Peyton, who would mostly be occupied with day care, preschool and her friends. On the other hand, Peyton was the person Marion really wanted to meet. Presumably, Julie would want to see her daughter, too. And Peyton had been begging him to take her to Disneyland. Half the kids in her preschool had been to that magical park, which wasn't far from the New Dawn Retreat.

"I'd need Monday to make arrangements at work," Eric said. "The earliest I could go is Tuesday morning."

Brad touched his chest and massaged it. "The sooner the better."

"For fun, I'll check the airline schedules." Air Canada and WestJet both had seats available on Tuesday. The most convenient one at a reasonable price would get them to Los Angeles in the late morning. Eric swivelled toward Brad. "The retreat says it's a mere two-hour drive from the airport. We'd be there after lunch."

Brad slumped into his chair, forehead dotted with sweat. His eyes, sunken into his face, pleaded with Eric. This could be him in thirty-four years with Peyton off to whatever-the-hell-place. He would want his future-ex-son-in-law to come through for them.

"I'll reread Delilah's email," he said. "Take a deeper look at the New Dawn website, although it seems skimpy. Maybe I'll read more blogs about the retreat."

"I'm grateful, Eric." Hope resurfaced in Brad's eyes.

"If it seems right for me to go, then okay. Peyton will get to see Disneyland."

* * *

In her office, Aurora revived herself with homemade tea. Her instinct to withdraw and cut the Sunday morning session short had been right. Fatigue had made opening her mouth an effort. Worse, she'd come close to fainting in the amphitheatre. What a horror that would have been for guests, especially on their first full day, when it was crucial to set the tone for the week.

A woman appeared in the door frame, and Aurora's heart skipped. Julie. Aurora thought once more how stunning her daughter looked in the mint-green robe, her auburn hair trickling down her bare shoulder.

Aurora motioned her to the chair across from her desk. "The hike finished early?"

"A guest with a sore leg overestimated her abilities," Julie said. "Sebastiano suggested we all turn back in support."

Aurora nodded. No doubt he had done this to impress Julie, to prove he had sensitivity. "What did you think of our hills?"

"They're great, but hiking is awkward in this getup."

Aurora inwardly cringed. Getup? Yesterday, she hadn't noticed such lack of refinement, which Julie would have acquired from Brad, his Fox relatives, and her engineering world. A few weeks at New Dawn would smooth those bumps.

Aurora sipped tea to build her courage. "Have you decided if you'll prolong your stay?" At breakfast, Julie had told her she wasn't sure if they'd leave after lunch.

Julie's fingers traced circles on the desktop, her cheeks flushed. From the hike or something else?

Aurora leaned forward. She felt a pull on her collarbone. "You have every right to blame me for abandoning you. And no business blaming yourself."

Julie's finger paused.

"My departure was all about me," Aurora said. "It had nothing, absolutely nothing, to do with you." Her eyes filled with tears, naturally, after years of connecting to retreat guests. "You must understand that."

"Understanding isn't the same as feeling a thing is true."

Aurora nodded. "New Dawn doesn't teach that feelings are truth. Understanding is a first step away from faulty feelings. Please stay with us." Her voice quivered with desperation. She had never begged anyone for anything. Marion had, but not Aurora.

"Delilah and I talked it over," Julie said. "She's keen on another night, although worried about not having our meds. So far, neither of us has developed withdrawal symptoms. I convinced her we could live without meds for a couple of days."

This was progress. Aurora glanced at the computer. "There's a job here for Delilah if she's interested. I need someone to handle the office and website."

"Delilah would be good at that, but she couldn't stay permanently."

"Why not?"

"For starters, she'd need to get a green card to work in the US."

Starters. Another crudity. And how unfortunate that Julie had inherited those narrow Fox eyes. Widely set eyes, like Delilah's, suggested warmth, a valuable trait in a leader. Delilah might balance Julie's tendency for resistance, another Fox trait.

"Green cards are easy to arrange with the right connections," Aurora said. The way the outside world worked, that was probably true.

"Did you become a US citizen?"

"For practical reasons, to buy the property." And with the help of the old lawyer, who had died to give them the money for their venture. Before that, working illegally was no problem. "What about you? Are you eager to return to your job?"

"Not particularly. I used to love work before…the postpartum. I might enjoy it again, once I get into it."

Julie had given birth four years ago. Despite what Aurora had implied to her yesterday about her own experience, postpartum depression didn't last that long. Hers had vanished when Julie started sleeping through the night. What woman could tolerate disrupted sleep, a baby's constant demands, and a husband's unwillingness to do his share?

"Did you choose engineering because it was your father's field?"

"Partly," Julie said. "I was good at science and math. I expect I also wanted to make a statement. It's still not common for women to go into engineering, especially chemical."

"I thought you were in petroleum?"

Julie's faint smile suggested she was pleased that Aurora had remembered. "After first year, I switched to petroleum to land a better job. Oil rules in Calgary, at least until the downturn a few years ago."

"A practical choice, but not your first love. Or, perhaps, second."

"It's too late to change course."

"It's never too late."

"For civil engineering, I'd have to go back to school and then take an entry-level job. I'm not that disillusioned with the oil patch."

"There's always an alternate path to your dreams."

Julie rubbed the shoulder clasp of her robe as though it were an irritant to expel, like a lump on a collarbone.

Aurora changed course. "Are you and Eric legally separated? Or divorced?"

"We've lived apart for ten months," Julie said, her lips tightening in the Fox way. "That's sufficiently separate."

"And you share custody of your child?"

"Eric has custody. I see her on weekends, under my parents' supervision. I mean…my father's and Rosemary's. My choice, I didn't—don't—trust myself with Peyton." Julie's chin quivered.

Aurora sustained her gentle gaze.

"In November, a few days before Peyton turned four, I tried to drown her in the bathtub." Julie's narrowed eyes challenged a response.

A mother should love unconditionally. Aurora willed her expression to remain unchanged.

"In my warped mind, I wanted to save her from future pain."

So, this was her secret, cloaked in childish anger at her own mother. Aurora was certain Julie had purposely mentioned Peyton's age to imply that Marion's departure was the cause of her psychotic break. Foxes weren't quick to forgive. It would take work to jettison the Fox out of her daughter.

"That's why I can't blame you for leaving," Julie said. "I did worse. I might have killed Peyton." Her voice shook. "My shrink suggested that I knew Eric was coming and would save Peyton. I don't believe that."

Julie let go of her shoulder clasp. She stared with the penitent expression Aurora had seen countless times on the faces of guests, whose sins ranged from trivial to greater than Julie's. One had pushed her younger brother down the stairs. He broke his neck and wound up permanently disabled. The woman had never told a soul she'd done it deliberately. Aurora pointed out that she had been a child, with the normal jealousy of a new sibling. Any child might have done the same without full awareness of the consequences. The guest left the retreat with greatly reduced self-hatred. If Julie were a guest, Aurora would reinforce her therapist's view, true or not, and point out that Peyton was alive and well.

"What happened has happened." She locked her gaze on Julie's. "We can't take back what we did. For your sake and your daughter's, I hope you'll forgive yourself and move forward. I'm no different. I may have left you as a child because I didn't trust myself with you."

Julie's brow creased. Aurora hoped her daughter was considering the truth—that Marion might well have killed someone had she remained in that wretched domestic situation.

"Sometimes we need to sacrifice our own wants for the benefit of another," Aurora said. "Difficult as that might be. I wanted to stay with you more than anything."

Julie rose, looking confused. "I should go and get ready for lunch."

"We don't say 'should' at New Dawn," Aurora said, standing as well.

They left the office and separated in the hall. Julie went upstairs while Aurora checked the dining room. The staff had set only one chair at the head table. She instructed a server to add two more places and then hurried through the herb garden to Sebastiano's cottage. She had a few minutes before the lunch bell to find out what he had gleaned from Julie.

She found him lying sideways on his bed, perusing one of his photo books.

"Don't you knock?" he said. "I might have been naked."

"I wouldn't have noticed." Her collarbone area throbbed. If she couldn't make it through the afternoon session, guests would start to wonder and gossip about her.

Sebastiano hopped off the bed. "I assume you're here for the scoop on your daughter and me."

Aurora tensed. "I heard Julie come upstairs not long after me last night. I trust she rejected any advances you made."

"Ha. She's worth waiting for," he said. "Julie's a terrific girl, I grant you that." He placed a hand on his abdomen and bowed to her. "In your maternal absence, you did an exceptional job of raising her."

Aurora crossed her arms to stop herself from slapping his face. "As you probably know, Julie's decided to stay at least one more night."

"I have my appeal."

She glanced at his book. "I've been thinking. Civil engineers were the architects of Rome."

He nodded. "I've suggested to Julie that she could take charge of constructing the new Roman-themed retreat—the buildings, landscapes, bridges, pools, and underground support structure. The grand project would occupy her for years."

Aurora turned away, so he wouldn't read the agreement on her face. Julie wouldn't need to earn a new university degree to plan the satellite retreat. She would learn on the job, do her own research, hire consultants as needed. If only this didn't fit so well with Sebastiano's vision for New Dawn. But keeping Julie here was more important than pride. *Pride is a barrier to relationships.* Advice for her as much as for the guests; she was not yet perfect and still capable of growth.

A bell chimed from the main building. Lunch. Aurora's next chance to subtly convince her daughter to remain in California.

Chapter Twenty-Two

Julie said good night to Aurora and continued down the hall with Delilah. They exited the main building and stepped into the herb garden. In darkness, Garth loitered in front of his cottage. Julie glanced at Delilah, whose face shone at the sight of Garth. No wonder she'd agreed so willingly to stay a third night.

Sebastiano emerged from his larger cottage. Earlier, he'd accompanied the guests to their residence across the lawn to "get the herd moving" so Aurora could rehash the day's sessions in the lounge with Julie and Delilah. Sessions turned out to be gatherings of ten to fifteen guests in the amphitheatre. Aurora would speak on an empowering topic, and then there were questions and discussion. Aurora didn't participate in hikes, but she eagerly listened to the gossip Julie and Delilah had picked up on the trails.

"I appreciate the insight into the guests," she'd said.

Julie could tackle the harder hikes thanks to the boots the seamstress had brought her from town. Francesca had also fitted her with a short robe, which Aurora called a Diana-the-huntress stola. Delilah had also gotten a Diana robe and boots, but she preferred the leisurely pace of the easy hikes.

"This way, you and Delilah, between you, can audit both of my daily sessions," Aurora said. "I welcome your constructive critique."

From what she'd seen so far, Julie couldn't think of a single improvement. Guests appeared enraptured by Aurora's speeches. They asked numerous questions, engaged in the discussions, shared personal stories that led some to tears, and gushed about the sessions on the hikes.

Both evenings, Aurora had brought the rehash to a quick close so she could get a proper night's sleep. As Aurora headed upstairs, Sebastiano arrived and invited Julie and Delilah for a stroll before bed. Delilah hesitated, until Julie shot her daggers. The past two days, Julie had felt herself getting closer and closer to Sebastiano. A walk alone with him under the stars was bound to end with him propositioning her. She needed Delilah on these walks as a chaperone. Tonight, Sebastiano had arranged the bedtime stroll in advance. Evidently, he'd lined up Garth to keep Delilah occupied.

The foursome crunched diagonally across the lawn to the tune of cricket chirps. Delilah and Garth slipped behind. Julie glanced up at her mother's dark bedroom window. She sensed Aurora was curious about her involvement with Sebastiano but held back from pressing her with questions. Was Aurora already in bed or had she turned off the lights so she could observe the lawn without being seen? Julie hadn't experienced a mother's overprotectiveness as a teenager. Rosemary had left rules about curfews and excessive worry to Brad when Julie dated. Julie found it strange now, in her late thirties, to feel a mother's hovering.

They approached the oak tree. Her shawl grazed the double swing. On the other side of the lawn, faces followed them from the lit guest-room windows. A couple of women waved. Sebastiano waved back. Julie liked that he didn't feel a need to force conversation with her. Somehow, he knew when she was in a mood to ruminate. They rounded the guest building to the path beside the vegetable and fruit garden. A few bedroom lights shone through the windows. Of all the guests, Julie had clicked the most with Nelson, the younger half of the gay couple. She often found herself next to him on the hikes or at the sessions.

"Have you decided how long you'll stay?" Sebastiano broke into her thoughts.

They had reached the lemon groves. Julie inhaled the citrus aromas mingled with Sebastiano's aftershave, which had started to grow on her. Ahead was the illuminated pool.

No one was swimming on this brisk night. Julie was glad her mother had insisted she borrow one of her shawls.

"I've avoided making up my mind," Julie said. "I told my mother I'll take it day by day."

"Works for me."

Julie looked back at Delilah, who was talking animatedly with Garth. She no longer wanted to drive to Santa Monica to get their belongings before they had to check out of the apartment on Friday.

"Five hours minimum in a car," Delilah had said. "Packing up everything. LA smog—when I could be here in this pristine environment. Plus, I feel okay without my meds, happier and more content than I've ever been. No withdrawal symptoms."

"Me neither." Julie was less sure about happy and content but liked the freedom from the daily pills.

Undoubtedly, Garth's presence at the retreat contributed to Delilah's reluctance to leave, even for half a day. Last night at the end of the evening walk, Delilah had looked at Julie as though to ask if they'd go into the men's respective cottages. Make your own choice, Julie mentally answered. Which had been Aurora's advice at the session earlier that day.

Sebastiano slowed their pace as they turned toward the main residence. He paused at the olive grove to gaze up at the stars. So many of them out tonight, and a bright moon on its way to becoming full. Aurora's bedroom was still dark. Delilah's and Garth's footsteps closed in. The four of them stepped onto the herb garden path and stopped at the crossroads to the main building and cottages.

"Well, good night," Delilah said and linked her arm with Garth's. She evaded Julie's questioning gaze. Delilah and Garth continued on the path to his cottage. The door closed behind them.

"Who'd have thunk it?" Sebastiano said.

Julie laughed. He'd told her he was completely baffled by Garth's new interest in romance.

"Everyone has their surprising side."

"Not me," he said. "I'm exactly what I seem."

"Oh yeah?" She cocked her head at him. "So, tell me, why would a dynamic, sociable, worldly man choose to live in this place, removed from civilization?"

Sebastiano tucked his thumbs into his tunic belt. Starlight speckled his face. "I get to spend my days doing what I like. Hiking, swimming, meeting an ever-changing variety of people who clue me in to new interests. Tai chi, for instance, was inspired by a guest." He whisked his hands from the belt, stretched out his arms, and moved them in slow-motion circles.

She laughed again. "I'd have assumed you preferred a more forceful martial art."

"A tai chi master can take any kung fu expert."

"Really?"

"In theory."

He lunged around her in a circle. The wafting aroma of his aftershave mixed with the scents of the herbs. She felt drawn to his complex scents. Eric hated male cologne. He would never wear tights and a tunic. She might join the tai chi group tomorrow morning if Aurora didn't waylay her after the sunrise service.

"I need to ask you something," Julie said. It had nagged her since she'd arrived and she had to be certain before moving forward.

He stopped in front of her. "Go ahead."

"Did you and my mother ever sleep together?"

"No." His eyes widened in surprise that looked genuine. "Why would you think that?" He hadn't hesitated in his reply, and his stare remained steady.

"Not once?" Julie said. "Even when you first met, and you were teaching her to surf?"

"We were never attracted that way."

"Because she's older?"

"Not only that. My best friend had a crush on her."

"That story is true?"

"You heard Aurora talk about it in her presentation."

"I don't know what's real around here or not."

"Does it matter?"

"In the regular world it does." Here, she wasn't sure. Obviously, he wanted sex, and she hadn't felt such tingling in her torso and legs since the early days with Eric. If this were to go beyond the physical, she'd have to tell him everything, and even the physical might not work with a man who couldn't accept who she was. But who wouldn't recoil from a woman who'd tried to kill a child? Not the kind of person she'd want to be with.

"My friend's crush made Aurora off-limits, even if I'd been interested," Sebastiano said. "He was a sensitive type. My involvement with her would have killed him. He was my brother. Not literally, but in the real sense."

"He committed suicide?"

"It knocked me out and changed my life." He scanned the two octagonal cottages framed in silhouetted trees that crept in from the woods. "Among other things, it taught me that our time on this planet is limited. Fill it with what you want, not with what others want for you."

His sleeve brushed her arm. Their noses touched. Sweet garden aromas embraced them. During their stroll last night, he'd admitted he occasionally slept with female guests.

"Holiday flings for them," he'd said. "Flings that mean nothing to either side. For fulfillment, I'm waiting…"

Julie wondered if he'd left the sentence dangling to spin her. "Don't let paranoia control you," her shrink always said.

Sebastiano kissed her. Fill it with what you want, not with what others want for you. Then Aurora's words. Make your own choice. His tongue entered her mouth. Her shawl slid down her arms. His pelvis pressed into her.

She pulled back. "We're outside, for God's sake."

"We can change that in an instant." He looked at his cottage.

Her mother's bedroom windows faced other directions. Last night, Sebastiano had denied any involvement with Cassandra. Julie didn't quite believe him. *Let it go.* Cassandra was gone. Aurora had dismissed her because she hadn't worked out as hoped.

Sebastiano kissed her neck. He touched the small of her back. The only window in the main building that faced this way was Delilah's, and Aurora certainly wouldn't be watching from there. And so what if she was? Julie let him guide her into his cottage. He flicked on the light above the table. A queen-sized bed angled into the room, dominating the space. Its comforter in swirling shades of blue, brown, and green echoed the abstract painting of a forest above his bed. Books lay on the table. Julie edged toward them. *Villas of Ancient Rome. Mediterranean Gardens. Planets and Stars.*

She looked out of the window behind the table, the view a straight line to the valley oak. Its silhouetted branches were perfectly still.

"I bet if I measured, I'd find the tree dead centre in the yard."

"Your mother loves symmetry," he said, from close behind her. "I prefer things a little off-balance."

He eased the shawl off her shoulders and set it on the table. His fingers grazed her arm, edged up to the clasp of her robe. They were really going through with this. With his other hand, he fumbled with her rope belt.

"Who tied this?" he asked.

"I was a Girl Guide."

"I could say I was a Boy Scout, but that wouldn't be true."

There was a second thing she had to know before the step, although she'd rather run and hide, anything but say this. "I'm a terrible parent."

"What parent isn't?" He nibbled her ear.

Tingles rushed to her shoulder and moved lower. "Some are worse than most."

"What makes you particularly bad?" He brushed her hair back and nipped her neck.

Her knees wavered. The words spilled out. "I had this dark depression after my daughter was born. Rather than work to make it lift, I bottled it up. It developed into psychosis that got so bad one day that I tried to drown her."

He stopped nibbling. No sounds, not even crickets from outside. Somehow, they'd moved to his dresser. She stared down at the comb and mirror set, which seemed too old-fashioned and feminine for a man like him.

"That's it?" he said.

"It's plenty." She stepped away from him. Was he too distracted to hear what she'd said?

"All of us go crazy and cause hurt sometimes."

She turned around and looked into his too-blue eyes. "Not like that."

"Why blame yourself? The psychosis did it, not you." He moved closer, a nose-length from her.

"The psychosis is me."

"No, it's not." His eyes, his whole face and body, contained not one speck of condemnation.

* * *

Delilah sat at Garth's table, while he marched between the foot of the bed and the back door. Each time he reached the exit, she expected him to bolt outside. This was a first, her being the less nervous one in this situation.

"I've never done it with anyone before," he said. "Not successfully."

She considered asking what he meant by that, but it might well send him stumbling into the forest. To her surprise, she didn't enjoy this upper hand any more than her usual pre-sex feelings of inadequacy. If she were in Garth's shoes, what would she want him to say?

"I've only been with two guys." Technically three, if she counted the one-night stand during university.

He halted by the bed. "Long-term relationships?"

"Is three months long?"

Garth brushed his hair from his eyes, reminding her of Eric, whom she'd barely thought of all day.

"I can't believe some guy hasn't snapped you up."

"It was my own fault."

"How come?"

Sharing her own weaknesses might make him feel less alone. "Eric," she said. "I had this stupid crush. It lasted years. Too many."

"Who's Eric?"

"Julie's—" No need for that detail. "The crush blinded me from noticing other men."

Garth's ears flushed. They had cute, pointy tips.

"I've never been in love like that."

"Consider yourself lucky."

"What made it end?"

"I don't know. I sank into a depression. When I resurfaced, in a new place, the obsession had vanished." Smart not to blurt out that she'd sunk into the depression four days ago, the new place was here, and the day before yesterday she still hadn't been completely sure she was over Eric.

Garth rubbed his hands as though they were freezing. If they were going to make it to the double bed, she would have to take the initiative.

"I really like you," Garth said.

"I like you, too." Mundane and fantastically true.

She rose, attempting to be graceful. He shuffled closer. She rested her hands on his shoulders. He touched her waist, his workman hands strong and permanently stained with earth. Her lips met his soft ones. If he were an amateur, she loved amateur.

He jerked back. "I..." he said between breaths. "No condoms." He gulped. "I mean, why would I? No need."

"We'll do without."

"Are you...?"

"On the pill? Not that kind."

"What other kind is there?"

She looked into his eyes, which in this light looked solid brown, not Eric-like hazel. "Antidepressants."

"Do they act as birth control?"

She laughed. The meds had diminished her libido, which was back after a couple of days without them.

Garth's ears went red. "Dumb of me to say that. I know about meds. Couldn't function without them in Chicago. I don't need them here."

"What I really meant was, most likely I can't have a kid, especially now that I'm getting older."

"You're not old."

She stepped sideways, hitting the mattress. "Years ago, a doctor told me my uterus was small. Or maybe he said it was big. Whatever. I got the impression it would be hard for me to have children and—"

Garth grabbed her waist. He kissed her.

At age thirty-eight, her odds of conceiving immediately were low.

Garth's tongue explored her mouth.

Or no more than a hundred to one. Her tongue met his. Maybe twenty to one. Or ten. This was probably her last chance.

* * *

Delilah forced open one eye. Garth stood by the bed slipping into his overalls. Dim light strained through the closed blinds.

"What time is it?" she asked.

"I tried not to wake you," he said. "I've got to get to work."

"So early?"

"It's late." He leaned over, kissed her forehead, and mumbled something.

"What?" she said.

"I hope Julie will decide you'll stay."

"Me too."

Delilah watched him pad to the door. He stopped and turned, and his face darkened with desire. No man had ever stared at her this way. She curled herself into a ball, his stickiness between her legs, and hugged her silly knees. Too early. Too early to know anything.

* * *

Julie woke to a chorus of birds. More than a chorus—a symphony. If sounds travelled outside as well as they did in, someone had probably heard them last night.

The room was still so dark she couldn't see Sebastiano, but she could smell his sweaty cologne and hear him breathing beside her. Was there a clock in here? Needing to use the bathroom, she rolled slowly onto her side. Her fingers touched the condom box on the bedside table.

"Hey." His body wrapped around her back and enveloped her in his flesh and scent. "You're insatiable."

"Just checking if they're expired," she teased, sort of.

"You don't trust me?"

"To check technical things like dates, no."

He stretched his arm past her and flicked on the lamp.

"Oww." The light blinded her. She blinked until the box came into focus. Checking wouldn't hurt. "They don't expire for years."

"Zero chance a single swimmer snuck through."

"When did you buy them? Last week?"

"You're the only one who matters now." He rolled onto her.

She felt him harden. His fingers sliding under her thong. God, she wanted him. He fumbled between her legs, pulled the cloth to the side, his bare flesh against her.

"No." She pulled away, reached for the box.

"You're a careful one."

She couldn't have another child, now, or ever again.

* * *

Again, light shone and dazzled her. Julie closed her eyes. She must have fallen back asleep after more amazing, and slower, sex and using the bathroom. Her eyes reopened to the sight of Sebastiano propped on one elbow, gazing down at her.

"Looks like we slept through the sunrise service," he said.

Sunlight streamed in from the window. "Your tai chi?"

"Cancelled, I presume, when I didn't show up."

"Morning hike?"

"Possibly time to make that." He kissed her.

"Has the breakfast bell chimed?"

"It woke me up."

Julie rolled out from under him. Her feet struck cold tile floor all the way to the bathroom. Her face in the mirror looked pasty, hair tangled in a bird's nest. She was glad he hadn't followed her in. Or was she disappointed he hadn't? She hadn't come so hard since before Peyton.

In the triangular shower stall, she savoured the hot water pouring over her skin. Outside the opaque glass, a figure shimmered. Sebastiano opened the shower door, stepped in, and latched it shut. Water flattened his black hair and flowed down his chest. He raised his hand, fingers clutching a packet. A condom. She smiled—he respected her needs.

"What about breakfast?"

He bit the packet open.

Chapter Twenty-Three

Eric wheeled his suitcase down the motel corridor. Peyton trotted beside him hauling her Paddington Bear case. The room was simple with two double beds, veneer furnishings, and prints of generic beaches. One remarkable feature was a balcony that looked out over natural parkland, with no snow. He'd found it rejuvenating to step out of the Los Angeles airport into heat and then drive the rental car past palm trees and flowers in bloom. At a milkshake joint, he and Peyton had changed into sandals and shorts.

She plopped on the bed and grabbed the TV remote while he set out their toiletries in the bathroom. The drive to New Dawn had taken them twice as long as expected, due to stretches of crawling traffic and the stop for fries and shakes. California time was 4:00 p.m. His Calgary body clock said five—still too early for dinner, but from everything he'd read about New Dawn, there were no restaurants on-site. Best to avoid Peyton getting hungry or cranky at the retreat. A cartoon character squawked from the TV.

"How about a bite at the restaurant next door?" he asked Peyton.

Her gaze remained fixed on the screen. Watching TV in bed was a novelty for her. Then a commercial blared.

Peyton looked over at him. "Can we go see Mommy now?"

"After dinner. Sweet, you've been watching screens all day."

She surprised him by flicking off the set. She must really want to see Julie. He hoped her mother would be happy to see her. And if Julie was annoyed by his interference, she'd have to tone it down in front of Peyton. He was glad he'd brought their daughter.

Outdoors, he found the sun low in the sky. It would set in about an hour. The route from this town to the retreat was along a country road that might have little, if any, lighting.

Bells clanged as they entered the restaurant. A gaggle of teenagers had crammed into a booth near the door. Farther back, a woman sipped water, alone. Eric opted for a booth between them. Since it had an angled view of the woman, he slid onto the bench seat facing away from her to avoid staring. The waitress brought them menus and a kids' paper placemat and crayons. Eric ordered a burrito. They were in Southern California, after all. Peyton chose chicken fingers.

"What brings you our way?" the waitress asked. The name tag on her large chest said 'Trish'.

"We're visiting my wife at the New Dawn Retreat."

Her pencilled eyebrows rose. "That's different."

"Why?"

She frowned, as though she hadn't considered this question before. "People don't usually get visitors. Never, I'd say. They tend to bunker in for the week."

He clasped his hands on the table. "I'm curious to see what the place is like."

"Me too. Folks they employ are vague about specifics."

"Do many people work there?"

"The retreat pretty much keeps us alive, along with orange farms and retirees." She turned to the clanging door. "Speak of the devil."

Eric craned his body sideways. A man strode toward them. Tall. Tanned.

Trish waved at him. "That's Sebastiano. He runs the retreat along with Aurora."

"Hey, girl." Sebastiano grinned at Trish. "What's up?"

"Same old, same old." Trish glanced at Eric. "This fellow's here to see his wife, who's staying with you this week."

Sebastiano cocked his head.

"Is there a problem?" Eric asked.

"I can't think of who might be expecting you."

Sebastiano's straight teeth were so white they had to be capped, although they looked natural from this distance.

"What would be a good time of day to come?" Eric said.

"Depends on what you arranged with your wife."

"I hear the evenings are quiet," Trish said. "No TV or internet. I'd go bonkers."

Peyton looked up from her colouring.

Sebastiano bent toward her. "Who is this cutie? Do you miss your mom?"

Peyton nodded. Eric's jaw hurt. He hated the man's perfect smile.

"Who needs television, when we can swim and play outside?" Sebastiano kept his gaze on Peyton. "In cold weather, people bundle up indoors and talk, read, and play board games. Some draw, but not as well as you." He smiled at her. "You're quite the artist."

Peyton beamed. Eric wanted to climb over the table and shield her from this creep. Had he ever hated anyone so much on sight? The temperature would turn cool once the sun went down. He couldn't talk to Julie tonight with a bunch of people around, and he was beat from the flight and drive. Plus, Peyton's body clock would be saying "bedtime" in a few hours. They'd both be fresher in the morning.

"What time do things get going tomorrow?" he asked Sebastiano.

"We're up with the sun," Sebastiano said. "Before breakfast, some of us do tai chi."

Julie wasn't into that. At least, she hadn't been.

Sebastiano leaned into Peyton. "When you come see your mommy, I'll give you a special tour of the retreat. It's nifty."

Nifty? Did this guy think the word was cool? Trish smiled adoringly at Sebastiano. Eric's stomach curdled. The creep was obviously full of himself. And smarmy. And far too attentive to Peyton. Sebastiano saluted the three of them and left. Trish scurried after him.

"It's about time," Eric heard the woman in the booth say. From the corner of his eye, he saw Sebastiano slither onto the bench across from her.

Eric strained to catch more of the conversation. If he faced them, he might glimpse the tops of their heads. "How about we change places, sweet," he said to Peyton.

"Why?"

"Because."

"Okay."

How great to accept things simply "because." From his new position, Eric had a clear view of the woman in the booth. She was in her early thirties, he guessed, and was doing most of the talking. He wished he could read lips. Trish returned with two glasses of water and a new paper placemat with elephants and clowns.

"Do you know that woman with Sebastiano?" Eric asked.

Trish twisted around. "Cassandra? Came as a guest and stayed on to work at New Dawn. Now she's taken a job at Ralphs, the supermarket."

"Do you know why she left?"

"Personal differences, she says, between her and Aurora. Beautiful, isn't she?"

"Aurora?"

"Cassandra. Aurora probably was too, in her day." Trish lowered her voice. "Between you and me and this table, I wonder if Aurora felt threatened."

"By a younger woman?"

"I get the sense she's something of a control freak."

Trish left to check on their meals. Eric glanced at the other booth again. Cassandra chatted and gestured as if she and Sebastiano were old friends. Her long face was asymmetrical. Eric would call it more interesting than pretty. Peyton coloured a clown's coat in her methodical way, carefully staying inside the lines.

After Brad and Rosemary had left on Saturday night, Eric spent hours reading blog posts about the New Dawn Retreat. Most were glowing reviews. A few noted that Aurora and Sebastiano complemented each other—Sebastiano focused on the body, Aurora the spirit. That left out the mind, but no one seemed concerned about it. Former guests rhapsodized about the retreat's idyllic atmosphere, its

Italianesque setting. Many claimed the week had changed their lives. They'd given up soul-destroying jobs, dumped oppressive spouses and partners, started new businesses and artistic endeavours. The retreat had released their creativity. This particular point had actually made Eric want to jump on a plane to unblock his poetry.

Then he'd read a post written by a woman who felt inspired to sever her ties with her whole family as a result of the retreat. That gave him pause. Yet, many talked of renewed family connections, marriages refreshed.

But one post that rambled with incoherent sentences and misspellings had stopped him cold. 'Aurora is a frod. Sebastiano screws everyone in robes or tunics. The New Dawn Retreat recked my life.'

Eric had attempted to comment on the site and ask for details. His entry failed to upload. The post had been written over a year ago and the blog, apparently, abandoned shortly afterwards. He tried to dismiss the complaint—the writer probably hadn't been bright enough to grasp the point of the retreat—but it nagged him into bed.

At 3:00 a.m., he had booked their plane tickets. An impulse, he realized in the morning; an overreaction to fears in the night. Nothing had a perfect track record. No doubt there were people who disliked his approach to dentistry and certainly many who didn't appreciate his poems. Most of the world, in fact.

He noticed Cassandra watching him. Had he been staring at her? He blinked and looked at Peyton. "Sweet, how about tonight we stay in and watch TV. There's a microwave to make popcorn. We'll go see Mommy first thing tomorrow."

Cassandra moved deeper into her booth, where Eric couldn't see her anymore. He wondered if she had shifted position on purpose.

* * *

"How are Aurora and Julie making out?" Cassandra asked.

"It's a real mother-and-child reunion," Sebastiano said, taking care to keep his tone light. "Aurora cut the afternoon session short to spend time with her."

"That's serious." Cassandra slurped her soda.

"The official reason was so guests could spend extra time in the pool before it turns cool later this week."

Trish arrived with his coffee and their burgers and fries.

"Thanks, darling." He gazed up at her.

Trish tossed him her usual flirty smile. He was confident she'd sleep with him if he asked. Equally certain she'd be furious when their fling ended; it was not worth losing this haven of non-retreat food and source of town information.

"You don't use such endearments with the women you sleep with," Cassandra said, after Trish left.

"Would you want me to?"

She dumped ketchup on her fries. "Stick with your usual approach."

Cassandra liked it rougher than Julie. He loved adapting to the variety of human ways. Sex was all about harmonizing with the other person. Aurora's messages had numerous applications.

"Here's to beef." Sebastiano held up his juicy, dripping burger. He had nothing against alfalfa sprouts, but how could Aurora live without tasting animal flesh on occasion? For non-vegetarian guests, the retreat offered chicken or fish three times a week, steak being environmentally harmful and expensive.

Cassandra chewed a fry. "Didn't you have a burger yesterday when you were in town?" As always, she talked and chewed at the same time, another habit she'd need to lose if she were to become a leader. Unlikely this nowhere town had someone who taught etiquette, but he'd ask Trish.

"That's why I can't see you tomorrow," he said. "Three town days in a row will make Aurora suspicious."

"So, I spend my days and nights toiling at Ralphs and watching TV alone?"

"Until everything is settled."

"When will that be?"

He bit into his burger, avoiding her stare. The mouth of the little girl in the booth reminded him of Julie's. But it was something about the way the child concentrated on her drawing that had convinced him Julie was the mother. Julie's family in Calgary hadn't wasted any time.

"Why are you frowning?" Cassandra said.

"Am I?" He wiped mustard from his lips, hoping she'd take the hint and do the same with the ketchup on hers. "Aurora's real reason for spending time with Julie this afternoon was to convince her to remain at the retreat."

Cassandra's eyes flashed. "I knew it."

"This doesn't mean you're out."

"It will if Aurora succeeds." Cassandra leaned out of the booth to get Trish's attention. She asked for a refill of Diet Coke. Trish nodded and left.

"Are the guy and kid still there?" Sebastiano asked.

"He looks like he's getting ready to go. So, you really think it's Julie's husband and child?"

Estranged husband. But if he clarified that, Cassandra might start wondering if Julie's marital status mattered to him.

"Yes. If they're at the motel, you're likely to see them around."

"You want me to chat him up?"

"Discreetly."

"For what purpose?"

"Depends on what he says. We'll figure out the use for it later."

Trish reappeared with Cassandra's drink. "What's new at New Dawn?"

"Not much since yesterday." Evidently, word of Aurora's long-lost daughter hadn't spread through town. Trish would chide him for keeping that detail secret. And instantly forgive him. He munched his burger until Trish took off, impressed that Cassandra hadn't spilled the news. She had an instinct for the right moment.

"I don't think there's space for both Julie and me at New Dawn," Cassandra said. "Especially since Aurora despises me."

"That's a strong word."

"Aurora's a strong person."

"She's also a mother who wants her daughter with her. If your presence will help Julie stay, Aurora will swallow her bile and take you back."

"How could my presence help?"

"I haven't worked out that part yet."

"Well, start soon, because I'm tired of living in Limbo.

"So that's the name of this town. I always wondered."

She slapped his hand.

"Careful," Sebastiano said, and picked up a fry. Julie had filled him in on her afternoon discussion with Aurora. He saw no reason not to share it with Cassandra. "Aurora told Julie of her plan to build a satellite retreat on the farm property. One built in the style of an ancient Roman villa."

"Isn't that your idea?"

"Seems Aurora has appropriated it as her own." He suppressed a grin. "Why set her straight? I just want it done. Aurora asked Julie to oversee the development. She'd have total control."

"With Aurora's meddling." Cassandra swirled a French fry in ketchup.

"Aurora dislikes mechanical matters. She might refrain."

"That would be a first." Cassandra continued swirling the fry. Good that she was giving this thought.

"By the time the project is completed, Aurora hopes Julie will be committed enough to lead the second retreat."

"Meanwhile, I'm long booted out." She flipped up the fry so fast that it spattered ketchup across the table, barely missing his shirt.

He was glad he hadn't flinched. "The thing is, I don't think Julie's the spiritual-leader type. Aurora is blind to that fact. I envision Julie and you in complementary roles, with Julie the architect, and you the leader."

"Aurora won't go for it."

"That's what we have to work on."

"How?" She nibbled the fry.

"Things often fall into place if you keep your eyes open for opportunity."

Cassandra looked almost convinced. It helped that what he'd told her was mostly true. Julie currently had no interest in succeeding her mother, but that could change as she got more involved in the retreat. A huge factor was Aurora's health. Sebastiano hadn't yet managed to reach her doctor, but he would make an extra effort to wrangle the real biopsy result from him tomorrow. Assuming the worst, that Aurora was cancer free, she would still eventually come to realize that two retreats required two leaders. One aging person spreading herself between the locations would dilute the energy and message. If Julie accepted a leadership role, she would probably opt for the new place, the one she'd built from scratch. Aurora would lead the original retreat until she collapsed from a heart attack or stroke in the amphitheatre.

He paused to picture Aurora dying at the sunrise service. She would love the drama cementing her legend.

The glitch for Cassandra was that any successor Aurora groomed would not be Cassandra, whom she did despise. For Sebastiano, the plan would work with any appealing protégé. Among the hundreds who passed through the retreat, he and Aurora would find one on which they could agree.

"But does Julie want to stay?" Cassandra asked.

He'd be wise to stick with the mostly true. "She sounded interested." She really had, to his surprise. "She's not super-keen on her job back home, and her husband has custody of their daughter."

Cassandra glanced toward Eric's table. "Why?"

"No clue."

"Makes you wonder what kind of person she is." Cassandra ran her finger over her plate to dredge up the cheese that had dripped from her burger. "I can't help thinking Julie's presence means I'm out on my tail."

"And a pretty tail it is."

She licked the cheese from her finger. Not exactly elegant, but sensual. "What time do you have to get back?"

"Dinner's in an hour. You leave here first. I'll go around to the motel's far side, where you can let me in."

"I don't like this sneaking around."

"Sure you do."

"Speak for yourself."

Sneaking enhanced the kick, but more important was the particular outcome, his two women leading retreats on either side of the hill. Ideally, they would be Julie and Cassandra. Keeping Cassandra in town was worthwhile in case they found the opportunity. But if forced to choose, he would go for Julie. She was the one for the retreat. Aurora was right about that.

Chapter Twenty-Four

"Every day is a new dawn, a chance to cast off the burdens of the past and pursue your dreams."

From the top row of the amphitheatre, Julie studied her mother behind the podium. Aurora spoke in front of a sky that was evolving from indigo to pale yellows, pinks, and oranges. Everyone in the rows below seemed transfixed. So did Delilah, who sat beside Julie. What a change in Delilah these past few days.

"I wonder if I could live without meds here," Delilah had mused.

Julie wondered too. Delilah had confided she was in love with Garth and that he'd said he loved her. Last week, Julie would have been skeptical; genuine love didn't happen this fast. But at New Dawn, this seemed possible. She was far from in love with Sebastiano, though. Doubts about him kept tiptoeing in. *He lies when he says I mean more to him than the others he's slept with. He's using me to implement his vision for the retreat.*

On the lawn, Sebastiano stretched and lunged, warming up for tai chi. He had joked he'd initiated the sessions as an excuse to skip the sunrise service. "After three or four hundred times, it can get repetitive."

Even though he didn't completely buy into the message, he was able to work for it. Financially, Sebastiano and her mother were equal partners in the business, but he was lower in the hierarchy, and a male. They had founded the retreat as an alternative to mainstream society, he'd said—real change required female leadership. And conveniently allows him to have fun and avoid responsibility.

"...a clean slate..." Aurora said.

When her mother emoted to the crowd like this, Julie thought of her as Aurora. During their private talks, "Mother" was starting to feel normal.

"Go with whatever feels right," Aurora had said.

Intellectually, Julie understood her mother's reasons for leaving her. Staying with Brad would have dragged Marion down until she had nothing to offer a child or herself. For sure, Marion and Brad would have separated during Julie's elementary school years. And her father's and grandmother's stubbornness and hostility toward Marion would have resulted in child-raising battles that might have scarred Julie as much as a mother's departure. But even though her mind understood, she couldn't let go of the pain. *Replace "can't" with "won't."* That was what Aurora had told the group at yesterday's session. You make the choice to cling to outmoded thoughts. Some of Eric's Fox poems carried a similar message.

"It's about the old stuff that controls you," he'd explained to Julie about a poem he called "The Duchess." The aristocrat with her fox stole lived a restricted life because she feared letting go of her archaic patterns.

This had felt like an accusation. Aurora's message built hope. Everyone is capable of becoming whomever she or he wants. Julie wondered if that was possible for her.

"Life is an opportunity waiting to be grabbed," Aurora said.

Another platitude Julie had heard before in a hundred variations. The guests in robes and tunics nodded in agreement, but how many would incorporate the message into their everyday lives? She supposed that even if only one or two did, that was something. The others would return home from a pleasant and memorable vacation, perhaps changed in a small way. Aurora was doing good work. Julie's work produced a product that drove the economy, raped the earth, and possibly caused cancers and other ailments. Her father and colleagues insisted the benefits of oil and gas outweighed potential negatives. Julie used to agree. Or she'd tried to, to justify her work. Aurora had suggested Julie's aversion to driving sprang from a subconscious rejection of gasoline. That seemed a little far-fetched.

"Remember when you were a child," Aurora said at the podium. "Every day promised a new adventure. The child is still in you, trapped in your adult skin. Release the child."

Aurora's spiel was certainly no worse than oil-patch propaganda. Designing a new retreat across the hill was an opportunity for Julie. Her mother had brushed off her concerns about obtaining a green card to work in the US.

"Julie, decide first what you want, then deal with the obstacles. Too many people focus on them as an excuse to abandon their dreams." She paused. "What are your dreams, Julie?"

Julie had shied away from answering. Compared to her mother's dreams, Julie's felt ordinary.

Love. She'd loved Eric once, and lost that connection. Her former excitement and warmth when she was with him were gone. Love didn't seem possible with Sebastiano. Sooner or later his eye would stray. Don't start with the obstacle. Choose the dream first. Did that mean risk loving him and find ways to keep his love?

A rewarding career. Developing a retreat would build her skills and provide a hands-on education with room and board, although no salary. But she didn't need money here, and Aurora would surely say money was a shallow goal.

Finding her mother—a dream fulfilled. But her other family relationships could use improvement, and that was already happening with Delilah. This journey together had made them almost friends. And she might actually get along better with her father and Rosemary if she lived farther away from them.

The biggest dream of all: a true bond with Peyton. That was the dark hole. Shared custody in Calgary would give her more time with her daughter. If she stayed here, she would see Peyton only on holidays. And she couldn't—that was, she wouldn't—ask Eric for unsupervised custody until she was certain of her mental stability.

Before the retreat, medication and therapy had been her only possible treatments. Now, she'd gone three days without meds. Garth had told Delilah he was a mess in Chicago but living here had cured his crippling anxiety. Julie couldn't believe that. *Damn doubts.* Delilah was already talking about staying here with him. That was too quick. *Cast off the old attitudes.*

"I keep hoping I'm pregnant" —Delilah's next shocker. "It's silly, I know, but we aren't using protection."

Julie had shuddered. Sebastiano's condom broke their second night. While he respected her worry, he seemed take-it-or-leave-it about the pregnancy possibility. Would he one day want her to produce an heir, a combination of him and her to lead the retreat or be the sidekick counterpart? She had to cast off these suspicions or they would drive her to paranoia, worse than she'd experienced in the past with Eric. What did clinging to the tired Julie model give her? Not an error-free life. She had so blatantly, horribly erred.

Aurora raised her arms. "Welcome the new day."

"Welcome" rippled through the amphitheatre from the rows below.

Beyond the oak tree, the sun peeked above the mountain, capped with snow despite the warmth of the valley.

Welcome, Mother. Welcome, Mom. Julie cringed saying it to herself, never mind aloud. She couldn't say it. Or wouldn't? *Let go of archaic resentments.* She chose to cling to them or not.

The bright ball rose behind Aurora. Julie leaned forward. *How wonderful to have a mother in her life.* A mother who understood her in ways no one ever had. In front of the glowing ball, Aurora's silhouette raised her arms to Julie.

"Welcome, Mom." Julie mouthed the words.

Love trickled down her throat and relaxed her stomach.

"Welcome, Mom," she whispered. Love fanned to her fingers and toes, warmed her whole body.

"That was really inspiring," Delilah said.

The spell broke. People shifted positions and spoke to their neighbours.

"Are you going to tai chi?" Delilah said. "I feel too lazy. Thought I'd get a book from the library."

Julie tried but couldn't recapture that moment of welcome love. Had it been a religious experience? The love hadn't come from a god. It had emanated from her mother, who was now circled by guests.

"Your mom's amazing," Delilah said.

They padded down the stairs, Julie's legs wobbly. A few guests were heading across the lawn to Sebastiano. Julie had planned to do tai chi, but it would feel like a distraction now. Aurora glided toward her. Aurora. Mother. Mom. A trinity. Aurora a goddess, three in one. *Don't be ridiculous.* The goddess was mother, daughter, ghost. *Get your head level.* Was this a delusion? Abrupt withdrawal from her meds could cause them.

A few stragglers lingered in the amphitheatre, keeping their distance from Aurora, Julie, and Delilah. Another trinity. Mother, daughter, stepdaughter. New patterns, not archaic.

"How did you escape from everyone?" Julie asked her mother as they walked to the path. "I sensed they wanted to approach you."

"You learn a few tricks. I make them feel my need to take a small break before breakfast."

Mother, daughter and a third entity, about which Julie wasn't sure. Was she developing schizophrenia, this connecting with her mother on three, constantly changing, levels?

"I'm doing your morning session," Delilah told Aurora. "After lunch, I'll drive to Santa Monica to pick up our things."

"I'll go with you," Julie said. "It's not fair that you do that long drive alone."

"That's thoughtful of you, Julie, but—" Aurora halted. "Who is that?"

A man and child approached from the parking lot. He held the girl's hand as she skipped alongside. Julie froze. Peyton broke free of Eric and raced toward them.

"Mommy!"

Julie scooped her up. What were they doing here? Julie's robe bunched around her child, who felt heavier than she remembered. Eric shambled up to them. His T-shirt and shorts looked strange, given her immersion in robes and tunics.

She squinted at his face, which was a pasty contrast to Sebastiano's tan, and tried to remain cool. "What are you doing here?" It came out snarly.

"Daddy and I came to see you." Peyton's hands enclosed Julie's neck.

Eric stared at Aurora.

Julie set Peyton down and took a deep breath. "Eric and Peyton," she said. "Meet my mother."

"My granddaughter." Aurora squatted in front of Peyton, who retreated into Eric. "I want to get to know you," she said. "But you are smart and right to be careful of strangers."

"How did you know where I was?" Julie asked Eric.

"Julie, I wrote him," Delilah said. "I meant to tell you."

Julie stomped her foot. Delilah had no right. She'd promised to let Julie take the lead on telling their family, which included Eric. Why was Delilah contacting him anyway?

"Daddy and I are going to Disneyland and the beach," Peyton said to Aurora.

"You lucky girl." Aurora remained at the child's eye level. She connected to everyone, regardless of age.

Peyton gazed up at Julie. "Daddy says you'll come with us to LEGOLAND."

"I only suggested you might be interested," Eric said to Julie.

She glared. He'd obviously come here to meddle.

"Can we talk?" he asked her.

Aurora grabbed Julie's wrist and pulled herself up, wincing. Her mother displayed so much energy in the amphitheatre that Julie kept forgetting she was almost sixty. Rosemary, around the same age, had back problems. Brad had high cholesterol. Odds were that her mother had a medical issue or two.

"I'll take my granddaughter to the kitchen. We might find a treat." Aurora fumbled for Peyton's hand. "Have you had breakfast yet?"

"We ate at the motel," Eric said.

The small hand secure, Aurora gazed down at Peyton. "I hope you'll join us for a second breakfast. Today is French toast with strawberries from our garden."

"Strawberries!" Peyton looked at Eric for permission.

Eric nodded. Julie continued glaring at him. Only an asshole would use a child to intrude this way. He could have left Peyton in Calgary and come to California on his own. Cowardly and manipulative.

"We'll talk later," Delilah said to Eric, and followed Aurora and Peyton into the building.

What was Delilah up to? Julie had thought they were friends.

"Does my father know you're here?" Julie asked.

"He's the one who urged me to come. From Delilah's description, he thought the retreat sounded like a cult." He scanned Julie from head to toe. "I can't disagree, seeing you in this outfit."

"It's no more an outfit than your T-shirt and shorts. People wear clothes to fit the place they're in."

"This must be some weird place." Eric's lip twitched in mockery, his face a mask of resistance similar to hers before her mother's love entered. If she tried to explain that to him, it would sound peculiar, even to her. Conversion, religious or otherwise, was faith beyond reason. Eric was mired in the rational, like she'd been.

"You have to be at New Dawn to understand," she said.

"I am here. No way am I wearing a dress."

She folded her arms.

"I was joking. Oh, there's someone in normal clothes."

Julie had missed seeing Garth, in the citrus on the hillside. Julie called him over and introduced him to Eric.

"Delilah's Eric?" Garth said, and blinked several times.

Eric's brow creased. Julie was equally puzzled. Delilah's Eric?

"Did you write to Delilah first?" Julie asked.

"Only because you didn't respond."

Julie looked at Garth. "What did you mean by 'Delilah's Eric'?"

Garth held up his basket. "I'm late picking oranges for breakfast." He scurried to the grove so fast he stumbled, but he managed to recover.

"Weird duck," Eric said.

"Can you not be critical for one second?"

He pinched his lips together. Ugly. A schoolmarm. "Julie, I'm here to talk about you and this retreat." He looked around—at the courtyard, the amphitheatre glimpsed through the cypress trees, Garth picking oranges.

"You are so judgmental," Julie said. "I don't know how I stood it before."

"Can we stick to the point?"

"Which is?"

"Firstly, how long are you staying here?"

Julie opened her mouth to respond, but Delilah rushed from the main building. "Eric, Aurora had this idea, if you agree. Peyton says you're on your way to a beach. Santa Monica has a great one. If you go there, you could stop at the apartment, pack up our things, and spend the night to save money on a hotel. Then you can take our things with you to Calgary. We don't need them here."

Eric's lower lip dropped. "You two are actually staying?"

Delilah glanced at Julie. "We changed our flights home to Monday, so I'd have more time to figure things out with Garth."

"The guy with the oranges?" Eric said.

Delilah brightened. "You've met him?"

"Garth said you told him about Eric," Julie said.

Delilah froze. "What did he tell you?"

"Is there something to tell?" Julie looked from Delilah's flushed face to Eric's pale one. What the hell was going on?

"Oh, Julie, it's over," Delilah said. "It was stupid and silly and now I realize it didn't mean anything."

"What's she talking about?" Julie asked Eric.

"I don't know," he said. "Unless she means staying over on Saturday night." His face flushed.

"After the poetry reading," Delilah said. "I told you I drove him home."

Julie sucked in the citrusy air to expand her tight chest. "You didn't add that you slept with him."

"I didn't." Delilah's face grew redder. Liars. "I'd had too much wine. Eric agreed I shouldn't drive." She looked at Eric. "Did you tell Garth about all that? Oh, Garth. Where is he?"

Eric motioned toward the orange grove. Up the hill, Garth moved between the trees.

"I have to talk to him, explain." Delilah hurried away, into the grove.

"I wish she'd explain to me," Eric said.

"It's perfectly clear. You pick her up at your reading and then ply her with liquor to get her into bed."

"That's crazy," Eric said. "Julie, she's your sister."

"Stepsister."

"I didn't plan anything," he said. "We just had a few drinks."

"As far as I'm concerned, you can screw whoever you wish."

Eric stepped back, perhaps shocked by her language. "That's generous, when, by your choice, we've been separated for ten months." He raised his hands, palms to her. "Julie, can we please stay on topic?"

"As defined by you. What did Delilah tell you in her email?"

He shrugged. "That you'd both fallen in love with this ridiculous place. It got me curious."

Delilah was talking to Garth, moving her arms wildly. His body sagged, as though her hand gestures were beating him down. Then he turned his back and lumbered to the trees by the amphitheatre and down to the main building.

Delilah emerged from the grove, her face scarlet. "Oh God, have I screwed this up."

"If it would help, I'll talk to him," Eric said.

"No. I need to take care of this myself. It's all my fault." She slunk into the main building.

"I wish you two would tell me the truth," Julie told Eric.

"Would you believe us if we did?" Eric stared over her shoulder. "Is that Sebastiano?"

Julie whirled toward the courtyard. The tai chi group had shifted into view. Everyone extended their arms and raised a leg, Sebastiano steady, the rest tottering. "How do you know him?"

"He was in the restaurant yesterday."

Sebastiano had told her he'd gone into town to buy hiking socks to replace his worn ones, which were causing a blister, and that he'd stopped at the restaurant for a non-healthy-food fix.

"Strange guy," Eric said. "I can't put my finger on it."

"Did you talk to him?"

"Part of it was the way he looked at Peyton."

"He's not a pedophile."

"It isn't that," Eric said with a frown. "Anyway, in the restaurant, he met a woman named Cassandra."

"Yes, he told me he ran into her."

"Their meeting seemed planned."

Julie's throat felt tight. "How would you know?"

"From what I overheard, I'm certain it was."

Liar. He'd said that to hurt her so she would respond and reveal her status with Sebastiano. "You were eavesdropping."

"I'm telling you this, so you'll know what you're dealing with."

Chills prickled Julie's arms. She crossed them, but they didn't warm up. A cloud had passed over the sun for what felt like the first time since she and Delilah had arrived in California.

"Cassandra's staying at my motel," Eric said. "I ran into her at breakfast."

"By accident or your intention?"

His flushed neck showed she'd hit the mark. He really had come to the retreat to snoop.

"Cassandra confirmed the official story," Eric said, his tone skeptical. Could he be more transparent? "She and Aurora clashed. A difference in style. She didn't have a bad word to say about Aurora or the retreat."

Julie could do sarcasm too. "How disappointing for you."

"She's working at the local supermarket. Why would she want a Joe job in a hick town?"

"Not everyone's ambitious, Eric." Julie flashed a condescending smile. Fortunately, Sebastiano had kept her in the loop. "Cassandra likes the rural atmosphere and is considering settling in the area. I like it too. It's incredibly peaceful."

He shook his head. "You used to tease me about growing up in boring Saskatchewan."

"The old me."

One eyebrow rose underneath his drooping bangs. "There's a new you?"

Her inspiration at the sunrise service had felt like a calling. To what? She couldn't puzzle that out in the midst of Eric's negativity. Her mother's message was all positive.

"Shit," Eric said. "The creep is on his way here."

A half-dozen women, and Nelson and his partner, Orrin, flanked Sebastiano, all of them laughing and chatting. Sebastiano's gaze lit on Julie and Eric.

"Go ahead without me, guys," he told the group. "Save me a spot at the table." He stopped beside Julie, facing Eric. "You look familiar." He snapped his fingers. "The restaurant. You were with a cute little girl. I knew she looked familiar. It didn't hit me until now. She's the image of Julie."

"Is that why you were staring at her?" Julie said.

"Was I? Sorry for that." Sebastiano looked at them both. "I must have been trying to place her."

Julie tossed Eric a smug glance. He scrunched his face, his body stiff. Petty.

"Is Peyton here, too?" Sebastiano said. "I can't wait to meet her, officially."

"I'll go see what she's up to." Eric strode away.

"Nice guy," Sebastiano said.

“He was rude.”

“I get the sense he’s protective of his daughter.”

“What does he have to protect her from? Me?”

“If he believes that, he’s an idiot.”

The breakfast bell chimed, melodious yet insistent. They walked into the main building, not touching, but Julie felt their bodies brush. Aurora would call it their auras mingling. Hours ago, Julie would have scoffed. She’d only half-listened to Aurora’s explanation about auras, something that involved colours.

In the lounge, women descended on Sebastiano. Robes of all tints swept him down the hall. Aurora stepped out of her office and linked her arm with Julie’s.

“Where’s Peyton?” Julie said.

“In the dining room. I wanted her to sit with us at the head table, but Eric objected most abruptly.”

The dining room buzzed with guests energized for the new day. The tai chi group gathered around the table at the back with Peyton and Eric, who talked with Orrin. Nelson held out a seat for Sebastiano. Next to Peyton was an empty chair.

“I should sit with my daughter,” Julie told Aurora.

“And let Eric get his way? He’s behaving like a stubborn child.”

A woman settled on the empty chair and leaned down to speak to Peyton, who answered. Their mouths moved in pantomime. Peyton’s lips spilled clouds of yellow, the woman’s, clouds of blues. The colours swirled into a healthy green. Was Julie going crazy? Or was a deeper power showing her how this stranger connected to Peyton better than Julie did or had in the past or ever could in the future. Peyton laughed a bright yellow bubble.

Aurora increased the pressure on Julie’s arm. Julie let her steer them past the table.

She belonged with Aurora; she didn’t belong with Peyton. She had to admit that, accept who she was, her true self, and focus on what she did well. Here, she could accomplish good work, create a new retreat, and acquire the skills to lead it. In the process, she'd strengthen her bond with her mother, her primary need for now.

This wasn't abandoning Peyton. Her daughter would know where she was and come for holidays. In between, Julie would make trips to Calgary and, overall, see Peyton as much as she did now. For all his narrowness, Eric was a decent man. One day he would find a wife suited to parenting, like the woman talking colours with Peyton. Julie would do her best to be supportive and become a positive, if different, model for her daughter. The retreat offered Julie the possibility of living, of loving, and of being herself. What Peyton needed most of all was a healthy mother.

"Julie?" Aurora leaned on her arm.

"I'm with you. Mom." Julie tried out the word, which felt awkward, this first time. "Mom." It flowed over her tongue. "Mom." Natural and easy.

Chapter Twenty-Five

"What does each colour mean?"

Over breakfast, Aurora had been answering Julie's questions about auras. "That's for you to interpret."

"How will I know if I interpret it right?"

"You develop a sense."

Aurora hadn't reached the level of auras. Her daughter had a gift—one Aurora deserved after her years of struggle and work. But she should be gracious toward Julie. That elusive gift had contributed to the change in her, a slight shift to Aurora's side.

Julie left the subject. "I'm worried about Delilah. It's not like her to miss a meal."

When Delilah hadn't appeared, Aurora had instructed a server to remove the third chair from the head table. This would be a permanent move. Delilah made a pleasant companion for Julie and would be useful for the office and social media, but she didn't deserve elevated status. Sebastiano sat with the guests. Aurora would delicately suggest to Delilah that, with her sociable and empathetic nature, she could fill a similar role of bonding with people at meals. And, in truth, she knew Delilah would be more comfortable there.

Guests filed out of the dining room, some to prepare for the morning hike, others to stroll or refresh themselves before Aurora's session. Julie left the head table to talk to Eric. The man reminded her too much of Brad, who dismissed anything that deviated from the so-called normal. Too often, women repeated their mothers' mistakes. The strong ones, like Julie, seized the opportunity for a second chance. Aurora followed Julie to the table at the back.

"What's next on today's agenda?" Eric asked, as Aurora approached. "Peyton's keen to hang around, if we're invited."

From Julie's rigid shoulders, it was clear she dreaded a prolonged visit from this husband she had rejected. Was there a way to keep Peyton here without him?

"The retreat works as a cohesive group," Aurora said. "Outsiders disturb the organic whole." She smiled at Peyton. "Outside adults, I mean. Children are always welcome."

Eric rubbed his jaw. "Peyton can't stay without me."

"I understood she came all this way to spend time with her mother."

Eric and Julie exchanged glances. Perhaps related to his supervised-visit requirement?

"Julie and I will spend time with her together," Aurora said. "When we're occupied, I'll assign someone to mind Peyton. We have a large staff."

"What's the point of leaving her here with a sitter?"

Julie's jaw tightened. "I'll give her my full attention while she's here."

Juliana, don't submit to the mother role. Aurora touched her daughter's arm, pleased by the name that had just come to her. "Juliana" suited a leader and sounded Italian. It would be best to introduce the name when Eric was gone, though. "Julie has plans to study my session and the farm property today."

Peyton perked up. "Does it have ponies?"

"Only a horse," Aurora said. "We'll buy you a pony for your next visit."

Eric's nostrils pinched as though he were sniffing manure. If Aurora could see auras, she was sure his would be black.

"Since when did you get into farming?" he asked Juliana.

"It's the site for the new retreat she's designing," Aurora said.

Eric's eyebrows rose. Juliana stared at him, not flinching. Good girl.

Peyton tugged at Juliana's robe. "I want to go to the farm."

"It's a grown-up hike." Aurora rolled her stiff shoulder. "We'll take you there on your own to see it later. For now, would you like us to make you a robe like your mommy's?"

"A princess dress?" Peyton asked.

Eric ruffled Peyton's hair. "Sweet, let's save it for another time. Mommy asked us to pick up her stuff at her apartment near the beach."

"Can Mommy come swimming with us?"

Eric looked at Juliana. "How about it?" His expression stayed casual, on the surface. Aurora didn't need to read auras to pick up his mental challenge.

"I'd rather play with Peyton here." Juliana also rubbed Peyton's hair. "I'll skip the session and hike."

"Peyton's heart is set on the beach today."

"I want the farm and princess dress," Peyton said.

"Later, sweet." Eric coaxed Peyton up from her chair. "We've got to get going."

"To the farm?"

"Julie," he said. "I'll need the address and keys for your Santa Monica place."

"The farm." Peyton stamped her foot.

"Delilah has them upstairs," Juliana said. "I'll get them."

Eric patted Peyton's head. "Next time, sweet. I promise."

Sweet. What a sickening word of affectation, so traditionally male. Eric's clinging to the child could be a hiccup in Aurora's plan, especially if he threatened to restrict Peyton's future visits to the retreat. A Canadian judge might accept Eric's twisted description of the retreat and side with him, forcing Juliana to go to Calgary to see her child. Each trip would pull Juliana away from New Dawn's sphere. Her shift wasn't yet solid enough for her to choose the retreat over Peyton. Aurora had to tip the scales, with Sebastiano's help.

While Juliana went upstairs, Aurora took Peyton and Eric to the lounge, even though it would make her late for the session. Upheavals threw the retreat off its track, but, as she told the guests, they promoted growth. Embrace disruptions.

Juliana returned with the keys and directions to the apartment. "Delilah's pretty upset."

"I'll talk to her next time," Eric said.

Had they established a next time? Aurora led them all out to the morning air. The older gay man walked toward them. Cicero was his mnemonic. Inexplicably, his name slipped her mind. She hoped Eric and Peyton's arrival was the last in this series of intrusions. *Embrace these disturbances.* They were sent by the heavens as help in working toward a solution for the retreat's future. Her goals and Sebastiano's had converged in the person of Juliana. Peyton, Aurora's granddaughter, was a smart, charming girl. Let Eric do the grunt work of raising her. At the right time, Peyton would come to Juliana, as Juliana had found Aurora.

How could one possibly transform the name "Peyton" into one suited to a leader?

When her granddaughter came to them, she would retrain her. So would Juliana. Peyton's leadership would carry the retreat long into this century. Further, if Peyton had a daughter.

Cicero nodded hello and handed a folded piece of paper to Eric. "Here's the thing I was telling you about."

"What's that?" Juliana said.

"A secret." He winked at Eric, who stuffed the paper in his pocket.

Juliana's brow knit.

Cicero waddled away. Some men weren't meant to wear togas, although on Cicero, tights and a tunic would be hideously worse. Eric could probably pull off either one, although in a tunic he wouldn't cut a figure like Sebastiano. Juliana could surely see that. Aurora hugged Peyton goodbye. Juliana did too, adding a kiss.

"See you," Juliana said to Eric. No hug or kiss.

He gripped Peyton's hand all the way to the parking lot.

"You'd think we were handing out poison around here," Juliana said.

Aurora smiled. Hostility between Julie and Eric was bound to be a positive.

"Peyton could probably have managed the easy hike," Juliana said. "But children do naturally draw attention to themselves and change a group's focus."

She'd almost sounded like Aurora when she said that. Juliana's understanding was growing by leaps.

Across the lawn, Sebastiano's hiking group milled beneath the valley oak tree, waiting, it would appear, for Sebastiano.

"He's rarely late for the hike," Aurora noted.

"Sebastiano had to make a phone call this morning," Juliana said. "He's due for a medical checkup."

Unlikely. Sebastiano considered himself too young and fit for an annual physical. Had her illness made him conscious of mortality? She doubted he would be that sensitive or prudent. Even she had delayed seeing a doctor about the lump. Cancer was Juliana's zodiac sign. Another connection that had brought Juliana to the retreat at this particular moment.

"Do you mind starting the session while I retrieve something from the office?" Aurora asked her.

"Start it how?" Juliana said.

"Talk about yourself and your journey."

Aurora left her to work this out and breezed into the lounge, now empty of people. She opened the door to the office. Sebastiano banged into her, on his way out. The muscle around her collarbone throbbed. Aurora stroked the pain, backed Sebastiano into the office and closed the soundproof door.

"I finally reached your doctor."

His candour startled her. "About what?"

"He refused to say if you were cancer free or not."

"Doctors have ethics."

"You'd let cancer consume you before you handed the retreat over to someone you feel unworthy."

"Cassandra?"

He rounded the desk and stopped in front of the bookcase. "I agree with you that Julie would make a better successor."

Aurora stifled a smile. She had won that round. "Are you and Juliana using protection?"

"Tut-tut, Mom. Daughters need their privacy," he said. Then his brow furrowed. "Juliana?"

"Pregnancy would interfere with her roles as leader and architect."

"Not to mention my enjoyment."

But could a pregnancy help with the long-term plan? Juliana was thirty-eight, still young enough to have a son to eventually replace Sebastiano. What a beautiful boy he would be. Tall, dark and athletic—Sebastiano's looks with Julie's brains. A grown-up Peyton, assisted by her younger half-brother in charge of New Dawn?

Aurora smiled. "I am cancer free."

His gaze bored into hers, and then his blue eyes relaxed in satisfaction. He believed her; and it was the truth, at the moment.

They were the perfect team. While Aurora was more vital to the retreat, New Dawn wouldn't function to its fullest without him. Juliana had reunited their vision. Aurora's head felt light. The heavens were giving her too much. *You don't deserve all this.* She did deserve it. She'd hoped she had jettisoned that nasty voice with the lump.

Sebastiano waited for her to continue, distracting himself by taking books from her shelf and returning them to the same place. She leaned against her desk and surveyed the room. Oval Tuscan window. Medieval tapestry carpet. Books of inspiration—the ones that had helped her most.

Her surgeon wouldn't declare her completely cancer free for five years. The disease could resurface in any organ or spot of flesh, or she might live in good health another twenty or thirty years. Whatever her fate, New Dawn was her life. She wanted to leave it securely in her daughter's hands.

"Do you like Juliana?" She squinted at Sebastiano, needing to read behind whatever he said.

"I do." He fanned a book on Buddhist teachings. "In fact, more than Cassandra, and as much as anyone in the past."

"How soon before you cheat on her?"

"I've no one in mind yet."

"I hear Cassandra has a job in town."

"She's tenacious." He shoved the book back into the shelf. "I've told her flatly and clearly it's over. Eventually, she'll give up."

"If you're still screwing her…"

"You think I'd do that and risk all our plans for Julie?"

Unfortunately, she was fairly certain he would. Life for him was a game. If tossing Cassandra into the brew added to his fun and raised the stakes, he would gamble the retreat. His prize, the two women of his choice, leading two retreats after Aurora was gone. She wished she could hate him for this. The problem was, during the last ten years, he had moved from being her lover to, in effect, her son. Her two children, Apollo and Diana. They were sun and moon, brother and sister who would continue the New Dawn Retreat into future generations through Peyton and a child he and Juliana might conceive.

Aurora pushed herself from the desk. "Guests are waiting for me at the session."

"My hikers will be stomping in their boots." Sebastiano smiled. "Can't these people learn to take care of themselves?"

"It's what makes us essential."

* * *

Julie rapped on Delilah's door. "Mind if I come in?" She heard rustlings from inside the room. "It's almost lunch."

"I'm not hungry." Delilah sounded hoarse.

Julie opened the door. Delilah's bedroom was about half the size of hers and looked out to the herb garden and cottages.

Delilah crawled up from the comforter, her amber robe a mass of creases, her eyes and nose red, skin blotchy. "Julie, honestly, nothing happened between Eric and me."

"Even if something did, Eric and I are separated. I don't care who he sleeps with." Except it bugged her to think of him with Delilah.

"He didn't sleep with me."

Liar. "Like I said, you have nothing to apologize for."

Julie turned toward the sound of footsteps in the hall. A maid carried a basket of laundry out of Cassandra's former bedroom. With all the laundry a retreat produced, any new one that Julie designed would include chutes to the basement laundry facilities. She closed Delilah's door.

Delilah sat on the edge of the bed. "Julie, what will I do about Garth?"

"Talk to him. Explain."

"I've tried. The last time, he got all hysterical and brushed me away."

Julie settled on an antique chair, which felt even harder than the one in her room. "If nothing happened, what's Garth's problem with you and Eric?"

"It's embarrassing. Eric dated me before you."

"A couple of times."

"It felt longer than that, emotionally. I'd been interested in him already for a…a few years."

"How many is a few?"

Delilah reached to her bedside table for a tissue to blow her nose. Evading the question. "After he broke up with me for you, I stayed hung up on him and…it didn't really end until last week."

"You never told me this." Julie's chest burned.

"How could I? Even my mom doesn't know."

Julie stared, her breath shallow. "Did you sleep with Eric during any of this time?"

"No. Never. Not once."

Too much protest.

"It was a dumb obsession," Delilah said.

"That lasted until last week. Is that why you emailed him from California?"

"He asked me to."

"After you slept together?"

"No, but that night I stayed over. I had no idea he'd tell our parents or show up with Peyton." Delilah stood up. "I have to phone my mother. She'll be wondering."

Julie blocked Delilah from leaving. "Tell me the truth. Did Eric ever come on to you after he was with me?"

"No, Julie. He hadn't a clue I was still interested." Delilah blew her nose. "I'm not anymore, I swear. I love Garth."

"But last week you loved Eric."

"That wasn't real love. I see that now." Delilah flung herself back down to the comforter. "Julie, how can I convince Garth? His head is like a rock."

Julie moved to the heavy dresser. The porcelain bowl on top was painted with a scene of a cottage surrounded by woods. This was what Delilah wanted, a peaceful, country life with Garth. Cast away your disbelief, Aurora might say. Delilah wasn't the type to cheat with a stepsister's boyfriend or husband. Julie touched the bowl. With her finger, she traced a crack that ran through a painted-on tree, slicing it up the middle.

That morning, Aurora had advised her to practice nurturing the guests. Her filling in for Aurora at the morning session had gone reasonably well. Guests had warmed to her and seemed receptive to her talk of coming to California to find her mother in part to understand herself. They'd laughed at her story of meeting Terry, the "stoner." She might have got them crying with Hank's tale of her mother's death if Aurora hadn't shown up to replace her. If Julie were Aurora, what would she say to nurture Delilah?

"I'll talk to Garth for you."

"Would you?" Delilah sat up.

"After the afternoon hike. I can't promise he'll listen."

"It couldn't make things worse."

Julie also wanted to talk to Orrin. She'd noticed him and Eric talking a lot at breakfast. And later, Orrin had given Eric a piece of paper, which Eric had quickly shoved in his pocket. What was the big secret?

Delilah slipped into her sandals. "Since Eric is taking our things in LA home, I'll drive to town for replacement meds. I'll get yours too, if you call your doctor. There must be a phone here that works."

"I'm doing fine without them," Julie said, and opened the door.

"I thought I was, too," Delilah said. They entered the hall. "I so hoped I was—until this mess with Garth."

At the top of the staircase, Julie grabbed the folds of her robe and lifted the skirt so she wouldn't trip. Her new retreat would have functional clothing for women.

* * *

After lunch, Julie changed into her taupe Diana robe. Its hem brushed her knees. Fresh air warmed her calves. She took a lunging step because she could. Freedom.

Sunshine glinted off the hikers' heads as they made their way up the orange grove. Only five guests had come along. The others were at Aurora's afternoon session or enjoying the pool. And one woman, the only female guest who always wore a short robe, had claimed a spot under an olive tree to write in her journal alone. Julie had wondered if she might hit it off with this woman, named Rachel, but she hadn't attended any sessions or hikes.

"As long as she's happy," Aurora had said, when Julie asked about her. "This is Rachel's third visit to the retreat. She knows what she wants from it."

Ahead of Julie, three forty-something women crowded around Sebastiano. They were friends, married with children, who had come for a girls' getaway that seemed to mainly involve giggling. The short one trotted to catch up to the others and lost her footing. Sebastiano grabbed her arm to save her from falling. Her friends laughed. One of them hiked with good skill, even in her flip-flops, but Julie suspected they would have opted for the pool were it not for Sebastiano's appeal. Last night, she'd teased Sebastiano about his groupies.

"All three together in my bed couldn't compete with you," he'd replied jokingly.

Julie had been considering taking a break from sex tonight, to get some sleep, but watching him bound up the hill, muscled thighs and calves smoothed by leggings, tunic bouncing against his firm ass—it made her want to drag him behind a tree.

Who was she kidding? She'd wind up in his bed tonight.

Behind Julie, Orrin wheezed, despite the gentle slope, and chatted with a woman in her thirties about chiropractors and masseuses. The woman's name was Kate. Cate. Cathy. Chatty Cathy. Aurora's mnemonic devices sometimes worked.

The path widened as they crested the hill, and Sebastiano stopped to let people catch their breath. Below, a road snaked through fields in the bottom of the bowl. Citrus trees crept up the hillsides.

Sebastiano pointed at the ranch house beside the road. "The former owner still lives there. We lease him the land. Our plan is to develop this as a second retreat with a Roman-villa theme."

"Cool," Flip-flops said. "We'd wear these same robes?"

"Absolutely."

Julie bristled. They'd see about that.

"At Retreat One," Sebastiano said, "the Tuscan style might change to Renaissance wear, low-cut bodices for women."

A giggle.

"The idea is to distinguish the two retreats. Give guests a choice."

"Sebastiano will have to stay Tuscan." Flip-flops' hip bumped his.

He smiled at Julie. "I might try a robe in a proper setting."

Flip-flops cocked her head at him. "You'd look cool in anything."

Chatty Cathy leaned in to Julie. "Someone has a crush. What do you think of that?"

Julie's knees sank, but she managed to straighten her legs. Why would she think anything? She turned away from Cathy. Earlier, while the group was assembling for the hike, Julie had pulled Sebastiano aside to ask if he thought anyone suspected their involvement. He assured her none did, and they had been careful. She went to his cottage after dark, when the guests had all retired to their residence, and left before dawn. During the day, she and Sebastiano acted like casual friends.

"We'll build a second amphitheatre on this side of the hill." Sebastiano continued his outline of the plans. "Four sessions a day, for more variety." His gaze caught Julie's. "The rest of the layout will depend on the architect."

While the others asked questions, Julie used the last minutes at the viewpoint to study the land. She'd keep the existing road in her design and do something exciting with that low hill in the southern part of the valley.

Sebastiano led them down a different path back to the retreat. Long grasses tickled Julie's calves. She slowed to Orrin's pace.

"Sorry to hold you all up," he said. "My lungs aren't what they used to be."

She glanced at his profile. He wasn't so old. Late forties, early fifties? "You're doing fine," she said. "I'm glad to catch you alone. When my husband, Eric, left this morning, I noticed you handed him something."

Orrin kept his gaze down, focused on taking careful steps.

She couldn't read his expression. "Did he ask you to keep it secret?"

"I had to promise and cross my heart." He looked up and laughed. "Poets. Who can figure them out? I said as much to Nelson." He stumbled, regained his footing and stepped faster. "We can't let the others leave us behind."

Julie remained at the back. Had Eric asked Orrin to report on her and Sebastiano? Was that the information in the note? Nelson might already be spreading gossip throughout the afternoon session. What did Eric hope to gain by this? He clearly didn't like Peyton's being here. Was he collecting rumours and lies to keep her away from the retreat? To have her declared an unfit mother?

At a fork in the orange groves, Julie split from the group. She met up with Sebastiano at the front of the pack.

"It's turning into a scorcher," he said. "Feel like a dip in the pool?"

"I didn't bring my suit, but my mother could loan me one."

He laughed. "Aurora in a bathing suit in front of her guests? She'd find it undignified."

"Then maybe I shouldn't swim."

A shrill laugh from behind made Julie whirl. Flip-flops and Chatty Cathy stared at her, smiling. What was the joke?

Farther down the hill, Sebastiano paused at the cypress trees lining the amphitheatre. A robed couple strolled through the yard, and two others rocked on the swing. "Aurora's session must have finished," he said. "Another short one today."

Julie scanned the area. "Any idea where Garth would be?"

"Puttering with his plants," Sebastiano said.

The hike continued to the path, where the group separated. The women went to their residence, Sebastiano to his cottage. Julie and Orrin crossed the lawn to the pool, where a half-dozen guests batted a volleyball back and forth above the water. Someone shrieked as a pair dove for the ball and collided. A woman reclining on a chair beside Nelson looked over at Julie and tapped Nelson's arm. He got up. As Julie turned to go and look for Garth in the garden behind the guest residence, Nelson approached. She noticed Orrin pad into the residence, presumably to get his swimsuit.

"I wanted to tell you," Nelson said. "I had the most interesting talk with your husband." Sunglasses blocked his eyes. His thong suit barely concealed the basics. "You've got a really cute daughter. I told him he's lucky to have her."

Julie glanced at the pool. Had he meant lucky to have Peyton alive and not drowned? Surely, Eric hadn't told this stranger she'd done that. Why would he? Except to drive Julie from the retreat, which he'd hated on sight. She hadn't seen such loathing in Eric's eyes since that afternoon he'd rushed into the bathroom and found her at the bathtub with Peyton.

"Are you all right?" Nelson said.

Julie rubbed her clammy brow. "A bit hot after the hike."

Flip-flops and another giggler emerged from the guest residence. They glanced at Julie, their expressions grim. Did they know about her too?

No. This was paranoid. Nuts.

"I have to go find the gardener," she told Nelson.

Conscious of him watching, she strode around the guest building and spotted Garth bent over the border of red, yellow, and orange flowers. As she drew close, he looked up and started. He held his spade to his chest like a shield.

"I want to explain about Delilah and Eric," she said, stopping in front of him. "Delilah never slept with him."

Garth lowered the spade and tapped it against his thigh. Dirt sprayed the ground. "She loved him."

"Loved?" Delilah had told Julie it hadn't been real love. Liar.

"For years and years and—"

"She's over him now."

"It lasted ten years—"

"More like twelve."

"Oh God." Garth fumbled with the brim of his straw hat. "A love that long vanishes two minutes before she meets me?"

Julie's stomach knotted. But if Aurora could set the personal aside to help others, so could she. "Give Delilah a chance. Listen to her. She's truly upset."

Garth raised the spade and whipped it around. Julie leapt back to avoid getting dinged.

"Would you all stop bothering me about this?" he said. "I have to take care of these weeds." He dropped to his knees and slammed his spade into the earth around the flowers.

Julie stared at the back of his hat. If Garth couldn't handle this first blip with Delilah, their relationship would never work.

She continued along the path and met Rachel coming out of the guest building. Rachel carried a book and journal close to her chest. Was Julie up for another stab at nurturing?

She smiled at the woman. "Aurora tells me this is your third visit." Strange, how she still thought of her mother as Aurora when referring to her leadership role.

"Yes, and Nelson told me that was your husband and daughter at breakfast."

"Former husband," Julie said. "We're separated."

Rachel nodded. "I heard."

So, people were talking. They set off along the path by the amphitheatre.

"You're a mother," Rachel said. "What kind of mother would do that to a child?"

Julie stopped. "Do what?"

"I'm sorry, it upsets me too much." Rachel marched toward the amphitheatre.

Julie's legs wobbled. If Rachel, who kept to herself, knew about Julie, then all of them did or would by tonight. Eric had used Orrin and Nelson to spread the story. Nelson, whom Julie had thought was a potential friend. This was Eric's plan. Drive her mad by getting everyone she lived with here talking about her, despising her, looking at her with disgust. That piece of paper, which Eric had hidden in his pants, had to be Orrin's reports on her behaviour. Eric was collecting evidence to have her declared unfit to look after her child, to achieve his goal of removing her completely from Peyton's life. The bastard. But he'd underestimated her support here. Two people knew the horrible thing she'd done and still believed in her goodness. Julie's legs grew steady. She wasn't alone. Not anymore. She had her mother and Sebastiano.

Chapter Twenty-Six

The supermarket was a blaze of bright packaging—boxes, cans, and jars. Delilah wandered the aisles, overwhelmed by the variety. What a contrast to the retreat's limited meal options, which were organic, prepared from scratch, and better tasting than processed food.

Soft drinks. Chips. Chocolate bars. Caffeine might lift her mood. Three Musketeers, Milky Way, M&M's. She couldn't decide. One of each? She'd need a few handfuls after Julie's failure with Garth.

"Let him stew on it alone and wait until he comes to his senses," Julie had concluded.

"What if he doesn't?"

"How will the two of you work out the big issues if he can't deal with this little thing?"

It wasn't little, though, given Garth's insecurity. And this insecurity was a part of him that Delilah loved. Being the strong one in the relationship for a change had felt good. If only she'd fudged the end date of her obsession with Eric and implied it was over years ago. She grabbed another bag of barbecue chips.

"Delilah?" a woman said.

Delilah jumped.

A Ralphs employee approached. Her long face looked familiar.

"I'm Cassandra." She extended her hand. "We met at New Dawn."

The woman who'd greeted them when they arrived. Aurora had dismissed Cassandra for some reason; incompetence, Delilah recalled Julie saying.

"I heard you went home," Delilah said.

"I was planning to, until I found this job. It's a perfect fit, with my experience in retail. I like this town better than the one I came from."

After the lushness of the retreat, the town's main street had struck Delilah as bland. She squeezed toward the shelf of popcorn boxes to let a man with a shopping cart pass. The retreat kitchen had to have a microwave. Scarfing popcorn while curled up with a book in the lounge might get her through this evening—except popcorn would make her crave a movie, and New Dawn had no TVs. Delilah could see why guests only stayed a week. Although if she was with Garth—

"How are Aurora and her daughter getting along?"

"Great," Delilah said. "Aurora's grooming Julie to take over."

"Julie wants to do this?"

"She's especially keen on designing the second retreat on the other side of the hill. Julie's got a knack for planning."

Another shopper stopped her cart beside them. The toddler perched in the basket reached for a jar of chocolate ice-cream topping. Delilah wouldn't mind a sundae tonight. The mother steered the cart away. Was it possible that she could be that mother three years from now, on a shopping excursion while living at the retreat? Ralphs' pharmacy section might carry pregnancy kits, but how early did they give results?

"Are Julie and Sebastiano hitting it off?" Cassandra's expression was neutral.

How much should Delilah reveal? Best to fudge. "They get along okay."

"I had the feeling there was a mutual attraction," Cassandra said. "Is he part of her reason for staying? Sebastiano's always had an eye for the guests. I'm surprised it hasn't got him into trouble."

"What do you mean?"

"You know how women can be." Cassandra smiled. "You sleep with a guy a few times and figure it's serious."

Delilah's stomach sank. Energy drained from her body. The pharmacist had told her he wasn't licensed to fill a prescription from a phone call to her Canadian doctor.

"Anyway, Ralphs will axe me if I don't get back to restocking shelves," Cassandra said. "Nice running into you."

Delilah grabbed a box of popcorn, five chocolate bars, and a six-pack of Diet Sprite and wheeled the cart back to the pharmacy section. She glanced around in case any retreat guests had jaunted into town. Sebastiano had made three trips since Saturday.

She found the pregnancy kits tucked in a side aisle and picked up a box. 'After your period is missed,' the box directions read. She wouldn't miss hers for another week or two, even three. Her periods were irregular. Her body wasn't made for pregnancy. A second kit also instructed her to wait for missed menses. She'd be home by then, unless Garth bubbled up from his stew of issues. Alone in Calgary, would she keep the child? Yes. Absolutely. No question. She would never have another chance. Her mother had raised her alone, with the help of Delilah's grandmother, whose husband had taken off with another woman when Rosemary was a toddler. Delilah had so wanted to break that pattern and have a child with a supportive man who didn't split at the first opportunity.

A third pregnancy kit, which cost twice as much as the others, produced results five days before a missed period. That could be as early as tomorrow. Or as late as two weeks from now. A waste of money if she used the kit too soon. A negative result tomorrow would mean nothing. The longer she could hold off taking the test, the better, but having the kit in her room might give her hope. After another scan for anyone watching, she dropped the box into her cart and covered it with the junk food.

A woman fiddling with the vitamin shelf waved. Cassandra. She worked in pharmacy? Shit. If she'd seen her pick up the pregnancy kit, she might tell a New Dawn employee who lived in this small town. So what? No one at the retreat cared about her, including Garth. He hated her now. Her mother, in Calgary, was the only one who cared. Delilah longed for a sympathetic shoulder and had her cell phone with her, but her mother would worry if she called. Delilah was stuck.

She returned to the retreat to find that Aurora had cancelled her pre-dinner yoga group due to the fine weather, which was calling people outside. Delilah settled alone in the lounge with a chocolate bar and *Wuthering Heights*, a novel that she'd always intended to read. Twenty minutes later she realized she'd read the first page a dozen times and had absorbed nothing. She turned to page two.

"Hi, Delilah."

She looked up. The woman wore tortoise-shell glasses and a knee-length robe. Delilah had seen her at meals, but they hadn't talked. What was her name? She held a thick tome under her arm. "Hi. What are you reading?"

The woman showed her the cover. Greek history. "It's really good if you're into the subject." She returned the book to the shelves beside the unlit fireplace. "Anything you recommend?"

Delilah glanced at *Wuthering Heights*. "I'm more into fiction than nonfiction."

"I alternate."

Delilah remembered noticing this guest on the swing and in the groves while everyone else was at sessions or on hikes. The retreat had its appeal to shy loners. Like Garth.

"You mainly like it here for some quiet time?" Delilah said.

"There's not much else to do."

"Sessions, hikes, yoga, tai chi."

The woman pulled out a book. "I did all those on my first two visits, except for tai chi. It's new." She turned the cover toward Delilah. *Middlemarch*. "I'll follow your classic example."

Delilah smiled. "I'm sorry, I've forgotten your name."

"Rachel. You're Delilah—Julie's stepsister?" Rachel stared through her lenses. "What do you think of Aurora?"

Delilah blanked. Her mental fog seemed to be getting worse.

Rachel clasped the book against her chest and continued. "Aurora was my hero. Sebastiano, he's obviously a jerk. But Aurora." Her voice trembled. "Since you're Julie's sister, what do you think of her taking off on her kid like that?"

Delilah closed *Wuthering Heights*. "Julie originally came here temporarily to find out about her mother. If she does stay, she plans to see Peyton regularly."

"Unlike her mother, who never even called to see if Julie was all right."

"You mean Aurora?" Delilah said. "She tried to contact Julie's family."

"Not very hard."

Delilah's head buzzed. "Aurora's explained it all to Julie, in depth. Julie understands and accepts her mother's leaving."

"I don't get that," Rachel said. "You were at the welcome dinner when Aurora told us the story. Did it make sense to you?"

It did at the time. Nothing made sense now.

"I felt like someone had clobbered me with a brick," Rachel said. "I loved Aurora. On my second visit, I left feeling right about myself. I'd always felt inadequate about not wanting children, like something was wrong with me. Aurora taught me that I'm okay, and I came to believe that in my heart. There were other things, too."

"I...the believing part is still good, I hope?"

"All I know is, this is my last stint here. Probably about time, too. We all need to move on."

The door chimed three women into the lounge—the friends who laughed together constantly.

"I'll see you at dinner," Rachel said, and left the lounge. The friends settled on a sofa and chair far from Delilah, who made another attempt at *Wuthering Heights*. From Julie's account of her talks with her mother, Aurora's abandoning her had seemed necessary, and almost beneficial to Julie. Why, exactly, was that? Delilah's brain was too foggy to puzzle it out.

* * *

"Daddy, look at the pretty ladies."

Eric stepped around his suitcase to peer at the living room's wall unit. Peyton stood on tiptoes, her hands pressed to the glass, and stared at the owner's collection of figurines. A woman stretched her bondage chains out from her naked body. A bosomy cancan dancer raised her leg. Luckily, she wore underwear. He guided Peyton away. Unlike the figurines, the prints hanging on the walls—nudes and couples engaged in sex—might qualify as art.

"I want to learn tap-dancing," Peyton said.

"Since when?"

She dance-stomped into the coffee table and tumbled to the floor. Eric helped her up.

"There's not much space here," he said. "We'll leave the dancing for our next hotel."

"A boy called me a clunk," Peyton said.

"He's an idiot. Let's get all Mommy's stuff packed."

Eric led her to the bedroom, where he rifled through drawers full of clothes in gaudy colours and wildlife designs that weren't Julie's taste. Since they didn't seem like Delilah's either, he assumed they belonged to the owner of this brothel. He came to a drawer with Julie's style of lingerie. Good to know there was one way she hadn't changed. He tossed her underwear to the bed and assigned Peyton the task of packing.

Someone thumped the side wall. Traffic sounds rumbled from the street. Santa Monica noise would keep him awake tonight, but he doubted he'd sleep anywhere. From the closet, he took the pastel and white clothing he guessed belonged to Julie or Delilah. If the retreat had cell coverage, he could phone Julie about the outfits he was dubious about, although she'd probably accuse him of checking up on her. The apartment owner could donate any clothing he left behind to charity.

"Disney tomorrow." Peyton twirled Julie's bra. "Disney. Disney."

"Pack," he said. "Was that a boy at school who called you a clunk?"

"He pushes me down."

Eric folded a shirt that smelled faintly of Julie.

"He's stupid," Peyton said.

"Ignore him, sweet; he's a bully."

Peyton dropped the bra into the suitcase.

"Or he likes you."

"Stupid." She tossed in Julie's underwear.

"Boys are like that. Let's pack this neater or there won't be space."

Peyton shuffled her feet forward and back in a semblance of dancing. He was tired from their afternoon of sunshine and sandcastles. Tomorrow at Disneyland would be worse.

He straightened Julie's underwear. "Do you really want to take tap lessons?"

"The other kids do."

"Who?"

"Him."

"The mean boy?" he said. "Ah."

Peyton was four years old. What was he in for over the next fourteen years, with no Julie to help him bring up a daughter?

Peyton stopped mid-foot-shuffle. "Mommy's toothbrush."

"Right." He'd forgotten the toiletries in the bathroom. The shower-curtain print, stiletto heels, must have given Julie a chuckle.

Her blue toiletry bag sat on the toilet tank. The beige case had to be Delilah's. From the ledge above the sink, he collected toothbrushes, toothpaste and floss. He opened the medicine cabinet. It was empty aside from two medicine bottles—one prescribed to Delilah, the other to Julie, by Dr. Kumar. He placed the antipsychotics in Julie's bag, the antidepressants in Delilah's. Eric's aunt with five cats was considered eccentric. That was as close as his family got to mental illness.

He zipped up the toiletry cases. Delilah had inherited her tendency toward depression from Rosemary. Julie's mother was plain weird. Aurora had founded a society that revolved around her. There was something pathological about that. He carried the cases to the bedroom and halted. Damn. Her antipsychotic meds were here, not with her at the retreat.

In the living room, he opened the sofa bed for Peyton.

"I'm not tired," she said.

"We have to get up early for Disney." That theme park had to be the world's biggest bribe.

"We'll take Mommy her suitcases before Disney?"

"No, sweet. We're taking them home."

"I want to see Mommy."

"You will, when she's back in Calgary."

"After Disney?"

"It's too far from the retreat."

"I hope my new grandma buys me a pony."

Aurora had made it clear she was in no hurry to see Eric again, but she'd appeared enamoured with Peyton. If he wanted an excuse for a repeat visit, he could say Peyton had begged him to take her. In winter, Disneyland closed at 5:00 p.m. With a stop for dinner, they could make it to the town near the retreat by bedtime. It was on the way to their next stop, LEGOLAND, give or take a hundred miles. No. That was wrong on so many levels. He did not want Peyton involved in the retreat. If Julie stayed at that place, he would insist she visit Peyton in Calgary. He'd get a court order, if he had to.

He struggled a wiggling Peyton into her pyjamas, counted out loud the thirty seconds she brushed her teeth, and then scrubbed the last grains of sand off her face. On the hide-a-bed, he read her a Disney-version Winnie-the-Pooh story.

"Lights out." He flicked the wall switch enclosed in a sinuous snake.

He needed to settle his mind with some reading before turning in. The book of Victorian poetry he'd brought wouldn't work—he'd barely been able to concentrate on

Pooh. What had he done with the poem the man at the retreat had given him? It should be easy reading, and, hopefully, not so terrible that he couldn't scrounge up a few positive comments. He found the piece of paper in his shorts pocket.

Orrin had confided that Nelson was an aspiring poet in that early stage of writing when he wouldn't show anyone his poems, not even Orrin. Eric suspected that Orrin had given him the poem without his partner's consent. Reluctance like Nelson's was sometimes a sign the poem was truly bad—but not always.

Eric stretched out on the bed, which wafted traces of Julie's aroma. He took a deep breath and, for a few seconds, imagined her puttering at the dresser, getting ready to join him. Instead, she was at that place, and off her meds for four days. Delilah was without hers too.

Outdoors, a siren shrilled. A stereo pounded from the apartment next door. Delivering the meds was another excuse to visit the retreat. It would be caring and responsible of him. Wrong. Julie would be pissed at his further intrusion. Peyton might get more sucked in by New Grandma. Or, in her child's wisdom, would she start to see through Aurora and smarmy Sebastiano? There was a lot to mull over tonight while not sleeping.

* * *

Sebastiano rocked his chair, legs propped on the bed, skimming his book on Roman architecture. Footsteps padded outside. Julie arriving, at last. But instead of coming closer to his cottage, the footsteps stopped in the garden. He left the chair and opened the window blind a crack. In darkness, Garth hunched over the herbs. Poor schlub. His collapse over Delilah's nothing-indiscretion proved him incapable of dealing with real life. Garth hadn't cloistered himself at the retreat for no reason.

Bye, bye, bye, Delilah. Pity they had to lose her. She'd have been useful in the office, as well as company for Julie. Women liked having girlfriends, apparently.

Sebastiano turned the page to a photo of a temple to Apollo. Should they have a temple in their Roman-style retreat, and, if so, for what purpose? Meditation? Yoga? Symbolic sacrifices—as in, cast off the cage of your past? Brainstorming with Julie would be fun, but too bad Cassandra wouldn't be taking over the office management.

Farewell, Cassandra. This one was bad timing. Were she to appear a few years from now, when they had two flourishing retreats, he would find a place for her. Three Alpha women in this one retreat was a crowd.

He flipped to a photo of a Roman bath. 'Frigidarium,' the caption read. Cold plunge followed by a leisurely soak in steaming water. What about baths at their new retreat? Sebastiano pictured Nelson's boyish hips sinking into a pool. Would Julie find his occasional gay flings less threatening than ones he'd have with women? Naturally, he'd do his best to keep flings of all types secret, but gossip shot through New Dawn like cricket chirps. One chirp had told him Nelson swung both ways. Sebastiano was pretty sure Cassandra would be game for a threesome.

The cottage door burst open. Julie. Sebastiano dropped the book to the table and wrapped her in his arms. The smell of the woods permeated her. Her body was stiff.

"What's wrong?" he said into her hair.

"Everyone knows about us."

"So?"

"Orrin gave Eric a piece of paper."

"What?" Sebastiano drew back. "What was the paper about?"

"My guess is it was his email address so he and Eric could trade information about me, to drive me nuts and prove I'm an unfit mother."

Sebastiano nibbled Julic's cxposed shoulder. He had hoped she'd wear the short robe tonight, but Aurora had persuaded her to change to this more elegant one for dinner. Would Julie's husband really send details about her to a guest? If so, did it matter? Nelson and his partner would be gone by the weekend, which meant he had only two more nights to fit in his encounter. Attractive, potentially available men were rare in this setting.

Julie stepped away from him. If she weren't in this peculiar mood, he'd raise her sweet bottom onto the tabletop.

"The worst is," she continued, "Eric told Orrin about my attempt to drown Peyton. He told Nelson, who spread it to everyone else."

"Didn't I say not to beat yourself up over that? You were sick."

"Most people blame me."

"Who cares what they think?"

"I do, if it costs me my daughter."

No chirping about her attempted drowning had reached him, and he usually picked up the gossip on the hikes. But her presence this afternoon might have inhibited the giggling crickets. Tomorrow, he'd sniff around.

"I hate people talking and whispering," she said.

"Take your mind off that with something outrageous and wild."

"Like what?"

"Anything. I don't know." His gaze lit on his abstract painting. "Have you ever considered a threesome?"

She laughed, relieving some tension, he hoped. "You, me and who else?" she said. "Not Cassandra?"

He tensed. Why had Julie thought of her? Intuition?

"Delilah ran into her in town," Julie said.

He feigned his best look of shock. "I thought Cassandra went home."

"She's working at the local grocery store."

"I can't think why." He added a touch of perplexed disinterest.

"How about one of your giggling women from the hike?"

"For our trio?" His wince was real. Julie's shoulders relaxed under his stroking fingers. Was she really open to this? "Why think of threesomes from the male perspective?" he said. "For your sake, I'd tolerate another man."

"You're too kind."

"Anything to please you." She'd taken it as a joke, but he'd planted the idea. A start. Now to reassure her. "I promise to suss people out, find out what they know. I'm sure it's nothing."

"You can't be sure."

"I am." He massaged her shoulder, her arms, felt them yielding.

Chapter Twenty-Seven

Julie spotted a dozen people underneath the valley oak tree, gathering for the morning hike. A few turned toward her. She balled her fists, vowed to not let their whispering get to her, and stopped beside Rachel.

"You two look fab in shorty robes," a woman told them. "I wish my calves weren't so thick."

Another woman looked at Julie. "Taupe is gorgeous on you."

"Julie could wear a bed sheet and look divine," a third said.

They laughed. All of them staring, staring, staring, staring.

Someone touched the back of Julie's hair. "I've never seen such an amazing red—so many varied tones. It can't be natural."

Julie spun around. "So what if it's fake."

"What I meant was it's too beautiful to be real."

"If that colour came from a box, I want the brand." A woman tittered.

"Hey, isn't your surname Fox?" Nelson said. "That is too cool, to match the colour to your name."

Julie turned away from them, to the amphitheatre, where the guests opting for Aurora's session assembled, among them Delilah.

Sebastiano strode toward them from his cottage. He clapped his hands. "Enough of the Julie fan club. Let's take a hike."

Nelson laughed. "So far, only a minority have done the hard hikes. Why's everyone here this morning?"

"I need exercise after a lazy day at the pool," a woman said.

"The air's perfectly fresh this morning for hiking," another said.

Sebastiano winked at them. "You mean the draw isn't my charms?"

"That too." Both women smiled up at him flirtatiously.

Rachel glanced at Julie and rolled her eyes. Even she'd joined in for a close-up look at the child-killing ogre with fraudulent hair. Sebastiano led the group to the olive grove, and they filed uphill to the deciduous forest. Some tree limbs were completely bare; leaves lingered on others. To keep her distance from Sebastiano, Julie slipped to the rear of the line, behind Nelson.

"Rachel," Nelson said, when the group stopped for a break. "What brings you out of hibernation?"

"I figured, I'm here. It's exercise." Rachel looked past him to Julie. "I was hoping Delilah would come."

"Nice girl, Delilah," Nelson said. "Orrin had a good chat with her."

About what? When? Delilah would certainly confirm Eric's story.

"I like her, too," Rachel said.

"Great praise, coming from Rachel," Nelson said. "She's less crazy about some of the others." He elbowed Julie.

So, they all preferred Delilah. What else was new? Sweet Delilah, the hypocrite, who had slept with Eric, possibly while he was with Julie.

They resumed walking and reached the crest, which reminded Julie of her hike with Sebastiano the first day. Everyone, except him, caught their breath while admiring the retreat in miniature below. How magical it had seemed to her then. And still magic, or would be again when this week's guests, Eric, and Delilah were gone. Julie was glad, now, that Garth wouldn't be keeping Delilah here. All was working out as it should for her.

The group continued up the slope to the second viewpoint. Sebastiano led them farther to a tree-filled ravine Julie hadn't seen before. She faked an ooh at the panoramic vista. He announced that from here, they'd hike up about twenty minutes then down to a creek in the state park that, technically, they couldn't enter without permits.

"We might get arrested," he added.

Several laughed.

"Why doesn't he spring for the lousy permit?" Rachel said to Julie and Nelson.

A half dozen said this was as far as they'd go. Evidently, they'd had their Julie fix. They'd wait here and enjoy the view. Julie and the others followed Sebastiano up the trail to a barbed-wire fence. He held up a weakened part for them to crawl under. Julie crouched to go first.

"If you can fit through, I can," Rachel said.

"Are you implying she's fat?" Nelson laughed.

"Tall." Rachel, five foot nothing, crawled underneath.

"You must have been a rabbit in another life," a woman said.

Nelson poked Julie. "Foxes chase rabbits for dinner."

What was he suggesting? In Eric's poems, the foxes were sometimes predators and other times prey. A double image, he'd told Julie. Depends on their situation. She would not be prey to these people.

On the other side, Nelson held the fence up for Sebastiano, who leaned back and limboed beneath with exaggerated grunts and groans. He grabbed Nelson's other hand, clearly pretending he needed a help up. Everyone chortled. Sebastiano patted Nelson's back in mock thanks and passed by Julie as though she meant no more to him than Rachel. Good for him to maintain their public guise. Keep the business and personal separate, like Aurora and Mom. Julie wondered how her mother's session was going. With the small numbers there, Delilah could seize the chance for more gossip with Orrin, Eric's contact at the retreat. Julie's muscles tensed. Delilah, the one person in the world Julie had been sure she could trust.

The downward trail into the ravine widened enough for two people to walk side by side. Julie stayed at the back and found herself beside Rachel.

"I talked to Delilah in the lounge last night," Rachel said.

"About what?"

"Books. And Aurora." Rachel kept her gaze fixed on the rocks and roots on the steep trail. At a stretch of gravel, her pace slowed. The others were far ahead.

"Do you mind if I hold on to your arm?" she said. "I'm not being a phony about it, like Sebastiano. I've got a terrible fear of falling and don't trust these poles." She transferred a pole to her outside hand and gripped Julie's arm.

"You sound like you hate Sebastiano."

"I don't hate anyone, really. It's a case of feeling let down, betrayed. You know what I mean?"

Yes. Delilah had betrayed her, a cruelty that cut worse than the rest. She wouldn't have wasted a minute last night corroborating Julie's drowning attempt of Peyton. Was Rachel fishing for a confession?

"People do things for different reasons," Julie said. "Unless you've been there, you can't understand."

"That's why I try not to judge. Still, I can't help my feelings about it."

They caught up with the group, which had stopped for a drink of water.

"This is killing my knees," Nelson said.

"The knees go first." Sebastiano laughed. Others joined in.

Rachel scowled and muttered to the woman beside her. As the hike started up again, Nelson lingered at the rear.

"I get the sense people are manoeuvring to talk to me." Julie smiled to imply she was joking.

"You're Aurora's daughter," he said. "People are intrigued."

"I'm nothing special."

"Oh, I wouldn't say that. Your husband was telling me you inspired his book."

"Did he mention what the poems were about?"

"Not in any detail. Imagine being a muse."

The last poems in Eric's book had referred to her postpartum depression. Nelson and Eric would have had plenty of time at their breakfast table to segue into her psychosis with Peyton in the bath.

"As Eric was leaving, I saw your partner give him something."

"What?" Nelson said.

"A piece of paper."

Nelson's neck muscles tightened. "Did he say what it was?"

"I asked Orrin."

"And?"

"He evaded the question."

"Good old Orrin." Nelson's neck muscles relaxed.

So, Nelson knew what the paper was about. He remained close by her, apart from the group, as Sebastiano paused at a creek. She kicked a wad of dry leaves. Today's weather was shifting from summer-like to fall. The seasons in California were all mixed up.

"This is gonna sound cornpone." Nelson's neck flushed. "I really love that guy."

"Orrin?" Julie said.

"We're thinking of adopting a child. One that's been mistreated or abused. The things people do to children, it's beyond comprehension." His eyes bored into Julie, eyes filled with horror. "You have no idea."

Nelson knew. Rachel, Orrin, everyone knew what she'd done to her child, to innocent Peyton. Julie tried to brush dirt from her robe but it clung, blended with the taupe.

"I'm sorry," she said. "So sorry."

* * *

"Mickey! Tigger! Piglet!" Peyton jumped on the motel room's mattress.

"Stop that before you break your neck," Eric said. A rotten thing to tell a kid, but he was drained from a day of chasing her from ride to ride at Disneyland. "It's a Small World" had played in his head the whole drive to town, while Peyton napped in the car.

She veered to the edge of the bed. He grabbed her. "Jammie time."

"I'm sleeping with Tigger tonight."

After a half hour of debate in the overpriced gift shop, she'd chosen Tigger as her souvenir.

"Teddy and Blankie and Pony will be jealous," he said. "They'll have to sleep with me."

He got Peyton into her pyjamas. Teeth brushed. Forget washing her face. Mechanically, he read her the Pooh bedtime story and tucked her and Tigger in. Seconds later, Peyton decided she couldn't leave out Teddy and Blankie and Pony.

"Daddy, you sleep alone."

The story of his life, present and future. He spent ages in the bathroom, to give her time to fall asleep, and then tiptoed back into the dark bedroom.

"Daddy, I'm not tired."

"I am."

Beyond tired. A wire of tension ran through him. Tomorrow would be his last chance to knock some sense into Julie before returning home.

"I'm going out on the balcony," he told Peyton. "When I'm back, I want you asleep."

He hoped that was firm but kind. If it didn't work, he'd try a bribe, which was terrible parenting. So many opportunities to screw up your kids. Hundreds a day. How did most children survive?

Outside, the air was refreshing and cool. He was glad he'd remembered to ask for a room on the motel's quiet back side. The balcony lights illuminated the forest park, turning the sycamore trees into ghostly silhouettes. Their naked, spindly arms lined a jogging path. If he and Julie were together, they'd take turns jogging tomorrow morning while the other stayed with Peyton. That's what their marriage should have been about, sharing the tasks, along with understanding each other's problems and doing whatever to help. He'd failed to understand Julie. He'd been attracted to her because she was different from the ordinary, and then he'd condemned her for it.

In the forest, something moved between two tree trunks. The creature passed through a beam of light. A person. A man, whose confident gait looked familiar. He cut from the forest to the motel parking lot. Sebastiano. He disappeared behind the motel's far end.

Inside, Peyton was asleep, her arm around Tigger. Could Eric leave her alone for a few minutes? More bad parenting.

He let himself into the hall, double-checked the door was locked, and ran down the corridor and stairs. Yes. There was an entrance at this end. He bet that Cassandra had been waiting to let the slime in.

* * *

In the motel breakfast room, Eric dawdled over his coffee, toast, cereal, and a banana while perusing the local tourist brochures he'd picked up at the front desk. A farm offered tours of orange cultivation, free samplings, and pony rides for children. They could postpone LEGOLAND until tomorrow.

A man with a briefcase entered.

Peyton swirled her fork in her syrup and soggy waffle. "When are we going to see Mommy?"

"Let's give her time to finish her breakfast."

"Can I eat with Mommy again? Strawberries?"

No way would he go through another meal with Aurora and Julie presiding over the room like queens. "How about I bring Tigger and your books to read down here while we wait for someone Daddy wants to talk to?"

Upstairs, he grabbed Peyton's stuff as quickly as he could so he wouldn't miss Cassandra in the breakfast room. He also dug out Nelson's poem for another review. The work was raw, but it had more heart than anything Eric had written in years. With a little technique, Nelson's message about fear of loving and being loved could reach people.

Back downstairs, a young couple had replaced the businessman. No Cassandra. Eric hoped she didn't have a late shift at Ralphs, or an early one—maybe she'd skipped breakfast. He pulled his chair next to Peyton's and absently read her book aloud, keeping his voice low to avoid disturbing the couple who leaned into each other like newlyweds. They were halfway through the story when a woman sauntered into the room. Purple shirt, black jeans, hair swept into a bun, long face and nose. Cassandra.

Eric handed Peyton the Pooh book. "You finish it." He met Cassandra by the toaster. "Hey," he said. "I thought I recognized you from the restaurant a couple of days ago. I hear you have some connection to the New Dawn Retreat, where my wife is staying."

She picked up some packets of cream cheese and looked at him. "Julie's husband. I assumed you'd gone."

So, the creep had told Cassandra. "Julie asked me to bring her some things from the place she rented in LA."

Cassandra grabbed tongs and plucked her bagel from the toasting tray. "I saw Delilah at Ralphs yesterday. You want to sit somewhere?"

Eric got them both coffees on their way to a table on the opposite side of the room from Peyton, who was absorbed in her book. She knew the story so well she believed she could read it. Cassandra smeared cream cheese on her bagel.

He plunged in to catch her instant response. "Was Sebastiano here last night?" he said. "I saw him on the jogging path."

She looked down and stared at the bagel. "You probably know Julie's involved with him."

Coffee curdled in his stomach.

Cassandra glanced up. "Delilah told me yesterday, indirectly. I'm sure he squeezed me in between dinner and Julie in his cottage."

"Does Julie know about you and him?"

"Would she put up with it if she did?"

"I doubt it," he said. Unless Julie had changed.

"Then he's obviously strung her along as deftly as he has me."

"I expect he's an expert at that."

Cassandra raised the bagel to her mouth. "As much as he's up front about how he is, he makes you think he's spinning everyone except you." She bit and chewed, as though stalling. "Delilah bought a pregnancy kit. Why would she need it, except for Julie?"

Oh God, not Julie and that man. "Well, Delilah has a thing going with the gardener."

"Garth? Are you joking?" Cassandra's eyebrows rose and then sank into a frown. "Damn that Sebastiano. He told me Julie was too skinny for him. Like a fool, I believed it."

"Daddy, can we go now?" Peyton appeared beside him.

"In a minute," he said. "Go back to your book."

A pregnancy kit. Neither sister had left birth control pills in the Santa Monica medicine cabinet. It made sense that Julie had gone off them. She hated taking medication.

"Daddy." Peyton batted Tigger against his leg.

Eric looked at Cassandra. "We have to be off."

"Let me know if you need any help," Cassandra said.

"With what?" he asked.

"Anything."

* * *

Slumped on a love seat in the lounge, Delilah opened *Pride and Prejudice*. She'd read it a half-dozen times and seen as many movie versions. Jane Austen was comfort literature. She nibbled her chocolate bar. When the door jangled, she tucked the bar under her robe. A man entered with a child. Eric and Peyton? Delilah stumbled to her feet and hugged Eric hello. She squatted to wrap Peyton in her arms, squishing her stuffed animal.

"How was Disneyland?"

Peyton extricated Tigger from between them. "We did rides and everything."

Eric looked around the room, down the hallway, at Aurora's closed office door.

Delilah eased up. "They're all out at the session or hike. I wasn't in the mood."

"We decided to bring your things here, rather than home," Eric said. "Your suitcases are in the car."

"Where's Mommy?" Peyton asked.

"Hiking," Delilah said. "She'll be back in a few minutes."

"Can I play on the swing?"

"Later, sweet," Eric said. "We have to wait here for Mommy."

"I'll take her while you wait." Any excuse to meet Garth on the lawn. Or maybe she'd see him in the flowerbeds, from which he might be tempted to the swing.

She took Peyton's small hand in hers. The feeling made her long to do the pregnancy test tonight. She suggested Eric help himself to a book.

"Let's see what crap they've got." He wandered to the bookshelves.

His digs at the retreat wouldn't help convince Julie to leave, if that was his motive for returning.

Outdoors, Delilah surveyed the yard. No Garth in the flowerbeds, on the grass, in the trees. She spotted Aurora in the amphitheatre, guests seated on the tiered seats.

Peyton skipped beside her to the swing. Delilah would love raising a girl. A boy would be strange territory. She had no brothers, no father on the scene until Brad, no husband.

They placed Tigger between them and glided on the double seat, in and out of the hatched shade of the valley oak. Peyton raved about Disneyland. "It's a Small World" was her favourite. And the "Pirates of the Caribbean." And the parade where Tigger, the real one, hopped right over and talked to her.

"He doesn't talk with words," Peyton said. "But you know." She'd met the character again near the teapots and given him a "hummugus" hug.

"I can hug you bigger." Delilah drew Peyton and Tigger onto her lap and squeezed them tight. A girl would be wonderful, but she'd get used to a boy. With Garth or without him, she wanted his child.

* * *

Julie left the olive grove exhausted from the hike. Sebastiano had promised the guests an especially challenging one for tomorrow, their last full day at the retreat. She'd inwardly groaned, although surely tonight she would sleep, after so many restless nights and this day in cooler, fresh air.

Go. Stay. She had to decide. Staying could mean losing her child. She owed it to Peyton to give the retreat up. But shouldn't her caring for Peyton feel more like love than duty? Help me understand my deepest self.

"Is that a kid on the swing with Delilah?" Sebastiano said, coming up beside her.

The child sat on Delilah's lap. Peyton? She was supposed to be in Disneyland or LEGOLAND or whatever-else-land with Eric.

Julie stormed across the lawn to the high-pitched voices and laughter. "What's going on here?"

"Mommy!"

"Julie," Delilah said. "I didn't see you. We were having so much fun." She wrapped her arms around Peyton, who giggled.

"Where's Eric?" Julie asked.

"In the lounge. He wants to talk to you."

"About what?"

"He brought our things from the apartment."

Peyton flapped her stuffed tiger's paw on Delilah's nose. Delilah laughed and sneezed, or pretended to. The lunch bell rang. From the amphitheatre, guests spilled into the yard. Julie tore past them and Aurora into the lounge. Eric looked up from the love seat by the window.

"Why are you here?"

He dropped the book to the cushion and rose. "At the apartment, I noticed some things you might need—"

"Cut the bullshit."

He glanced at the people entering the lounge.

"Is it about the paper the guy gave you?"

"What paper?"

"I saw him slip it to you when you left."

"Oh yeah, that. I have to talk to him, too."

"You don't even deny it?"

"Can we go somewhere private, to talk?"

People stared. Sebastiano insisted none of them knew about her act, but he said that to pacify her. In any case, he'd added, tomorrow their week here was up and she would start fresh with a new crop. So, let them watch and gape. "This is private enough."

Eric edged toward the fireplace. She stayed put, her gaze on his Mickey Mouse T-shirt. He moved back and met her eye. Point one for her.

"We spent last night at the motel in town," he said. "I saw Cassandra at breakfast. We talked."

"Did you wheedle information from her?"

His eyes darted sideways, proving her guess right. "She told me a few interesting things."

"Such as?"

"Did you know she's sleeping with Sebastiano?"

Julie forced her gaze to stay steady; her legs wavered. The watchers had all gone to the dining room, but the door chimed a lone figure in. Rachel paused, studying them.

Eric looked from her to Julie. "If I had to choose, I'd take these shorter robes. You actually look pretty cool in this one." He relaxed onto one hip, his head cocked. Was that supposed to be flirting?

Julie waited for Rachel to leave. "Cassandra told you that?"

"As a matter of fact, yes." His chin jutted forward.

"And you believed her?"

"I saw him sneak into the motel last night."

"Spying again?"

He scowled. "The guy is an asshole."

"Why do you hate him so much?"

"Why can't you see through him?" That nasty curled jaw. How had she ever found him attractive?

"He's on my side," she said. "All you do is turn everyone against me."

Eric's lips opened, but the door chimed before he could snap at her. Delilah entered.

"So many friggin' bells around here," he said. "Don't you hate the control?"

"Where's Peyton?" Julie asked Delilah.

"Aurora took her to the dining room." Delilah turned to Eric. "She assumes you're staying for lunch too."

"I didn't see them come in," Eric said.

"She used the garden entrance so Peyton could pick a special herb."

"A poison one?" Eric asked.

"You don't need to be sarcastic," Julie said.

"I have to dash up to the bathroom," Delilah told Eric. "I'd use the one downstairs, but Aurora doesn't want guests knowing we have bodily functions." She hurried away.

He chuckled.

"It's not a joke," Julie said.

"This whole place is a joke."

"You always conveniently turn up for meals."

"Trust me. The food isn't that great. And the atmosphere in the banquet hall is worse."

Julie crossed her arms. "What are you up to, Eric?"

"I told you, I brought—"

"Why are you here?"

"In the grand scheme?" he said. "I wouldn't mind taking you home."

So he had a scheme. "It's despicable for you to use Peyton to gain access to me and my place."

"Your place?" He raised a brow. "It's come to that?"

The door chimed Nelson and Orrin into the lounge. Orrin poked Nelson. They started to walk toward Eric, who shook his head. Nelson got the message, and both men waved and disappeared into the hall.

"What was that about?" Julie asked.

"Nothing of interest to you." Eric leaned over the love seat, looking down so she couldn't read his face. "I'll apologize to Delilah for finishing her chocolate bar." He picked up a book.

Julie read the title aloud. "*Pride and Prejudice*. Perfect for you."

"I admit I'm prejudiced against this joint and the gang in charge."

She jutted her chin out, to mimic his smugness. "The gang leader being my mother."

"And here I thought I'd escaped mother-in-law jokes." He smirked.

"Not funny." She tried to think of a clever, dismissive retort while watching Delilah emerge from the staircase and flit into the dining room. "I need to use the washroom, too, before lunch."

"As a mere mortal, I'll grab the downstairs one." Eric smirked again.

Julie glared.

"I know," he said. "That was mean to put your mother down. It's just that, for my taste, Rosemary's a hell of a lot better for a mother-in-law."

Julie trod up the stairs, not giving him the satisfaction of looking back. For once, Eric was right. Rosemary was more suited to motherhood than Marion. By taking Marion's place, she had enabled Marion to become Aurora. Was Delilah destined to do the same for Julie? Delilah and Peyton had sat so close on the swing, talking and laughing naturally in a way Julie never would. Delilah wanted a child. She loved Peyton and didn't fool Julie with her protests she was over Eric. Aurora had made the sacrifice, given up Julie to a better mother. Did Julie have the courage to do the same? Not yet, but she would work on it with Aurora's help. Delilah's mother was Julie's stepmother. Delilah becoming Peyton's stepmother was fitting, serendipitous. If Delilah was pregnant, Peyton would have a little sister or brother. Eric once said he'd like two children. Aurora, grant me the serenity to accept what's best for Peyton.

Downstairs, she met Eric on his way out of the kitchen. "I was talking with the staff."

More snooping? Raise me above his tiny mind. In the dining room, guests were already eating their soup. At the sight of Peyton at the head table with Aurora, Eric's jaw clenched. He lunged forward.

"Planning to make a scene?" Julie said.

He stopped, his body rigid. "She is not sitting up there."

Sebastiano sauntered in and stopped next to her and Eric. Everyone looked up from their soup bowls, some with eyes growing wide. One of the gigglers poked her friend. Sebastiano touched Eric's arm and motioned toward Delilah, who was taking a seat at the round table of guests closest to the podium. "There's a place for us there, man."

Eric shook him off and stepped to the back table. Some guests kept staring at him, others resumed eating and talking to their neighbours. Talking about Julie? Nelson, at the back table, pointed at the vacant chair beside him.

"Should I join them?" Sebastiano asked Julie.

"Eric would hate that."

Sebastiano smiled. He grabbed a spare chair and squeezed it between Nelson and Orrin. She smirked, and gloated all the way to the head table, where Peyton gazed up at Aurora, apparently absorbed in whatever her grandmother was saying. The watchers would all know Peyton was the child Julie had tried to drown. But she'd show them she loved her daughter, despite her terrible act, and that Aurora and Peyton loved and forgave her. Brilliant move by Aurora to bring Eric in here to witness this.

After dessert, her triumph secure, Julie brought Peyton to Eric's table. Sebastiano had taken off after the main course. She'd been looking forward to laughing with him about how Eric had snubbed him through lunch.

Peyton jumped on his lap. "New Grandma says I can swim in the pool."

"We can't, sweet," Eric said. "Our suits are at the motel."

"Go get them, Daddy."

Nelson smiled. "Good luck convincing her, Eric. And thanks."

This was about that piece of paper Orrin had passed to Eric. "For what?" Julie probed.

Nelson nudged Eric. "Our secret."

"Please, Daddy, please."

"It's too cold today for swimming."

"Not for a child," Aurora said.

Julie hadn't realized Aurora was behind her. Stealthy movement was another skill to learn from her.

"I'll mind Peyton," Aurora said. "You get the suits while Julie and Delilah unpack their suitcases you kindly brought."

Eric's arms surrounded Peyton, protectively.

"Daddy."

Eric slowly let go and Aurora lifted Peyton with a grimace that, once more, reminded Julie her mother wasn't young. She left Peyton with her new grandma to walk with Eric to his car.

"What did you give Nelson?" Julie asked him.

"It's no big deal."

Secrets hold meaning, Aurora had told the guests at yesterday's session. Unlock them. "I don't care what it is."

"Good."

Julie glanced at Delilah, who trailed behind them. "How long are you planning to hang around?"

"Until your mother is tired of Peyton."

"She asked her to stay overnight."

Eric halted. "When did she ask? At that snob table? I knew letting Peyton sit up there was a mistake."

Peyton had looked excited by her grandmother's offer but told her she had to ask Daddy, despite Julie's sitting right there. Even Peyton recognized her peripheral motherhood role.

Delilah drew up to Eric's other side. "I'll help look after Peyton while Aurora is at her session."

Help. Code for "supervise" because Julie couldn't handle her daughter alone, couldn't be trusted. They continued to the rental car. Eric hoisted the suitcases from the trunk.

"Delilah and I can carry them upstairs," Julie said.

"You aren't taking yours to Sebastiano's cabin?" Eric asked, sounding like he'd genuinely expected this.

Julie hadn't considered moving into the cottage, which would be small for them both. For the new retreat, she'd have to design one that was larger but still unobtrusive. The project would have so many interesting challenges. Eric stepped from side to side. She wouldn't satisfy him with a reply.

"I'll be back with the bathing suits in forty-five minutes."

The minimum time to the town and back. In Eric's mind she'd never move past her one enormous failure. "Don't dare leave her alone with me a second longer."

Eric and Delilah shared a glance. Julie shot Delilah a look that asked what the fuck she was up to.

"You go ahead." Delilah ignored her and looked down at her robe. "Eric and I haven't had a chance to talk." She fiddled with her sleeve. "Nothing important. I want to ask how Mom's doing."

Lies. Lies. Julie yanked her suitcase across the parking lot, down the stone path. Those two. Those fiends. Plotting their life together before she was cold.

Inside, she wrestled her suitcase through the lounge and up the stairs. Thump. Thump. Thump. Cassandra's former room had a view of the parking lot. From the window, Julie watched the two conspirators. Eric gestured toward the cottages and main building, clearly pumping Delilah for details about Julie and the retreat. Delilah was answering his questions with her pretense of support for Julie. No need to hear a word they said to know what those demons were up to.

Chapter Twenty-Eight

Eric pulled into the empty motel parking lot. He dashed up to his room and collected the bathing suits, towels, and Peyton's water wings. The sooner he was back at the retreat, the sooner he and Peyton could leave it. He would not give in to another dining room meal, and he'd refuse to let his daughter spend the night.

Out again in the bright haze, he remembered the sunscreen. Damn. Aurora surely kept a supply, unless her godliness protected her from burning. He smiled, glad he could see humour in this miserable situation, and dumped the swimming gear in the car. Sebastiano probably oiled himself to enhance his deep tan. He'd be a shrivelled raisin at age fifty. Eric drove to the lot exit and checked for traffic in the direction of Ralphs. Was Cassandra still working her shift there? Suntan lotion would be an excuse to pop in.

In the grocery store, Eric grabbed a hand basket and darted past produce and baked goods to the pharmacy section. Sunblock, 60 SPF, waterproof, kid friendly. No sign of Cassandra, but he needed fruit and granola bars for LEGOLAND tomorrow anyway, and microwave meals and popcorn for tonight. Peyton would get a kick out of eating in their motel room and choosing their pay TV movie. He spied Cassandra in the frozen food aisle, restocking pizzas.

"You're still here?" she said.

He leaned onto one hip to appear nonchalant. "We decided to stick around to take in the local tourist attractions." He peered into a glass door to show he was here for pizza. "Which of these work in microwaves?"

"How'd it go at New Dawn?"

A Ralphs employee and a customer passed by. Eric waited until they stopped two cabinets down, out of earshot. "We had lunch and got an invite for a swim."

Cassandra's hand lingered on a door handle. "Aurora invited you? Why?"

"To spend time with her granddaughter."

"I mean what's her real reason for the swim? With Aurora there's always subtext."

Eric's stomach rolled over. What subtext? "You don't like Aurora much?"

"I admire her." Cassandra pulled the door open and stacked boxes on the shelves.

"What's your plan for the retreat?"

"Me? I'm no longer involved." The door closed, and she wheeled the trolley to the next cabinet. Indifferent or feigning it? She picked up a box from the cart. "I've microwaved this kind. The Hawaiian is good."

Eric drew close to her. "Are you hanging around, waiting to pounce?"

"If you buy two, they're on special."

No food appealed to him now, and dinner at the café might be a chance to pump Trish, the waitress. "You know, I think we'll eat out after all." Eric opened the cabinet door for her. "Me anyway. Aurora wants Peyton to stay overnight."

Cassandra paused, a pile of boxes in her hands. Then she stashed them in the cabinet.

"What?" Eric asked.

She turned around. "I get off at six and plan to eat at Rita's Café."

* * *

Julie knocked on Aurora's office door. No answer. Of course, Aurora wouldn't hear. The soundproofing added to the feeling that she was invading her mother's sanctuary. No one entered Aurora's office unless invited, except Sebastiano—and Aurora seemed irritated when he did. Julie turned the knob and nudged the door open.

Aurora sat cross-legged on the floor, her robe draped over her legs. Peyton knelt over a sheet of butcher-block paper, colouring. Crayons lay scattered over the carpet.

A memory flashed through Julie's mind, *sitting at the kitchen table holding a periwinkle crayon.*

"Try magenta," the woman sitting beside her had said. "It's brighter and prettier and more exciting." A young woman's voice. Marion or a babysitter? If the woman was Marion, this was Julie's one true memory of her mother before she left.

Julie squatted to look at Peyton's picture. "That's good," she said. "Is it a zebra?"

"Tigger," Peyton said. "Riding my pony."

Julie stared at the horse-like creature. "Those coloured spots make your pony brighter and prettier and more exciting." She glanced at her mother.

"Why go for the ordinary?" Aurora said. Her expression remained neutral. With a groan, she raised herself from the floor. "That's enough colouring for today," she told Peyton. "Clean this up, and I'll read you a book."

Peyton started drawing rainbow stripes on Tigger. Julie itched to leave so she could process this, her one confirmed memory. But what about duty?

"I'll read to her," she said.

Aurora frowned at Julie's short robe. "Aren't you helping me with the session?"

"I can't. Peyton wants to swim."

"People are expecting you," Aurora said.

Always duty.

"Where is Delilah?" Aurora asked.

"In her bedroom."

"Tell her to come down right away. She's supposed to mind Peyton until Eric gets here."

And then he'd find Julie evading her motherhood task. "I'm looking after Peyton."

Aurora looked at the floor. "Peyton, put away those crayons and paper and choose a book from my shelf."

Julie shuffled from foot to foot. Her mother or her daughter, whose need came first in this situation? Peyton didn't care who read to her. "Okay, I'll start the session."

"Change into your long robe first, and send Delilah down here right now."

Delilah would come in her own time. *Fuck the long restrictive robe.* Julie escaped through the lounge to the outside air, sunshine, and warmth. Sebastiano and the afternoon hikers set out from the oak tree. She longed to join them, to move, move, move. Maybe she could do something animated at the session.

About fifteen people sat staggered on the amphitheatre's tiered seats, including the three gigglers and others Julie would have expected to do the afternoon's easy hike. Once more, most of the guests flocked to her, adjusting their activities to match hers.

Her head high, Julie took her position beside the podium. "Aurora suggested we start today's session with calisthenics." This used to work at Girl Guide camp.

"Too much work," a giggler called out.

"Not Aurora's style," someone else said.

"It's my style," Julie said.

Nelson leapt to his feet. "You go, girl."

Julie began with stretches. People rose, followed her movements—extended their arms, wrapped their hands around their shoulders. She led them through bicep curls. "Imagine the resistance." Now tricep curls, fists tight, use your body for resistance. "Feel the pressure."

A few groans. Several women shuffled down the steps. Leave me if you want. Fine. Julie jogged on the spot, sweating, glad she'd stayed in the short, loose robe. She focused on the memory of the young woman watching her colour; attentive, encouraging. "Go girl," her mother might have said in a later era.

"I'm done," the last giggler whined, and flip-flopped away.

Only Nelson and a woman whose name Julie forgot remained for the jumping jacks.

"Twenty-three." Julie jumped up and down, sweat rolling down her face. "Twenty-four."

She was sure the woman in the memory was Marion. So what if everyone else scorned and abandoned her? She had her mother.

* * *

"Andy, Mandy and Candy laughed all the way home." The story over at last, Aurora closed the picture book. She tried to roll her chair out of the sunlight pouring in from the window, but it wouldn't move with this weight on her lap.

Peyton wriggled. "Grandma, read another one."

"Three are enough." Aurora set the book on her desk. Children never quit. She had forgotten how exhausting the demands were, twenty-four hours a day. Juliana had been better at entertaining herself than Peyton. Eric spoiled the child, who was now used to constant attention. Brad's benign neglect had made Juliana independent.

Peyton wrapped her arms around Aurora's neck. Were there women who genuinely enjoyed the clinging? Or was every last one of them conditioned to think if she didn't love it, she was inferior? A retreat leader had to stand above the lemmings.

"I hope you'll remember us here when you leave with your daddy," Aurora said.

"Can I stay?"

"You have to go back to your school." Only nursery school—and just as well that Eric would never leave Peyton with Juliana full-time. Otherwise, the retreat would have to deal with busing Peyton to kindergarten next year or hiring a tutor for home schooling, so she wouldn't distract Juliana from her retreat roles. Leaving the man with the child-raising drudgery had worked for Marion. Eric could have Peyton, provided he allowed her enough visits here to satisfy Juliana. She would need to feel she was being a good mother, and they would also want to nurture Peyton into her future retreat leadership. The girl stirred, but her body felt heavier.

"Are you asleep?" Aurora said.

"I'm dreaming."

"About what?"

"My pony."

Oh yes. Aurora had forgotten her offer. "We'll buy you one when you come for a long visit."

Peyton raised her head. "When's that?"

"Whenever your daddy lets you."

Knowing what she did about Eric already, she was certain he'd keep the visits minimal. Let him be the bad guy who says no. Juliana would be the fun parent whom Peyton looked forward to seeing a few times a year.

Peyton flopped to Aurora's chest. No ache stabbed her collarbone area. A good sign she was recuperating. Peyton's arms remained around her neck, although the grip had loosened.

"I want Mommy home."

Children only thought of themselves. "Your mommy has work to do here."

"She goes to work at home."

"Here she gets to build a whole village, like you do with your LEGO, except it's real life and important."

"Daddy's taking me to LEGOLAND."

Once Peyton returned to her routine—playmates, toys, and nursery school—she would hardly miss Juliana. Plus, she had doting grandparents nearby.

"Rosemary tried to become my mother," Juliana had told Aurora. "I didn't accept her."

Because Juliana had longed for Marion. Evidently, so had Brad—enough to initiate the search for her in California. Delilah had hinted Rosemary felt threatened by the possibility of the former wife resurfacing. What if Aurora showed up at their door? *Almost worth it to see Brad tremble and blanch.* She chuckled, making her shoulder throb. Peyton squirmed and snuggled into her chest.

Delilah was close to her mother, possibly codependent. Single mothers, like Rosemary had been, often turned their daughters into confidants. Single fathers, like Brad and Eric, tended to keep a greater distance—much better for the child. In any case, Eric would find a new wife or partner sooner rather than later, Aurora predicted. His pursuit of Juliana suggested he wasn't a man who relished being alone, and he earned a healthy income and was good-looking enough to be viewed as a catch.

Eric and Delilah? Aurora sat upright. Her shoulder pulsed. Delilah, with her strong maternal instincts. Aurora looked across the desk at the computer. A shame to lose Delilah in the office, but it would be easier to find a trustworthy clerk than the right mother to raise Peyton, the long-term future of New Dawn. Were Delilah and Garth definitely finished? Probably not or Delilah would have left. She must still have hope.

Peyton's head banged Aurora's chin. "Can we read another story?"

Aurora thanked the gods that hard head had missed her collarbone. "I have something better for you. A present."

"For me?"

Me. Me. Me. Aurora peeled off the child's arms, and the weight slid from her lap. She opened her desk drawer and took out the toy she'd asked the cook to buy in town.

Peyton grabbed the bulky bag. Her eyes growing bright, she yanked out the box and peered at its pictures of animals next to a scarlet barn. "A cow, chickens, sheep. My pony!"

Juliana had said she left Calgary in the midst of crafting a farm as a surprise for her daughter. Peyton getting her farm would give Juliana one less reason to return.

"Don't open it until you get home or you'll lose some pieces," Aurora said.

Peyton's pudgy finger picked at the cardboard flap.

"I said later." Aurora took deep, even breaths, mentally counting to ten. Marion would have slapped the brat. Fortunately, Julie didn't remember this. Aurora placed her hands in Peyton's armpits to lift her up. Pain seared her collarbone area as she pulled the child higher. Peyton's foot struck her thigh.

"Sorry, Grandma."

Aurora was certain that kick had been on purpose. The poor passive-aggressive child would be hurt when Juliana left Calgary for good. But it was often best to rip the Band-

Aid off. Peyton's father, grandparents, and future mother would soothe the pain. In the end, little Peyton would be fine. She took the girl's hand, deposited her and her present with a housemaid in the lounge, and hurried to the afternoon session.

Guests strolled in the yard. Three rocked on the swing. Had Sebastiano cancelled the hike? The only people in the amphitheatre were Julie, Nelson and Sheepy-Sheena, all doing lunges.

Aurora gulped for air. "What is going on?"

Juliana paused by the podium and performed a pirouette. Sheena tripped on a step. Nelson caught her before she tumbled down the rows.

Nelson laughed. "Sheena, next time, wear a shorty robe like Julie's."

"There won't be a next time." Aurora dug her fingernails into her palm. "Juliana, I told you the plan for starting the session."

"I changed it."

Juliana jumped up five stairs, spun around and began squats. Completely undignified. Aurora could see up her thighs. Herbal tea would take care of this madness. Strong herbal tea. First, the session had to be returned to order.

"I'll collect the absent guests and we'll begin again," Aurora said.

"I'll help you, Aurora," Sheena said.

Nelson, down a row from Julie, squatted in unison with her. "Calisthenics are more fun."

Aurora's nails dug deeper into her flesh. Sharp pains shot through her collarbone area. She glared at Juliana, willing her to stop squatting.

Juliana straightened. "I'm tired of this anyway." She marched down the stairs, past Aurora without a glance, and out of the amphitheatre.

Childish. As bad as four-year-old Peyton. Nelson took giant steps along a bench seat and down to the next row of seats and next. Now Garth would have to wipe them all.

"Would you find the gardener and bring him here?" Aurora asked Nelson.

He jumped to the front of the amphitheatre and strode out to the lawn without replying. Rude, but Nelson didn't matter like Juliana. Her obstinacy might require more than tea.

* * *

Eric tossed the ball over Peyton's head. Julie leapt up from the pool and caught it.

"It touched the water," he shouted.

"Did not."

"Did so." Peyton paddled in circles between them, her water wings keeping her afloat.

He ducked as Julie hurled the ball at him. Then she dove under and swam to Peyton.

"Ohh." Peyton spewed. "Shark."

Julie surfaced inches from him. Water dripped from her hair down her nose. He'd reach out and kiss her, if she let him. No chance of that.

He looked past Julie at their daughter. "Let's get out and dry off."

"I want to swimmmmmm." Peyton whirled in circles.

"You've been in an hour." An exaggeration, but he wanted them gone from the pool area before guests showed up after their sessions and hikes.

Julie gripped the side of the pool and raised her body out of the water. Her wet ponytail flopped against the small of her back. More than a kiss, he longed to grab her and press her tightly to him, their bathing suits dripping between them. Peyton paddled away from them, along the perimeter of the pool.

A towel over her shoulders, Julie stretched out on a chair, her high-cut suit accenting her long legs. Eric settled on a lounger beside her. Above, puffy clouds flitted across the afternoon sky. Birds chirped in the lemony scented trees.

"Heaven," he said.

"I don't know why you won't let her stay one night, when I won't be seeing her for months."

So much for the last half hour of play, when Julie had been her normal self, and he'd almost forgotten they were in this wretched place.

"Are you really serious about moving here?"

"Why not?"

"What about your job?"

"I have a job here now."

"Not a real one." He wished he could see her eyes behind the wraparound frames she was wearing. "What does it pay? It won't build your credentials."

"Work's not all about money and status, Eric."

"I hope you extend your leave of absence, rather than quit, in case you change your mind."

Her mouth was set in a straight line that reminded him of Aurora. He shivered. Julie was part of that woman's flesh and blood. So was Peyton, who was starting a second lap of the pool.

"She's a little fish," he said, shifting to an amiable topic.

"Water wings create bad swimming habits."

"They give her independence until you finish teaching her to swim."

"Remind me of that, again, why don't you?"

"Of what?"

Julie stared ahead. "Will you ever let me forget it?"

The bathtub. That image. Julie leaning over the tub, drowning their daughter. "I wasn't thinking of that, honest."

"You'll always throw it in my face."

"Julie, I swear—"

"No matter what I do or how much I improve, it will be in your mind. You'll hurl it against me after every mistake. I get that. You'll never trust me."

That was true, although he would try not to hurl it. The psychosis wasn't Julie's fault, but it could happen again any second. What responsible human being would feel completely comfortable leaving a kid in her care? Peyton paddled toward them, her teeth chattering.

Eric shifted forward on the lounger. "Sweet, you're cold. You have to get out now."

Peyton circled away.

"I wish you'd stop calling her that."

"What?"

"Sweet. How do you expect her to grow up to be a strong woman when you shower her with girly terms like princess?"

"I never say princess. That's Rosemary."

"Never?"

"Hardly ever. You call her sweet sometimes. Or sweetheart."

"Everything you buy for her is pink."

"It's her favourite colour. She chooses pink. The girls' sections of stores blare pink. What choice do I have?"

"You always have a choice, Eric."

He felt a lump in his stomach. Her nitpicking was unfair. "Rosemary buys most of the pink stuff."

"Blame Rosemary for everything."

He had to show Julie his willingness to try, that he was open to giving her mother's retreat a chance, and even that he trusted her since it was possible he might with time. This would be their only hope of ever getting back together.

"Okay," he said.

"What?"

"Peyton can stay tonight."

"Don't do me any favours."

The lump grew harder. He was fed up. Why had he thought there was any hope? Peyton floundered to them, her lips blue. Eric slid off the lounger and squatted to coax her out.

"One more swim," she said.

He grabbed Peyton under the water wings and lifted her, kicking, from the pool. As he'd grabbed and lifted her from the bathtub that horrible day. Peyton's skin felt hot then. Now it was freezing against his chest, which had warmed and dried in the sun. He slid off the water wings, enclosed her in a towel and stared into her hazel eyes. She should be safe here with Delilah and so many others around. "Do you want to sleep over with Mommy tonight?"

"You too."

“I’ll spend a boring night in the motel watching a grown-up movie.” Which sounded terrific, compared to the rest of this vacation.

The three of them left the lemon grove and squeaked over California grass. People milled outside the amphitheatre. Aurora’s session had ended. A man in a tunic separated from the robes. Nelson met them by the swing.

“Thanks again,” he said to Eric. “You don’t know how much I appreciate your taking the time.”

“For what?” Julie asked.

“You too, Julie, for the calisthenics,” Nelson said. “Aurora’s sessions needed the shakeup.”

Julie looked from him to Eric. “What are you up to?”

Nelson looked away, at the oak tree. Eric was amazed someone so outgoing would be shy about revealing he wrote poetry. Peyton crawled onto the swing.

“Can I rock too?” Nelson said.

She nodded. Nelson sat down beside her.

Yet, Eric was equally bad. He hadn’t told Julie he was writing the Fox poems until a publisher accepted his manuscript. He was afraid she’d think his poems were crap. She didn’t get most of them, but a few she liked. Mainly, she’d said, she was mad at him for exploiting her postpartum depression and not telling her he was doing it.

“Do you want me to withdraw the manuscript?” he’d asked.

“No, Eric, I won’t spoil your little dream.”

Little. He was furious. But, why wouldn’t she be mad? If he could, he’d take back the whole book. Whatever he’d gained from that publication hadn’t been worth it.

“There’s Orrin.” Nelson helped Peyton off the swing as hikers emerged from the orange trees. A woman at the rear held on to Sebastiano’s arm. He separated from her and headed their way, Orrin behind them.

“How was the swim?” Sebastiano asked Julie and Peyton, ignoring Eric.

Eric balled his fists.

“How was the hike?’ Nelson asked, before either of them could answer.

"A woman felt faint," Orrin said. "Sebastiano managed to get her down the hill."

"Is she all right now?" Julie asked.

"A little dehydrated." Sebastiano's teeth gleamed in the sun. "Aurora's elixir will fix her up."

Eric strained for a closer look at his dental work.

"Homemade herbal sports drink," Sebastiano explained, as though Eric cared.

"Eric's a skeptic," Julie said. "Did you enjoy the pool?" a voice beside him asked.

Aurora. How had she moved so silently on the rubbery grass?

Peyton tugged Aurora's robe. "Daddy says I can sleep here."

Eric gritted his teeth as everyone looked at him. He'd been stupid to agree, but going back on his offer would fuel Julie's view he was prejudiced against this wacky place.

"Sure," he said. "I could use a quiet night." With Peyton staying over, surely Julie would sleep in the main building rather than with Sebastiano. Any decent parent would. At least this would keep her from the vulture for one night.

Aurora bent toward Peyton. "Since you'll be with us, how about we make you a robe?"

"A princess dress?" Peyton asked.

"You can call it that," Aurora said. "What colour would you like?"

"Pink."

"How did I guess?"

Eric looked at Julie. When it came to gender bias, Aurora was no improvement on Rosemary or him.

"You don't have to smirk," Julie said.

"It's Eric's natural expression." Sebastiano laughed, baring his fake teeth. "Suits him."

Eric turned to the oak tree to hide whatever negative expression he was shooting out now. He would love to punch in that dental work.

* * *

Julie helped Peyton put on the pink robe the seamstress had whipped up while they were in the pool. Aurora had guessed not only the colour Peyton would choose but also her size and a style perfect for her.

"The guests are dying to see how cute you look," Aurora told Peyton. "Now, my yoga group is waiting for me."

Aurora glided from the room. Julie adjusted the short sleeves of Peyton's pink robe. Ribbons of darker pink formed an X across her chest and cinched her waist. The hem ended at her calf. Aurora's design was inspired by a fairy in a storybook she'd read to Peyton. Fairies were magic and powerful, Aurora had said, but she'd agreed with Julie that Peyton would need a tunic for playing.

Peyton skipped around the room and bumped into the IKEA dresser that seemed an oddity at the retreat.

This had been Cassandra's bedroom, before Aurora dismissed her. Every day Julie had asked Sebastiano if he'd slept with her and he denied it. She couldn't quite believe him but was sure he wasn't cheating with Cassandra now. Eric and Cassandra were lying. Julie didn't care about Cassandra's motive, but Eric's, obviously, was to destroy Julie's trust in Sebastiano. Eric knew her weak points included fear of abandonment. Her jealousy of his poetry groupies had driven her over the edge last year. Now, he was accusing Sebastiano to twist the knife, to drive her nuts again and prove she was unfit to look after Peyton. The worst of it was, Eric was right. She didn't trust herself with Peyton either.

She swallowed the knot in her throat. Her eyes watered. Peyton became a blur, rifling through the closet's robes of assorted shades, left behind because Cassandra didn't need them in town. Screw jealousy, especially when it originated in lies about Sebastiano. Cassandra was history. Aurora had judged her unsuited to be a leader. Sebastiano prefers me.

Peyton strapped on a pair of sandals and tapped on the hardwood floor, managing not to trip despite the floppy shoes. Cassandra was no Cinderella.

Julie had a knack for life at the retreat. Aurora had said she now felt as though she'd created New Dawn for Julie, in preparation for her arrival. True, this was before the calisthenics. She knew that beneath her calm exterior, Aurora had been ticked. But conflict between mothers and daughters was normal. Julie had grown up missing the teenage rebellion phase with her mother and might be cruising through it now, at high speed, as her mother dropped from goddess to mortal in her view. Aurora was a little distant with guests; she stood too much on a pedestal. Julie would get to know them as friends. Nelson, Orrin, Rachel, and Sheena, whom she'd encourage to be more assertive.

"Mommy, can we open this now?" Peyton held up a box.

"What's that?"

"New Grandma gave it to me."

My Little Farm was written on the sides. Animals, a barn, fences. Julie yanked the box from Peyton's hand.

"You'll help me build it?" Peyton asked.

Julie leaned close to the tiny writing on the box. Some assembly required. Not suitable for children under three. Plastic pieces.

The room started to spin. Julie dropped the box to the floor.

"Mommy, can I play with my farm?"

"It's yours. She gave it to you."

Peyton sat down, ripped open the end flap and dumped the plastic pieces to the floor. This was wrong, Julie knew, but she didn't know why. Grandparents didn't need to consult the parent on every present. The farm wasn't a pet or something enormous like a trip. Yet, it was wrong.

Julie strode out and knocked on Delilah's bedroom door.

"What?" Delilah sounded as if she had a cold.

"Can you watch Peyton while I go talk to Aurora?"

Delilah sniffed. "Give me a sec."

Peyton was four. She'd be fine alone with the toy for a few seconds. Downstairs, Julie found no Aurora or yoga group in the lounge. Noises flowed from the kitchen. Aurora always dropped in to supervise meal preparations. But no Aurora there or across the hall in the dining room. Her office door was shut. Julie's office in the new retreat would be approachable. She pushed the door open. Aurora's desk and computer chairs were empty.

"Looking for something?" a voice said from behind her.

Julie spun toward the cleaning woman.

"Aurora went for a walk before yoga."

"She said…"

A staff person near the fireplace was moving a chair to the wall, to clear space for yoga. The cleaning woman dashed over to help her hoist a love seat. It appeared yoga wasn't due to start for a while. Aurora had made that excuse to get away from her and Peyton.

The door chimed Julie outside. Her mother couldn't have gone far. Julie could walk this whole world in twenty minutes.

Chapter Twenty-Nine

Sebastiano rocked his chair in time to Aurora's pacing between his bed and closet, as she recapped Eric's latest visit to the retreat. She reached the point where he left Peyton with them and stopped by the bathroom door.

"Thank the gods we won't see that man until tomorrow. He causes Juliana stress."

Sebastiano still couldn't adapt to Julie's new name. "Your daughter thinks he spreads nasty stories about her to all the guests."

Aurora stopped by the bathroom door. "Has he?"

"My spot-check of the guests says no. I think it's in Julie's head."

Aurora's forehead veins pulsed.

Sebastiano steadied the chair to read her thinking. *Good to keep Julie against Eric, so she'll believe we're the only ones on her side.* Moreover, if he argued with Julie about her delusions, she'd lump him into the conspiracy. Years of dealing with guests prone to paranoia were coming in handy.

"Juliana will be fine once her husband and those chemicals are out of her system," Aurora said. "She finds my herbal tea soothing."

"More than my affections?"

Aurora glanced at the painting above his bed. "Your insistence on clinging to that piece of art makes me wonder if you've got a soft spot hidden inside."

"Half the time I don't notice it." He studied the erratic shapes painted by the suicidal guest during the retreat's brief experiment with art sessions. "The work has energy, passion."

"Like the artist?"

After their passion in his cottage, she'd slipped back to her bathroom in the guest residence and cut her wrists. Another guest found her after she didn't turn up for breakfast. Aurora had handled the situation deftly at lunch. "She came to us deeply troubled, beyond our help."

"I barely remember her."

"I hope you remember my daughter better."

"Is Julie going somewhere?"

"Juliana." Aurora corrected him. "Not if you do your part to keep her here."

He stroked the book on his table, *Villas of Ancient Rome*. Julie had suggested the new retreat include a villa with space for them and her daughter, when she visited during school holidays, assuming Eric would let Peyton come here.

"Eric hates the retreat, and most of all you," she'd said.

Of course he did. The guy was in love with her. No need to point that out to Julie, though.

"What is the status of Delilah and Garth's tiff?" Aurora asked.

"Last I heard he still hasn't forgiven her for pining for Eric."

Aurora balled her fists. "What's so special about Eric? He almost makes Brad look exciting."

Sebastiano cocked his head. "Thoughts of flying up to Calgary to disrupt the second marriage?"

"Wouldn't that shock his new wife?" Aurora's forehead pulsed again.

He knew she was debating the pro of sucking her ex-husband back in and dropping him cold versus the con of leaving the retreat for the time it would take. Her forehead veins settled. He was certain the retreat, her new husband, had won. New Dawn consumed all her energy, including sexual. Had Aurora seen from the start it would be like that? The day his cottage was finished, she proposed they abandon their sexual relationship. The minute she said it, he realized this would free him for their guests. How they had fucked like rabbits that night on this bed, one last time.

Aurora stared out of the window, in the direction of the olive grove. He hoped Julie wouldn't become married to her retreat—like mother, like daughter. All the more reason for him to keep this cottage. If he was careful, Julie wouldn't find out about his trysts with guests on this side of the hill. By the time rumours spread to her retreat, the week would be up and a fresh crop arriving. This concept of continuous renewal helped New Dawn, and him.

"I'd like you to talk to Garth," Aurora said. "He looks up to you, for some reason."

Sebastiano couldn't think why the guy did, aside from the obvious. Geeks like Garth wanted to be Sebastiano. So did responsible Eric-types.

"I'll tell him to stop being a fool about Delilah."

"Reinforce Garth's view that she's in love with Eric and dreams of returning with him to Calgary, becoming Peyton's stepmother."

Sebastiano raised an eyebrow. He wanted to get up and walk around, but sitting felt like the power position now. He listened as Aurora explained that Julie was bound to be initially upset about Delilah's replacing her but would come to see it as best for the child. Sebastiano agreed it would hurt Julie to lose her child to Delilah—she cared about her kid, or wanted to care. She tried to care. Unlike her own mother. Pity he couldn't explain this distinction to Julie, so she'd stop believing herself a monster. It bugged him that she suffered for this when there were mothers way worse. But the truth—that Aurora cared about Julie only as her successor—would make Julie leave the retreat. That wouldn't suit him at all.

After Aurora left, Sebastiano found Garth hunched over the spider plants along the far side of the guest building. At the sight of Sebastiano, he jerked up straight as a flagpole.

"How are the spiders making out?" Sebastiano said.

"A bit droopy on account of no rain. They love the sun."

"Don't we all?"

The strap of Garth's overalls drooped over his shoulder. The schlump didn't stand a chance.

"I am sorry it didn't work for you with Delilah."

"I've been thinking that over."

"Women can be manipulative."

"What do you mean?"

"Delilah pretended to come to California to support Julie," Sebastiano said. "It's obvious her real motive was to make Eric realize how much he missed her, so he'd follow her here."

"I thought he came for Julie."

"That's his excuse. For all I know, he believes it. You know how we guys are. We conceal our true feelings, even to ourselves. Especially to ourselves."

Garth's brow furrowed in contemplation. His face was pale for someone who spent his days in the sun. His hands, the only tanned part of him, were scratching each other as if to wipe off the permanent dirt stains.

"I really believed Delilah had feelings for me."

Sebastiano paused in apparent reflection. "I'm sure she did, in the moment, but could the feelings of a few days extinguish a passion of so many years? Delilah was convinced she had no chance with Eric and, naturally, latched on to the closest guy around. You can't blame her. Love makes people desperate."

Garth's Adam's apple bobbed. "I guess so."

Too easy.

Garth dropped to the spider plant and attacked the surrounding earth with his spade. Poor sap. He'd never get laid again. That's how it was for the world's Garths.

Sebastiano rounded the guest residence. Guests strolled on the path and lawn. Robes everywhere, but where was Nelson in his tunic? Deducing that Julie would spend the night with Peyton in the main building, Sebastiano had dropped Nelson a hint to meet in the olive grove after supper.

Under the oak tree, a small person sat on the swing. Julie's daughter.

"Hey, kid." Sebastiano eased up to her. "Why are you here all alone?"

Peyton craned her head back. "Aunt Delilah's tired. Mommy's talking to Grandma."

"Mind if I join you?"

She clutched her stuffed animal to her chest. A tiger with orange and black stripes.

"Tigger?" he said. "He was my favourite. I had the whole gang of Pooh animals when I was your age. Tigger was the best. Pooh was too brooding, Piglet a follower, Eeyore mopey. Tigger bounced all over the place having fun." He hadn't thought of those books in years.

Peyton edged sideways, making space for him on the bench. Her body bounced as he sat down.

"You look beautiful in that pink robe," he said.

"It's a princess dress."

"You bet it is." Good for you, kid. Don't adopt Aurora's Roman fantasies. Stick to your own. "What are you and your mom planning for tonight?"

"I wish Mommy would come home."

She moved her legs that didn't reach the ground. He pushed his long legs forward and back to glide the swing. Kids of divorce always had this dream they'd be happier if their parents got back together. His family life hadn't been better before his parents split. They spent their time bickering and arguing about his father's affairs and ignoring Sebastiano and his sister. The kindest thing they ever did was buy him a gerbil for Christmas instead of the parrot he wanted.

"Noisy, messy, ugly bird," his mother had said.

"Do you like parrots?" he asked Peyton.

She looked ahead, swinging, mouth tight. He didn't understand children well enough to read her.

"Parrots live a long time," he said. Presumably his mother was still alive. He'd made sure his sister knew how to contact him at the retreat so he'd get part two of his inheritance when the old bat croaked. At his father's funeral, his mother had shot him a glance that made him wonder, for a second, if she suspected his part in the old man's death. Which would place her way ahead of the cops, who'd accepted Sebastiano's answers and Aurora's alibi for him that he was with her at the beach house that whole evening. Last he'd heard, the murder remained unsolved. While it might have been fun to have the second wife implicated—

one thing he and his mother would agree on—he was glad that the old man's death hadn't dragged down an innocent service person. Come to think of it, part two would be convenient now. He wondered if the old bat had cut him out, as his father had intended.

"You are the luckiest kid in the world," he said.

Peyton started but didn't say anything.

"You've got a dad who loves you and takes you to fun places like Disneyland," Sebastiano said. "You've got your grandparents in Canada, a mommy here to love you, a new grandma. Your favourite aunt, Delilah. And, whenever you want it, you've got all this." His arm motion swept the lawn, trees, buildings, flowers, blue sky, and amphitheatre. He pointed to the hill leading to the farm. "Your smart mommy will build a new retreat with fountains, statues, and a pool so big it will take you an hour to swim across."

"An hour?" She looked dubious.

"Her retreat will have miles and miles of grass for you to play on."

"With a pony?"

"Whatever animals you want. Even parrots."

She scrunched her face, looking puzzled.

"They're big birds that talk and have colourful feathers."

"I know what parrots are."

"Sure you do. I knew that." Don't talk down to kids. "It will be your own personal Disneyland."

Her face glowed a rosy shade, reflecting the sun sinking to the horizon. Aurora had cancelled tonight's sunset service. Too much going on, she'd said. She'd be glad when things returned to normal. He liked the status quo too, but disruptions were a fun change.

"When you're a teenager," he said, "we'll build a third retreat. You'll be in charge of the design and can make it your own fantasy."

"Mine?"

"Totally."

"A farm for my pony."

What was this with ponies and farms? He pictured guests slogging through mud, dressed in overalls like Garth. Flannel checked shirts. The women wearing bib aprons. Well, he had years to work with Peyton to improve that concept. He could go for women in Daisy Dukes and halter tops, their cute asses bouncing on ponies and the resident wild bull.

"I want to go see Mommy," Peyton said.

He dug his heels into the ground to stop the swing. They hopped off. He reached for her hand, brushing her tiny fingers. She accepted his firm clasp. Peyton believed him, and why wouldn't she? He had told her the truth.

They found Julie in the lounge standing apart from Aurora's yoga group.

"Not joining in?" Sebastiano asked her.

"While I was walking all over the retreat, looking for her, my mother got the yoga started."

Peyton looked up at Julie. "I tried building my farm. The pieces won't stick together."

Julie continued staring at Aurora, who was leading the group through a stretch. Orrin waved his chubby arm at Sebastiano. Was Nelson at the pool?

"Mommy." Peyton grabbed the hem of Julie's robe.

"What?"

"Can we go up to build my farm?"

Enough with farms, parents, and kids. Time to show off his new thong swimsuit to Nelson. He said his farewells and sauntered toward the hall.

* * *

Eric entered the restaurant and scanned the tables and booths. Grey-haired couples. A Latino family. From a booth near the back, Cassandra waved at him.

"You decided to let your daughter stay over?" she asked.

"Was I wrong?"

"Since we're both alone, you might as well join me."

He slid into the bench seat across from her. Cassandra bit into her burger. Trish, the same waitress as last time, brought him a menu, but Cassandra's burger and fries looked so good he immediately ordered the same.

"I was hoping you'd turn up." Cassandra's floral blouse with a scooped neck and capped sleeves was an improvement over her Ralphs polo shirt. A pendant shaped like a hot pepper dangled from her necklace chain. "I've been talking about New Dawn to people I run into during the day. Ralphs customers, motel staff, clerks in other stores."

"Did you learn anything new?"

Trish arrived with Eric's water. Cassandra slurped her Coke until the waitress left.

"Trish has been helpful," Cassandra said. "Like almost everyone, she has nothing but praise for New Dawn. This really is a one-industry town. You know, I'd vote for changing the name of New Dawn. It sounds like a dish detergent."

"You said almost everyone."

"A few gripes about the increased traffic. Some don't like newcomers, especially Mexicans, coming here for jobs. They miss the former tranquility. Quiet is dead, if you ask me."

"So why do you want to live at the retreat?" he asked. "It's as tranquil as it gets."

"For the guests. Aurora, Sebastiano, and their helpers make the whole operation run seamlessly minute by minute, week after week. Imagine the challenge."

She stared into her Coke, perhaps regretting she'd revealed that much. Petty gripes by townies were nothing. If only her snooping had unearthed a horror. No, better it hadn't, with Peyton there tonight, and Julie intending to stay indefinitely or permanently.

Cassandra glanced sideways, probably checking for the waitress's presence. "Trish clued me into Meggie Bell."

"Who?"

"I'd have saved myself a lot of time if I'd pumped Trish first. I suppose I didn't because she's chummy with Sebastiano and might tell him. Anyway, Trish mentioned

Meggie as the only person she knew who truly hated the retreat. Trish didn't know why. Meggie's old, kind of a recluse. She gets her groceries delivered from Ralphs. She worked at the retreat in the beginning. My hunch was she clashed with Aurora."

"Like you?"

"Meggie lives in a bungalow past the edge of town, a long walk."

Cassandra's habit of ignoring his questions kept him constantly off guard. Was that her purpose?

"It made me wish I'd bought a secondhand car, but who knows if I'll be here long enough for the expense?"

"How did you get to the retreat without a car?" he asked, not expecting a reply.

"Shuttle. They arrange all that. See what I mean about managing the operation? A screw-up with airport transfers could put someone off their whole week's stay. I've never heard of it ever happening."

He shifted her back on topic. "What did you learn from Meggie?"

Cassandra nibbled some fries. Considering her answer? Dramatic effect? Either approach would make her a good successor to Aurora, if that was her ambition. Her family was likely working class, or they'd have splurged to get her buck teeth fixed. Running the retreat would be a step up for Cassandra.

"It took ages for Meggie to answer her door," Cassandra said. "When she finally did, I convinced her to let me in even though I must have looked like a dishevelled rat from the walk."

Trish appeared with Eric's burger and fries. He wanted to ask for vinegar, but that would necessitate a return visit from the waitress. Trish left him to his food and thoughts. He bit into the burger. Cassandra had been persuasive with someone reluctant. Another Aurora trait. If a retreat leader had a job description, Cassandra would get a lot of check marks. Even her teeth didn't detract from her impressive looks. The malocclusion wasn't harmful, and he wouldn't recommend orthodontic treatment unless it made her self-conscious.

The restaurant hummed with chatter. It drew a good crowd on this Friday night, thanks to New Dawn's economic injection into the town.

"Meggie's house was a typical old person's nest of trinkets and doilies collecting dust. There was a weird smell. Maybe urine."

He set his burger on the plate. Too much detail.

"At first, Meggie denied she had issues with New Dawn. 'The hogwash they spout doesn't hurt no one,' she said."

Cassandra's expression remained neutral. Eric wondered if she thought the retreat's message was hogwash or the answer to people's problems.

"I think Meggie's lonely and liked talking to me, once she got going," Cassandra continued. "When Aurora and Sebastiano started building New Dawn, they hired Meggie to cook, clean, do laundry, and buy groceries while they got on with the important things, like supervising construction, landscaping, and selecting fixtures. They built the two cottages first. The one Garth lives in now served as their kitchen and eating space. So, get this." She paused and set down the remnants of her burger. "Meggie said Aurora and Sebastiano were both sleeping in his cottage."

"Where he lives now?"

She nodded. "The main building was still under construction. There was only one bed in the cottage. Meggie saw it delivered. Sebastiano swore to me he and Aurora had never had sex. In all my time at the retreat and from all the town people I've talked to, including Trish, I haven't heard a single rumour about him and Aurora before this."

"How reliable is Meggie?"

Cassandra shrugged. "I'm certain he and Aurora aren't sleeping together now, and I don't care what they did in the past."

"Julie would."

"You can be sure Sebastiano lied to her about that, as much as he lied to me."

Eric chewed a fry, pondering this development. The Julie he knew would be appalled by the thought of being with a man who had slept with her mother. But would it be a deal-breaker for the Julie now smitten with the retreat and its charms?

"There's more."

Eric's jaw tensed. Please, no details about Sebastiano and Aurora's sex life.

"The official story is that the money to build the retreat came from Sebastiano's family and Aurora's savings and investments," Cassandra said. "Not so, according to an argument between them that Meggie overheard."

Trish swooped in to ask if they wanted dessert. Cassandra ordered apple pie with ice cream and coffee. Eric would be lucky to get through this first course. Trish sashayed to the kitchen.

"She's curious about what we're discussing," Cassandra said.

"Not merely an efficient waitress?"

Cassandra smirked. "Anyway, the windfall to buy the property came from a con job in LA." She munched a few fries. Again, keeping him dangling for dramatic effect? "Aurora got friendly with this rich old widower, roping him in with love and sex. Sebastiano played the role of her son to make her story plausible. They got him to revise his will leaving Aurora a bundle. Meggie wonders if they slipped him an overdose of his own medicine to speed up her inheritance."

"Does she have proof of this?"

"Nothing more specific than his children contested the will and failed. Meggie's nephew, who's a lawyer, advised her to let it drop. Even if she found out the man's name, all she could add was hearsay evidence."

"You'd think Meggie would have blabbed this all over town if she hates them so much."

Cassandra drank her Coke. "The few she told initially said, 'So what, the retreat provides jobs.' Meggie quit working there after that argument because she felt Aurora and Sebastiano watching her and thinks they suspected she'd heard them. It gave her the creeps. For years, she was afraid they'd come after her. I think that's the real reason she stopped telling people. She worried it would get back to them. Meggie implied this led to her reclusiveness."

"What could they do to her?"

"She thinks Sebastiano would kill her to keep her quiet."

Eric squeezed a fry.

"A friend she told about this called her paranoid," Cassandra said. "I kind of agree. Sebastiano's no saint, but he wouldn't kill."

"Meggie thought he did."

"Well, yes, I can see him going along with Aurora's plan to off the old man with his medications or herbs."

"That's killing, direct or as an accessory."

Cassandra shook her glass, clinking the ice. "Sebastiano told me the inheritance from his father covered the retreat development. The buildings, furniture, and landscaping would have cost hundreds of thousands. The money came at an opportune time."

"Too opportune?" Eric pictured Sebastiano's perfect, grinning teeth. "Is anything chance with that pair?"

"What do you mean?"

Eric pushed his plate away. What an idiot he'd been to leave Peyton with those criminals. He wouldn't relax or sleep a minute until he got her out of there, first thing in the morning, or earlier.

"Whatever," Cassandra said. "I don't care about their past ethics."

Julie would care—the old Julie would. If he told her this, would it plant suspicion? Or would she accuse him of making it up to get her away from the place and Sebastiano? Would it be fair of him to damage Julie's relationship with her mother with hearsay information that had come from Meggie and Cassandra, two women who'd been hurt by Aurora and Sebastiano?

Cassandra wiped her lips. "All this time, Sebastiano has been leading me on, making me believe Aurora's going to welcome me with open arms when Julie gets tired of the retreat. The reality is, he'll do whatever it takes to keep Julie, and Julie isn't the type to share. While she's in, I'm out."

What did "whatever it takes" include? Julie could take care of herself, but Peyton?

Cassandra banged her fork on her plate. "I can't believe how stupid I've been, twiddling my fingers at Ralphs, waiting for—"

"Is my daughter safe there tonight?"

"Safe? Why not?"

Cassandra's puzzled eyes relaxed him, a little. What could happen in one night?

A lot.

He'd left Julie with Peyton one weekend and she'd tried to drown her. You'll never forgive me for that, Julie would say. He couldn't, not with Peyton at stake. What if Sebastiano, Aurora, and the retreat pushed Julie beyond her breaking point?

Trish arrived with Cassandra's coffee and pie. Eric discovered he'd finished his burger and tasteless fries. He asked for a coffee. Trish took his empty plate and left.

"Let's go out there and cause a stink," Cassandra said.

"At the retreat?"

Cassandra rammed her fork into the ice cream. "Julie doesn't know half the shit that's going on. I'll throw it in all of their faces."

"You mean, about her mother with Sebastiano?" Eric folded his hands on the table. "And the old guy they might have killed?"

She swirled ice cream over the pie, apparently reflecting. "In the evening, guests are usually in their residence and most of the staff is gone. We don't want them around so Aurora can recruit them to her side by calling us crazy and vindictive. It will be you and me against the pair of them. An even match."

"I'm not sure about even." Eric winced at an image of the giant couple staring them down. "I also don't want my daughter involved." He glanced at his watch. 7:00 p.m. Peyton was on holiday time and likely to be up for another hour or more.

Trish interrupted with his coffee. She rambled about the sudden change to cold weather. Eric sipped the hot drink until she was gone.

"I've got nothing to lose," Cassandra said.

"A shitfest will make things worse for you."

"I'm gone, either way. Aurora hates me too much."

'Throwing it in Julie's face' would hurt her. Sebastiano and Aurora would deflect their accusations. "We don't stand a chance against them."

"It will be worth it to get even," she said. "Something for them to remember me by. Leave with a bang."

A bang might wake Julie up. How else could he make her listen? "That much commotion will disturb Peyton asleep upstairs."

"We'll steer them into the vault."

"Huh?"

"Aurora's office is soundproof," Cassandra said and frowned. "Hmm. There are no accidents with those two. It's all starting to make sense."

Manoeuvring Aurora, Sebastiano, and Julie into "the vault" hardly seemed doable. But with Peyton tucked in, they might find Julie and Aurora in the lounge, maybe with Sebastiano and Delilah. From nervousness, Eric chuckled at an image of the foursome playing bridge. Delilah would listen to him and see reason. She'd help keep Peyton upstairs and calm, if necessary.

Eric stared across the table at Cassandra. "This plan for your shitfest," he said. "Run it by me again."

* * *

"Delilah." The closed bedroom door muffled a woman's voice. "Why aren't you down at supper?"

"I have a headache."

Seconds, minutes passed. Delilah's stomach rumbled. She dragged herself out from the covers. The room felt cooler than it had the previous nights. She put on a sweater and looked in the mirror. The sweater and robe combination looked bizarre. She picked up her watch. 7:05 p.m. Since the sweater had already spoiled her style, she strapped the watch on and shuffled from the room and down the stairs. At the landing, she met Julie and Peyton on their way up.

"We saved you a plate of leftovers," Julie said.

Delilah bent toward Peyton. "Bedtime?"

Peyton looked up at Julie. "Can we play with my farm first?"

Delilah left them. She continued to the hall and decided to save her dinner until after talking to Garth. If it killed her, she'd give them this last chance. Light shone from his cottage. She padded through the herb garden. How she'd love to go to bed every night with these scents wafting through his open window. And wake to them each morning.

She knocked on Garth's door. No reply. Had he seen her through the Venetian blinds and chosen to avoid her? He might be on his back patio reading. Life would be perfect with a guy to sit outside with, both of them consumed in books. She followed the beaten path between the cottages.

No Garth on the patio. His treehouse would be a warm place tonight for his reading, or better, brooding about her. She made her way into the woods and climbed the ladder to the treehouse. The dark space was vacant aside from a pile of pillows. From the treehouse window, she looked through the trees at the two octagonal cottages, their thatch roofs black spikes in the indigo sky. Sebastiano's bathroom light was on. She couldn't see Garth's windows from this angle, but he might have been showering when she knocked. Or out doing evening chores.

Something flitted behind Sebastiano's cottage. An animal? A person. Sebastiano had left his cottage by the back entrance and was heading up the hill. His third hike today. How much energy did the man have? Garth was active but also able to take it easy and stay still. Delilah preferred that.

She stepped partway down the ladder and peered through bare and leafy branches. Sebastiano's silhouette lingered in the trees. What was she doing spying on him? This was none of her business—although, from the start, her purpose on this trip had been to look out for Julie. She had promised her mother, Brad, and Eric. Along the way, she'd gotten sidetracked by herself.

Sebastiano cocked his head, as though listening for something. Was he out spotting owls or other night creatures? Perhaps he had more depth than she gave him credit for. If she stayed with Garth—oh, what was the chance?—Sebastiano might become her friend, on a certain level.

What was that? A second silhouette appeared. Also in a tunic. The men merged.

Merged?

They moved up the hill and vanished.

Delilah wobbled down the ladder. She crunched to the herb garden path, each step a cannonball in her head. Aside from Sebastiano, the only person here who wore a tunic was Nelson. Both were vigorous hikers. They must be going on an evening hike. Except that their "merge" had looked like a kiss.

Sebastiano was cheating on Julie. Nelson was cheating on his nice partner. Should she tell Julie?

Delilah banged on Garth's door. To her surprise, it opened. Garth was dressed in pyjamas, his sandy hair slick. It seemed he'd just gotten out of the shower. So, he hadn't ignored her knocks. She struggled to remember what she'd come here to say. Garth shifted from bare foot to bare foot. He made no motion to invite her in. Oh hell, blurt it out before he shut the door against her.

"Garth, I swear, I care nothing for Eric."

"I can't believe that."

"He's no more than a friend and my relative by marriage."

"You've loved him for years and years. That doesn't end in an instant."

"It does. When you're ready, I guess."

Garth blinked. Rapidly. Wildly. As if he was going to cry. A lump lodged in her throat.

"You'll be happier with Eric," he said.

"I don't want him."

"You only say that because you think you can't get him."

Delilah folded her arms for warmth. What if Eric drove here and begged her to marry him? Would she say yes?

No. She wouldn't. If she hadn't been one hundred percent free of him before, she was now.

"That's exactly what I mean," Garth said.

Oh no—he'd misinterpreted her hesitation. "Garth, I am certain. Eric isn't the one I want. It's you."

"Go away."

"Please let me explain."

"Leave me alone." He slammed the door in her face.

She knocked on it and pounded until her knuckles ached. "Alone!" she yelled. Could he hear through the door? "Alone is where you'll be. Forever and ever." That was cruel, but he deserved it for his obstinacy. She raised her voice. "No wonder you wound up in this place. You can't handle the real world."

Silence inside. She imagined Garth on his bed, rocking, trying to comfort himself. She turned the doorknob. Locked.

"Garth," she shouted through his door. "I didn't mean that. I'm sorry."

Still no answer or sounds within. She hoped he hadn't heard her.

She stumbled down the herb garden path, into the main building and up the stairs. Behind Peyton's closed door, Julie spoke in harsh tones. How could she be angry with a child she'd had with a man she once loved? Delilah bolted into her own bedroom, threw herself on her bed, and collapsed.

Chapter Thirty

"I want that farm put away now. All of it, in the box."

Peyton trotted the pig through the air, ignoring the barn pieces strewn on the floor. Julie gritted her teeth and squatted to collect the plastic shapes. She still had to talk to her mother, before Aurora escaped to her bedroom. There had been no chance after yoga with guests clinging to her, or during dinner, where Peyton sat between them. After dinner, Aurora had slipped into her office and locked the door. Technically, it hadn't been wrong for her to give Peyton the farm set to replace the one Julie would never finish if she stayed at the retreat. If. That was what bothered her. She hadn't decided yet. The gift seemed, at best, an assumption, and at worst, an attempt to direct her choice.

"I told you not to open that."

Julie jumped at the voice. Her mother stood in the doorframe. She held a children's book as though preparing to swat a fly.

"Mommy helped me," Peyton told Aurora.

"The present was for you to take home."

"Peyton already has a farm set at home." Julie dumped the last pieces into the ripped box, which would need taping. "A solid, hand-made one. Not cheap plastic."

"I have a farm?" Peyton said.

"Let's get you out of that robe and into bed," Julie said. Peyton would have to sleep in her underwear.

"A farm. A farm." Peyton clapped her hands.

"How about we use the robe as a nightie?" Julie said.

"And get it wrinkled?" Her mother frowned.

"So what?" Julie said. "She's leaving tomorrow."

"Peyton needs to look good at breakfast."

"I'll get up early and iron it," Julie said. "I can skip your precious sunrise service."

Her mother took a deep breath, her face tight. "I put a pink toothbrush in the bathroom for Peyton."

"Pink." Julie inhaled, like Aurora. Smooth things over, don't pick a fight over small issues. "She'll be more comfortable sleeping in her undies." Julie patted Peyton's behind. "Off you go to brush your teeth and use the toilet. Remember to wash your hands."

Peyton bolted from the room.

"She won't brush properly," Julie said to her mother. Work at bonding. "Eric makes her count to thirty every time, but we won't tell him."

Her mother clasped the book with both hands, her body stiff. "I brought Peyton the story we read this afternoon. Children like repetition."

"How would you know?" So much for smoothing things over.

"I beg your pardon."

"How would you know what children like? You weren't around when I was her age."

"Yes, I was."

They stood facing one another. Lines bracketed her mother's eyes. Her nose and mouth reminded Julie of her own when she looked in the mirror, except downward lines flared from her mother's lips.

"You left right after my fourth birthday. Peyton is four years and two months."

"That's quibbling."

"I can quibble if I want."

"Juliana, I told you—"

"You told me a lot of things."

Peyton appeared in the door frame. Julie hoped she hadn't overheard.

"Did you brush your teeth?" Julie said.

"We don't want your daddy complaining," her mother added.

Too late, Mom. You lost your chance to ally against Eric. Julie's chest hurt. "Grandma will read to you and tuck you in."

"Mommy, you read."

"This is Grandma's last night with you for a long, long time."

It was probably Julie's last night with her too. She couldn't speak, her chest was so tight. She ran into the hall, down the stairs, and outdoors.

* * *

Sebastiano watched Nelson recede through the trees. The sex had been incredible. So good that he wouldn't need another shot of guy stuff for months—long enough for Julie to settle into retreat life. Starting tomorrow, he'd focus his attention on her. With her husband, kid, and the stress they caused gone, he and Julie could plunge into the design for the new retreat, topped by hot romance at night. Maybe a fresh location. The ledge up the hill had worked for Nelson and him. Doing it with Julie in that spot would recall the memory, enhance the intensity; almost as good as a threesome.

By now Nelson would be safely in the guest building. Sebastiano trotted down the slope to the lawn. No one out strolling tonight. The slightest drop in temperature and guests retreated to their lounge for an evening of reading, talking, and emoting.

This cool, clear night was perfect for viewing stars. He really had to convince Aurora to buy a telescope. He'd get Julie to support him on that. A robed figure glided down the stone path by the amphitheatre. Aurora? No, that was Julie striding to the swing, her head forward, as though on a mission. Sebastiano hid behind an olive tree.

Julie circled the swing and tree in a figure-eight loop. She paced to the edge of the amphitheatre, and then back to the swing. More figure eights. Obsessive-compulsive. This wasn't good. He would talk to her, calm her down, after his shower. Pity to wash away the musky aroma of Nelson, but

Julie came first from now on, above his other women and men. One day Julie would understand those dalliances didn't affect the core of him and her. Cassandra had gotten that right away. What a girl.

Julie circled the swing and tree again, her shoulders stiff. Her whole body looked like a firecracker ready to explode. He'd make it a quick shower.

* * *

From under the covers, Delilah heard a tap on her door.

"Could you do us a favour?" Aurora's voice.

Delilah poked her head out. She grabbed a tissue and blew her nose. "What?"

"I have to talk to Julie. Would you mind reading to Peyton?"

"All right."

Delilah crawled to her feet and glanced in the mirror. Her eyes were red from the crying, her face blotchy. She brushed her robe, which was creased from hours spent curled into a fetal position. If Peyton noticed her blotches, she'd accept whatever explanation Delilah dreamed up and return to the world of her children's book. Kids were wonderfully innocent.

Delilah nudged her door open. To her relief, Aurora was gone and wouldn't see her looking a mess. Why wasn't Julie putting Peyton to bed? This could be her last evening with her child for months. Was she with Sebastiano? No, he was with Nelson. Delilah decided to keep her mouth shut about that. Julie was already agitated enough.

Peyton lay on the single bed, a book propped on her knees. Delilah squeezed beside her, under the comforter. Peyton's skin felt warm and her body tiny, fragile.

Delilah looked at the book cover. "*Andy, Mandy and Candy*. I haven't heard of it." If she had a child, she'd make sure she was up-to-date on kids' books and TV shows. Well, not TV if she stayed at the retreat, but that wasn't going to happen. Emptiness swept through her body.

“I don’t want to read this.” Peyton reached across Delilah to get a thicker book from the bedside table. “Mommy brought me this one.”

Where the Sidewalk Ends by Shel Silverstein. Delilah had noticed it in the library downstairs, presumably left by a guest. Her mother had read her the poems when she was a kid and laughed as much as Delilah did. In fact, she and her mother had introduced them to Julie after their parents got together.

Delilah opened the book and read the poems, her mind outside the room, in her ideal life. The retreat was her opportunity to raise a child with a decent man, to easily juggle motherhood and work. A woman from town could come to babysit while Delilah commuted through the herb garden to her job in Aurora’s office. She’d work independently, although supervised—she suspected heavily—by Aurora. The absence of television would free up a lot of time for healthy activities like helping Garth garden. She’d learn all the flower names. Gardening would be their common interest in addition to reading and their child. He wasn’t much for talking, which was fine. Not like she was used to having a man to converse with.

At New Dawn, she would have her meals provided, dishes cleaned, laundry done, Julie for a next-door neighbour and friend. She would live in a pastoral setting and take occasional trips to town for appointments, chocolates, books, and coffee in a shop with internet. For the rare times she craved more, towns with movie theatres and big-box stores were only a two-hour drive away. A few times a year she’d fly to Calgary to see her mother, who might enjoy a holiday at New Dawn. More likely not, with Aurora here. She’d assure her mother she needn’t be jealous. Aurora was successful and impressive, a mother to guests who came here week after week, but she lacked—

“Auntie Delilah,” Peyton said sharply.

“What, honey?”

“You stopped reading.”

Delilah scanned the words on the page. “Where were we?”

Peyton's hand dropped to a line of words. Delilah picked up her rote reading.

Aurora lacked warmth. Brad must have learned that during his time with her. He would never dump Rosemary for Marion. Delilah had to tell her mother that.

"Auntie Delilah," Peyton said. "Move your hand. I need to turn the page."

"Sorry, Peyton."

What if Garth burst into the room, got down on his knees to Delilah, said he loved her and pleaded with her to stay? If it turned out she wasn't pregnant and could never have a child, would she choose this domestic idyll with Garth?

Before her crying jag, she would have answered yes. She loved him and New Dawn life. But her love had been an infatuation with them and the possibility of motherhood.

"Delilah."

"One last poem—all right, honey?"

Delilah forced her concentration on the poem that morphed into three more poems before she convinced Peyton it was time for sleep. If she couldn't have a child of her own, she would be the best aunt. Eric would appreciate her help, with Julie away most of the year at the retreat. She could take Peyton shopping, to the library, and to kiddie movies.

She tucked the comforter around Peyton's neck and kissed her soft brow. "Your mommy will be here soon to say good night." Surely Julie wouldn't miss that special moment with Peyton.

Delilah tiptoed down the hall. No voices from Julie's bedroom. She rapped on the door. No reply. Julie might be in Aurora's bedroom, but Delilah didn't dare knock. She went downstairs and paused in the hall. No buzz of workers in the kitchen or dining room. The lounge was empty. Aurora's office door was closed, as usual. She and Julie must be talking in there.

The front doorbell chimed. Delilah whirled. Sebastiano walked into the lounge and stopped beside a chair.

"Have you seen Julie?" she asked.

"She's outside, strolling through the lawn with Aurora, deep in conversation. I decided to leave them be." He sauntered to the fireplace. "Shall we get this thing lit? It's a cold night."

* * *

Aurora paused on the path between the guest residence and vegetable garden. She hoped Juliana would take the hint and slow her exhausting pace. They had walked the entire property and her daughter still hadn't explained why her buying Peyton a tiny present was such an issue.

"If you don't understand…" Juliana's steps quickened.

Aurora stood her ground. The stress of Peyton and Eric's visit had clearly made Juliana irrational. That would be over with tomorrow, thank the gods. Aurora wrapped her shawl tighter against the chill and considered adding the extra shawl she'd brought for Juliana, who refused to wear it. This was like dealing with a stubborn child. Guests sometimes talked of sinking to a childish level when disagreeing with their parents. She wanted Juliana to be mature and strong while, of course, recognizing Aurora's senior position. Was that too much to ask?

To the west, the orange groves rose up the hill and farm beyond. Never mind toy farms. Aurora was giving her daughter a life-size one to redesign. Few parents were that generous. She deserved gratitude, not tantrums. Juliana doubled back. Not giving in had worked.

Juliana faced her, eyes as wide as those narrow Fox eyes could be. "What was it like for you the day you left our home for California?"

They had covered this the first afternoon, when Juliana arrived at the retreat. Why beat the dead horse?

"Gut-wrenching." Aurora stepped up the emotion. "The saddest moment of my life. It took every effort to tear myself away, yet I knew I had to go."

"Why?"

Aurora took a deep breath. When she'd explained it all on Saturday, Juliana had appeared to understand. And over the last six days, she'd shown no sign of being a chronic whiner unable to move past a childhood hurt. Brad's and his bitter mother's prejudice against Marion might run deep, but Aurora's daughter was better than this.

"I have this memory," Juliana said. "A woman hugging me, holding me close, telling me to be brave, that I was a big girl. I sensed the woman was going far, far away."

Juliana talked faster and faster. Aurora had to concentrate to catch the words.

"Was the woman you?" Juliana said. "Or someone else, like Grandma Fox leaving on a trip to visit my uncle? Was it the day you left, or an ordinary day you went downtown and I was being a clingy kid? I don't know if the memory is real or something Grandma or Dad once told me." Her voice trembled. "Maybe I made it up to fill the gap."

Aurora's recollection of that day was equally vague. She had stood on the front porch listening to Brad call her selfish and worse. Juliana, in the house, either hadn't heard or didn't remember that. Marion would have hugged Juliana goodbye. The message to be a brave, big girl sounded like something she would say.

Aurora touched Juliana's cold hand. "I hugged you so hard, didn't want to let go. You were brave and strong. Even then, I could see that in you, Juliana."

"Julie."

Aurora pressed her lips together.

"I was barely four years old."

Previously, Juliana had said she had no memories of her mother aside from the possible one of Marion watching her draw. She might have withheld this other memory because it hurt the most. Juliana's raising it now meant she felt closer to her. Clichés were often true. This was the darkness before the dawn. A new dawn. They would work through this crisis.

"What did your father tell you about that day?" Aurora said.

"You know Dad. He doesn't talk about things."

"You must realize this was part of my problem with him. Expressing myself to Brad was like hitting a wall."

"I get that." Juliana rubbed her arms.

Aurora held out the shawl.

Juliana hugged her arms to her abdomen. “Why didn’t you think of me during all those years?”

“I thought of you every day.” Would Juliana balk if Aurora tenderly draped the shawl over her shoulders? Best not to risk it. She added the layer of warmth to her own shawl.

“How could you not phone or write?”

“It wasn’t nearly so convenient in those days before email.”

“Bullshit.”

Aurora jerked back at the word and struck an orange tree. Pain seared her shoulder. Juliana tore into the yard, toward the valley oak. Aurora followed. Those bursts of profanity would have to go. Eric and Peyton’s showing up had unbalanced Juliana. The child’s presence constantly reminded Juliana of her failure, just as toddler-Julie had reminded Marion she didn’t measure up to the motherhood ideal. Eric’s arrival tomorrow morning to take Peyton away couldn’t come soon enough.

Aurora longed to rest on the swing, but Juliana bolted past it. Should she hold her ground again and coax her daughter to sit? Juliana in this mood might swing the chair hard enough to make Aurora sick. On purpose, perhaps. Thank the gods she’d missed those years of raising a rebellious child.

Her feet sore, she followed Juliana through the lemon grove to the pool shimmering with turquoise light. No swimmers this cool evening. How beautiful the pool looked enclosed in darkness. Her retreat was a marvellous creation with unlimited possibilities.

“It’s wrong for me to leave Peyton,” Juliana said.

“Whose view is that?” Aurora asked. “Society’s? Your ex-husband’s? Your father’s?”

“Did you ever sleep with Sebastiano?”

Aurora recoiled. “No.” She would kill Sebastiano if he had stupidly confessed this to Juliana.

“He insists you didn’t,” Juliana said. “I don’t know how truthful he is.”

Juliana's suspicious nature would challenge Sebastiano's lying expertise, but Aurora felt confident he was up to it.

"No matter how nuts I go," Juliana continued, gazing at the pool, "I don't think I'd try to drown Peyton again or deliberately hurt her in another serious way."

"Juliana, I know you won't. That's progress, your belief in yourself."

"I might do worse, though."

"What would be worse?"

Juliana looked at her. "See, you think what I did to Peyton was the worst possible thing."

Don't manipulate my words. "Peyton wasn't damaged by your action," Aurora said. "Peyton is strong."

"She's a little girl."

"She's bright. Peyton will understand—"

"She will never understand why I don't love her. Not really. Not deep in her gut."

Was this Juliana's root problem with her child? Aurora would solve it by assuring her not all women were naturals and this apparent lack was a sign of Juliana's higher purpose.

Juliana darted into the lemon grove. She zigzagged out of the trees and jogged across the lawn back to the valley oak tree. Aurora followed, exhausted. Daughters were harder to handle than guests. She approached Juliana, who stood beside the double swing.

"Leave me alone here, to think," Juliana said.

Aurora's feet ached and two shawls weren't warming her shoulders. She'd leave her daughter alone to come to her senses and brew herself a tea that was good for circulation.

She took the garden route to the main building. Engulfed in the fresh scents, she plucked the needed herbs. Sebastiano might enjoy a cup too. Before Juliana's arrival, when Sebastiano wasn't sleeping with some guest, they would sit by the fire on winter nights, discuss the day, and plan for the next one. Life had been easier.

* * *

Julie climbed onto the swing and spread her feet apart to keep it steady. She reached up and touched a branch of the oak tree. It felt solid, unbending, and was the ideal height. Across the lawn, lights glowed from the guest building windows. The main building was dark. Peyton's room was on the opposite side. Julie wished she'd tucked her in rather than delegate the task to her mother, who had pawned it off on Delilah. Peyton's one night here. A normal mother would have given her daughter that tidbit of time. Instead, Julie had wasted the hours on thoughts and arguments with no answers.

She should return to Calgary to be Peyton's mother.

Don't say should.

Aurora was right. This retreat was Julie's place. She ran her fingers along her belt and played with its rope knot. The problem was she wasn't sure she wanted to stay here. Right now, she was neglecting and ignoring her daughter as much as her own mother had done to her for thirty-four years. Aurora was full of excuses and explanations that made sense on the surface, but no outside force had kept her away. She hadn't been addled by drugs or drink. Aurora was resourceful to the core and could have found a way to contact Julie, if she'd wanted.

Marion, Aurora, Mother, Mom. Not one of them loved Julie. Julie didn't love Peyton. Break the negative pattern. Julie had put her heart into trying to love her child. She hadn't managed it. Never would. Break the pattern.

The belt came loose from Julie's waist. She clutched the twisted rope, raised it up her chest. Silky yet tough, the long rope grazed her neck, caressed her skin. She knew how to tie a knot that wouldn't slip. Break the pattern.

Despite the drowning attempt, Peyton was still innocent, capable of love. Julie hadn't ruined her yet. Peyton loved Eric, her Aunt Delilah, Rosemary, Brad. All of them loved Peyton like Julie couldn't. Left in their care, Peyton would grow up loving, steady, able to take on the world.

Julie looked at the main building again. Delilah was somewhere inside. *I bequeath my daughter to you.* When Julie's sick influence was out of the way, Peyton would flourish with Eric's and Delilah's nurturing. Break the pattern. Too late for Julie, but she could save Peyton. Julie could give her no better gift. Break the pattern. Break it. Break it. The belt, soft and strong. Tie the rope around her neck. Secure it to the branch. Kick the swing away.

But the swing would keep gliding back, pounding her legs like her sickness that would never end. If she chickened out, her toes could grab a foothold.

A pool chair. Strong to stand on, flimsy enough to kick far away from her feet.

Chapter Thirty-One

Eric parked beside Aurora's Beetle. "What's the plan?"

"See who we find and wing it?"

Cassandra had shown up in the motel lobby dressed for the event in a thigh-length sarong with a wild print of shiny swirls, white capris, and 'high heels to match Julie's height,' she'd said, tossing her head to dangle the earrings that kissed her shoulders.

He'd thrown in his lot with a vengeful drama queen. On the drive from town, they had debated strategies. Eric had considered backing out, but Cassandra on her own might make things worse for Julie and Peyton. This way, he would be there to defuse the blowout.

The clanging door announced their entry into the retreat lounge. Sebastiano rose from a chair by the fireplace. *My luck to encounter the creep first.* Delilah popped up from an adjacent chair and rushed over and hugged Eric. Then he spotted Aurora standing beside Sebastiano.

"We came to see Julie," Eric said.

"And you." Cassandra glared at Sebastiano.

"Is she upstairs with Peyton?"

Delilah glanced at the ceiling. "Peyton should be asleep by now."

Aurora's gaze flashed between Eric and Cassandra. "I might have expected you two to ally against Julie's best interests."

"We have news that might interest her," Cassandra said.

Eric touched Cassandra's arm, as a message to wait. Before walking into this vulture den, he should have insisted on a plan with a semblance of organization. "Where is Julie?"

"I was just going to check," Sebastiano said.

“Liar.” Cassandra grabbed his tunic. “You swore you weren’t sleeping with her.”

Sebastiano didn’t flinch or frown.

“I left her to sulk in the yard,” Aurora said.

Cassandra pounded Sebastiano’s chest. “You liar. Manipulator. User. You…”

Her tirade became a roar of words while Julie was outside alone. Eric bolted to the door.

* * *

Julie steadied herself on the pool chair and reached up to the oak tree branch. She wrapped one end of her rope belt around the sturdy limb, far from the trunk so she couldn’t clutch it in a final few seconds of losing her courage. The knot tied, she yanked the rope to test it was secure. She draped the other end of the rope around her neck.

Would the first arrivals for the sunrise service spot her tomorrow before dawn? Some might see her earlier from their bedroom windows. Aside from Julie’s bedroom and the dining room, the only rooms in the main building with a view of the yard were Aurora’s office and bedroom. Aurora might be up before everyone, to prepare for the sunrise service. Julie pictured her mother glancing out of her bedroom window, surveying her world that waited to greet the new day. Her gaze would light on this tree and the figure of a woman hanging from a branch—Julie, her daughter. Aurora would scream, barrel down the stairs, cry, “No, Julie, no.”

Perfect.

Julie looped the rope into a knot at her neck. She hoped she wasn’t doing this to force her mother to prove her love. That would be childish. And stupid. Too late. What good would her mother’s love be when she was dead?

Peyton often got up early. In this unfamiliar place, she would likely go to Julie’s room to crawl in with her. When she found no Julie in the bed, she’d try Delilah. Actually, Peyton might go to Delilah first, her true mother. But what if instead of seeking comfort, Peyton felt keen to explore and trotted down the stairs, out to the yard to the swing and tree and found—No. No. No. There was little chance of this. Peyton would be cuddled with loving Aunt Delilah while other people cut Julie down.

But there was a chance. A small chance Peyton would see her mother's body, dead. The image burned forever in her eyes. Julie couldn't risk it, couldn't do that to her child. She was trapped, stuck in life. Eyes burning, she pulled on the rope knot to loosen it.

From the main building, through the darkness, someone ran toward her. A man. Sebastiano? Smaller. No tunic. Street clothes. Eric. He stopped in front of her, gasped for breath.

She brushed the rope from her neck. "Can't you trust me alone with Peyton for one night?"

Eric scanned her body, the chair, the rope, the tree. "I need to tell you a few things."

No doubt he'd ask what she'd been up to out here. "That can wait until morning." Julie glanced up at Aurora's window. This understanding was more important now. "At last I get it."

"Me too."

"Do you know how sumptuous my mother's bedroom is compared with the rest of this place?"

"You should know Cassandra's been questioning people in town."

Julie untied the rope from the tree limb. "Her office shuts her off from everyone." She tied the rope back around her waist, jumped off the chair, and marched toward the main building. Eric's footsteps crunched behind her on the rubbery grass. Cricket chirps engulfed them. All this time outside tonight, she hadn't heard their music.

She entered the lounge. Delilah rushed over and squeezed Julie to her chest.

"What's that for?" Julie asked.

Eric drew up beside her, and Cassandra clacked toward them. From the love seat by the window, Sebastiano saluted her.

"Where's my mother?"

Cassandra nodded at the office door. "She can't stand hearing the truth."

Eric's hand pressed against Julie's back. "Let's sit."

"I'll stand."

"Eric's right." Delilah touched her arm to guide her to a chair.

Julie sloughed them off. "Stop treating me like a child. What's going on?"

Cassandra waved her hands through the air. "Shall we begin with the terrible, the criminal, or the worst?"

"I want to talk to my mother." The office door was probably locked, but she turned the handle. The door jerked open, making her stumble forward. Aurora sat behind her desk.

Cassandra pushed up behind Julie to enter, but Julie slammed the door against her and bolted the lock. Her mother laughed.

"What's so funny?" Julie said.

"Those two clowns turn up here with their stories. As if a smart girl like you would believe them."

"I'm not a girl."

"I know." Her mother stood up. "But you'll always be my little girl."

"I was never your girl," Julie said. "You dumped me."

Her mother eased around the desk. "Juliana, don't talk like that."

"I'm not Juliana."

"You are becoming her."

"You didn't love me."

"They're jealous and want to ruin you."

"You never did." Julie's voice wavered.

"Don't let them turn you against me."

"You didn't call or write in thirty-four years." She felt her voice return. "Did I cross your mind once that whole time?"

"Juliana."

"Julie."

"What can I do or say to convince you?"

Her mother's warm fingers grazed her arm. Julie shoved them off. "I understand not loving your child. Of course I do.

I understand you getting on with your life and re-creating yourself. Child out of sight, out of mind."

"Julie, it wasn't like that."

"I understand all that in the past. I accept it."

"Understanding and acceptance." Her mother's Aurora voice. "That's a beginning for you, a start."

"Do you love me now?"

"More than anything in the world."

"Do you?" Her feeble voice cracked.

Her mother's face radiated love, as it did to twenty-two strangers every week. "Cassandra and Eric are angry, bitter people. They want to drive you from me and New Dawn, your destiny."

"All I am to you is your ideal successor."

"You're a natural, my flesh and blood."

"My father's too."

"Those Fox features need smoothing, but they will make you better than I could ever be."

Her mother's hands reached out. Her mother wanted her, accepted her.

A memory, a hand slapping her face, her mother saying, "You're a bad girl. You deserved that. You're rotten to the quick."

Julie knocked Aurora's hands back to her face. Her mother clutched her cheek.

Good. *Hurt her the way she hurt me.* Good. Good. Good.

"You hit me like that. You hit me, a little kid." Julie's knees buckled. She grabbed the edge of the desk. "You used me. How could you do that?"

"We can discuss this when you calm down," her mother said.

"I don't want to calm down."

"Stop being a child."

"I am a child. I was a child. You walked away from an innocent little girl."

Her mother stared. "Be glad I didn't try to drown you."

Julie let go of the desk, her chest heaving. She looked into her mother's eyes. Julie's miniature face stared back from the pools of blue-grey.

"Forgive me, Julie, I didn't mean to…"

"Yes you did. You craft every word you say."

"That's cruel."

"Who did I get that from?" Julie shivered. "You shift the bad onto everyone else, including me. You stab me for the drowning, slide in the knife on purpose to hurt…" Her voice gave out. *Don't show weakness.* She strode to the door, struggled with the handle.

"Juliana, I realize you need to blame me for what you did to Peyton."

"I am not Juliana." Julie yanked the unyielding handle, tried to twist it. "Fuck." *Bad.* Her mother's voice in her head. *Rotten. You deserved that.*

"When you're feeling better, we'll discuss this rationally, over tea."

The door jerked into Julie. She tottered backwards, regained her balance, and lunged into the lounge. Eric, Delilah, and Cassandra zoomed toward her.

"Go away."

Sebastiano hovered behind the trio, legs planted apart.

"Leave me alone." Julie sensed her mother behind her.

Bad, bad, bad, worthless. Marion's hand slapped little Julie to the floor.

"Mommy?" Beyond Sebastiano, a girl stood in the hall, her pink robe rumpled. Peyton. Julie's body sank. Her baby, her Peyton.

"I'm sorry, Peyton," Julie said. "I won't hurt you again." She lurched forward.

Eric blocked her. Her knees buckled. She veered left. Eric slid in front of her.

"Let me by."

She forced her legs straight, tore between Eric and Delilah and hit Sebastiano's chest. She couldn't see Peyton. Where was Peyton?

"No," Julie screamed.

Peyton floating under water, her eyes glazed.

"No. No. No. No."

A child in a glass casket.

"No."

Drowned, dead by her hand.

"No. No."

"Julie." Eric's voice.

She spun around. Her mother, Delilah, Eric, and Cassandra reached for her. Round and round, her vision blurred. The wall of arms and hands closed in. She couldn't get past them, get past it, she would never get past it all. Her legs gave out. The arms would get her when she struck the floor. She slid by Aurora and fell into Delilah.

Chapter Thirty-Two

Eric dodged Sebastiano and scooped up Peyton's small body into his arms. His daughter hid her face in his chest, her shoulders heaving in synch to Julie's and Delilah's across the room. Aurora stared at the sisters clutched together, her expression fathomless. She wrapped her shawl around her shoulders and strode out the front door, into the night. Peyton's clasp on his neck tightened.

"Are you okay, sweet?"

She wriggled, not looking up. Sebastiano drew Cassandra to the fireplace. Some hero he'd turned out to be. Not that Eric had been a huge improvement, right from the start. A better person would have viewed Julie's near drowning of Peyton as a sickness, an aberration, and helped her move beyond it to become the real Julie again. Instead, his condemnation had contributed to her feeling subhuman. No wonder when it really counted, she'd chosen Delilah over him.

Julie and Delilah pulled themselves away from each other. They still looked shaky as they settled on a love seat.

Slimy as it was, the retreat had given Julie the support Eric hadn't. If she stayed here, he would do his best to make it work. He wouldn't withhold Peyton from her or use other tactics out of a desire to make her miserable and prove she'd made the wrong choice. As long as Peyton was safe, he would let go and move on with his own life.

By the fireplace, Cassandra and Sebastiano talked, she with elaborate hand gestures, he leaning against the bookshelf. They focused on each other, with no glances at Julie. If Julie was done with Sebastiano, Eric might win her back, if he could ever get past seeing her try to drown Peyton or hang herself on that tree. And her sleeping with

Sebastiano. She'd been attracted to the despicable man. Eric's stomach turned. Had she found the sex better than it ever was or could be with him?

And more, Delilah had bought a pregnancy kit for someone. What if Julie came home but she was pregnant with Sebastiano's child? Eric doubted Sebastiano would give a hoot about the girl or boy's upbringing, but the child was bound to inherit some of the father's physical traits and, perhaps, emotional ones. Was pathology in the genes?

Other people loved children who hadn't come from them. Eric wouldn't find it hard to love a child who looked like Julie, but what if the child turned out to be a clone of Sebastiano? Eric hugged Peyton closer. He imagined a boy her age with curly black hair, skin tanned from playing outdoors, grinning mischievously with perfect teeth, up to no good. A daily reminder of Julie with Sebastiano.

Peyton raised her head. Through reddened eyes, she looked across the room. "I want Mommy."

Eric nodded and took her to Julie.

* * *

Aurora paced from the front row of the amphitheatre to the podium then back to the tiered seats, and then repeated the steps. What a disappointment Julie had turned out to be.

Julie. She wasn't worthy of Juliana.

It wasn't her emotional fragility. Aurora could cure that with herbs and ministry after the husband and child were gone. Neither was it Julie's histrionics. A sense of drama gave a retreat leader style. If Aurora had a flaw, it might be a lack of outward passion that drew people to her and her message. Julie, potentially, had that charisma. Aurora hadn't lied when she'd told her daughter that Juliana might surpass even Aurora.

Julie's flaw, what made her unsuitable, was the insolence from her challenges and hostility after Aurora had explained and apologized a dozen times. What more did Julie want? Aurora paced. She had welcomed her long-lost daughter, overlooked her annoying traits inherited from

Brad—stubbornness and conventionality, among others. Brad and mainstream society had beat Julie down for her failing. Aurora alone had forgiven her daughter's worst sins. Gods in the past smote those who showed them no respect. History was full of leaders who passed over weak children and handed the torch to their true heirs. New Dawn would not crumble without Julie.

Aurora leaned on the podium for support. She was tired. So very tired. Was it the cancer resurfacing? No. She was cancer free but had to preserve her resistance or the sickness would creep back in. Stress wore down the body. Evil seized the slightest opportunity.

If Julie wanted to stay, Aurora would lay down ground rules. If her daughter refused to accept them, she could return to her child and Eric or fly to the moon, for all Aurora cared.

But how long would the retreat survive? Aurora was almost sixty. Somewhere in her body, cancer or another illness lurked, preparing to pounce. Sebastiano had his strengths, but without a woman in charge, New Dawn would die.

Cassandra? Aurora hadn't recognized her at first in that ridiculous costume. Like cancer, Cassandra lurked. She'd found an ally in Eric and taken action to get what she wanted, just as long-ago Marion and Stuart had done what was needed to achieve their dream. Cassandra was tenacious, determined.

* * *

Delilah left Julie and Eric on the love seat, Julie holding Peyton. By the fireplace, Sebastiano talked in whispers to Cassandra. Aurora had left the building. No one was here for Delilah. She made her way down the hall.

Cassandra caught up with her at the back door. "I'm off to the cottage."

"Sebastiano's?"

They exited to the herb garden and stopped at the path crossroads.

“Good luck with him,” Delilah said as Cassandra left her.

“You make your own luck, Aurora says.”

A light shone from Garth’s cottage window. He was probably inside reading. Delilah had so wanted those evenings spent with him and their books.

Garth answered her knock in his bib jeans smeared with earth. “Delilah.” His neck flushed.

She took a deep breath. “Garth. I think you’re a really nice man. The best. You’ve made a good life for yourself here.” She touched her chest. “One that isn’t for me.”

He blinked several times. Why add that she didn’t really love him and wouldn’t want him without a child?

“Goodbye, Delilah,” he said, and closed his door.

Delilah returned to the path and those wonderful aromas. She might plant a garden this spring, but first she would find a job. Some bookstore or related business was bound to be hiring. If “the gods were with her,” to quote Aurora, and she was pregnant, she would raise the child, with her mother’s help. Julie’s too, perhaps. While they’d talked on the love seat, Julie had mentioned, calmly, that Sebastiano’s condom had broken one night.

“I hope to God I’m not pregnant,” Julie had said. “Regardless, what would you think of finishing your basement into a suite for me? You could hang out with Peyton when she visits.”

Delilah understood. Julie would prefer her supervision to that of their parents, and Delilah would get a housemate for practical, economical, and companionship benefits. Her unselfish side prayed that Julie and Eric would somehow work things out. Either way, Delilah was glad to have Julie for a sister. What a waste it had been to feel jealous and intimidated by her all those years.

Even with Julie in her basement or coming over to lend a hand, raising a child would be busy and crazy. But Delilah welcomed the challenge.

* * *

Sebastiano approached the spectre in the amphitheatre. The stars illuminated Aurora, who stood beside the podium. No surprise she would retreat to this spot from which she radiated her greatest strength.

At his approach, she wrapped her shawl tighter around her arms. "What's happening inside?"

"Julie is cocooned with her family."

"Trust Cassandra to come up with that scheme."

"She had no clue it would play out like this."

"You don't sound disturbed," Aurora said. "I thought you cared for my daughter."

"I did. I do. Cassandra offers different pleasures."

While he enjoyed Julie, she'd have restricted him. Cassandra was more eager for him and the retreat, hence more willing to accommodate his desires. She also had her surprises.

In the lounge, while pounding his chest, Cassandra had ranted, "You'd kill your own father if it suited your purpose."

He'd started, only an instant, but she'd caught his expression. Cassandra knew—her damn intuition—and accepted this.

"She's no architect, though," he said. "We'll need to find another one for the new retreat."

Aurora's gaze travelled up the amphitheatre's seats to the hilltop. "I have never liked Cassandra."

"She'll grow on you."

"Her ambition is to replace me."

"That's true of any successor. We don't live forever."

"You included." She edged behind the podium.

"I'm well aware."

"So you do your utmost to enjoy your time."

He shrugged. "What else is there?"

Aurora scanned the seats fanning upward. He knew she was imagining the rows filled with guests at her next sunrise service. Cassandra had learned to mimic Aurora's style. From this, Cassandra's own style would emerge and solidify, different, yet as effective as Aurora's.

“We’ll try her out in the office and at occasional services and sessions,” Aurora said. “The slightest hint of her stabbing me in the back and she’s out the door.”

Sebastiano touched Aurora’s shawl. “I’d call that reasonable.”

* * *

Julie and Peyton nuzzled noses.

“Off to bed,” Julie said.

“I’m not tired.” Peyton yawned.

Eric chuckled. Julie noticed Delilah in the hall and motioned her over to the love seat.

“Eric and Peyton invited us to tag along on the rest of their trip,” Julie told her. “LEGOLAND on Sunday followed by a beach day.”

“Don’t feel sorry for me,” Delilah said. “I’ll survive Garth.”

“It’s not that,” Eric said. “We want you along.”

Eric’s ready agreement to Julie’s suggestion they include her implied that he too would appreciate Delilah’s presence as a buffer between them and help in keeping the holiday light for Peyton. Julie and Eric would need to tread carefully toward any possible reconciliation.

Julie looked up at Delilah. “Tomorrow at breakfast I want to talk to some of the people here. Nelson, Orrin, Rachel. I owe them an explanation.”

“What for?” Delilah said.

“Treating them, at best, weirdly.”

“Oh, Julie. Aurora, Sebastiano, and everything pushed you to it.”

“After breakfast, Eric suggested we check out the local sights with him and Peyton.”

“Daddy’s taking me for a pony ride.” Peyton stumbled up to her feet. Balanced on Julie’s thighs, she grabbed Delilah around the neck, yanking her awkwardly lower.

Julie hoped she was done with paranoid thoughts, especially the one about Delilah trying to steal Peyton and Eric. There was certainly a lot to discuss with Dr. Kumar when she got home. Julie hugged and kissed Peyton good night, her love flowing, as though an invisible hand inside her had flicked a switch to release it. She couldn't wait to tell her psychiatrist he'd been right. He was the only person who'd known she was blocked besides Aurora, who had used that confession to manipulate her.

Delilah offered to take Peyton back up to bed, and they disappeared into the stairwell.

Julie looked at Eric. "I was naïve to let them suck me in."

"Aurora played the convincing mother," he said. "Sebastiano the lover. Who wouldn't fall for that?"

Eric's face, which had struck her as pale after Sebastiano's, now took on heightened colour tinged with flickers from the fireplace. She liked how his hair fell casually. He never preened, and she preferred his natural aroma to gobs of aftershave. It was impossible that he still loved her after all she'd put him through, all she'd done to Peyton. She wasn't sure she could love him again. The miracle was her love for her child.

She smiled wistfully. "I'll miss the work they offered me here," she said. "Designing and building a new world, my own LEGOLAND."

"You can find an equivalent in your job back home."

"In oil and gas?"

"You could transfer to another department, change companies, or switch to a different area of engineering. There're tons of opportunities. It's not like dentistry."

"You aren't stuck there, either."

"It's tolerable with poetry on the side," he said. "Next time I won't use you as material, I swear."

"Write whatever you want." She glanced around the lounge to Aurora's office door and couldn't help but laugh a little. "This retreat is a minefield of material."

"Time I dug into myself." Eric rubbed his jaw. "Root canals. I've got the germ of an idea."

Julie smoothed her robe over her legs, which now felt steady enough for standing. Would she be able to leave this place for good? Aurora was still her mother, after all.

Sebastiano? She might not be totally disinterested, but if she ever visited the retreat, she'd be smart enough not to give in to him again. Right now, she wanted to get one matter out with Eric. "You have to know," she said. "There's a small chance I might be pregnant by him."

"Sebastiano?" Eric blanched.

Julie studied his face, to gauge his response.

He swallowed. "If you are, whatever you do about it, I'll be there for you, if you want."

"I think I'd keep the baby."

He looked away. "I've always wanted a brother or sister for Peyton."

"Even a child of Sebastiano?"

His gaze returned to her. "I don't know."

"That's honest," she said. If that was testing him, he'd done not badly. "Suppose I should call my dad."

"He must be driving Rosemary nuts with worry. I'll email them when I get back to the motel."

Julie shook her head. "Rosemary tried so hard to reach me. All I did was push her away."

The outer door chimed Aurora into the lounge. She clutched her shawl around her chest, her hair shining silver. Julie stood up. She moved toward her mother, whose cheeks looked hollow. Was there something physically wrong with her? Tomorrow, at breakfast, she'd press Sebastiano for a straight answer.

Aurora stared at Julie, her expression neutral. "Sebastiano's in his cottage with Cassandra."

Julie knew that underneath the flat tone lay an intentional stab, aimed at both her and Eric. She felt not one pinprick of jealousy or regret about Sebastiano and Cassandra. "They're suited to each other."

Aurora looked away from her. "Are you staying with us?"

"I'll be more comfortable at the motel," Eric said.

Aurora glanced at him. "I don't care about you."

Julie laughed. Eric's hand grazed hers.

"What's funny?" Aurora asked.

"That was a rude thing to say to your guest."

"I didn't invite him," Aurora said. "I assume you're going with him."

"Don't assume anything about me. You know fuck all."

"You need a lesson in manners, Julie Fox."

"Not from you."

Her mother didn't love her. She never had, she never would.

Julie took Eric's hand. "Let's go check on Peyton."

Chapter Thirty-Three

Julie cleared the shelves of her medicine cabinet. Tylenol. Band-Aids. Children's cough syrup. She dumped everything into the tote bag. Her antipsychotic medication went into her purse, so it wouldn't get lost in the move. The pills were working, presumably, with no obvious side effects, but she hated the daily reminder she was sick. She'd asked her psychiatrist if she'd ever get off them.

"We'll see," Dr. Kumar had said.

"Let's make that sooner rather than later."

Watching her, he'd scribbled a note. "We'll work on it."

Something clunked in the next room. Eric folding the craft table. Peyton loved the farm she'd made for her. They were taking it to Delilah's house for the three of them to play with. Well, four, since Peyton expected the new baby to be her playmate from the minute he or she was born.

Julie emptied the cupboards under the sink and packed the towels into a box destined for a charity. She wanted to be rid of all of this bathroom's reminders, and they wouldn't match the towels at Delilah's place. Julie still thought of the house as Delilah's, even though she'd spent the past three months renovating the basement into her own suite. On weekends, Eric and Brad joined her to hammer, lay floorboards, and paint. Rosemary kept Peyton out of their way and helped Delilah, who was constantly tired, nauseous and the happiest she'd been in her life.

Footsteps in the hall padded toward the bathroom. Peyton entered, her hands behind her back.

"What's that you've got there?" Julie asked.

Peyton slowly brought her hands in front of her. Julie moved in for a closer look at the piece of red plastic on Peyton's palm.

"A chicken?" Julie said.

"From that farm set your mother gave her." Eric appeared in the door frame. "I found the box in Peyton's suitcase when we got home."

"I purposely left it at the retreat," Julie said.

"Peyton swears she didn't pack it."

Their daughter shoved the chicken in her jeans pocket and scooted around Eric. Then her footsteps disappeared down the hall.

"My guess is Sebastiano slipped the box in," Eric said.

"Why would he?"

"It's an asinine thing he'd do to bug us."

Julie's neck tensed. Eric's put-downs of Sebastiano felt like a slur against her for her foolishness in falling for a cad. "He wouldn't care enough, once he knew I was out of his life," she said. "Sneaking the farm in is more my mother's style."

"So her granddaughter will remember her?"

"You think she has that much heart?"

"Not really," Eric said. "Maybe she meant it for you—a message you can't escape her."

Julie folded the top of the box. "I told Dr. Kumar that Aurora will always make me feel I'm not worthy of a mother's love."

"Julie, that's stupid."

"Yeah, that's what he said, in his shrink words. I'm starting to believe it, sometimes."

"Make that all the time."

Julie stepped into the tub to collect the shampoos, soaps, and sponges. Eric went to get a plastic bag. During their renovation work, Eric had hinted he viewed Julie's move to Delilah's as temporary. He wanted Julie back with him and Peyton and had shown enough trust in her to leave Peyton alone with her on Saturdays, and last weekend overnight. But Julie had sensed his relief Sunday morning when he picked Peyton up. How could she blame him? She also doubted Eric would be so eager to patch things up if she had turned out to be pregnant with Sebastiano's child.

"That wouldn't have been fair to the innocent kid," she'd said to Dr. Kumar. "Shouldn't Eric accept me baggage and all?"

"Nobody's perfect," Dr. Kumar had replied.

"Are you talking about Eric or me?"

"You might cut people slack, including yourself."

Eric returned with the bag and held it open. Julie tossed in the bottles. She threw the last one to his left. He dove and caught it in the bag.

Julie turned away from the tub, the site of her worst afternoon, glad to be leaving it forever. She and Eric were sure Peyton didn't realize Julie had tried to drown her, but her child had certainly absorbed the full repercussions that followed. When Peyton was older, Julie would explain and apologize.

"You remember that website we started?" she asked Eric. "The one we'd hoped my absent mother might stumble across? Delilah and I were talking about turning it into a blog for mental health, assuming she has the time on top of her bookstore job and baby."

"Delilah's always been into writing."

"We'd both write about our experiences and post other people's thoughts and information," Julie said. "Delilah came up with a name for the blog. Foxtrotting, from our surnames and your poem. We trot out our stuff."

He groaned.

"Okay, bad idea."

"Not the blog but its name."

"You stole me as material." She smiled. "My turn now."

"That's fair."

Peyton's footsteps pounded toward the bathroom again.

"What happened to her delicate feet?" Eric asked.

She thumped into the room wearing the soccer shoes and knee socks Julie had bought her last weekend and packed away for the move. They'd signed her up for a team, and Julie had volunteered to coach.

Julie lifted her up and set her on the edge of the tub. "Let's get these shoes off before you trip on the laces. We'll save them to wear outside." She peeled off the shoes and socks.

Peyton slid to the floor. She padded to Eric and punched his arm. "Daddy, you're it."

Eric whirled. "I'm gonna get you." He tore after Peyton into the hall.

Julie scanned the bathroom. Nothing left but a last scour of the counter and sink. Peyton shrieked from the living area. Julie picked up the liquid cleaner and put it down. Work could wait. She jogged toward the shouts and squeals of Peyton chasing Eric around the dining table. Peyton bumped into a chair, wobbled, recovered. Eric closed in on her. Julie ran the other way and met Peyton head-on.

"Mommy!"

Julie scooped her up. Peyton clung to her neck and laughed while Julie waltzed them through the living room. Her daughter, her baby, her love, her life. Safe.

The End

Dear Reader. Reviews mean everything to an author. They determine the placement of the book, and thus how many potential readers will see the book. I will be so grateful if you will take a minute of your time and return to the site where you purchased this book to leave a review, even just a two-line review. It doesn't matter how long, just that the book is reviewed and rated.
Thank you so much, Susan

BWL Author
Susan Calder

Susan Calder is a Calgary writer who grew up in Montreal. She has published two mystery novels, *Deadly Fall* and *Ten Days in Summer*, both set in Calgary and featuring insurance investigator sleuth Paula Savard. Her short stories, poems, and articles have appeared in magazines and anthologies.

Susan teaches fiction writing courses at the Alexandra Writers Centre Society. She is a member of Crime Writers of Canada and serves on the board of Calgary's When Words Collide Festival for Readers and Writers as the liaison with the Writers' Guild of Alberta. Her favourite non-writing activities include travelling and hiking in the mountains near Calgary.

Please visit Susan at www.susancalder.com
Facebook: Susan Calder
Twitter: @Susan_Calder
BWL Author Page
http://bookswelove.net/authors/calder-susan-mystery/